The messenger appeared in the entry of the King's Tower. He bore the Duke of Norfolk's cognisance of the Silver Lion at his breast. He hurried forward. "My liege," he said gravely, bending a knee, "the Duke of Norfolk bids me inform you that the tidings I bear are of a most serious, distressing, and confidential nature, and cannot wait."

Anne halted in her steps. Jack stiffened, and Francis, conversing with a pretty young woman, broke off in mid-sentence. All along the way, among those within earshot of the messenger, smiles died, movement ceased. Anne was reminded of the picnic on the Ure when the messenger from London had brought the tidings of King Edward's death and Bess Woodville's conspiracy to steal power. Her breath caught in her throat.

"What's the matter, Mama?" demanded Ned. "You look strange. Do you have a fever too?"

"No, dearest," Anne said, forcing a smile to mask her misgivings. But from the corner of her eye, she saw Richard drop the children's hands and stride into the Tower, Francis, Jack, and Rob at his heels.

The messenger rushed to follow.

BOOKS BY SANDRA WORTH

The Rose of York ***series***
Love & War
Crown of Destiny
Fall from Grace

THE ROSE OF YORK
FALL FROM GRACE

SPEAKING VOLUMES, LLC
NAPLES, FLORIDA
2020

The Rose of York: Fall from Grace

This is a work of fiction based on real people and real events. Details that cannot be historically verified are the product of the author's imagination.

ISBN 978-1-64540-233-6

THE ROSE OF YORK
FALL FROM GRACE

SANDRA WORTH

Acknowledgements

I wish to thank my editor and publisher, Kurt Florman of End Table Books, for his excellent work on this manuscript and David Major, partner and art director of End Table Books, for the stunning art work he has produced on all three books in *The Rose of York* series. My thanks go out to fellow End Table Books author Wendy Dunn and my wonderful agent, Irene Kraas of the Irene Kraas Literary Agency, for their support and faith in my books. Last, but never least, I wish to thank the Richard III Society and my friends and family.

Dedication

For my daughter, Erica

"Though truth for a time rest and be put to silence,
yet it rotteth not, nor shall it perish."
—Richard, Duke of York, father of King Richard III, circa 1455

"It is by suffering that God has most nearly approached to man.
It is by suffering that man draws most near to God."
—Inscription at Stanford University Memorial Church

Background

In 1399, the childless King Richard II was deposed and murdered by Henry of Bolingbroke who became Henry IV and gave birth to the Lancastrian dynasty. For three generations the House of Lancaster ruled England: Henry IV, efficiently; Henry V, gloriously; and Henry VI, disastrously. Weary of injustice, men turned for relief to the blood heir of Richard II: Richard Plantagenet, Duke of York. Thus began the Wars of the Roses, the dynastic conflict between the Houses of York and Lancaster for the Crown of England, which brought to the throne the Yorkist kings Edward IV and Richard III.

Principal Characters

In a tumultuous era marked by peril and intrigue, reversals of fortune and violent death, the passions of a few rule the destiny of England and change the course of history…

***Richard**:* Distinguished by loyalty to his brother the King, and a tender love for his childhood sweetheart, Anne, he has known exile, loss, tragedy and betrayal. But his loyalty is first challenged by war, then by the ambitions of a scheming queen. Time and again he must choose between those he loves, until Destiny makes the final decision for him.

***Edward**:* A golden warrior-king, reckless, wanton, he can have any woman he wants, but he wants the only one he can't have. When he marries her secretly and makes her his queen, he dooms himself and all whom he loves. (Deceased as story opens.)

***Bess**:* Edward's detested and ambitious queen. Gilt-haired, cunning and vindictive, she has a heart as dark as her face is fair.

***George**:* Richard's brother. Handsome, charming and consumed with hatred and greed, he will do anything it takes to get everything he wants. (Deceased as story opens.)

***Warwick the Kingmaker**:* Richard's famed cousin, maker and destroyer of kings. More powerful and richer than King Edward himself, he attracts the jealousy of the queen and seals his fate. (Deceased as story opens.)

***John**:* The Kingmaker's brother. Valiant and honourable, he is Richard's beloved kinsman and Edward's truest subject, but when the queen whispers in the king's ear, he is forced to confront what no man should have to face… (Deceased as story opens.)

***Anne**:* The Kingmaker's beautiful daughter. She is Richard's only love, his light, his life…

The Houses of York, Lancaster and Neville, 1399 to 1485

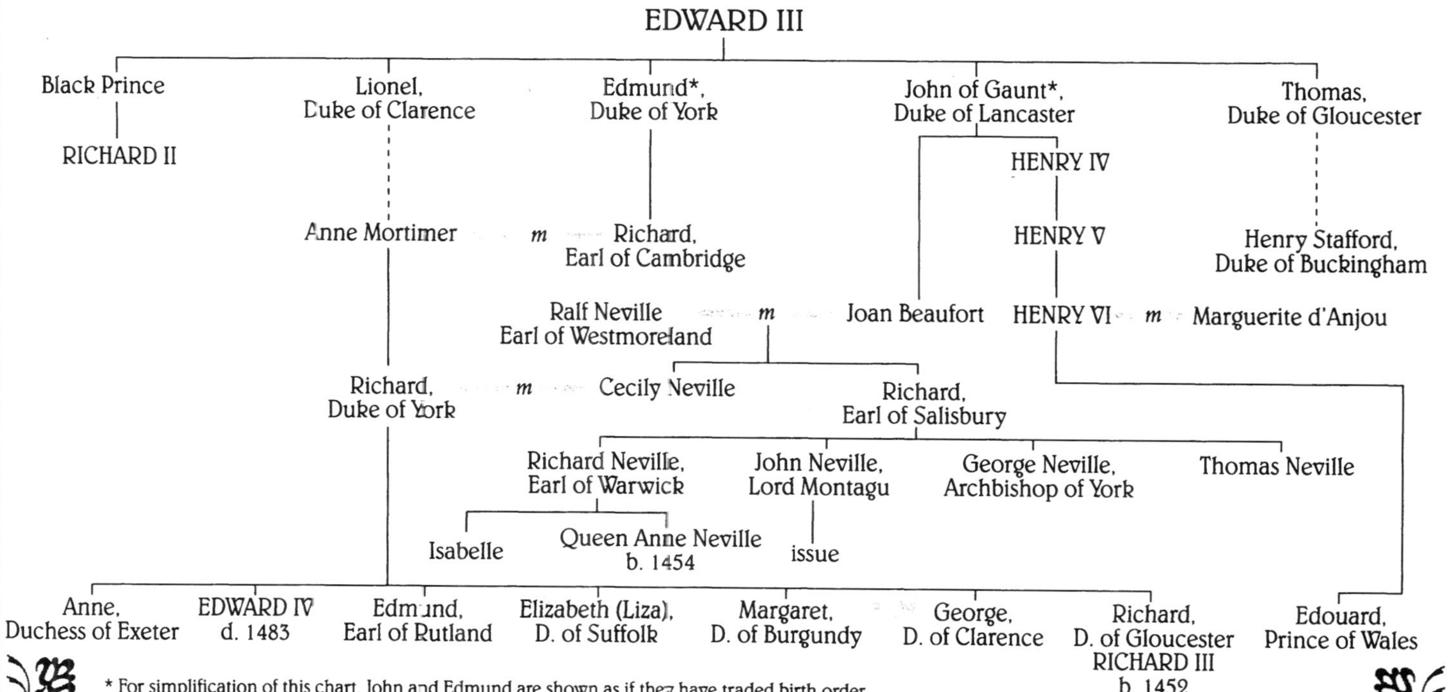

* For simplification of this chart, John and Edmund are shown as if they have traded birth order.
Missing lines denote missing generations.

Historical Characters

House of York

Richard Plantagenet, Duke of York (Deceased as story opens)

Cicely Neville, Duchess of York, his wife

King Edward IV, their eldest son (Deceased as story opens)

Elizabeth Woodville (Bess), Edward's queen

Elizabeth, eldest daughter of King Edward and Bess Woodville

Edward, elder son of King Edward and Bess Woodville

Richard, their younger son

Thomas Grey, Marquess of Dorset, Bess's elder son by her first marriage to Sir John Grey

Richard Grey, Bess's younger son by her first marriage to Sir John Grey

King Richard III, formerly Duke of Gloucester, youngest son of Richard, Duke of York

George, Duke of Clarence, Richard's older brother (Deceased as story opens)

Margaret, Duchess of Burgundy, Richard's youngest sister

Ann, (Nan), Richard's eldest sister, married to Sir Thomas St. Leger

Elizabeth, Duchess of Suffolk, Richard's elder sister

John de la Pole, (Jack), Earl of Lincoln, her eldest son, Richard's nephew, later his heir to the throne

Richard Neville, Earl of Warwick nicknamed "Kingmaker", Richard's father-in-law. (Deceased as story opens)

Anne Beauchamp, Countess of Warwick, his wife and Richard's mother-in-law.

Anne Neville, Warwick's daughter and Richard's queen

Edward (Ned), Anne and Richard's only child

Isabelle Neville (Bella), Anne's older sister and wife to Richard's brother George (deceased)

Edward, Earl of Warwick, Bella and George's son

Margaret (Maggie), Bella and George's daughter

Katherine, Richard's illegitimate daughter

John of Gloucester (Johnnie), Richard's illegitimate son.

House of Lancaster

Henry Stafford, Duke of Buckingham

Henry Tudor, Earl of Richmond, later Henry VII

Lady Margaret Beaufort, mother of Henry Tudor and wife of Lord Thomas Stanley

Introduction

Much has been written about Richard III, and many readers are familiar with Shakespeare's portrayal of him as England's most reviled and villainous monarch. What is not as widely known is that Richard III gave us a body of laws that forms the foundation of modern Western society. His legacy includes bail, the presumption of innocence, the protections in the jury system against bribery and tainted verdicts, and "Blind Justice"—the concept that all men should be seen as equal in the eyes of the law. He was the first king to proclaim his laws in English, so the poor could know their rights, and the first to raise a Jew to England's knighthood.

Such ideas were revolutionary in the fifteenth century. They alienated many in the nobility and the Church and played no small part in Richard's ultimate fate. Two hundred years later, when it was safe to do so, men questioned the traditional view of Richard bequeathed to them by the Tudors and found themselves unable to reconcile the justician with the villain, the man with the myth. In the early twentieth century, such men came together to form the Richard III Society.

Two of Richard's most well known contemporary critics, Alison Weir and Desmond Seward, subscribe to Shakespeare's depiction of him as a hunchbacked serial killer. In his book *Royal Blood: Richard III and the Mystery of the Princes,* Bertram Fields, a prominent U.S. attorney and author, examines the school of thought represented by Weir and exposes the inconsistencies and deficiencies of the traditional view.

Richard III caught my imagination when I first saw his portrait in the National Gallery in London. Then I read Josephine Tey's *The Daughter of Time.* This compelling mystery inspired me to consume whatever I could find on Richard and to make several research trips to England in search of the true Richard. It was in Paul Murray Kendall's *Richard The Third* that I finally found him. Kendall, a Shakespearean scholar and professor of English Literature, provides a most convincing and illuminating portrayal of Richard and his times, and it is his interpretation of events that is reflected in this book.

While Shakespeare was a great dramatist, he never claimed to be a historian. In an age of torture and beheadings, he wrote to please the Tudors. The authority Shakespeare drew on was Sir Thomas More's *History of King Richard III*, a derisive account of the last Plantagenet king, which More never finished. One of history's enduring mysteries is why More broke off in mid-sentence and mid-dialogue to hide his manuscript. Fifteen years after his death, it was found by his nephew, translated from the Latin, and published. Had Sir Thomas More discovered the dangerous truth that the true villain was not Richard III, but the first of the Tudors, Henry VII?

The question remains, and the debate continues.

What Went Before...

Fall From Grace is the third and *last book* in *The Rose of York* series, following *Love & War* and *Crown of Destiny*. Each book in the series is self contained and may be read without reference to what went before, or what is to come. Each book has won its own individual awards without the judges being aware that the book they were reading was part of a larger series. This last book, *Fall From Grace*, has garnered the most substantial of these writing prizes: a fifteen hundred dollar award of the Bay Area Writers League of Texas for best unpublished work in their 2003 Open Manuscript Competition. However, for those readers who are coming to this part of the epic drama that makes up the Wars of the Roses without knowledge of the first two books in the collection and who would like to know what went before, and also for those readers of *Love & War* and *Crown of Destiny* who would like a re-telling of these stories, I present a synopsis here.

Commencing in 1452, the Houses of York and Lancaster began their feud for the Crown of England. Each side chose the rose as their emblem: York chose the white, and Lancaster the red. Against this turbulent backdrop of the Wars of the Roses, the orphaned nine-year-old Richard Plantagenet goes to live with his famed and much older cousin, the Earl of Warwick, nicknamed "Kingmaker." There he meets his cousin Anne Neville, the Kingmaker's daughter. Richard and Anne grow up and fall in love. But thanks to Edward's avaricious and detested Queen, Elizabeth Woodville, a commoner whom King Edward has married in a scandalous secret marriage, tensions between Richard's brother, King Edward IV, and Anne's father, the Kingmaker, erupt into war in 1471.

Richard remains loyal to his brother King Edward IV. The House of Neville falls. Two of the three Neville brothers whom Richard had loved are slain at the Battle of Barnet, where they fought for the Lancastrian side. The third, an Archbishop, is imprisoned by King Edward. Richard later obtaines his release, but he dies soon afterward.

Meanwhile, Richard's brother George, who is married to the

Kingmaker's elder daughter, Bella, schemes to prevent Richard's marriage to Anne. The two young lovers elope, thwarting George's attempts to keep them apart. Now George turns his attention back to plotting for the Crown that he has desperately desired all his life. For these efforts he is finally executed by his brother, King Edward. Upon King Edward's own sudden and premature death in 1483, England faces bloody civil war once again as the King Edward's odious queen, Bess Woodville, plots to set aside King Edward's will that makes Richard the Protector of the Realm during her son's minority. However, it is soon evident that Destiny has larger plans for Richard.

During the tumultuous, confusing and divisive events of 1483 following King Edward's death a secret is revealed that changes the succession to the throne: Edward was married when he wed Elizabeth Woodville, and his bigamy makes his heirs illegitimate. As England teeters on the edge of war once again, the three estates of government urge Richard, now the true heir, to accept the throne that he has so far refused. Torn between duty to his dead brother Edward and duty to the land, Richard agonizes over his predicament. Finally, he realizes he has no choice. A reluctant king, he accepts the crown, determined to bring peace and justice to his people at last....

Fall from Grace

1483 -1485

Chapter One

"God bless the King, and all his fellowship!"

The day dawned brilliant with sunshine for the first double coronation in two hundred years. At the hour of Prime, as church bells pealed across London, with Anne's train following his, Richard of Gloucester left Westminster Hall for the crowning at the Abbey. Removing his shoes, he walked barefoot on the red carpet, heralds trumpeting the way, followed by his lords and a procession of priests, abbots, bishops, and a cardinal bearing a great Cross high over his head.

Richard's gaze fell on ginger-bearded Lord Stanley, who was carrying the mace. He remembered his own words: "One thing men can rely on, as surely as spring follows winter—a Stanley will ride at the winner's side, no matter what his sin." He hadn't intended to reward Stanley for his treason, yet he had. To appease his own guilt for taking the life of a better man, he supposed, wincing at the memory of Lord Hastings. Even Stanley's wife, Margaret Beaufort, had been greatly honoured this day. Harry Buckingham, a good friend and cousin whom he'd entrusted with the coronation, had arranged for her to carry Anne's train—she, the mother of Henry Tudor, who, now that all true Lancastrian claimants were dead, had become their claimant merely because he lived! The world was indeed a strange place.

Richard wondered how Anne fared. Suffering from a chill and fever on the previous day, she'd been carried in a litter for the traditional journey of the monarch from the Tower of London to Westminster Palace. Much to his relief, she had felt well enough this morning to walk in the ceremony, and now followed him into Westminster Abbey. At least this once the wagging tongues that sought evil omens would be stilled. No one would have guessed she had been so ill, for she looked beautiful in her crimson velvet mantle furred with miniver with her hair flowing down her back, giving no hint of her recent illness. His sister Liza walked behind her, trailed by more noble ladies and a line of knights. His eldest sister, Nan, however, was absent. Of course, his mother had not come. She had even refused her blessing. He forced the memory away. But the entire peerage of England was here. That was much to be grateful for. It meant that England accepted him with good heart.

They approached the west door of the Abbey. The sign of the Red Pale in the courtyard of the almonry swung in the breeze. Here in 1476, William Caxton, that old mercer of Bruges, had come to print his books with the help of the Gutenberg press that he'd brought from Germany. It was a long way they'd travelled together since that wintry afternoon in the Bruges tavern, Richard thought, marvelling at the caprices of life. He'd been a youth of seventeen then, broken-hearted, hungry and poor, an exile from the land of his birth, with little hope. Now he would be King.

His gaze moved from Caxton's shop to his friend Francis Lovell, carrying the Sword of Justice, and he remembered a question Francis had posed when they were boys. "If you could be anyone in King Arthur's court, who would you be?" He'd had no answer then. Lancelot, whom he'd admired as the embodiment of his valiant cousin John Neville, had seemed out of reach to him. Later, torn between love and loyalty, he had felt himself more like Lancelot than any of Arthur's knights, for Lancelot had been the most flawed.

I can answer you at last, Francis, he thought. *I shall be Arthur, reigning with mercy and justice.*

***

The high, pure voices of the choristers lifted in praise. Song burst forth from the church, *Domine in virtute*—

Richard and Anne entered the nave and proceeded down the aisle. Hundreds of candles flickered and incense filled the air with a rich, heavy scent, sending curls of smoke wafting into the gloomy nave. At the high altar, Anne watched as Richard knelt to be anointed with the holy Chrism, and rose to be vested in his regal garments of black and gold. Girded with the sword of state, he knelt again. Old Cardinal Bourchier picked up the crown of St. Edward and placed it on his head.

From the corner of her eye, Anne saw Richard's cousin Harry

Buckingham turn away. *As if he can't bear the sight,* she thought. Why wouldn't this moment fill him with joy when he had been Richard's staunchest ally, instrumental in gaining him the throne? His labours were crowned with Richard's crowning—*unless... unless...*

She had no time to finish the thought. Richard's sister Liza was arranging her hair and Cardinal Bourchier was coming forward to anoint her forehead with oil. She felt his cold touch with a shiver. He held the crown over her. She tensed in its shadow. He set it down on her brow and the weight felt like a sudden blow. The sceptre and rod were thrust into her hands, and a hundred voices broke into a *Te Deum.* The song filled the cathedral, resounded against the stone pillars, coloured windows, and soaring arches, but in her throbbing head the chant dissolved into a chorus of jarring chords. She rose, and moved with Richard to their thrones in St. Edward's Shrine for Mass.

Stanley's wife, Margaret Beaufort, appeared at her side.

Anne felt a sudden chill. In the dimness, Margaret Beaufort's narrow wolfish face had taken on a cruel look. Her smile seemed forced, strangely twisted, and her deep-set eyes glittered with menace. Anne chastised herself for her uncharitable thought. *Margaret Beaufort has stepped between me and the candles,* she told herself, *throwing her shadow over me momentarily and moving into darkness herself.* That was all. She was a good woman, known for her piety, and favoured by God. At the age of ten she had received a vision....

Her head ached from the noise of the ceremony. The air in the Abbey was musty and cloying, reeking of incense and the stale perfumes of the nobles. She closed her eyes and tried to remember the rush of the cool wind sweeping her beloved Yorkshire moors, but all she could feel was the weight of the crown. Cardinal Bourchier's voice droned on.

She opened her eyes. Her glance fell on Stanley's square, bulky figure. Why had Buckingham insisted on giving Stanley the honour of carrying the mace, which rightly belonged elsewhere? Why had he heaped Stanley and his new wife, Henry Tudor's mother, with such honours? She turned the question over in her mind, making no sense of it. Because it defied reason, it acquired a suspicious and sinister aspect. *Buckingham...* He reminded her so much of Richard's dead brother George. The same smile, the same golden curls, arrogance, eloquence, need for attention. The same shallowness and ambition. She couldn't trust him, yet she knew Richard trusted him implicitly. *As my own father once trusted George.* She blinked, lifted a hand to her brow. Something was wrong with her sight. Shadows were everywhere, all around her and Richard. It was the fatigue and the noise. They made her mind play tricks on her. She wished the ceremony would end. But it continued. There was still Holy Communion.

At last, Richard offered the crown of St. Edward and other relics at the shrine. Anne sighed with relief. It was over. She prepared to rise. Clarions sounded. She turned her eyes on Richard. His face was pale and grave. At that instant the knowledge struck her with full force. Richard was King of England.

Blessed Mother, and she was Queen!

Queen. What her father had dreamed. What she had never wanted. Now it was thrust upon her! She put out a hand to the shrine of St. Edward for support, and whispered a prayer.

Chapter Two

"In the dead night, grim faces came and went."

The Thames shone like satin in the twilight of the sultry night. Richard stood at an open window in his privy suite at Windsor, listening to the music flowing from the piper and harpist in the corner of the chamber. These two had been among the minstrels who had played at his coronation banquet. How splendid the evening had been! His friends Rob Percy and Francis Lovell had served him from dishes of silver and gold, and the King's champion had ridden into the hall in pure white armour on a horse with trappings of red and white silk. As drums thundered and cymbals clashed, he had delivered his traditional challenge and the hall had rung with the cry, "Long live King Richard III!"

King Richard.

He rested his hand on the stone embrasure. So must have stood every Plantagenet king before him, gazing on the mighty river and listening to the murmur of its tide. So must his brother Edward have stood.

He winced.

Lights glimmered in the city. *I should get back to work,* he thought. While much had been accomplished this past week—a treaty broached with Isabella of Spain, an embassy received from Scotland to discuss a truce—much still remained to be done. He needed to address problems in Ireland and to persuade Duke Francis of Brittany, who harboured the former queen's brother, Edward Woodville, and his Lancastrian enemy, Henry Tudor, to deliver them up to England. As for France, he had sent Louis XI an announcement of his assumption of the throne by his herald, Blanc Sanglier. *Jesu,* how much had happened since he left Middleham three months ago.

"I wish Ned were here," said Anne at his shoulder.

Richard turned from the window. Anne looked wan and pale, and it troubled him that she had lost weight in these weeks. Illness and the demands of the coronation had sapped her energies. But then, London had never agreed with her. He knew she was lonely and he felt a stab of guilt for neglecting her. The pressures of state never ceased. Her sole purpose in coming to London was to bring him comfort, yet he'd been unable to spend much time with her. "Go to him, Anne. Though London will be the worse without you." He took her hand, remembering with an ache the picnic on the River Ure before his brother's premature death changed their lives. How long ago those golden hours seemed now!

"But you've been gone from Middleham even longer than I, Richard… Can you not come with me? The change would do you good."

Richard was about to refuse, then changed his mind, suddenly buoyant. "Indeed I shall! We'll go together, dear Anne. We'll have a progress to meet the people and let them see their new king. A progress north—to Middleham!" Already it was as if the fresh wind of the moors had touched her cheeks. Colour flooded them, and light returned to her dull eyes.

"Oh, Richard! I shall write Ned and tell him…"

"Stay while I dictate a letter to Kendall, Anne. Work always seems less arduous when you are with me." Anne smiled, raised on tiptoe and kissed the cleft in his chin. "There's embroidery I must finish… A banner for Ned." She went to a chest and removed a roll of colourful cloth. "He wants one just like yours."

Richard's mouth lifted in a smile as he called for his secretary. "Kendall, my good man, take a letter to the Earl of Desmond." John Kendall went to his desk and Richard began his customary pacing. After requesting his friend to administer the oath of allegiance to the people of Ireland, he sent instructions on various state matters.

"And it gives me much pleasure," he concluded, "to send you this collar worked in gold of the Suns and Roses of York, with my White Boar appended—" He halted, his gaze on the dark river curving towards Westminster. A sudden stillness had fallen and the lapping of the river came to him clearly; lapping as it had that night long ago when he'd sat by the water's edge as a child and overheard Anne's father Warwick, and Desmond's father, Thomas Fitzgerald, in conversation about Edward's odious queen, Bess

Woodville. Their words were to prove fatal to them both.

"Your father's service to my father, the Duke of York, is warmly remembered," he added quietly, "but we, their sons, are also bound together by a common tie of sorrow. For those who encompassed your father's death are the same who encompassed the death of my brother, George, Duke of Clarence. If you desire to prosecute the guilty parties to the full extent of the law, I promise you the opportunity."

He glanced at Anne. She had bowed her head and halted in her embroidery. To the charges against Bess Woodville could be added another: the destruction of Anne's family, the Nevilles...

He couldn't undo the past; he could only learn from it. If his brother Edward had not been ungrateful to Anne's father, the man who'd made him King, might it all have come out differently? He was determined not to make the same mistake. "Make a note, Kendall... The Duke of Buckingham is to be appointed Constable and Chamberlain of England and to receive the de Bohun estates, which are now the property of the Crown."

Anne's head jerked up. "Is that not excessive, my lord?"

"He helped me gain the throne. He should share in the glory as well as the responsibility. I cherish his loyalty and wish him to know it," Richard said roughly.

Anne bit her lip, thrust her needle and scarlet thread into the silk cloth and yanked it through. If only loyalty weren't Richard's strongest trait! It made him blind to the faults so clear to others. That could be dangerous in a king, but there was no reasoning with him. How she wished to be wrong about Buckingham! *Maybe I've rushed into judgement? Maybe, this once, my instincts have failed me?* she thought hopefully. Buckingham might well be guilty of nothing more than a physical resemblance to the man who had charmed her father then turned his coat and helped destroy him. At least she could hope that was the case.

There was a rap at the door. A smiling Buckingham entered the privy chamber. He bowed to Anne. Richard brightened.

"Ah, Harry, speak of the devil! You're the first to know: Anne and I have decided to make a progress north. Isn't that a splendid idea? We'll spend a few days at Warwick Castle and stop at Minster

Lovell to visit Francis. I want you at my side, naturally."

Buckingham didn't respond. Anne noted that he was taken aback and seemed strangely thoughtful. *He has been strangely thoughtful too often of late,* she thought.

"When do you plan to go?" Buckingham inquired with a raised eyebrow.

"In about ten days."

"Dickon, I can't leave that soon. Can I meet you on the way?"

"What keeps you in foul London, Harry? Nothing unpleasant, I hope."

"No… but I've had scant time to attend to my own affairs in these past weeks."

"Then so it shall be, Harry!"

Anne watched Buckingham leave, more disturbed than ever. Her instincts told her something was very wrong.

***

That night in bed Anne tossed and turned fitfully.

"What's the matter, my sweet?" asked Richard, lifting up on an elbow. He could see her dimly in the moonlight flowing in through the open windows. "What troubles you?"

"Nothing, Richard, nothing—" she said, and the hand that lay along his thigh dug into his flesh.

"Anne, tell me."

"I mustn't, Richard. It's not my place—it would be an intrusion."

"An intrusion? Nothing you could say would be an intrusion, Anne. You can't think that!"

When Anne still hesitated, Richard reached for her hand. With a smile in his voice, He said, "Tell me, my lady. 'Tis a royal command."

"It's Edward's boys, Richard," Anne replied softly.

Richard's smile vanished. He dropped her hand, lay back down, and stared at the silk canopy overhead. "They're well treated, Anne, I assure you. Surely you don't think otherwise?"

"No, Richard." Anne sat up in bed. Now she couldn't rest until she'd spoken her mind. "I know you'd always do your best for your brother's children but…"

Richard waited.

"The plots by the Lancastrians and the Woodville sympathisers to deliver them from the Tower and use them to foment rebellion against your rule—that's why you've forbidden them visitors and to play in the garden, isn't it?"

"Aye. 'Tis necessity, not malice, that obliges me, Anne."

"I know, my love. But they're children. Little Dickon is only nine—Ned's age, Richard."

Richard threw back the covers. "Christ, Anne, well do I know that! Do you not think I'm troubled by what I must do?"

"Richard, I believe I've found the solution that will solve your problem and still permit the boys a measure of freedom."

Richard rose and went to the window, regretting he had opened the door to the subject. Women understood nothing of such matters and Anne's feelings would be hurt when he refused to heed her suggestion, as he surely must.

It was a beautiful, clear night; the sky sparkled with stars and a cool breeze stirred. Anne appeared beside him and shut the window. He looked at her with surprise. She was the one who insisted on sleeping with the windows open and the bed curtains drawn back. She met his gaze boldly, not shyly from beneath her lashes with her head lowered as she was accustomed to do. He was caught off guard.

"No one must hear this," she said. Then she unfolded her plan.

The solution was so simple, lying there all along, so clear...Why hadn't he thought of it himself?

"There's one more thing, my love," Anne said.

"Aye?" he said in wonderment.

"Entrust the task to Francis." She hesitated. "And don't tell Buckingham."

"But Buckingham's my blood, my ally. I owe my throne to Buckingham—"

"Call it a foolish whim, Richard. It would mean much to me."

In the moonlight, in her white filmy shift with her fair hair streaming down to her waist, she looked more than beautiful: she looked ethereal, and he was struck as never before that she was heaven's gift to him.

"I can deny you nothing, flower-eyes," he said, and drew her to him.

Chapter Three

"To ride abroad redressing human wrongs."

"Rule fairly in your region," Richard told his lords before setting out on his progress two weeks after his coronation. "Allow no oppression of the people." He rose from his throne. "I thank you for your loyal support. All who wish to leave are dismissed."

There was a murmur. His nephew Jack de la Pole, Earl of Lincoln, pushed forward. "But my royal uncle, will you not require an armed escort?"

"There is no need. I rule by the will of the people."

"But, Sire—" It was Anne's kinsman, Lord Scrope of Bolton. "To go abroad without men-at-arms is dangerous, even in times of peace."

"Nevertheless, I am decided. My throne must rest on loyalty, not force."

Scrope exchanged an anxious glance with the others. "My lord, I choose to stay."

"So do I," said Richard's boyhood friend Rob Percy.

"So do I," echoed Jack.

Richard descended the dais. "I shall be glad of your company, my good friends."

"M-m-may I c-come, too, L-lord Uncle?" stuttered a small voice at his waist. Richard looked down at his brother's son, whose mother had been Anne's sister, Bella. His heart twisted with pity. With his rosy cheeks, bright blue Neville eyes and wealth of wheat-coloured curls, his brother George's son—yet another Edward—was a beautiful child and exceptionally sweet-tempered. But thanks to the neglect of his guardian, the Woodville queen's son, the Marquess of Dorset, he was a timid, dull-witted boy, unable to comprehend at eight what most understood at five.

"Of course you may, Edward, if only to meet your cousin, my own little Edward," said Richard gently. He tousled his fair hair. "From now on, you'll come with me everywhere I go, won't he, Gower?" He exchanged a knowing look with little Edward's new squire, Thomas Gower, who had been squire first to Anne's uncle, John Neville, and then to John's young son, George, until their deaths.

"Aye, sire," answered Gower with soft eyes. Richard managed a smile, and his glance, moving over his company of friends, passed to one who stood apart: Lord Stanley.

Clearly reluctant to be there, alone at the back of the group, Stanley was watching him warily. *You, too, will come with me, my wily fox,* thought Richard. *Everywhere I go.*

***

In the glaring sunshine of the July morning, Richard set out with his entourage, trumpets blowing, dogs barking, baggage carts creaking. He was accompanied by those of his lords who had chosen to stay and a great train of bishops, justices, and officers of his household. The crowds were sparse in the streets and the procession only drew the curious, but those present remarked on the King's lack of an armed escort.

Everywhere along the way, through the towns and villages, Richard was welcomed with pageants and processions, and offered gifts of money. He could have put these to good use defraying his expenses. Money had been a constant problem from the day the Woodvilles had absconded with half the treasury. But he refused. "I would rather have your hearts than your money," was his common refrain. Instead, he made them gifts of his own. In Woodstock, it was a grant of royal forest land that Bess had appropriated for her own pleasure and that he knew would greatly ease the people's burden gathering food for their families; in Gloucester, it was a charter of liberties. And everywhere, it was justice.

Tirelessly, Richard presided at the local courts, heard the complaints of the poor, and punished offenders. In Oxford, his second stop after leaving Windsor, Richard, whose scholastic tastes ran to moral philosophy and Latin theology, lingered two days to engage in lively discourse with the Chancellor and eminent doctors before leaving for Gloucester. But the visit was marred by ill tidings. Another plot had been discovered, hatched around Bess Woodville.

Her daughters were to be smuggled abroad to join Tudor so that they might marry princes willing to carry on the fight against Richard.

In their lodgings at Magdalen College, Anne exchanged a weary glance with his close friend Rob Percy as the messenger from Westminster apprised Richard of events. Conspiracies swirled around Bess. She was a born plotter who thrived on discord. To live peaceably went against her nature. Richard's Chancellor, John Russell, had crushed the plot swiftly, but more were sure to be hatched in spite of the strong guard placed around Bess.

The next morning Richard and Anne set out in a pelting rain to visit Francis at his ancestral home in Oxfordshire. The skies cleared as they rode westward, the sun came out, and the dewy green slopes glittered like emeralds. They passed shiny fruit orchards and old churches; they crossed stone bridges and gurgling waterfalls. Gradually the conspiracy faded from their minds and smiles replaced their strained looks. Dusk was falling when they arrived at Minster Lovell.

"I forget how beautiful it is here, Francis," breathed Anne. She fingered a white rose in full bloom on a trellis running up the stone of the manor house and bent her head to its perfume.

"Here a troubadour might well think himself in heaven, Francis," smiled Richard, pausing to admire the magnificent view. To the trilling of larks, swans glided past with their cygnets on the smoothly flowing river that glittered silver in the fading light. Tall cypresses, in relief against the darkening sky, defined the spacious walks leading to a splashing fountain, and butterflies flitted among the profusion of white Persian lilies, purple pansies, and violets, their brilliance heightened by evening.

"I must admit I have been driven to song on occasion," said Francis Lovell softly, "especially at night. Nothing is more beautiful than the night, when nightingales sing and the moon hangs high and bright, and stars fall in the sky."

Richard clapped a hand on Francis' shoulder and gave Anne a smile. "See, what did I tell you, Anne? I was right from the first; he's a troubadour at heart."

A troubadour who sang of love, and knew none in his own life,

Anne thought, her gentle glance touching for an instant on Francis' club foot. No children, no true wife. No one to embrace him when he came home. Anne released the rose she held. Its petals dropped away, baring its empty yellow heart. With an elusive, undefined regret, she entered Francis' lovely manor home.

They made themselves comfortable in their chamber, a spacious room adjoining the chapel, lit by traceried windows along one wall and a deep oriel that opened on the view of the river. Richard began sorting through the day's business with Kendall. Anne settled into a chair with her embroidery, and young Edward came to sit by her skirts to play with his new puppy, Gawain. Servants moved quietly about the room bringing bowls of fruit and nuts and offering sweet wines to the lords who had divided themselves into groups. The hum of their manly conversation was punctuated with bursts of laughter, almost drowning out the soft notes of the lyre plucked by the minstrel in the corner.

"—Brittany won't give Tudor up," said the newcomer to the royal circle, Richard Ratcliffe, a Neville kinsman by marriage whom Richard had made an intimate. Not only had Ratcliffe proved his loyalty during the difficult early days in London when the Woodville queen had tried to seize power, but he had turned out to be a man of rare intellect as well as honour. Richard was drawn to him both for advice and friendship.

"Brittany's had Tudor since the Battle of Tewkesbury and wouldn't let King Edward have him, so what's changed?" Ratcliffe continued with a guarded glance at Stanley, conversing with one of his own henchmen across the room. Mindful that Stanley's wife was Henry Tudor's mother, he lowered his voice. "Tudor's a valuable pawn. France wants him, England wants him, and Brittany has him. I wager Brittany will keep him."

Richard's twenty-year-old nephew Jack grinned. "How much?" he demanded, startling Ratcliffe, who had no idea what he meant.

"How much will you wager, Dick? I'm good for a gold noble—" He took one from his purse and slapped it on the table. The royal nephew Jack, Earl of Lincoln, had grown from a merry child into an apple-cheeked lad with dark curls too unruly for his own liking, and a quick smile that had endeared him to all the household. A descendant of Geoffrey Chaucer, he was no man of letters; his zest was for the wager.

Ratcliffe laughed. "That's too rich for my blood, Jack. How about something more modest—a few groats, maybe? I fear the harvest won't be so good this year. Anyway, Tudor's not worth a full noble."

Hoofs sounded on the gravel path below. Jack jumped up to look out the window. "A messenger from Westminster! Good news, or bad; anyone willing to bet?" This elicited only laughter from the others.

Anne put down her embroidery and watched as the messenger entered and delivered the letter to Richard.

"It's from King Louis..." Richard cut the seal with his dagger, bent his head to read, and looked up with fury. "The devil take him!" he cursed.

"What is it, my lord?" demanded Anne.

"How dare he insult me!"

The messenger paled. He had not been privy to its contents, and he hesitated a moment, debating whether to respond. "Sire," he finally offered, "'King Louis is dying. He is sinking fast and may already be dead. He may not have been in his right mind when he wrote the missive."

"If he's dead, he's no loss to anyone but his dogs!"

Under different circumstances, Anne would have smiled. Louis' affection for his retinue of dogs, who were said to be closer to him than his courtiers, had made him the butt of many a jest. She went to Richard's side and read over his shoulder. Louis' letter was offensively brief and veered from custom in addressing Richard merely as "Cousin" instead of "Brother England" or "Most High and Mighty Prince," the language of kings. Clearly he had never forgiven him for refusing his bribe in Amiens years earlier when Edward had invaded France and, against Richard's objections, was paid off by Louis to leave without a fight.

Richard crumpled the letter and hurled it against the wall. It landed at Francis' feet. Francis picked it up and smoothed the parchment. Everyone except Stanley gathered around to read.

"How dare he—the damnable black Spider!" Richard spat, using the French king's grotesque nickname.

This time there was no doubt in the messenger's mind that no answer was to be made. Richard strode to the writing desk, seized the pen, dipped it into the ink pot, and scribbled furiously. "If France doesn't care about Anglo-French relations, neither does England. And if Louis doesn't stop seizing English ships on the high seas in violation of our truce, I shall send a fleet against the French privateers. Two can play this game."

"And farewell to you, Monsieur mon cousin," he added at the end, affixing his signature with a grand flourish. "Send this to Louis by a groom of my stable!" The messenger paled, retreated with a bow. Richard gave a grim laugh. "That should show Louis how he ranks with me, if he's not in hell yet."

His lords smiled, but nervously, without mirth. Anne sank back in her chair, remembering Louis. She didn't think that was wise of Richard, but he was direct and forthright by nature, unable to employ honied words with those he disliked, and what did she know about statecraft? Besides, Louis had no right to insult him. She picked up her embroidery and pushed the needle through.

***

They rode to Gloucester through the peaceful hillsides dotted with woolly sheep. On their arrival at the Abbot's lodging in St. Peter's Abbey, Richard found another messenger waiting with a saddlebag of letters and state business from Westminster. He began wading through them with Kendall.

The news was not as good as he might have wished. Already one plot to free King Edward's bastard son, young Edward, from the Tower had been narrowly averted. Old Jack Howard, the friend he had come to love like an adopted father since John Neville's death and whom he had left behind to help the council rule in his absence, had written of unrest and conspiracies in the southern counties aimed at abducting young Edward from the Tower. He believed the threat to be serious since there were many diehard Lancastrians about, along with malcontents in the pay of Henry Tudor and the French who would be only too happy to see Richard dethroned. There were also those who believed Richard had lied about the princes' bastardy. Clearly, the Woodvilles were not without friends. The queen's despicable son, the Marquess of Dorset, was still at large; her brother, Bishop Lionel, had escaped from Sanctuary; and her brother Edward Woodville had found safe harbour in Brittany.

"Make a note to strengthen the guard around young Edward, Kendall," said Richard. He picked up another letter from the pile. "Welladay, I'll be damned," he whistled through his teeth.

Anne looked up from her casket where she had been sorting through her jewels, and Edward stopped rolling the ball to his new puppy, blue eyes wide. Stanley, standing apart in a corner of the room, put down his own mail. "What is it, Uncle?" demanded Jack abandoning the window seat where he'd lounged with Rob, Ratcliffe, and Scrope of Bolton.

Richard slapped the letter in his hand. "I can scarce believe it. My royal Solicitor, Thomas Lynom, requests permission to wed Jane Shore!"

Anne was too dumbfounded for words. Like everyone there, she stared in disbelief. Jane Shore had been King Edward's whore and had taken up with the queen's son, Dorset, immediately after Edward's death. After aiding Dorset's escape, she had wasted no time bedding another great lord and enlisting him in the treasonous plot hatched by the Woodville queen against Richard. That lord, William Hastings, King Edward's bosom companion of many years, had invoked Richard's fury and paid with his head for his treason.

Scrope of Bolton was the first to speak. "How can a man in his position entertain such a ridiculous notion? The woman's nothing but a harlot."

"They say she's very beautiful, and very kind," Anne offered.

"But a bawd, nevertheless," said Richard with disgust. "I can't understand it."

Ratcliffe said softly, "Love spares no one, not the aged, the infirm, nor even the dour. Tom Lynom is a lucky man to have found it, though I would wish, for his sake, that it hadn't been with Dorset's leavings."

From behind a pillar came a sudden whimpering. Huddling behind a chair, little Edward rubbed his eyes tearfully. Anne went to him, knelt down. She put her arms around him and laid her cheek against his fair curls. "What is it, my sweet? What ails you?"

He clutched her neck. "D-do I h-have to go? P-p-please, Auntie, d-don't m-m-make me... me go—"

"Go where, my sweet? Where should you go?" His little arms clung to her so tightly they hurt, but she had not the heart to disengage them. The child's stutter was never this pronounced. She knew it meant he was terribly distressed. "I p-promise to be g-g-good. D-don't make me g-go..."

"Tell me where that is," coaxed Anne gently.

"To D-d-dorset... M-marquess of D-d-dorset..."

Anne looked up, met Richard's eyes. They were stormy and a muscle twitched in his jaw. Ratcliffe's innocent reference to Bess' son had stirred the child's deepest fears. *"Damn him,"* Richard muttered under his breath. "Damn him to hell!"

But it was not Dorset Anne blamed. No one expected better from a Woodville. It was Richard's brother King Edward. He had handed his own nephew to Dorset as his ward, so Dorset could profit from the boy's rich holdings, plunder the boy's lands, and fill his coffers. Such things happened when a child was left orphaned and heir to great estates with no one to protect him.

No one to protect him, dear God, when his own uncle was King! The child had been delivered by his own royal uncle into the Woodville's greedy hands to be milked, with no consideration of his welfare, only of their profit.

"My sweet little one," said Anne, stroking the child's curls, "you must never think of the Marquess of Dorset again. He is gone now and those days are over. You are safe with us, and we who love you will never give you up." She put her hand under his chin and made him meet her eyes. "Never, sweet nephew. Do you understand?" She drew her silk handkerchief from her sleeve and gently, very gently, dried his tears. Gathering him to her, she rocked him in her arms.

***

The Benedictine monastery of St. Peter's Abbey where Richard and Anne lodged in Gloucester was a quiet place, sheltered from the noise and bustle of the outside world by high, encircling walls. "If it were not for Ned, I should be sorry to leave tomorrow," said Anne, reaching for Richard's hand as they sat with Edward on the settle in the Abbot's private gallery after reading a letter from Ned.

A bustle at the door gave Richard no chance to answer.

"Harry!" exclaimed Richard, rising. He embraced Buckingham. "Good to see you, cousin! Did you conclude your private business in London?"

"Aye," replied Buckingham, avoiding Richard's eyes. "That went well—"

Anne watched, the old feeling of dread stealing over her again. Buckingham seemed preoccupied and was flushed, as if he'd been drinking. He answered Richard's questions and he bantered with him, but something was clearly wrong. His gaze kept shifting and he looked like a man living on the edge of highly strung nerves. "What's the matter, Harry? You're as jumpy as a gnat about to be swatted," Richard said at last.

"Nothing, Dickon, nothing—" Buckingham cleared his throat. "No. That's not true. There is something." He glanced at Anne and little Edward uncomfortably. Anne folded the letter from Ned that she had been delighting over and slipped it into her bosom. She rose from the settle. "By your leave, my lords, Edward and I shall take Gawain for a stroll in the garden." Richard inclined his head. Buckingham gave a bow and watched as they left. Anne heard the door shut firmly behind her. As she came out of the residence, she heard the thud of the window as that, too, was firmly closed to eavesdroppers. She had been right, then. Something was amiss.

With little Edward's hand in hers, she made her way to a stone bench by the freshwater pond. The scent of herbs and flowers hung heavy in the small garden and a songbird warbled in a mulberry tree. She sat quietly, listening. Edward soon tired of sitting and ran off with Gawain to explore behind the hedges. The sweetness of the garden lulled her into a mood of drowsy peace. She closed her eyes.

All at once came shouts and the shrillness of angry voices. She turned in time to see Buckingham stride out of the residence, his face dark as thunder. Richard followed. Even from the distance, she saw that he trembled with rage. Buckingham took swiftly to horse and galloped off, his entourage in pursuit. Richard stood and watched darkly. Neither raised a hand in farewell.

She came to her feet, her hand clenched to her breast. What in God's name could have made Richard so angry, their argument so fierce? It was not like him to lose control! Only once before had it happened, and then it had cost a man's life.

Gathering her skirts, she hurried to him.

***

Anne never learned what had taken place between Richard and Buckingham. Richard refused to speak of it and his eyes darkened dangerously whenever she neared the subject. All along the way, as they followed the Severn to Tewkesbury, he rode silently. When they approached Tewkesbury, it was Anne who fell silent. For at Tewkesbury, the site of that fateful battle, her sister Bella, and Bella's husband, George, were buried behind the altar.

And somewhere beneath the stones of the choir lay the body of her own first husband, the Lancastrian Edouard of Lancaster.

Richard reached for Anne's hand as she rode beside him. She clenched her fingers around his. Twelve years melted away and she was back in the tortured past... the flight to Calais and Bella's dead baby thrown into the sea... Louis of France watching her like a deadly spider as she was presented to Marguerite d'Anjou and Edouard... Her father, Warwick the Kingmaker, and her beloved uncle, John Neville, Marquess of Montagu, fighting valiantly to their deaths at Barnet... the journey in the cart as she was borne along by Marguerite's fleeing army, ailing in body and spirit... And Tewkesbury, the site of the final battle. Here, Edouard, unarmed, had been brutally cut down by Richard's brother George. And here, in an ironic twist of fate, George was buried with her sister, poor Bella. She closed her eyes and dug her nails into her palms until it hurt. The ghosts receded.

Louis had indeed been near death when he'd written that note. Early that morning they had received word that the old man-eating Spider had died in terror after desperately trying to bribe the Virgin, the Pope, and the Saints into extending his life. How ironic that King Louis of France and King Edward of England should ascend the throne together, and die together. Louis, too, had left a minor as his heir. Life was full of seemingly meaningless coincidences, like a map drawn in duplicate and superimposed, blurring the lines and rendering the map unreadable.

"My dear lady, we have arrived," said Richard.

She looked up. Before her rose the abbey church. Doves cooed, the sun shone. All was serene and tranquil. Richard helped her dismount. She took his hand and walked slowly up to the great Norman door. She hesitated, looked at Richard for strength. He pressed a kiss to her hand. Her gaze went to her silver laurel-leaf ring which he had given her in childhood. *Aye,* she told herself; *the chain of sorrows is finally broken.* As Richard kept reminding her, the dark past was dead and buried, and the future beckoned bright with promise. She braced herself and stepped through the door.

Chapter Four

"For were I dead who is it would weep for me?"

Galloping along the main road from Gloucester to Hereford, Harry Stafford, Duke of Buckingham, lashed his horse in anger. Richard had turned insolent, ungrateful, no longer thankful for his guidance. The tamed boar, so mild at first, had proven vicious after all, goring him and throwing him aside, as if he, Buckingham, the premier duke of the land, were no more than a dog. After all he'd done, to be treated thus!

Thus.

Richard was a fool. He refused to see reason, to do what needed to be done. He wasn't fit to rule, would never survive as king. Soft as woman's breast, he lacked the iron it took for kingship. He dug in his spurs. The lathered animal spurted forward, frothing at the mouth. He gave it another lash for good measure. What an arse he'd been, to have put his destiny in Richard's hands! *What a damned arse.* He'd not only delivered Richard a throne, but secured it for him, and what were his thanks? Richard had flown into a hideous rage at the mere suggestion. Had he known that it was already a *fait accompli—*

Buckingham shuddered. He'd have ended up like Hastings. His head on a log. He had no doubt of that. The wind felt good in his face; exhilarating, invigorating. He gave a bounce in his saddle and almost shouted for joy, so relieved was he to be alive.

***

In his castle of Brecon, Buckingham sought out his prisoner, Richard's enemy, Bishop Morton.

"Ah, my Lord Duke, what a great honour," smiled the cleric, placing his plump palms together in greeting and inclining his head. Buckingham threw his gauntlets across the table and sat down. A servant lad brought him a goblet of Madeira and, at his command, one for Morton. "I thought we might dine together tonight. Would you like that, Morton?" He eyed the black-clad bishop.

Morton's small mouth stretched into a smile. "Your Grace, you flatter me—I am overcome."

Buckingham called to the servants milling around lighting tapers and torches. "I'll take dinner here. And be quick about it. I'm so famished, I could eat a boar!"

Morton met his eyes, gave a laugh. The Boar was Richard's badge. "That is too clever, my Lord Duke. Too clever by far. You've had a disagreement with our noble sovereign, I gather?"

Buckingham guffawed. "You could call it that."

"Don't take it to heart, Your Grace. A hog cannot be expected to appreciate a pearl."

It was Buckingham's turn to smile. "My dear Morton, at least tonight I have good company." He tilted his chair back, regarded him thoughtfully. "Let's say—merely for the sake of argument, you understand—that I have changed my mind about my royal cousin. There's nothing to be done about it, is there? He's popular, loved by the people."

Buckingham was baiting him and Morton knew it. He linked his ringed fingers over his ample belly and gave the pretty duke a long appraising look. Buckingham's face was flushed and his eyes held a brilliant, frightening glitter that suggested suppressed fury. Morton decided to bite. "Indeed, the King goes about the land like Arthur, righting wrongs of the poor and powerless—" he leaned forward, lowered his voice to a whisper, "—but what of the powerful, my Duke? 'Tis from them he takes. While he worries about corrupt judges and the poor getting their due, their disaffection grows. And without the support of his lords, a king cannot survive."

"Neither can a king survive when he's a weakling," added Buckingham sullenly, upending his wine cup. He slammed down his cup, saying hotly, "He hasn't the courage or the stomach to do what it takes to keep the throne. I told him to get rid of his nephews and he told me to go to hell. He's not fit to wear the crown!"

Morton threw a glance around. Thankfully, only the servant boy was in the room to have heard this last treasonous remark. He lowered his voice to a bare whisper. "Frankly, I have never seen a head more closely fitted to a crown than yours, or a quicker mind. Both by the merit of ability, and the merit of your claim, you deserve to be king if Richard is deposed."

"'Tis what I've come to believe myself."

They fell silent again as servants appeared with trays of stuffed piglet and blancmanger, herbed jelly, milk pudding, and a selection of cheeses and grapes. The table was covered with a white cloth and set with silver trenchers. The servant lad refilled their cups with spiced wine. Morton leaned so close to Buckingham that they were almost nose to nose. "Even imprisoned as I am, I've heard the murmurings of unrest," he whispered, his small mouth barely moving. "I shall let you in on a secret: There will soon be a rebellion."

Buckingham drew a sharp inward breath. "And I shall be put forward as king?"

"Regretfully, no. As long as King Edward's sons are alive, the throne must go to them."

"And... if they were dead?"

"Ahh... That would be an entirely different matter, would it not?" Morton sank back into his chair, scrutinized Buckingham. "Pity, pity... Had we but known that you were willing to join your cause to ours! Alas, one other has been put forward in the dread eventuality of the princes' death."

"Who?"

"Henry Tudor, Earl of Richmond."

Buckingham gave a scornful laugh. "He's a bastard—the grandson of a lowly Welsh squire who was lucky enough to bed a widowed queen! Even on the paternal, his lineage is tainted with illegitimacy for his descent from John of Gaunt and his mistress. While I—" He emphasised his words with a crash of a fist on the table, spilling his wine, "—am a true prince of the blood, descended from a long line of Lancastrians." The servant lad cleaned up the mess. They fell silent and waited for the boy to resume his stance by the wall.

"But Tudor's mother, Margaret Beaufort, has been a prime mover of the conspiracy," hissed Morton. "We can't tell her just now that she can't put her son forward. When Richard is deposed, the nobles will see the rightness of your claim… And if not, at the very worst, you will be hailed *Kingmaker.*"

"Kings do not remain grateful to their makers. Look at Edward. Look at Richard. He owes me his crown and now he treats me like a varlet! What makes Tudor different?"

"The difference, my Lord Harry—may I call you that? For I can no longer see you as my gaoler, but as my friend—is that Tudor is no fool." He leaned back in his chair and cradled his belly with his ringed fingers.

"And Richard is, for sure."

"Let us count the ways. He has declared himself a champion of the poor, yet the poor cannot help him keep his throne, while the nobles can take it from him. He's inflexible, makes enemies when compromise would win him friends. There is only right and wrong, he says…" He gave a derisive laugh. "He refuses to hand the Duke of Albany back to Scotland, though to do so would secure peace. That would be the betrayal of an ally, he says. *Bah!* Albany can do nothing for him and he's too much a fool to know that kings must act in their own self-interest. In France he refused Louis' gifts. Bribes, he called them, and to Louis' face, no less. His insults only gained him France's undying enmity. Brittany doesn't trust him because they don't understand him. An honourable king is a dangerous king. He goes against his own self-interest, therefore one can never anticipate what he'll do next."

He gave Buckingham a cynical smile. "So you see, my friend, France, Scotland, and Brittany will lose no chance to use the disaffection in the realm against him. And there is much disaffection, I assure you, for kingship is not about right and wrong; it's about power." He raised his eyes to Buckingham's face, unable to suppress the urge to flick his tongue over his lips in the manner of a lizard about to devour a juicy, unsuspecting beetle. "Richard's days on the throne of England are numbered. Those who are wise will abandon ship while it is still afloat."

It was then that Buckingham made up his mind. He picked up his goblet. He drank. And he told Morton what until that moment, no other man knew.

Chapter Five

"A star in heaven, a star within the mere!
...And one will ever shine, and one will pass."

After Tewkesbury, Richard and Anne spent five nights at Warwick Castle, Anne's birthplace. For Anne, memories swirled around its mighty walls and along its passageways since her father's presence still seemed to fill the castle he had regarded as the jewel of his estates. While there, they made a day's visit to Newbold Revel and the widow of Sir Thomas Malory, a Warwickshire knight. A good friend to Anne's father to the bitter end, and dearly loved by her uncle John, Malory had died with them at Barnet. He had been thrown into prison by Marguerite of Anjou on a false charge politically motivated in the fifties. Released for a short time, he was again imprisoned in 1465 by Edward's odious queen, Bess Woodville for a remark at which she had taken offence. During the years of his imprisonment he wrote his tales of an historic King Arthur that he entitled *The Book of King Arthur and His Noble Knights.*

"What happened to Sir Thomas is an outrage," Richard told his widow. "I wish you to know, dear lady, that never again shall anyone spend ten years in prison for a crime they didn't commit. They shall not spend even a single day, for I intend to amend the law to protect the innocent from such abuse."

A smile softened the old lady's wrinkled face. "His faith in you was not misplaced, my Liege. He remembered you from Middleham Castle when you were but a boy, and from that time forth, he always spoke well of you, Sire." She curtseyed, and they bid her farewell.

Soon afterward, two days before the Feast of St. Bartholemew, in the brilliant sunshine of a fine August morning, Anne and Richard were reunited with young Ned at Pontefract Castle. He had been ill again and so he was brought there by chariot, accompanied by Anne's mother, the Countess of Warwick, who never left his side. The joyous reunion stained Anne's cheeks with happy tears. Not only was she beside herself to behold her child again after so long an absence and so troubled a period in their lives, but it was on this occasion that Ned finally met his cousins, Bella's and George's children. Eight-year-old Edward gave him a tight hug, and ten-year-old Margaret—Maggie—who had arrived from the south, curtsied shyly. Though Ned still grieved the loss of his cousin George Neville—as she herself would do for ever more—Anne knew that the friendship between the two little Edwards would help take Ned's mind off his loss. As other friendships had.

A smile curved Anne's lips as she stood beneath the shade of an enormous beech in the upper bailey by the east gate of the castle watching the reunion between Richard and his bastard son and daughter. Twelve-year-old Katherine and eleven-year-old Johnnie were lovable children and Ned had been filled with joy to discover his new-found brother and sister. Over the past year a deep affection had blossomed to seal the bond of kinship between the three playmates. She remembered a tender moment in the solar at Middleham. "How it brings back memories," her mother had sighed, watching them romp among the wildflowers that dotted the grassy mound behind the castle walls. "It's as if time flew backwards, and it is you, and Richard, and Francis, playing there..." Anne had come to her side and placed an arm around her shoulder. "God has not left us bereft, my mother. He has seen fit to take, but He has also given in return."

Now Anne watched as Johnnie and Katherine ran to Richard and threw themselves into his arms with shrieks of delight. Richard turned his gaze on her and gratitude glistened in his eyes. How glad she was that she'd agreed to take the children! Richard's infidelity had wounded her deeply, but somehow she had found the strength to forgive. After all, Johnnie and Katherine had been conceived during the years of war when their families had broken with one another and she had been forced to wed another. Richard had thought her lost to him. Her heart melted to see how they fought Maggie for his hand as they danced around him, skipping and jumping, blurting their news with excitement. Even Bella's Edward participated in the game, performing cartwheels to steal Richard's attention away from the others.

As she walked beside Ned's rattling litter past the little Norman chapel to the King's Tower, smiling at her boy and holding his hand, she thanked the Blessed Mother for tender mercies. Jack came to join their side to entertain Ned by taking mincing steps and pretending to be a girl. Laughing merrily, they turned the corner of the chapel.

The messenger appeared in the entry of the King's Tower. He bore the Duke of Norfolk's cognisance of the Silver Lion at his breast. He hurried forward. "My liege," he said gravely, bending a knee, "the Duke of Norfolk bids me inform you that the tidings I bear are of a most serious, distressing, and confidential nature, and cannot wait."

Anne halted in her steps. Jack stiffened, and Francis, conversing with a pretty young woman, broke off in mid-sentence. All along the way, among those within earshot of the messenger, smiles died, movement ceased. Anne was reminded of the picnic on the Ure when the messenger from London had brought the tidings of King Edward's death and Bess Woodville's conspiracy to steal power. Her breath caught in her throat.

"What's the matter, Mama?" demanded Ned. "You look strange. Do you have a fever too?"

"No, dearest," Anne said, forcing a smile to mask her misgivings. But from the corner of her eye, she saw Richard drop the children's hands and stride into the Tower, Francis, Jack, and Rob at his heels.

The messenger rushed to follow.

***

In Richard's bedchamber, Anne stood gripping the bedpost tightly so Richard would not see how her hands trembled. "Gone?" she whispered for the second time.

Richard gave a nod.

"But how?"

"We've been over it a hundred times, my councillors and I, Anne. We don't know how it happened. But it did."

"Edward's servant boy, too?"

"Both of them. I suppose whoever is responsible mistook young Edward's little companion for his brother Richard in the dark. Both have vanished."

She dragged her eyes to Richard's face. He looked dreadful. Pale, drawn, older—far older than he had any right to look. "What are you going to do?"

"I don't know. I have no idea. They could be… could be…" He made himself say the word. "Dead." He sank down on the edge of the bed. "We're searching for them." He cradled his head in his hands.

She went to his side, sank beside him. "You mustn't blame yourself. If Edward hadn't been ill with an infection of the jaw when you moved little Richard to Barnard's Castle he'd be safe with his brother now."

"How am I going to tell the boy about Edward, Anne?" He looked at her with anguished eyes. "Why should Richard believe me? Others don't. They think I lied for the throne. Now they'll think I killed for it—"

"Those who know you will never believe that. *You* know you didn't… *God* knows you didn't. Isn't that what counts in the end, that God knows?"

After a long moment, his hand slipped into hers. She raised it to her lips, pressed a kiss against the bronzed skin, and held it tenderly against her cheek.

***

No further word was forthcoming from London. The investigation yielded nothing, shed no light on the matter of the two boys in the Tower. It was as if young Edward and his servant lad had vanished into thin air. Their disappearance hung like a heavy cloud over what would otherwise have been a flawlessly happy time for the Gloucester household.

When Anne awoke on the last morning of August, Richard was gone. She hurried out of bed, threw on her chamber robe, belted it, and slipped on her shoes. She knew where he was. She ran up the tower stairs after him. Richard had taken Edward's disappearance harder than even she had expected. He was often distracted, brooding, and he slept fitfully, mumbling and crying out in his dreams. It troubled her that he suffered so.

She reached the open doorway of the battlements and paused,

panting for breath. Richard had not sensed her presence and she took a moment to observe him unnoticed. He stood with his back to her, gazing out over the sweep of cliff, hills, dales, and forests, a forlorn figure against the grey skies in his dark hose and white shirt. The wind tore at him, whipping his hair. She pushed her own wild locks back from her face, went to him, rested a hand on his sleeve. "We must try to dwell on the blessings, Richard, and give thanks that little Richard is safe. It was illness that kept young Edward from leaving for Barnard. It was not your fault."

Richard's mouth worked with emotion. "My brother Edward said something once, when I tried to dissuade him from our royal cousin Henry's murder… He said—" He broke off, swallowed. "He said, 'To be a king, you have to kill a king.'" He inhaled sharply, turned his pained eyes on her. "That's what I did, Anne. By deposing young Edward, I killed him. I'm responsible for his death—"

"You don't know that he's dead."

"What else? He stands between Henry Tudor and the crown Tudor craves. If Tudor has him, the boy's as good as dead. If the Woodvilles have him, why haven't they produced him? He must be dead."

"And little Richard lives! Think of that, Richard. He lives!… *Because of you!*" The wind was chill, and she shivered.

He turned, took her face into his strong hands and held it as the wind blew her long hair about her. "No, Anne. Because of you… Dear God, I don't know what I'd ever do without you. You're all that makes sense in this senseless world." He gathered her into his arms and held her close. Together, against the wind, they watched as a bleak dawn broke across the land.

***

A week later, accompanied by the children and a splendid retinue of lords, which included the Scottish Duke of Albany who had sought refuge in England, Richard and Anne entered York. Their welcome was delirious. The entire city had turned out to greet them. A deafening cheer erupted from a thousand throats when the scarlet-clad mayor and aldermen came to receive them outside the city walls, followed by the council and chief citizens in red and others in blue velvet. As they entered on the south, by the twin-turreted towers and chief gateway of Micklegate Bar, the crowds on the walls flung rose petals that fluttered down like coloured rain. Doves were released and flew off into the falling petals with a thunderous flapping of wings.

Riding between his parents on his chestnut palfrey, Ned looked up at his mother, eyes round with delight. Anne smiled at him, and then over his head at Richard. Happiness and pride had relaxed Richard's taut features, eased the lines around his mouth, and lent a shine to his grey eyes, which now gazed at her clear and untroubled beneath the glittering circlet of gold on his dark head. He sat tall in the saddle and looked more handsome than ever before. In his rich riding jacket of gold and crimson furred with sable, he was every inch as majestic as Edward had ever been, she thought. Now that his brother was no longer around to dwarf him with his monstrous height, Richard did not seem short to anyone but himself.

Once they entered the city, it became evident to what lengths York had gone to give them a welcome they would never forget. The streets had been scrubbed, flowers and candles had been placed in every window of the timber-framed houses, and brightly coloured arras had been hung in the streets. The city had prepared three pageants for them: one at the gate, another on the bridge over the Ouse river, and a third at Stayngate. In the evening, they banqueted at the royal castle of York.

"What a greeting," said Anne drowsily as she nestled in Richard's arms that night.

"Never did I expect such a welcome," replied Richard. "I wish there were some way to show our appreciation."

"Hmmm..." murmured Anne, as she fell asleep.

***

Richard did find a way to thank the city. Not only would he reduce their taxes, but here, in their beloved York, surrounded by those who knew them and shared their happiness, Ned would be invested as Prince of Wales in a ceremony so splendid it might well be reported as a second coronation.

The September morning was overcast, but at least there was no rain. Amid the blaze of a thousand pennons, golden banners, satins, and cloth of gold, Ned was invested as Prince of Wales by the Archbishop of York in the cool and solemn dimness of York Minster. With minstrels playing, he walked from the Minster between his parents, his golden rod in his hand, his golden wreath on his brow. The people cheered lustily and sang in the streets to behold their King and Queen in their glittering crowns and ermine-trimmed velvet robes of state, trailed by a train of nobles, knights, and clerics such as York had never seen in living memory. But Ned was unaccustomed to spectacle and noise, and though there was much to marvel at, including the fountain by the Archbishop's palace that splashed sparkling white wine for him to drink, he was frightened by the fuss being made of him and the roar of the crowds. He tightened his hold on his mother's hand.

"I wish Tristan could have come, Mama," he whispered. "I miss him."

Anne laughed at the thought of a hound walking in a royal procession. "I know you do, my sweet. But it won't be much longer, I promise. If you are good, maybe Papa will knight him when we get home."

Ned turned his head to his father so quickly that his wreath almost fell off his silky locks. "Oh, Papa! Could you? Would you? Oh, Papa, I believe Tristan would be proud!"

"What are fathers for?" Richard replied with a twinkle in his eyes, meeting Anne's gaze over his head.

Anne gave a laugh.

***

Richard and Anne spent a contented two weeks with their family at their castle of Sherriff Hutton, near York, where they had spent many happy days as children themselves. The castle was crowded with chatter and music but Richard still struggled with the burden of guilt that had descended on him with young Edward's disappearance, and more bad news arrived to dim the glow of Ned's investiture. The council had written that all was not well. The rumblings of unrest were growing too loud to ignore, and measures had to be taken. In mid-September Richard dispatched writs to London with orders to appoint commissioners to hear cases of treason. He put Buckingham at the head of this commission.

Richard had long since forgiven Buckingham for suggesting, at Gloucester, that he do away with his two nephews for the security of his throne. He had received the suggestion in horror, seen it as an attack on his honour, and in his fury had practically thrown his cousin out with his own bare hands. But time had spent his anger. However misguided Buckingham had shown himself to be, he was kin and they shared the same blood. There was no doubt that his cousin had made the suggestion in Richard's best interest. It was one of those terrible ironies of life that young Edward had disappeared at the same time, as if plans to abduct him had been implemented by the plotters even as he and Buckingham stood arguing about the boy's fate.

Picnicking with his children by the edge of a pond on the castle grounds, Richard heaved an inward sigh. Buckingham had written him in the meanwhile, expressing horror at the boys' disappearance. The letter had been cleverly done, couched in language oblique enough to disguise its meaning from a casual reader, yet clear to him.

Richard leaned back on his elbows, felt the grass tickle his palms. He turned his head skyward to watch the quiet flight of ducks descending on the water. How pleasant it was here! He was determined to enjoy this brief interlude, the first opportunity he'd had to spend time with George's two children. Strange how different they were, he thought, watching little Edward chase butterflies at the water's edge and Maggie read. They scarcely seemed brother and sister. In contrast to poor, dim Edward, Maggie was a normal, healthy little girl, contemplative and intelligent, with a love of books and rarely to be found without one, as now. He picked up a pebble and threw it into the pond. Ned's hound, newly knighted Sir Tristan, went barking after it, while their old wolf-hound, Roland, now thirteen, who had belonged to Anne's dead uncle John Neville, opened a sleepy eye to watch.

"My lord father—" said Ned.

"Aye, fair son?"

"Why does Evil always vanquish Good?"

Richard had a sudden vision of young Edward at the inn in Stony Stratford soon after King Edward's death. He flinched. Ned was gazing at him with dark, thoughtful blue eyes. John's eyes. The past was everywhere at once. "But it doesn't, Ned. Whatever gave you that idea?"

"King Arthur dies in the end."

"Aye, 'tis a sad tale. Yet it lifts our hearts. Even now, seven hundred years later, we still recount Arthur's deeds of arms and remember his courage and his dream. So, in truth, he didn't die, did he?"

Ned was silent. Richard knew the idea was too insubstantial for his young mind to grasp.

"Virtue always prevails, my son, and the world is proof of it. In Roman times, man was enslaved, the human condition one of greatest misery. Now, men are free. They have rights, laws to protect them. In another few hundred years, their lot may be even kinder. It shall not come about because evil prevails, but because good men made a difference. Whether they live or die as a result of their efforts is immaterial..." He picked up a stone and threw it into the pond. "See that ripple? A stone fell in and disappeared so that you might think it did no good. But if for a thousand years men sit on these banks and throw pebbles into the mere, one day, there will be no mere."

"One day there will be no evil?"

"There will always be evil, for human nature does not change. But if enough of us are true to our conscience and seek to do good here on earth, our actions, which seem to count for little while we live, in the end can change the world. You are blessed, Ned. You'll have the power to make a difference one day, for you will be king after me."

"Dear Papa, I'd rather die than live without you!"

"Why, Ned, 'tis unnatural that a son die before the father. You will be king after me and do great works, and I shall look down from heaven and be proud." Ned threw his arms around Richard's neck and buried his dark head against his father's shoulder. "Oh Papa... I love you so! I'd be afraid without you!"

As his son's soft arms clasped him tightly, Richard was flooded with warmth and fatherly love, but he also felt a certain fearful vulnerability. In this small, precious child dwelt his hopes and dreams, all joy, all meaning in life. Ned was their future, his and Anne's. How he wished his cheeks were rosier, his lips redder, his eyes merrier! Richard slid his strong arms around his boy. It was for Ned, in large part, that he had taken the Crown. The world was filled with evil and danger, and Ned was so delicate...

Chapter Six

"Then a long silence came upon the hall
And Mordred thought, 'The time is hard at hand.'"

The time had come to leave York. Over the next week Richard placed little Edward and Maggie into Jack's care and appointed him head of the Council of the North in his absence. Then he turned his attention to his own preparations for departure.

St. Matthew's Day dawned glorious and bright. Richard pushed back the bed curtains and went to the window. "What a fine morning!" he called out. "Listen to the lark, Anne. 'Tis unusual that he sings so fierce."

Anne stirred sleepily. "It's not the lark," she mumbled, "it's the nightingale… Come to bed."

Richard returned, stood looking down at her. His shadow fell on her face, blotting out the sun and bringing back the comforting dark so that she smiled in drowsy contentment. He sat down on the edge of the bed and stroked her hair. "My love, the night's candles are all burned out. 'Tis indeed the lark. Come, rise and listen with me…"

She opened unfocused eyes. "If it's the lark," she grumbled, "then he sings out of tune."

Richard laughed. Anne raised a limp hand and caught at his shirt. "It can't be morning yet, Richard… If it's morning, we must part today."

"Aye, my little bird, I fear our time in York has run out. You must go to Middleham with Ned, and I must return to London."

She struggled up in bed. "Can you not stay for your birthday? It's only two weeks away."

"No, dear Anne," Richard sighed. "I'm needed in London. There's unrest in the land and much business awaits. I'll send for you as soon as I can, dear heart."

***

The autumn evening had turned chill and a great fire roared in the hall of the fine manor house in Gainsborough where Richard and his friends enjoyed wine with their host, Sir Thomas de Burgh. Reluctant to leave after supper, they lounged while the servants dismantled the trestle tables around them. A messenger interrupted the mood. Richard took the letter, read briefly, and passed it to Francis.

"It's Brittany's reply regarding Edward Woodville and Henry Tudor," Richard said, his tone resigned.

"Will we get Tudor?" inquired Rob.

As Richard offered no reply, Francis answered. "Duke Francis of Brittany says Woodville is inconsequential, but if Richard wants Tudor, he'll have to send Brittany help against France. A war is brewing and he needs at least a thousand archers."

Rob whistled.

Will Conyers, a Neville kinsman of Anne's who had journeyed with Richard from York, left the fire where he had been warming his hands and came to Richard's side. Richard was fond of his elder statesman. Though Conyer's kinship to the Nevilles was by marriage and not blood, he was as tall and broad-shouldered as John and Warwick had been, a handsome man with a high forehead and an eagle nose. His dark hair was silvering now, for he was at least fifteen years older, this kin of John's who had been Robin of Redesdale when the rest of them had been whelps.

"You should get that Tudor, Richard," he said quietly. "At all cost."

"There's nothing I'd like better, Will," Richard said, kicking out a chair for him. "But I'm in no position to offend France or provide an army for Brittany. We haven't the money. Edward Woodville stole the treasury, remember?"

"But if France gets hold of him—" Conyers broke off, unable to finish the thought.

"My lord king is right. Tudor's an expensive trinket. Much as we want him, we can't afford him," offered Richard's secretary, John Kendall.

"Not a trinket," corrected Will Conyers. "More like one of those new-fangled guns that shoots mischief from a distance."

"It doesn't change anything. There's still no money," replied Kendall.

Richard rose wearily. The hall was hot and stuffy from heat and smoke. He went to a window, flung it open. The blast of cold air was refreshing. He leaned against the stone embrasure and listened to the loud rustling of the wind sweeping autumn leaves across the grounds. A line from Malory came to him: "And when King Arthur made His Table Round, and all men's hearts became Clean for a season, surely he had thought That now the Holy Grail would come. But sin broke out."

He looked up at the sky. There were fewer stars than he expected for such an apparently clear night. He didn't know why, but he had felt despondent all evening despite the warm camaraderie of his friends. Brittany's letter had not helped his mood. So this was what it meant to be king, this state business that wore on at a petty pace, rarely to resolve with a satisfactory conclusion; this separation from Anne, who from now would have to divide her time between Ned and him. He had never shirked his duty, but sometimes duty seemed an onerous burden.

"Maybe the money will be there next year," said Francis, joining him at the window.

Richard inhaled deeply. It was too late in the day to dwell on Tudor, and useless in any case. "Hard to believe how quickly time passes... It's already the tenth of October. Last week was my birthday. I was thirty-one." He gave Francis a wistful look. "We're getting old, Francis."

"Speak for yourself," Francis grinned. "I'm as handsome as ever. You're the one who's a bit careworn at the edges, Richard."

Richard attempted a smile. He shut the window. "See you in the morning, old friend."

***

At the Archbishop's palace in Lincoln, the fresh morning air rang with the clangour of bells and the song of monks at Prime. After chapel, Richard strode into the great hall for breakfast. The smell of the freshly baked bread he loved made his stomach growl. As soon as he sat down, he tore himself a large slice, dipped it into a bowl of black treacle, and washed it down with mead. A steaming platter of pike was set before him; he lifted his dagger, attacked it with relish, then downed his favourite cheese and sweetened his palate with a serving of stewed figs. He had almost finished his breakfast and raised his dagger for one last slice of cheese when two red-faced messengers ran in and knelt at his feet.

"My Lord King," one panted, "a rebellion has broken out! The Duke of Buckingham has risen in revolt against you!"

Richard smiled. "Who sent you to me in this jest?"

The two men exchanged glances. "We're sent by Lord Howard, Duke of Norfolk, Sire," said the first messenger grimly. "'Tis no jest, my lord!"

For Richard, past and present converged and into his mind's eye flashed the image of Edward, laughing at the news that his loyal cousin John had revolted against him.

"The Duke of Buckingham has issued a public proclamation throughout the land—" the second messenger said, "that he has repented of his former conduct and joins the rebellion to free the princes!"

Richard listened blankly, his dagger limp in his hand, his blood pounding in his head. His mind told him it was no mistake while his heart refused to believe. Most news was made up of rumour, hearsay, innuendo, omens, and hasty judgements given flavour by perception. Buckingham was his friend, his ally, his blood. Never would he betray him.

Or would he?

He pushed away from the table. "Follow me," he commanded, and led the way to his council chamber.

***

During the course of the day, more messengers arrived. From London, Wiltshire, Kent, and Wales they came; two knights, half a dozen squires, a herald, even a lowly serving lad, confirming the first reports. Gradually the tale emerged. The Marquess of Dorset and his uncle Lionel, Bishop of Salisbury, had gathered their supporters and fomented rebellion in Salisbury, Wiltshire, Kent, Surrey, and Exeter. Most were friends and kin of the Woodvilles, like Sir John Fogge, whom Richard had pardoned and taken to his breast early in his reign. Others were old Lancastrians, yet others men who had lost their positions at court to Richard's appointments, like Sir John Cheyney, replaced by Sir James Tyrell as the King's Master of the Horse. Morton, the ambitious and wily Bishop of Ely, fell into two of these categories, being both a Lancastrian at heart and one who found himself out of favour with the new King. To this rebellion, the Duke of Buckingham was a latecomer. Sometime in August, he had made his decision to throw in his lot with them.

Richard looked from face to face, struggling to comprehend. "But… he had everything…"

"He had not the Crown, my lord," said Sir Marmaduke Constable, a Neville kin and John's old friend whom Howard had dispatched from Westminster to brief Richard. "The Duke of Buckingham considered himself next in line to the throne by virtue of his double descent from Edward the Third. By discrediting you, he felt he could gain the Crown for his own head. This much we learned from a serving lad who was privy to their treasonous plotting and came to us with the information."

"It makes no sense," said Richard. "He stands to lose everything by backing Tudor—an adventurer with no true claim, and fewer prospects."

"My lord, all we know is that Morton told him this and Buckingham went along with him, in spite of the fact that Buckingham himself preferred the Crown."

Richard made no response. He turned away to the window, seeing in its coloured glass a reflection of the black-robed, dark-eyed bishop and bright golden-haired Buckingham sitting over wine at a table in a dimly-lit room.

His best friend, and his worst enemy.

The old wound from Barnet began to throb in his right shoulder and his head ached. He became aware that Scrope of Bolton was speaking. The words came to him muted, as if they carried through fog. "…that foul traitor… God rot his soul! …after the King made him Lord Constable, Great Chamberlain, Chief Justice of Wales, gave him the crown estates of de Bohun and everything else he asked for!"

"Everything but the Crown." Francis' voice. "What baffles me is why he gives his support to Tudor. Surely he won't be content playing kingmaker?"

"Arrogant Buckingham doesn't intend to put Tudor on the throne," replied Scrope. "He's merely using him to topple Richard. No doubt he figures that when the throne is empty, it'll be the man with the best claim and biggest army at his back who'll wear the crown!"

Richard shook himself from his lethargy, tried to concentrate on what was being said.

"Those who have met Tudor say he is a wily devil, much like Louis of France," Marmaduke Constable said. "He's a penniless exile, forced to live by his wits. Intrigue is all that's left to him. Since he's been reared among the French, no doubt he's learned their ways."

"God damn him; he's timed his revolt well and caught us unprepared!" Francis exclaimed. "We've no army with us. The King's supporters who came on the progress returned to their households long ago."

A man-at-arms entered, and announced the Constable of the Tower, Sir Robert Brackenbury. Silence fell. Everyone turned to the door. Brackenbury strode in, his helmet under his arm. "Sire," he said, bending a knee.

Richard stared at the gentle knight. The long wavy white hair framing his face flowed from his crown to his shoulders like that of Merlin in an old illuminated manuscript. Aye, he could use a Merlin now; to turn time back, to set everything right. Mutely he motioned for him to tell what he knew.

"Sire, the Duke of Buckingham came to me at the Tower late on Lammas Day. He said he was there to carry out your bidding regarding the princes, and that, the matter being highly secret, only his men were to go with him to the royal apartments. All others were to be dismissed for the night. I was to ask no questions, he said... I could not deny him, Sire, for he was Constable of England and I, only Constable of the Tower, and you have long evidenced great faith in my lord of Buckingham—"

Richard inclined his head, absolving Brackenbury of blame.

"In any case, I had no cause to suspect wrongdoing since I knew how you felt about your royal nephew, and for certain, so did the Duke." Brackenbury cleared his throat nervously. "The Duke was there much of the night, and by morning he and his men had departed. I went straightway to the royal apartments, but they were empty... No sign of the Lord Bastard or his serving lad to be found anywhere. However, in the White Tower, under the foot of the stairs that leads from the royal apartments to the chapel, there was an area newly covered with mortar, still wet. We didn't know what to make of it." He looked at Richard with a pained expression. "Sire, if 'tis true that my lord of Buckingham did the foul deed, that could be where he hid the babes' bodies."

Richard's lassitude vanished, replaced by explosive anger. His blood boiled in his veins. With an oath he kicked a chair over, hurled the table on its side, pulled down the tapestries around the room, and grabbed the wine flagon from the sideboard. He pounded it against the stone sill and flung the battered silver piece across the room. He swung around, eyes blazing with murderous rage. "Kendall! Make a public proclamation! Buckingham is a traitor and all my subjects are to be ready to take up arms on my behalf! Write Chancellor Russell; tell him we leave for Grantham in the morning and to send the Great Seal there immediately!"

Kendall hastily upended the table with the help of the others. Someone offered him a chair and he fell into it. When Kendall was done, in a rush of feeling, Richard seized the pen from Kendall's hand and added a postscript:

And here, God be loved, is clear at last the malice of him that had best cause to be true, the Duke of Buckingham, the most untrue creature living, whom we with God's Grace shall soon bring to justice.

He flung the pen back on the table and rose. "Gather your clerks and send out a summons to arms across the land, all of you!" He sagged against the hearth and leaned his head on the mantle.

Francis went to him, placed a hand on his sleeve. Richard looked at him with wounded eyes. "How could he do it, Francis?"

Francis had no answer. "If we produce little Richard, the rebellion will collapse," he offered.

"It would make no difference to their purpose. We'd merely be toying with the child's life. Tudor would dispatch him in order to seize the throne. I can't take the chance." In a choked voice, Richard said, "I killed him, Francis."

"No, Richard. Edward died because he was too ill to be moved. But for his fever, I'd have taken him to Barnard with his brother. He was mortally ill. The infection in his jaw was spreading. In time it would have reached his brain. The boy didn't expect to live himself. He took confession daily and was preparing himself for death. As for the serving lad, it was not you but Buckingham who took his life. And remember, Richard of York lives—because of you."

"Not I… Anne alone. She suspected what I was too blind to see."

"It was Anne's idea to move the boys to Barnard's Castle, but you gave the order."

Richard put out a hand, gripped his shoulder. "'To be a king, you have to kill a king'… 'Tis my cross, Francis."

Chapter Seven

"I shudder, someone steps across my grave."

October drew to a close. The weather turned chill and wet. Never had England seen such torrential downpours. For a fortnight it rained without pause, turning roads into muddy quagmires and flooding many. Nevertheless, Richard's muster was complete. He was ready to leave Leicester for Coventry, heartened to learn that, contrary to what he had feared, the rebellion was not widespread but confined to the south. Standing in the great hall of Leicester Castle by a window overlooking the rain-driven River Soar, Richard dictated a second proclamation to John Kendall.

"As I, King Richard III, swore before God to rule with mercy and justice, therefore I grant to all my subjects my full pardon for any treasons into which they have been led by the traitor and adulterer the Marquess of Dorset and"—he clenched his fist—"that most vile traitor, the former Duke of Buckingham, Henry Stafford." His glance, moving across the rain-drenched gardens, fixed on the royal bedchamber in the round tower to the east behind the machiolated walls and battlements of the castle. There, a hundred years before, had died his great-grandfather, John of Gaunt, Duke of Lancaster, from whom both he and Buckingham were descended. Though the good duke's loyalty had been sorely tested by his nephew Richard II John of Gaunt had remained true to his king. Loyalty and honour had counted for something then… How times had changed. Richard dragged his eyes away.

"Further, I offer a reward for the capture of the Duke of Buckingham of one thousand pounds, or lands worth one hundred pounds per year—" Gasps went around the room. Aye, it was a royal sum, and no doubt would do the job quickly, but it was a sum his purse could ill afford and they all knew it. "For the Marquess of Dorset, I offer—"

The clatter of hoofs drew Richard's attention to a drenched knight dismounting in the courtyard below. A crack of thunder made the man look up and Richard saw that it was the grey-bearded messenger he had sent to Duke Francis of Brittany. The man strode into the building. Moments later he appeared in the hall.

"Urgent tidings, my lord," said Thomas Hutton, bending a knee. "I have hastened from Brittany to warn you that Henry Tudor intends to invade England with the help of Duke Francis."

"My thanks to you, Hutton. By good fortune, we were appraised of his intent some time ago and have set guard on the southern coast. As for ourselves, we are ready to march," Richard looked up at the dark skies, "foul weather though it be."

"No need!" called Francis, lumbering in, accompanied by a soaked, shivering young man. "Howard sends news." He grinned broadly.

"Sire," panted the messenger from London, "His Grace the Duke of Norfolk bids me tell you the rebellion has evaporated!"

Richard stared at the man in stunned disbelief.

"The Duke of Buckingham was unable to raise much support except by threats and force. It seems he is a much hated man. His castle of Brecon was looted as soon as he left, and his flank was harassed by a local chieftain as he marched east. A large and loyal band fought bravely for you—and right cleverly—to cut the Duke from bridges and to block the passes along his way. The foul weather sent by heaven played no small part in bogging him down. In the end the Duke was deserted by his men."

"Under whose captaincy did this loyal band fight so bravely against Buckingham?"

"Under Humphrey Stafford, his cousin, Sire."

"Ah." Richard made a mental note of the name and filed it away. "And the local chieftain?"

"A Welshman by the name of Rhys Ap Thomas, Sire."

"What about Buckingham?"

"Buckingham has fled; we know not where."

"And Morton, Dorset, Lionel Woodville? The rest of the plotters?"

"Morton deserted the Duke, my lord. 'Twas then the traitor Buckingham realised all was lost. It is believed the bishop fled to the fen country where he has friends. Men are on his trail."

"Well done," said Richard. But he had no smile. There was still Morton, and in the shadowy recesses of his mind lurked the dark knowledge that Morton was a dangerous man.

***

They went south, to Salisbury. More messengers caught up with the royal cavalcade along the way. The plotters had scattered. Some, like Dorset and Lionel Woodville, fled England for Brittany while others sought sanctuary with friends. It was in Salisbury that news came of Buckingham. The messenger was beaming. "I am sent by the Sheriff of Shropshire, Sire. The Duke of Buckingham has been apprehended!"

Richard rose from the council table in the privy chamber of the Bishop's Palace where he had been discussing strategy with his lords. "How was he found?"

"He took refuge with a servant in Wem and the servant turned him in, Sire."

"Judas, betrayed by Judas… As soon as he's brought in, he is to be tried by Sir Ralph Ashton." Richard ground the words out between his teeth, aware of the glances his men exchanged with each other at mention of Ashton. Dubbed the Black Knight on account of his armour, Ralph Ashton was as feared for his cruelty as Tiptoft, the Butcher of England, had been during the wars between King Edward and the Kingmaker. One of his favourite punishments for minor infractions of the law was to roll men downhill in barrels filled with spikes. That, Richard thought, dismissing the messenger and turning back to his lords, should put the fear of God into Harry, the pretty duke of Buckingham.

***

On All Hallow's Eve, the day after Buckingham was delivered to Salisbury, Ralph Ashton came to Richard. He was a man large in build, with pale yellow hair and rheumy hazel eyes. His features were so sharply etched and impassive, they seemed carved of rock, and he clanged as he walked, for he carried a sword at his side that slapped against the nails in his black leather outfit.

"Buckingham has confessed. He lost no time when he realised I was in charge of matters." Ashton's mouth thinned into a cold smile. "He begs one boon, however."

Standing on the dais in the silk-curtained hall of the Bishop's palace, his lords and knights gathered around him on the lower steps, Richard eyed Ashton without warmth. He preferred not to have such men in his service, but he could no longer pick and choose. The realm had been torn by strife for thirty years. First England had been ripped apart over York and Lancaster; then the Yorkist party had divided itself between King Edward and Warwick the Kingmaker. On Edward's death, it had divided again between those who wanted Richard and those who wished to see King Edward's sons on the throne. Now Edward's party had thrown in their lot with Buckingham and the Lancastrian Tudor, and that included much of southern England, for the South had hated the North ever since Ludlow when Henry's ferocious French-born queen, Marguerite d'Anjou, and her northern hordes had invaded them, burning, raping, and pillaging as they went. And to the South, he was a Northerner. Winning their trust would take time. In the meanwhile, his base of support had been shaved perilously thin and he had to reward loyalty wherever he found it.

"What does he ask?" Richard demanded.

"To see you, my lord."

"Never," Richard spat.

"'Tis what I told him, but he begs an audience. He is most desperate, my liege. I've seen men die, but none so fearful. He is beside himself, weeping, hysterical, half out of his mind. What should I tell him?"

"Tell him he is to be executed on All Soul's Day and to make ready."

A shocked murmur of protest arose from his men. "All Soul's Day falls on the Sabbath, my lord!"

"I don't care if it falls on doomsday!" roared Richard, his grey eyes dark, glittering. "He dies on All Soul's Day, and that's final!"

They were all staring at him as if he'd gone mad. Desperate to get away, he fled the dais. His heart racing, he halted in the passageway to catch his breath and leaned his head against the damp stone and closed his eyes. All Soul's Day, the second day of November, had been young Edward's birthday.

***

Men hammered in the drizzling rain, erecting a new scaffold in the marketplace for Buckingham's execution. Richard was conscious of the din as he listened to Ralph Ashton. "My lord, the traitor beseeches you to see him. He has lost all dignity. He is feverish, filled with abject terror, and wildly implores this one boon."

Richard looked at the scaffold rising in the shadow of Salisbury Cathedral and let his gaze drift upwards, to the spire standing dark against the grey skies. "You may tell him that well should he be filled with terror, for on Sunday he will be judged by God."

"My lord, he says there is something you need to know."

Richard hesitated. Then anger swept him. "Never again will I see his vile face in this world!"

Richard didn't sleep that night but lay in his bed listening to the chanting of the townsfolk. It was All Hallow's Eve and evil spirits were about. The castle servants had fastened hazel branches over the doors and windows to keep out witches and the souls of the wicked departed. In town, after an evening of apple-bobbing and fortune-telling around the half-finished scaffold in the market square, people were circling their homes with lighted candles for the same purpose. At the castle there had been mummery and entertainment for the servants, and in a light moment Richard had allowed his fortune to be told by a wise-woman. He would die young, she said, like all the men of his line, and his time would come soon after he saw the castle of Rougement.

Welladay, what else was new? Only Edward had died in his bed. Everyone else he had known and loved had died before his time, and violently. On Sunday there would be one more.

***

All Soul's Day blew in with freezing rain and a blustery wind. After Mass, as the mighty cathedral clock tolled the hour of noon, Henry Stafford, second Duke of Buckingham, was led into the crowded market square. From a small chamber high in the palace, Richard heard the axe fall and the pigeons scatter skyward.

As his lords talked among themselves that evening, he sat quietly around a table in the great hall staring into his wine, trying to understand the sense of loss that dogged him. Why had Buckingham's death affected him so? Maybe because he had felt alone at Edward's death, and then came Buckingham with Edward's merry laugh and George's golden curls. In a moment, he became everything.

There was something else. A sense of unfinished business nagged at him. What had Buckingham wanted to say? Might there have been more to young Edward's murder than he had confessed to Ashton?

Maybe he should have heard him out. And maybe it was nothing, just more lies... Maybe all he'd wanted was one last chance to beg for his life. Whatever it was, it was too late now. He'd never know.

He shook himself to dispel his gloom. A messenger had arrived. Richard lifted his head and forced himself to concentrate on what the man said... Henry Tudor had appeared near Dorset harbour with only two ships. They had tried to lure him to shore by waving lanterns and shouting that the rebellion had prospered and that the Duke of Buckingham had sent them to conduct him to his camp. But Tudor, sensing danger, had sailed away. "He was probably awaiting a password," offered the messenger.

The old sea-dog, Howard, who had joined them after taking care of the rebels, slapped a hand against his ample thigh and growled, "By God I wish I'd been there! I'd have given him a password he'd ne'er have forgotten!"

"I wish you'd been there, too, Howard," Richard said dully. "Tudor's the only threat left. We've survived the others... No doubt we'll take care of him soon enough."

"My lord, may I speak?" requested a man in a loose russet robe down the table. It was Thomas Hutton, who had returned from the court of Brittany. His brown eyes burned in his lined, bearded face, and his tone held urgency. Richard inclined his head.

"I observed Henry Tudor in Brittany and gained a sense of the man," said Hutton, leaning close and speaking low. "As so few here at court have met him, I request permission to speak bluntly, my lord, for it would be wise for all concerned to know what they are up against."

Richard motioned him to his side and he slipped in between Francis and Scrope. "'Tis not surprising that Tudor didn't fall into the trap," Hutton went on, "and—if I may give a word of warning, Sire—he will not be easy to trap. He has the suspicious wariness of a hunted animal, for in a sense, 'tis what he is."

His voice was deep and carried a unique force. Silence fell like a mantle over the table. His gaze moved from Catesby to Howard, from Jack to Ratcliffe, and lingered on Francis. A strange look came over his face. Then Hutton met Richard's gaze. In the flickering candlelight those penetrating dark eyes might have been the eyes of a seer, for they seemed to hold wisdom beyond understanding. So might Moses have looked, Richard thought, seeing all… knowing all.

Hutton continued. "He is a man both clever and devious, an adventurer with nothing to lose. He will risk all for his dream, which is the Crown of England. His word is writ on water, and having run for his life, most of his life, he is an unnatural man, bound by none of the rules which bind others." His thick brows drew together in a frown. "His head is filled with intrigue. He has few scruples and is consumed by ambition and greed. There is nothing he will not say, and nothing he will not do, to gain his end." He looked at Richard with his solemn, capturing eyes. "It would be a mistake to underestimate him, Sire. Tudor is a dangerous man—" Hutton's voice fell to a chilling whisper "a man to fear, as one would fear Lucifer's own."

No one moved. A shiver ran down Richard's spine. He made the sign of the Cross. His lords followed his example. Keeping all inflection from his voice with great effort, he said, "I thank you for your council, Hutton, and assure you, it'll not be forgotten." He rose to his feet, and with a confidence he did not feel, strode from the room.

That night he dreamt of the frightful dragon of his childhood nightmares with its cruel yellow eyes and fiery red breath. Screaming the wise-woman's prophecy of violent, premature death, its vicious fangs tore into his flesh. He awoke in a feverish sweat, the name *Tudor* on his lips.

How strange… He had forgotten. Tudor's emblem was the Red Dragon. *Damn Tudor*, he thought. Until Brittany handed him over, he'd have no peace.

Chapter Eight

"A moral child without the craft to rule."

Thoughts of dragons and prophecies soon evaporated as Richard learned in Exeter that another leader of the rebellion had been captured. Thomas St. Leger was his brother-in-law, married to his eldest sister, Nan.

She had begun a liaison with St. Leger when her Lancastrian husband, the Duke of Exeter, fled to France after the Battle of Towton that put Edward on the throne. Exeter, who had commanded Warwick's left wing at Barnet, was captured at Tewkesbury, sent to the Tower, and released years later, in time to accompany Edward on his invasion of France. At some point along the sea journey, he had disappeared. Foul play was rumoured. With her husband dead, Nan had married St. Leger on his return to England.

Richard found the whole business distasteful. But then, he'd never been close to his haughty oldest sister, and she had always kept aloof from him. He remembered how his beloved sister Meg had assured him, when he was small, that Nan was distant with everyone, but he'd had his doubts, even then. He knew exactly how he felt about St. Leger's treason, however. His sister's husband had hatefully, shamefully, betrayed the family ties and defiled the bond of kinship. He deserved to die. Richard immediately ordered his execution.

Within hours he was besieged by his sister's messengers offering large sums of money for his release. He refused. The next day she arrived in person to beg for his life. She had requested a private audience and Richard received her in a small chamber at the Bishop's palace in Exeter, with only Gower present,

"As he chose to become an agent of the Woodvilles, I see no reason to spare his life," said Richard.

"I love him!" she cried. "Do you know what love is?"

Richard stared at her. Now he admitted to himself what loyalty had suppressed all these years: He didn't care much for this woman, sister though she was. Age had heightened her stern demeanour by slashing deep grooves into her cheeks and pulling down the edges of her mouth. Nor did her dress soften her harshness. She had clad herself in a riding habit of brown and green and hidden her hair beneath a matronly wimple. Indeed, it surprised him that such a woman had ever found love. Clearly, she thought the same of him. Now he knew she'd never given a care to his predicament during the troubles with Warwick. He'd been seventeen, forced to choose between his brother and the girl he'd loved, and she had not spared him a thought in his misery.

Yet in spite of everything—in spite of her disregard for him, and though treachery was the most heinous crime a man could commit—he could still have forgiven St. Leger, if St. Leger had had his excuse. What made his treason more heinous was that he was kin, without cause to turn against him. Like Buckingham—

"Never did I wrong St. Leger! Never did I deny him favour. Always he was welcome and honoured in my court. He chose to be a traitor, and for no good cause—certainly no cause that I ever gave him. Such a man does not deserve to live!"

For a bare instant his sister said nothing, didn't even move. Then she lunged at him, screaming and pounding wildly against his breast. He seized her wrists in an iron grip and turned her over to Gower. Adjusting his velvet cap with the boar badge and straightening his doublet, he strode past her. In a voice low with disgust, he said, "Where is your dignity, sister?"

"Where is your heart?" she shrieked. Shaking Gower off, she ran after him. "I'll not call you 'brother'—you boar, you beast—you vile murderer of innocent babes! May God destroy you for what you've done—*Usurper!*"

Richard froze in his steps. Though he kept himself under rigid control, inwardly he felt as if a stake had been driven through his heart. It was not her curse that affected him as much as her words, which had scratched the secret core deep within his soul where he had buried the doubts, guilts, and fears of a lifetime. He clenched his fists and fled the chamber.

***

In late November Richard returned the Great Seal to Chancellor Russell in the Star Chamber at Westminster. The business of the rebellion was concluded; rebels punished, loyalty rewarded. Richard dealt with the rebels with a light hand, executing only ten men and offering pardons to most of the leaders of the conspiracy, including Morton and Dorset. Even Sir John Fogge, who had repaid Richard's kindness with treason, was pardoned and promised restoration to his estates. With Stanley's wife, Margaret Beaufort, the prime mover of the rebellion, he was exceptionally lenient. Though she was stripped of her titles, he gave them to her husband to enjoy. As for Stanley, Richard rewarded him so lavishly that he raised eyebrows even among those who knew him well.

"Is it wise, my lord?" asked Anne who came down to Westminster to be with him. Swathed in furs against the cold winter wind, they strolled along the garden walk to the river in the fading twilight. "Twice you've not only forgiven the Stanleys their treasons, but have granted them more power." She spoke softly, taking care to fall silent when others passed. "Stanley's brother, Sir William, is Chief Justice of North Wales, and Stanley himself is Constable of England, as Buckingham was. Everyone knows he's a man of uncertain loyalty, this 'Wily Fox.' You've placed him in a position to do you great harm if he chooses."

Richard looked at her delicate face, at the lovely violet eyes wide with concern for him. It was a joy to see her again after so long, but it troubled him that she had been ill with more frequency than usual this winter and had not regained the weight she'd lost the year before. He felt a stab of guilt; the disruption of their happy life at Middleham, the trauma of events and the enforced separation from their beloved Ned was to blame. If he hadn't taken the Crown—

He banished the thought. He'd had no choice. "I must keep Stanley's support. The only way to do so is to load him with wealth and titles so that he has too much to lose by supporting Tudor."

"That didn't work for Buckingham." Anne saw Richard flinch and instantly regretted her words. Yet they needed to be said. She spoke frankly nowadays. Grateful for the advice that had saved his nephew's life, Richard sought her counsel. "One cannot forget," she added, "that Stanley is Henry Tudor's stepfather."

"I've considered that. No, Anne, Stanley is too calculating a man to risk his neck for a bastard with no claim to the throne, even if he is married to the mother."

They had reached a bench overlooking the river near the watergate. Fatigued and out of breath, she took a seat. Richard hadn't dispelled her fears and the dark thoughts kept coming. "Nor do I trust Henry Percy, whom you've made Great Chamberlain."

Richard took her hand into his and smiled at her with twinkling eyes. "That, my dear lady, is because you are a Neville."

"Aye..." she sighed, unable to return his smile, "I am... and would feel safer if a Neville were still Earl of Northumberland, my love."

Richard looked down at the curve of the trusting cheek that now rested against his fur-clad shoulder, and the lightness he had enjoyed a moment before evaporated. Anne's uncle, John Neville, had always been true to York, and for his loyal service Edward had rewarded him with the earldom of Northumberland which had belonged to the traitorous Percys. After John's brother Warwick raised a rebellion against Edward and joined with the Lancastrian cause, Edward had stripped John of his title and returned it to Percy, though John had remained faithful to York and had fought for Edward against his own brothers. Eight months later, humiliated, broken-hearted, and nearly penniless, John had joined his brother's rebellion and died at Barnet.

Richard shifted his gaze to the river, which had turned deep blue in the twilight. The colour of John's eyes. "My lady... I know," he said roughly beneath his breath. Lifting an arm, he drew her tight against him, and they sat silently by the water's edge, watching the quiet Thames flow past.

Chapter Nine

"And still she looked, and still the terror grew,
Of that strange bright and dreadful thing, a court."

Christmas of 1483 was a happy affair at Windsor, a celebration of Richard's accession to the throne and his victory in crushing a rebellion without bloodshed. The castle was decorated with evergreens, strewn with dried rose petals and violets, and lit by hundreds of torches and yule candles. Snow fell softly outside, while inside the castle minstrels played in the gallery, fires crackled in the hearths, and the aroma of spiced apples and roasted chestnuts wafted through the merry halls crowded with laughing guests.

But as Richard sat on his throne watching the mummery, his heart was not as light as he would have wished. Brittany and Tudor preyed on his mind. A wool fleet bound for Calais had been forced to return to England to avoid capture by Brittany, and Tudor still haunted his nightmares. As soon as the Christmas festivities ended he would have to force Duke Francis to make peace—and hand over that Lancastrian remnant. Maybe all he needed was to give his admiral, that fierce old sea-dog and master of naval warfare, Howard, enough money to launch a serious campaign. Surely he would make Duke Francis see reason…

The thought might have banished his care had it not been for a certain emptiness. Ned was not with them. He was ill again and they dared not bring him to foul London, so full of pestilence and plague. Needing to reassure Anne, whom he knew pined for her child, he leaned close and took her hand. "We would have kept Christmas at Middleham had affairs not been so pressing, my love. But I must take care not to appear too much a Northerner to the South… Next year, God willing, we can hold our Christmas there."

"Oh, Richard, I know it's no one's fault. It's just such a concern when Ned is ill."

"Now, my little bird, remember—"

Anne turned her large eyes on him. With a faint smile, she recited dutifully, "'Richard liveth yet.'"

Richard thumbed his own broad chest. "Aye. This is the sickly babe who was expected to die. And so it will be for Ned."

He looked suddenly boyish with his cleft chin, a smile on his lips, and a happy look in his clear, grey eyes. "Did I ever tell you that I love you?" Anne whispered.

"Not lately. As I recall, I had a rebellion to quell, and you had embroidery to finish."

"Indeed, my lord. There's little time for embroidery these days," she said, feigning offence. "I start the day with the chamberlain and steward of the castle going over finances, crops, and animals. I arbitrate quarrels between servants, answer letters from supplicants, visit the sick, entertain your lords and otherwise run your estates in your absence. For two hours in the afternoon I see petitioners. Only after Vespers do I enjoy the luxury of needlework and Ned's company."

"It has been a burdensome pace for us both, my love," Richard admitted, his bantering tone gone. "We must snatch our small joys when we can, for time passes all too quickly."

The performance was over. They lifted their hands to clap and Anne's gaze passed over their guests. There was Margaret, jolly old John Howard's second wife, of whom she was very fond. With her was Howard's only son, Thomas, Earl of Surrey, who had miraculously survived his wounds at Barnet. *He is a fine young man, much like his father,* she thought. Her eyes sought Howard. The genial white-haired baron was threading his way through the throng, back to his wife's side. He pecked her lightly on the cheek and laughed.

Anne's eyes softened. She hoped that she and Richard would grow old together. Nearly sixty Howard was, but with a heart as merry as any twenty-year-old. As usual, he was not dressed soberly as became his years, but in a bright strawberry gown edged in miniver. Her eyes touched on his rotund stomach. She couldn't suppress a smile. No doubt the Colchester oysters he loved so well had much to do with his girth. He was devouring them now with evident relish while a page waited with a half-emptied platter. From experience she knew he would not stop until none were left in the castle.

Anne was flooded with affection. Howard was much like Richard: a fond husband and father. Dutiful. Hard-working. Energetic. In battle he was brave; with ladies always chivalrous. Like Richard he was a man of exceptional abilities, and like Richard he had married Margaret for love, not for titles or connections. Both appreciated music and learning, and were generous to the poor. Wherever he travelled, Howard opened his purse to those in need, and his workmen and ships' crews always received something extra above their wages for drink. At his own expense Howard had sent many a deserving lad to Oxford or to learn a trade. They had shared much together, many happy hours, their two tiny families.

She withdrew her gaze and looked around the room.

Richard's nephew Jack was dancing the pavane with one of the Bourchier girls while his three young brothers watched and his mother, Liza, bounced her youngest on her knee. Rob and Francis stood together laughing about something with their new friend, Humphrey Stafford, who had fought for Richard against his cousin Buckingham. Stafford was another genial young man, Anne thought; nothing like Buckingham. Down farther stood a group of Neville kinsmen and friends, the two Scrope cousins, Bolton and Masham, and William Conyers. With them was Richard's squire, Gower, who had once been squire to her uncle John. Below the gallery, against the wall, Richard Ratcliffe and his lovely wife were gazing into one another's eyes and laughing as they drank from a single wine cup. A smile softened Anne's lips.

Her gaze moved along several of Richard's Knights of the Body, and touched on Richard's trusted retainer, the gallant Sir Richard Clarendon, whose tall shining head attracted many a sidelong glance from the ladies. At the back of the great hall, past the line of dancers, she saw the Stanleys. She stiffened.

Margaret Beaufort, her husband, and their henchman Reginald Bray stood apart by a traceried window, observing the dancers and whispering together. Bray had been Margaret Beaufort's go-between in her treason with Buckingham, but Richard had pardoned him also. She watched as they all nodded at something Stanley said. Her eye moved to Stanley's brother, Sir William, who emerged from the crowd on the far side of the hall and strode across to join them.

How little he and Stanley resembled one another. Stanley was tall and thin; William, short and stocky. Stanley's bushy hair was a flaming red; William's wispy hair barely ginger. Stanley and his wife also made an odd couple. Margaret Beaufort was a tiny woman with a disproportionately long face that made her look top-heavy, almost dwarfish. He was jovial, and she was austere in manner and dress. Anne knew Richard found her fascinating. What was it he'd once said about her? That she both repelled and attracted at the same time, like a jagged rock that signals both land and danger to a sailor in a storm.

She was indeed a striking figure in her usual black velvet and ermine gown, but hard. Her face was wolfish, sharply pointed at nose and chin, and her pale deep-set eyes held a vigilant expression. Once upon a time Margaret Beaufort had fooled her as she now fooled others, but Anne had come to know her in these troubled months. She strove to look a martyr with her wimple and pious ways, but she was too pious for true piety and her treasons spoke of a heart far too worldly. Richard kept forgiving her because virtue moved his admiration, but he was an innocent in some ways. He couldn't believe that devotion in Margaret Beaufort might be pretence. Anne's eye fell on a book the Beaufort woman held in her hands. She wouldn't be surprised if it were a psalter. *Blessed Mother Mary, the Devil assumes many guises,* she thought, crossing herself.

***

Had she known what Margaret Beaufort whispered about, Anne would have realised her anxiety had good cause. It would be two more days before Richard and Anne received the news responsible for the smile on Margaret Beaufort's thin lips. Earlier that day, on Christmas morning in the Cathedral at Rennes, her son Henry Tudor had sworn an oath to marry King Edward's eldest daughter, Elizabeth of York, and unite the red rose with the white.

"It was Morton's idea," said Margaret Beaufort in a low voice as she stood watching the dancers from a distance. Her speech had a staccato ring to it, for she enunciated her words with the same precision and meticulous care she gave to everything she undertook. "And he has several more. One is very clever indeed."

To mislead anyone who might have overheard that remark, Lord Stanley gave a roar of laughter and called out to a dancer as she passed, "*Clever* devil, isn't he? Be careful he doesn't trip you, my dear lady!"

Margaret Beaufort looked pointedly at the dais and said quietly, "Ned is a sickly boy. His death would be an irretrievable disaster for the dynasty."

Lord Stanley blew his nose into a handkerchief. "I pray I haven't caught my son's cold," he said loudly to no one in particular. "George has been *sickly,* you know, *very sickly!*"

"Many would see such a death as divine retribution for the death of King Edward's sons," murmured their henchman, Reginald Bray, flashing his horse-teeth and feigning a smile designed to fool those watching.

Margaret Beaufort's eyes lit. "Divine retribution. What a nice touch. I hadn't thought of that."

Sir William Stanley joined them at that moment and Bray was unable to respond. As the two brothers exchanged remarks on the weather, Bray edged close to Margaret Beaufort. "But how?" he whispered. "He is well guarded." A group of young people approached, laughing.

Margaret Beaufort waited until they had passed. "The music tonight is charming, isn't it?" she said in a conversational tone. "But that is scarcely surprising. Our noble King is a great lover of music." She looked at Bray meaningfully. "*As is the Prince of Wales,*" she added pointedly. She turned to her husband. "My lord, I believe the King would find much pleasure in our minstrels. You must offer to send them to Middleham to entertain the Prince." She met Bray's pebble-hard black eyes, her own filled with meaning. "Our finest minstrels," she said carefully, enunciating every syllable.

Bray understood. A cold smile spread over his thick lips.

Margaret Beaufort turned to her brother-by-marriage. "My lord, you seem a trifle melancholy this evening. Are the festivities not to your liking?"

"Nay, lady, lavish they may be, but given by a babe-killer,"

William Stanley muttered.

Lord Stanley made a pretence of roaring with laughter. He slipped an arm around his brother's shoulder. His lips fixed in a smile, he said quickly, "Guard your tongue, watch your step, and keep your head, brother." He raised his wine cup in a mock salute.

William frowned. "You mean, keep a foot in all camps like you, brother?" Then, before Stanley could answer, he announced brightly, "Ah, there's good Percy!" He bade his brother farewell and bowed over Margaret Beaufort's hand.

She watched him leave. William's rashness was the reason she had excluded him from their plots, and he did not know her role in the deed at the Tower. Since Richard had as yet made no public statement about the boys' disappearance, William Stanley, like many others, assumed they had been put to death on Richard's orders. There lay William's value: as a weather vane testing the direction of the wind. If a man who had not been deeply committed to King Edward blamed Richard for the princes' disappearance, so did many others. Clearly, removing the boys—distressing as it was!—had proved a brilliant move. Good Buckingham had done them a great service.

Or perhaps the credit should go to Morton? she thought wryly. He was the one who first discerned Buckingham's fear that the princes, if they lived, might one day be restored to the throne and exact revenge for his part in the death of their favourite uncle, Anthony Woodville. Morton had planted the suggestion in Buckingham's mind early on, without the vain duke ever realising it was not his own idea. The he'd played on the fear until he drove Buckingham to the deed. Clever man!

Her mouth twitched with the need to laugh. By God, Morton deserved a cardinal's hat for his services! In getting Buckingham to murder the princes he had put Richard in an unenviable predicament. Whether or not Richard exposed the murders, he bore the blame. The princes had disappeared during his watch; that placed the responsibility squarely on his shoulders. Even if he made Buckingham's confession public, confessions were routinely extracted under torture and lacked credence. Besides, Buckingham had been Richard's right arm. No one would believe he had acted without Richard's knowledge.

There was one thing, however... Buckingham had said he thought the younger boy with Edward may not have been Richard of York. She crushed the thought and the unease that accompanied it. If it wasn't little Richard, who could it have been? Ridiculous. Buckingham was a fool.

Across the crowded room where William Stanley had disappeared, Margaret Beaufort's sharp eyes caught Richard emerging. She put on her best smile as he approached. Stanley and Bray bowed, and she bent into a curtsy.

"My lord and lady, I am pleased you chose to celebrate Christmas with us this year," said Richard.

The fact that Stanley had not requested permission to return to his estates since his pardon for his part in Hastings' plot had been heartening. The powerful baron had great experience of affairs, both military and civil, and had proved himself a valuable asset in Richard's government. He needed Stanley, but the winning of his loyalty went beyond need. It was a measure of the secret test that he had set himself. The Wily Fox had served Edward loyally for over a decade. If the baron chose to give him his loyalty, it meant Richard had succeeded in proving himself worthy of the Crown he had taken from Edward's son.

Stanley's red beard spread into a smile. "You are most kind to invite us, my lord."

"And why not? We are kin, after all." Richard regarded Margaret Beaufort. The only child of the deceased Duke of Somerset, Margaret Beaufort, like Richard and Anne, was descended from the great Duke of Lancaster, John of Gaunt. Edmund Tudor had been her second husband and Stanley her fourth. She had borne only one child, Henry Tudor, now a man about Richard's own age whom he had never met. As for Stanley, it was rumoured that she shunned his bed, having committed her person to God. Richard regarded her a saintly woman, for she had once been blessed with a vision.

"Dear lady, I know we've had our differences in the past, but I wish to assure you in the spirit of this holy day, that I hold no grudges and wish only for our amity."

Margaret Beaufort inclined her head graciously. "I thank you, my lord."

"Our great-grandfathers, the Dukes of Lancaster and of York, were the closest of brothers and dear to one another's hearts, so I am told."

"Indeed, my lord."

"Fair Cousin Margaret," Richard said softly, "surely it would please them in heaven to see us put aside the enmity that has rent our houses so grievously?"

"My lord, on my part I shall do all I can to bring about the unity of York and Lancaster, and may God in His Grace grant England the blessed peace for which we all pray."

A rare smile touched Richard's lips. His eyes moved from the heavy gold crucifix around her neck to the psalter she held in her hand. Anne was wrong. Margaret Beaufort was a woman of sincerity and good intent, for where there was such piety there could not be malice. "Joy to you, Lord and Lady Stanley… Bray." He turned to leave. Margaret Beaufort swept into a deep curtsy; Stanley and Bray bowed.

"You did well," said Stanley to his wife as soon as Richard was out of earshot.

"I did not lie," said Margaret Beaufort under her breath. Her mouth twisted into a cold smile. "I am indeed doing all I can to bring about the union of York and Lancaster."

Chapter Ten

"The blameless King... cast his eye
On each of all whom Uther left in charge
Long since to guard the justice of the King
....and found them wanting."

After the Twelfth Night feast in the White Hall of Westminster, Richard sat at his desk, going over papers in his bedchamber. Anne watched him from the corner of her eye as a lady-in-waiting brushed her long fair hair and another scented her with rosewater. There was a subject she had wanted to broach with him all Christmas but she had not yet dared to bring it up. The moment was never right. She sighed inwardly, wondering if it would ever be. Richard allowed himself no respite from work and would labour through half the night unless she found a way to stop him. The morning would bring another exhausting day; another late night. Quietly she had the servants set a pallet, a tray of spiced wine, and Richard's favourite cheese by the fire. She came up behind him and kissed the back of his neck.

"Nay, lady love," he chuckled. "I can't concentrate when you do that."

"'Tis my aim," Anne smiled, taking his hand and drawing him away.

"Lady, I have orders to sign for men, arms, ships; letters from kings to answer; appointments to decide you must not tempt me away—"

"All can wait a day, Richard. They'll not know the difference, I promise you." She dismissed the servants and drew him to a silk pallet. She unbuttoned his grey velvet doublet trimmed with fur and silver tissue, untied the silk shirt beneath, and laid them aside. Averting her gaze from the ugly jagged white scar from his injury at Barnet that had left his right shoulder slightly lower than the left, she massaged the hard-corded muscles of his back with smooth kneading movements. Richard gave a deep sigh of pleasure.

"See, you were tense and badly in need of a woman's touch."

She helped him into a brocaded robe and handed him a goblet of spiced wine. He planted a kiss on her smooth brow.

"My Flower-eyes."

"My King Arthur," she smiled. "In all ways but one."

"And what way is that?" demanded Richard gruffly.

"You have a son and heir." Her eyes misted.

"Aye, I know, sweet heart... As soon as we can, we'll go north, but I fear that can't be until after Parliament meets in January."

Two more months before she saw Ned again! She sipped her wine, trying not to let her heartache show. Rain pattered gently at the window and the fire roared, sending out warmth and light. Such a lovely fire, but soon it would consume all its wood, she thought with a stab of inexplicable sadness. She leaned forward, picked up a small log and threw it into the hearth.

"Anne," Richard said, munching on a slice of his favourite cheese, "do you care to hear my plans for Parliament?" He leaned back on an elbow. "The realm is restless, Anne... Strong measures would secure it quickly, but I've decided that's not the right way to go. I know you disagree and think I should not have pardoned the Stanleys, but I have good reason for leniency. Though, of course, to discourage treason, I must draw the line somewhere, attaint some of the rebels—"

"And their wives and children, Richard?"

He reached out and gently traced the outline of her cheek with his knuckles. "Nay, Flower-eyes. Their wives and children shall not be left penniless. I do not punish innocents." Anne kissed the ringed fingers against her cheek.

"As to my policy, I've decided to be as lenient as I can with the traitors, in part because I have no stomach for ruthless measures; in part because I wasn't born to the throne. I came into it—some say unjustly—so I must prove them wrong, Anne. I must *earn* my right to rule by winning the hearts of my people—and those of my enemies. I hope to do that by showing forgiveness and correcting injustice."

Anne found it strange that Richard should doubt himself, yet she had often noted that those who were truly good were never assured of their own goodness, while others, banal and wicked, held themselves in high regard, confident of their own worth. "Your right to the Crown is unquestioned, Richard, both by merit and inheritance. I know you'll win England, as you've won the North."

"The North is a small region and I had ten years to do it, Anne. England will take a very long time. Yet time is what we do not have."

A log fell from its high perch in the hearth with a crack like thunder and split into two, shattering the tranquillity of the night. Anne gave a start but Richard, absorbed in thoughts, didn't notice.

"First I shall explain why I have taken the throne," he said, "for I want everyone to understand. Beyond that, I propose to turn Parliament into a body representing all the people instead of letting it remain as it is: the King's High Court. That I shall do by the enactment of an entirely new body of laws—"

Anne's glance strayed to a book on Richard's desk, *The Vision of Piers Plowman* by William Langland was a tale about a weary wanderer who falls asleep and dreams of a better world where the corruption and injustices of daily life are laid bare and remedied. The cover was plain and unadorned, and the pages well worn by use. The book was one of Richard's favourites, and clearly he had heeded its plea.

She turned her gaze back on Richard. His enthusiasm was contagious. His eyes shone, his deep voice resonated. How she loved that wonderful voice! It was almost like listening to music, so fluid, melodic, and tender. She roused herself from her thoughts, forced herself to concentrate on his words. He spoke of banning benevolences, of limiting the powers of bailiffs, of dealing with unscrupulous sellers of land who sold the same property to more than one buyer. He spoke of statutes to correct economic injustices and protect innocent men from abuses of the law. At first she listened uncritically, then a disturbing thought began to form.

"You realise that many nobles and gentry will disapprove of your measures?" she said.

"Aye, to give justice to the poor, I must take power from the mighty, many of whom have used the system to prey on the weak." Fidgeting with his signet ring in the old manner from his childhood, he twisted it around his finger. "But I must hope there are enough men of good will to outweigh those who will resent me for doing what I know is right… what I feel compelled to do."

"If—the Saints forfend!—there were another battle, you would have need of all your barons. Can you afford to alienate them, given the narrow margin of support left to you, my love?"

"I'm well aware of the perils of my policy. But I can't condone what I know is wrong, yet by doing nothing, I condone it. Therefore, I have no choice."

"You can't right all the wrongs in the world by yourself."

"Who else is there?"

When she said nothing, Richard took her hand. "The strong must serve the weak, Anne."

King Arthur. Aye, it was what she had seen, and loved, in Richard from the very first. She squeezed his hand in understanding. "As his lady said, Sir Thomas Malory would have approved of your kingship, Richard."

For a long while they sat together, gazing at the dancing flames, drinking the spiced wine. The doubts faded and she found herself once more savouring the tranquillity of the night, unwilling to bring up the subject on her mind. Then the Abbey bells chimed one, reminding her of the lateness of the hour. She set her goblet down. "Richard, there is a favour I would ask of you, though you will not like it."

He chuckled, regarded her tenderly. "My silly Flower-eyes, why should I not like it?"

"It regards the queen."

"The queen?" He released her hand and sat very still for a long moment, his grey eyes hard as flint. He heaved an audible breath. "Forgive me, Anne… What would you ask of me that concerns Dame Grey?" Richard had taken to calling Bess by her first husband's name to drive home the point that Bess Woodville was never truly wed to Edward.

"Her daughters have been in Sanctuary since May. Seven months, Richard. The three oldest—" She broke off, plaited and unplaited a fold in her white shift. "I was their age when I was in France." Richard took her hand and pressed it to his lips. Anne rushed on before she lost her courage. "It's hard for them, Richard.

They're young. They wish to dance, to wear pretty gowns, to be admired by young men. Instead, they're locked up in an abbey—" She forced back the memories. "They must be so lonely. I would make them welcome at court. Can you not persuade Bess to let them leave Sanctuary?"

"You know I've tried. She's a stubborn woman. She thinks I'll do her harm and I can't make her believe otherwise."

"Because she thinks you've harmed her sons. There is a way to persuade her."

Anne met his eyes, and he read her thoughts.

"I'm responsible for Edward's death, Anne. I can't let anyone know little Richard lives—especially his mother. It would encourage her to plot again, and if Tudor found out the boy was alive, he'd try to harm him."

"'Tis a boon you'd do Bess to let her know her son lives. It would change everything between you… Richard, I know. I am a mother."

The fire crackled and hissed. Richard stared at the rain-spattered window, watched a droplet weave a path down a dark pane. With great difficulty he'd smuggled the boy north and kept him safe all these months. He hadn't exhibited him even to give the lie to Buckingham's rebellion and Tudor's rumours, because that was dangerous for the child. Now Anne was urging him to let little Richard risk a journey back to London that was fraught with peril and might well cost him his life. Or might hearten his Woodville mother to scheme again for the throne.

Or Anne might be right. Bess Woodville might give up the Sanctuary that was a reproach to him and his rule.

The Abbey clock clanged the half-hour.

"At first light, I shall make arrangements to bring him from Barnard's Castle." Drawing Anne to him so that her cheek lay in the hollow of his neck, Richard gazed at the fire, feeling its warmth surge through him. He kissed the top of her head. "What would I do without you, my Flower-eyes?"

Anne nestled in his arms, watching the dying embers. The last log had fragmented into glowing splinters, and the splinters were burning away, dissolving into ashes. She felt suddenly cold.

"You're shivering, Anne—" Richard put an arm around her and

poked at the ashes with a cherry branch. "Let's go to bed, my sweet. The day is done… the fire is almost out. "

Chapter Eleven

"He rooted out the slothful officer
Or guilty, who for bribe had winked at wrong...
Clear'd the dark places and let in the law."

Throughout the Christmas festivities, Richard focused his attention on the problem of Brittany and the external security of the realm. He bought more ships, manned them, and devised a system for protecting the merchant convoys. Before the new year of 1484 struck, he sent Howard and Sir Edward Brampton to harass the Bretons.

Finally he was able to focus on the internal peace of the land. Anxious to present himself to the people and give them a chance to assess him personally, he decided to make a progress south, to Kent, a seat of insurrection against the Crown since the days of Holy Harry. On his first day in Canterbury, after a private prayer vigil at the high altar, he returned to his chambers in the Bishop's palace and prepared a proclamation. He handed it to Anne for her approval.

As Anne read, she was overcome with emotion. The words were nearly an echo of those Richard had spoken to her on that starry night in Middleham during their first married summer together. She could see him in the moonlight, hear his voice: *I have a dream, Anne, I dream of justice for all...*

I am determined that everyone shall receive justice, he had written. *Extortion and oppression will be punished, and anyone who has been grieved, oppressed, or unlawfully wronged may come to me and I will see that justice is done... All my subjects shall enjoy their lands, property, and goods, according to law, and I order that no one, no matter how exalted or what his degree, can rob, hurt, or wrong a man... upon pain of death or imprisonment.* She handed the proclamation back to him without looking up.

Richard rose from his desk. "What is it, my sweet? What ails you?" With a gentle touch, he wiped a tear from her cheek.

Anne raised her head. His face sparkled as though she gazed at him through crystals. "Forgive your foolish wife, Richard," she smiled, lifting her chin. "They are tears of pride, beloved."

***

On the twenty-third day of January in the new year of 1484, as Abbey bells rang for Tierce, Richard opened Parliament in the Painted Chamber at Westminster Palace. After the Archbishop's speech, he rose from his canopied throne and addressed the members.

"In the past, innocent men have been thrown into prison solely by accusation," Richard said, his thoughts turning to poor Cook, the merchant who had had the misfortune to own a tapestry coveted by Edward's greedy queen. "And kept there for years," he added, remembering Sir Thomas Malory who, on one ruse or another, had been kept in prison and denied a trial for years because he had caught the evil eye of first Marguerite, then Bess Woodville. "That must change. Every accused must be granted bail until proven guilty. His property must not be seized until he stands convicted. The law must cease to be an instrument of extortion and oppression," There was a stunned silence, then a few cheers and everyone began to talk at once. Voices were raised against the measure, but in the end, they relented. From the dark looks around him, Richard knew he had failed to win these men over. They had abandoned their opposition only because he was King and they felt they had no choice.

Now to the yeoman, Brecher, who'd given him shelter one long ago summer's day when he and Anne had disguised themselves as peasants, fled Barnard's Castle, and were lost in the rain.

"Corrupt juries obstruct justice. Therefore, every man serving on a jury must be of good repute. To ensure that he has a vested interest in his community, he must own property. Verdicts of unqualified jurors are to be declared void, and tampering with jurors must be a felony." More cheers. More dissension. Finally, it was agreed; the wording strengthened.

One by one, in addition to the grant of bail to the innocent and improvements in the jury system, the rights dear to his heart were debated and adopted into law. These included economic protections against unscrupulous sellers of land, and the protection of the art of printing, which was hotly contested by the prelates. Book writing had long been the sole preserve of the Church.

"One last item," declared Richard in his resonant voice. "My laws are to be enacted in the common English, not Latin, so that the poor may know their rights." He noted Archbishop Rotherham's glum expression and the many glowering faces among the clergy. In one sweep, this measure stripped the Church of a power it had enjoyed for centuries and deprived it of another rich source of revenue. Richard realised he had made few friends here this day.

Finally, Acts of Attainder were passed against the chief rebels of Buckingham's uprising, but as he had promised Anne, their wives were given full protection against the loss of their property. Only one had her property confiscated: the former queen, Bess Woodville.

***

It snowed heavily in London on the first day of March as a bearded knight with kindly eyes rode into Westminster Palace. Richard watched him from the window of his privy suite where he waited with Francis. He had chosen Sir James Tyrell for this urgent business, knowing Tyrell would not fail him. He was related to Francis, and others of his kin had sided with Warwick in his rebellion against Edward. Yet he had fought for Edward against his kin, and with such bravery, that he had been knighted on the field of battle.

The knight strode into the chamber and knelt in homage. Richard held up a hand for silence until Francis had shut the door. "Speak softly, my good Tyrell," Richard whispered, motioning him to rise. "In castles even murals have ears."

"All is ready, Sire. Metcalfe awaits your command."

"Are the lodgings safe?"

"Aye, my lord. He is with kin of Sir Marmaduke Constable."

"Very good. Send my squire to announce my arrival and have Metcalfe bring him to the Abbey. We shall await him there."

"So far, so good," Richard said to Francis when Tyrell was gone. "I pray we can return him to the North without anyone discovering his identity." Francis assisted Richard into his furred mantle, grabbed his own, and followed him to the cloisters.

An icy wind blew, lifting swirls of snow in the courtyard, yet the North Walk was lined with clerics sitting on benches by tables and bookcases, and along the West Walk, others were washing. The sound of splashing water and the voice of the Master of Novices instructing his charges filled the cloisters, but Richard knew all attention was on him. Heads turned as he passed the long row of rush-strewn chambers with doors cracked open for air, emitting welcome drafts of warm air from their charcoal braziers. At the East Walk, which led to the Chapter House, he parted company with Francis and a hush fell over the cloisters. The last time he had come to Bess Woodville, it was to remove her son from her custody. Even then he had not gone to see her personally but had sent John Howard and Archbishop Bourchier.

The Captain of the Guard snapped to attention at the door.

"Let Metcalfe in when he gets here," commanded Richard in a low voice.

"Aye, my lord." The man unlocked the door to the Chapter House and threw it open.

Clad in blue velvet trimmed with ermine, Bess stood rigidly erect near the central pillar in the octagonal room. The chamber was crammed with the treasures she had carted from the palace, the glowing tiled floor scuffed by the heavy coffers and partially obscured by the Saracen carpets she had laid out. The brilliant wall-paintings were nicked and marred by chests she had stacked one on top of the other, then moved again. More coffers, more rolled carpets, and piles of tapestries and plate were set on top of these. Richard remembered with disgust how she had broken down walls in order to speed the delivery of her goods into Sanctuary.

Bess Woodville glared at him with the haughtiness she had always mistaken for dignity. He thought her a pathetic figure. Her hair was dyed, her cheeks over-rouged, and her scanty lashes blackened with charcoal. Even her mass of glittering jewels couldn't hide the fact that she was no longer beautiful, for in these months of confinement she had lost a front tooth and her figure had run to fat. Richard's gaze went to the corner where his five nieces cowered together like mice before a snake. They were all pretty girls with fair hair and bright eyes, the oldest eighteen, the youngest barely four. With shame he realised that to them he was the monster who had killed their brothers. *Anne was right*, Richard thought. He was glad he had come.

"Dame Grey, I wish to set matters right between us," he said.

"Indeed? Do you intend taking your life?" she snarled.

Richard clenched a fist at his side, maintained control by force of will. "You do me an injustice."

"*You*—you dare to speak to *me* of injustice? You who set aside my marriage to Edward, who imprisoned me here and took the throne from my son!"

"Lady, you knew of my royal brother's bigamy long before the rest of us. You even committed murder to protect your secret. As to your so-called 'imprisonment'—guilt drove you into Sanctuary. You disregarded the King's will and tried to seize power. That is treason by any definition, and well you know it."

"Are we to be blamed for protecting ourselves?" she wailed.

"By pointing a false finger first? That, Madame, is how you have always justified your crimes against others."

"And you've always been against us... Now, by your hand, my sons are dead! May God punish you in eternity—you murderer of babes!"

"Lady, you condemn yourself. Unlike you, I have not steeped my hands in infants' blood, as you'll soon learn from the lips of your son, Richard of York."

Her mouth fell open. She stared at him with disbelieving eyes. "Dickon?" she murmured feebly, shuffling towards him on unsteady legs. She searched his face. "My Dickon is alive?"

There was something unnatural about hearing his own name drop with reverence from such lips, and Richard retreated a step. At that moment the door was thrust open and a grimy stone mason entered, carrying a pail and tools, his boy helper at his side. The door slammed shut behind them and Bess Woodville swayed where she stood. "*Dickon!*" she cried, stumbling towards him, opening her arms wide. "Dickon!"

"*Mother, mother!*" cried little Richard, running into them.

Bess fell to her knees. Her body racked by sobs, she clasped her child to her breast and held him tight. The girls in the corner of the room dropped their hold of one another and stared in frozen, dumbfounded silence.

Had Bess been a stranger, Richard would have been moved to pity by her maternal devotion and tearful joy, but he knew her too well, so his heart remained untouched. Greed had brought her here. Greed for money and shiny things to fill the hollowness of her soul. For all her vicious cunning, all her sly and devious ways, all her clever schemes for power and gain, she was a stupid woman. Only the stupid never learned from their mistakes. He averted his gaze to grant mother and child a measure of privacy, but pity he could not feel. Not for this woman. This *Woodville*. Carnage she had demanded. Carnage she had wrought.

He lifted his eyes to the twinkling coloured glass in the window high above, and silently, in his heart, whispered a prayer for those she had destroyed: his brother, George; his father's friend, Desmond; for Warwick who had sheltered him, and John, who had taught him honour. And for the many others whom he had loved, and many others still whose faces he had never known, who had perished in the battles of her creation.

Chapter Twelve

"No light! so late! and dark and chill the night!"

At Westminster, Richard gazed out over the Thames, silver in the early morning light. Anne was always right, he thought. As she'd promised, he'd won Bess over, and with terms that were generous but not extravagant. As a result, no one could say he'd lured the greedy queen out of Sanctuary and into a country house by promise of the gold she had worshipped all her life. Then he dispatched her guard to sea to fight the Britons. His action proclaimed that the queen was no longer an enemy, or regarded him as one. *Too bad about Dorset, though*, he thought toying with his signet ring. Bess had sent her son a secret message in Brittany that all was well and he could return to England, and Dorset had tried to flee Paris in the night. But before he could embark ship, he'd been caught by Henry Tudor's men and "persuaded" to return. A pity. They could have learned much from him about Tudor's plans.

"My lord."

Richard turned. It was Kendall. "Ah, my good man, take a seat, let us see what we can do to help the humble folk..."

A prior who couldn't afford the eight pounds for a royal licence had it waived; a man who had had himself elected vicar-general by false means in Exeter was replaced by the man he had cheated out of office. A bricklayer in Twicknam who lost everything when his house burned down and could no longer afford to care for the poor he had previously housed, was given money. Richard even took care of Buckingham's unpaid debts to small creditors, including one for bread and ale delivered by a baker to Brecon. Many other misfortunes were noted and corrected. Richard enjoyed being generous. Despite his depleted purse, he passed out a number of grants. His faithful secretary, Kendall, was a recipient, and there were many others. Even old servants who had long since left his service were not forgotten.

"Finally, my dearest lady, we can set our sights on Middleham," said Richard to Anne early in the first week of March, "as I promised." A rare smile spread across his face. "We shall soon see Ned—and take care of problems along the way, of course, we must do that, but we are on our way to Ned!"

Spring was in the air. They felt it in the touch of the sun on their skin, caught it in the scented breeze that brushed their cheeks as they rode across the valleys and the fields. They saw it in the half-melted snow and the blueness of the vast skies overhead where frothy white clouds floated. They heard it in the cries of birds soaring across the hills. Richard and Anne exchanged many a happy glance as they rode together. *What a relief it is,* their glances said, *to be gone from Westminster, to be in the saddle again, heading north, north, north...*

For pure pleasure they tarried two days in Cambridge while Richard discoursed on divinity with learned doctors.

"Sometimes I find myself dwelling on what a holy man once told me," said Richard to a doctor of sacred theology. "There is no purpose to suffering. It merely happens."

"'Twas said by a man of little faith, Sire," replied the good man. "There is purpose in suffering even if we cannot divine it. We must simply resign ourselves to things that pass our understanding."

"But Scripture does say, 'The race is not to the swift, nor the battle to the brave, but time and chance happeneth to them all.' Is that not what is meant?"

"You are questioning the injustice of life, and for that, we are offered no answer. Scripture merely relates how it seems to us, not necessarily how it is. As Socrates explained, man sees shadows and mistakes them for reality, for man has never seen anything else. *Faith,* Sire... We shall know the truth someday. But on this earth we must have faith."

With that, Richard had to be content. Even so, their visit to Cambridge was a delight, a serene interlude. Before leaving, Richard and Anne bestowed generous grants on the university, then, on a dreary, drizzling morning in mid-March, they rode up the hills encircling Nottingham, their retinue clattering behind them. High above towered the massive fortress of Nottingham Castle built on a jutting outcrop of rock that glistened black in the rain. Anne reined in her palfrey.

"What's the matter, dear lady?" inquired Richard.

"I don't know, Richard... It must be the weather. Nottingham seems gloomier than ever this day."

"Aye, 'tis indeed a dismal place despite all the money Edward and I have poured into it. Even my new tower with its spacious royal apartments and oriel window scarcely seems to have brightened it up."

"'Tis not a place that can be brightened, Richard. It has an air about it."

Richard gave her a smile. "We'll not stay long, my love." He squeezed her hand.

Anne inhaled deeply, braced herself and nudged her palfrey forward.

***

Affairs kept Richard and Anne in Nottingham longer than Richard had anticipated. It was not all unpleasant, however, for they were able to steal time now and again for hunting and hawking in the woods where Robin Hood had once roamed robbing the rich to give to the poor. Watching Richard canter with White Surrey through the dappled forest, his gerfalcon, Balin, on his wrist, a smile touched Anne's lips. There was a bit of Robin Hood in Richard, she thought, for he had robbed the nobles of power to better the lot of the poor. *May God bless him*, she added to herself, spurring her chestnut palfrey after his mighty white charger.

March gave way to April and still they could not leave for Middleham. Easter found them at Nottingham, and it was at Nottingham they observed the thirteenth anniversary of the death of Anne's father and uncle John at Barnet. But the Feast of St. George that followed that sombre day banished gloom with its joyous celebrations and feasting in the great hall.

Anne's gaze fell on Bess Woodville's daughter, Elizabeth, dancing with Jack. "Your niece is a lovely girl," said Anne to Richard.

Richard made no response. Anne looked at him. "How can you not like her, Richard? She's nothing like her mother and there is much of Edward in her."

"Certainly she's tall like him," replied Richard.

Anne threw him a wry, indulgent glance. Richard had never cared for tall women. "Aye, Elizabeth is tall, but not ungainly so. She's at least a finger shorter than you and a full head shorter than Jack. And she has Edward's eyes. But I wasn't thinking of her appearance as much as her character. She bears herself with grace and utters not a word of complaint about her hardships."

"She is politic, then."

"Not merely that, Richard. She looks on the bright side of things. 'Tis a good gift to have… Edward had it."

Into Richard's mind flashed the memory of the sea voyage to Burgundy after John Neville changed sides, forcing Edward to flee for his life. Edward had made a jest of his poverty and merrily offered his furred cape to the captain in payment. He could always laugh in the face of cruel fortune. "That he did."

"And she's generous like Edward. Already she's given away one of her three new dresses to a poor knight's lady. She said she didn't need three anyway."

"Maybe she's filled with guile and knows that's the way to win your favours," Richard replied, raising an eyebrow. Anne reached for his hand. "She's a Plantagenet, Richard, not a Woodville. You do her wrong."

Richard turned his eyes back on Elizabeth, remembering the long-gone day when Elizabeth the child had danced with her father at her little brother's wedding. Everyone had remarked on the charming scene, but all he could think about was his own brother George down the river, in the Tower, waiting to die. Because of Elizabeth's mother. That witch. That *Woodville.*

He came out of his thoughts abruptly. Elizabeth was laughing merrily at something Jack said as she did a twirl under his raised hand. For a moment he thought of Edward and his heart twisted. Perhaps Anne was right about the girl, but it made no difference. He would endure her. He would find a gentleman to marry her. He would endow her, and treat her with respect. Not because he liked or trusted her, but because she was Edward's daughter and he owed that to his brother. The minstrels broke into a pavane. Tired of discussing Elizabeth, in whom he had no interest, Richard offered his hand to Anne. "Will you dance with me, my lady?"

They took their places on the floor. Richard noted that his head minstrel had thoughtfully slowed the pace for Anne's sake. It was evident to everyone that Anne had grown more delicate during the past year; so much so that even this small exertion was tiring her. The melody over, she panted, "My lord, it seems I'm getting old and must leave the dancing to others."

Richard led her back to her chair on the dais and took his seat beside her. "Twenty-seven years can scarcely be said to be old, Flower-eyes." He smiled, hiding his concern. "Not when you still have some teeth."

His teasing had the desired effect. Anne's mouth twitched with a smile. "You shall not be so rude again after the punishment I shall mete out to you," she scolded.

Richard took her hand and tilted his brows uncertainly, "Dear heart, if it's what I think it is, I beg your forgiveness most fervently, for I could not bear to be banished from your bed even for a night."

"And if I choose not to pardon you, my lord?"

"Then, dear lady, you'll leave me no choice. I shall command you to pardon me, for I am King and you must do as I say."

Laughing, they turned their heads from one another. As they did so, their smiles died on their lips. At the back of the hall, coming towards them, was Anne's mother. Clad in a black robe and mantle, unadorned by jewellery and leaning on a retainer's arm for support, she dragged herself forward, her face contorted in anguish. Her dark figure contrasted so strangely with the glittering jewel-coloured silks and velvets of the other guests that it struck an unnatural note, like a sweet melody foully ended by a loud, jarring chord. The minstrels ceased their song and a hush fell over the hall. The guests stared, opened a path for her. Slowly, so slowly they didn't realize they'd moved, Richard and Anne rose from their chairs, their eyes riveted on the Countess, a single thought on their minds.

Ned!

She had never left Ned's side in all these ten years.

The Countess stood before them, eyes filled with tears, mouth working with emotion. "Ned," she finally managed, "our beautiful boy… is dead—"

"No!" moaned Richard through bloodless, trembling lips. He stepped back and his chair crashed to the floor. *"No! O God, God, no—"* Thunder exploded in his mind and broke into a tumult that threatened to bring him to his knees. He covered his ears but the din rose to a crescendo of intolerable pain. He staggered to the wall. Reaching out blindly in his agony, he caught the cold stone mantelpiece as his knees gave way.

Anne felt as if her blood boiled in her veins. She let out a long, guttural half-human wail and, driven by a pain of excruciating agony, fled down the dais, a quivering madwoman, running from wall to wall like a cornered animal until there was no breath left in her. With wild eyes she cast about, but there was nothing but blackness all around. Unable to see where she was, where she was going, she put out trembling hands before her and fumbled forward. Her knees collapsed beneath her and she felt herself falling down, down, down… into a deep, dark well without hope and without end.

***

Anne lay in her bed in a deep, drugged sleep, dreaming of gargoyles. But now it was not her father who stood wavering on the steeple, begging for the help she could not give, it was Ned. And now, the laughing, fiendish gargoyles were not Marguerite d'Anjou, but bore the narrow, wolfish face of Margaret Beaufort. Anne tossed wildly and cried out for Richard. She dimly heard him answer, but why did he keep saying, "Forgive me," and where was he? She couldn't see him…

Sleepless in his chair, and transfixed by pain in his breast so heavy and acute he could barely move, Richard held Anne's hand, keeping vigil at her side. Flooded by memories, each a dagger thrust to the heart, he stared at her. Stared at her, and saw Ned, sleeping in his cradle, tiny fists on his pillow… Ned, at two, chasing yellow butterflies along the grassy hills of Middleham… Ned, Prince of Wales, walking solemnly in the procession at York…

Ned was gone.

Richard gasped for breath and closed his eyes. Was it the

judgement of God? Had God taken his son because he had taken a Crown from his brother's son? Anne had never wanted the Crown. From the beginning she had feared it. "Forgive me, Anne," he murmured. "Forgive me—"

Along with the physician and the servants ministering to the King and Queen, the Countess moved about the gloomy chamber like one risen from the dead, bringing food and drink, which was returned untouched. She had been orphaned; she had been widowed. She had buried a daughter and lived to see the destruction of the great House of Neville. But nothing she had endured compared to this; this shattering grief. She had raised Ned from babyhood, had known him as she'd never known her own children, had loved him as she'd never thought she could love anyone in this world. Now he was gone.

Her eyes touched on her daughter asleep in the curtained four-poster bed and moved to Richard, whose silent grieving she found harder to bear than Anne's tears. How much worse it was for him, she thought; to be a king, to lose an heir; to go on with kingly duties as though nothing had happened. He had put aside those duties for two days now, but soon they would clamour for his attention. Pity tugged at her heart. He looked slovenly, unkempt; not much like a king at all or even the old fastidious Richard she knew. For two days he had not shaved or bathed, and his white shirt, dingy and stained with perspiration, hung open at his neck. The stark pallor of his face heightened the darkness of the growth shadowing his chin as his stricken grey eyes stared mutely at Anne. Sometimes his lips moved, but she couldn't make out the words.

She brought her gaze back to her daughter. Anne's brow was feverish, her cheeks stained with dried tears, her lids purple and discoloured. The Countess drew in her breath. It wasn't only their child they had lost. They had lost their future and their hope. In silence she reached down, drew a blanket over Anne's shoulders, and mopped her damp brow. She took a cup of water to Richard and forced him to sip. Gently, hesitantly, she touched his sleeve. "My lord, it has been two days… we must go to Middleham."

***

Middleham, Richard thought, gazing at the castle that rose up before him. *Middleham...*

It was the sixth of May. Ned's birthday. The child whose hand he had held in the darkness was gone.

Sunlight filtered through an opening in the clouds like rays sent from heaven, illuminating the black-draped castle in a strange light. He remembered its pearly glow the first time he had come to Middleham and met Anne. He had been nine then. Ned's age. It had been May then, too.

He glanced behind him, at the litter bearing Anne. The trip from Nottingham had been ponderously slow and taken a week, for Anne was very ill and could not travel more than two or three hours a day in the bumpy litter.

The Countess appeared at his side. "How is my lady?" he asked.

"As well as can be expected, my lord," the Countess replied. She bit her lip, and didn't add, *for a mother who has lost her only child; for a woman who can never bear another.*

Richard looked back up at the castle. "Middleham... 'Tis a place where I was always happy." He stiffened his back and tightened his hold on the reins as they began the ascent to the castle. The portcullis creaked open. Followed by his dark-garbed retinue, he clanged over the drawbridge and passed through the arched stone gateway into the castle. Servants, friends, and nobles stood in the courtyard in sombre dress and countenance. He was conscious of an eerie stillness as he approached, then they bowed and curtsied and there was the rustle of fabric and jingling of chains. Here and there he heard sobbing. His mind turned back the years to the glittering gaily-garbed, smiling courtiers who had gathered to greet him the first time ever he came to Middleham. There, on those steps ahead, at the foot of the massive stone Keep, had stood the great Earl of Warwick and his brothers, George and John Neville. "Welcome to Camelot, fair cousin," John had said, winning Richard's heart with a smile framed between two dimples.

Richard blinked. The ghosts vanished.

Slowly, inexorably, his eye crept from the steps of the massive ivy-mantled Keep up to the highest window where two swallows pecked in the vines, building a nest below the black-draped stone sill. There, in that peaceful, sun-drenched chamber above, Ned had been born.

There, he had died.

Birds chirped; the wind rushed through the trees with the same rustle it always had, carrying the scent of fir and beechnut that Richard remembered so well. But there was also something else. He sniffed the air. Something faintly pungent and disturbing; a fume that grew stronger the nearer he approached the Keep. White Surrey snorted. Richard turned his head to his left, towards the chapel where Ned lay.

His heart twisted in his breast.

It was the sickly-sweet smell of incense, and it did little to mask the violent, putrid stench of rotting human flesh.

Chapter Thirteen

"Sing, and unbind my heart that I may weep."

There was no relief for Richard and Anne. Ned had died, and neither of them had been with him. Even harder to bear was the knowledge that he had suffered. Anne sat in a carved chair on the dais in the great hall clutching Ned's worn velvet blanket while Richard stood stiffly at her side, white-knuckled and unmoving, his face ashen. Together they listened to a procession of doctors, clerics, and servants who related the terrible details of Ned's passing.

He had fallen ill with a bellyache in the middle of the night on Easter Monday after a pleasant dinner and evening of music, and the doctors could do nothing for him. He was in great pain to the end and had cried out for his mother. Anne swayed in her chair. He had died two days later.

Richard had to practically carry Anne from the room, for her legs trembled so that she could barely stand. In their bedchamber where Ned used to play chess with them and read poetry, his love-child Johnnie sat with Bella's Edward by the empty fireplace. Eyes red-rimmed, their cheeks tear-stained, they stroked Ned's dog, Sir Tristan, as Gawain and old Roland looked on. Even the hounds mourned Ned, for they lay silent, chins flat on the cold tiled floor, a knowing, sorrowful expression in their eyes. In the corner where Richard's suit of armour hung beneath a tapestry of the Siege of Jerusalem, Maggie, his niece, and Katherine, his natural daughter, knelt at the black-draped prie-dieu together.

When Richard and Anne reached the threshold of their room, they halted. Directly ahead, in full view of the window, stood the tall elm where Ned's archery target still hung. The boys rose slowly, followed their gaze, saw the tree. Their faces crumpled. Young Edward ran to them, threw his arms around Anne's skirts. "L-Lady a-aunt," he cried in a strangled voice, unable to control his stutter, "w-w-why did N-Ned have to go? D-Did God n-not k-know I w-would have g-g-gone for him?"

Anne sank to her knees, bursting into tears. She clasped her sister's child to her breast and opened her embrace to young Johnnie, who rushed to her. Kate and Maggie ran to her, too, and Richard knelt and put his strong arms around them all. Together they huddled on the floor, all weeping, except for Richard, who stared over their heads with a blank expression, while the Countess drooped against the stone wall, tears pouring down her cheeks. Coming upon this scene, King Edward's daughter, Elizabeth, with aching heart and a depth of pity, shut the chamber door.

***

As Ned's funeral cortege clanged over the drawbridge of Middleham Castle and wound down the hillside, Richard looked back one last time; a long lingering look. White clouds sped across the blue sky, whipped by the roaring wind. Birds squawked, leaves rustled, and the bells of Jerveaulx Abbey chimed over the dales. His throat constricted. He would never return. Middleham, always his joy, was now forever draped in black. He jerked his reins and spurred White Surrey into a downward gallop.

Ned was taken to Sherriff Hutton to be buried near his young cousin George Neville. Anne had not wanted him to be alone. On May 24th, as bells tolled across all the North, his little body was laid to rest in the north chapel of the parish church of St. Helen and the Holy Cross, across from George, whom he had loved so well in life.

In their bedchamber that night, Anne was again tormented by her dream of fiendish gargoyles. As they had done since Ned's death, they bore Margaret Tudor's face. This time her yellow eyes blazed with triumph, and when she laughed, her lips formed a word: *Poison!*

Anne bolted upright, chest heaving. "Poison! It was poison!"

Richard sat up beside her and put his arms around her trembling shoulders. "Hush, dearest, you've had a bad dream."

"No!—'Tis the truth!" She turned wild, feverish eyes on him. "We didn't see it before! We didn't see it because we couldn't let ourselves see it! Ned was poisoned. *Poisoned—*" She broke off with a choked sound.

"No, cannot be! Ned was but a babe. No one would do such

a thing."

"Tudor would do it," whispered Anne in a strange, hoarse voice. "For the love of the Crown for the love of the Crown for—"

Richard slapped her. She stared at him, mouth agape. He looked at her mutely. Then he gathered her in his arms. She clutched at his chest, but there was no comfort this time. Unable to breathe, she pushed away, lay back against the pillows.

Richard gazed into the darkness. Hutton's words on the eve of Buckingham's execution echoed in his mind. *There is nothing Tudor will not do to gain his end.* Horror, chill and black, numbed him, and for the instant that he believed, he felt as if he had fallen into a lake of burning ice. *No, cannot be!* He flung back the velvet bed curtains, rose from bed. He went to the window and looked up at the dark sky.

Had he taken a Crown to which he had no right? Had God punished him by taking Ned? Was it Tudor's poison, or God's retribution? Or merely cruel fortune? He passed a hand through his hair and bowed his throbbing head.

***

The North mourned with them, but in the rest of England men murmured that Ned's death was divine retribution. Had he not died on Easter Monday, a year to the day of King Edward's death? In the taverns, the blacksmith shops, on the farms and in the manor houses, people crossed themselves and muttered that never before was the hand of God seen so clearly. Some who had not believed Richard had done the princes to death before, were persuaded now.

Richard was not told what his people said, but he knew. He had heard the whisperings in the castle, read the condemnation in the eyes of the villagers and townsfolk the nearer he rode to London. Even harder to bear was the mute pity on the faces of those who believed Ned had been poisoned. Out of nowhere had come this rumour, to be added to the rest.

Richard closed his eyes, let the steady clippity-clop of horses hoofs fill his head and numb his senses. John Neville's words of long ago came back to him: *Don't look back. In last year's nest there are no eggs.*

That had been good advice once, had kept his face turned to the future. But where was the future now?

He threw a glance back. Anne's litter wobbled along behind him. His heart twisted in his breast. It was August, three full months since Ned's passing, and Anne was ailing, unable to ride, with scarcely enough strength to sit up. It was no wonder. She didn't eat, didn't sleep. He had removed her from the oppression of Middleham as soon as he could and taken her to Barnard's Castle, but to no avail. Next, he moved her to York, where the townsfolk had surrounded her with an outpouring of love, then to the hills of Pontefract where the air was cool; then to the sea at Scarborough, where it was fresh. Nothing had helped. Since Ned's death they had not made love, not laughed. There had been no music, no joy to be found in the cold, hollow world.

Sounds of coughing came from the litter and he saw the Countess, Katherine, and Elizabeth exchange anxious looks as they rode together beside Anne's cart. He bit his lip, turned away. What if God took Anne? Then he would face a lightless future, pointless and irrelevant. His throat tightened. Where had he gone wrong? The image of the inn at Stony Stratford rose in his mind's eye. He saw Buckingham arrive, swing his long legs over the bench, heard his merry laughter. He saw the dimly lit room and young Edward carefully scratching out his name and Buckingham adding his motto and signature below. *What should I have done differently?*

Maybe there had been no right choice.

His throat ached. He'd taken the throne with the consent of the people to save the land from civil strife. Now men condemned him for it, said he had coveted it all along. That he, Richard, who had always remained steadfastly loyal to family, had murdered his brother's sons for it. Those lying rumours had fuelled Buckingham's rebellion and torn him from Ned back to London. And Ned had died, without his ever seeing him again.

Those lying rumours, spread by Henry Tudor.

Tudor. The word rattled in his head like an adder. Tudor was the source of their misery. That whoreson had spread the vile rumour that Ned's death was divine retribution. Perhaps he was responsible for Ned's death... *Poison*...

The thought writhed inside him like a maggot. He shuddered, drew a sharp breath. He could not—would not—believe such a thing! But Anne did. Her conviction that Tudor had poisoned Ned was destroying her. Of all Tudor's wicked cruelties, this was the worst, God damn him!

Richard clenched his fists around White Surrey's reins. A vision of Hutton's face rose before his eyes, lips forming a single word: *Lucifer*. He blinked. Aye, Tudor might well be one of Lucifer's own, for he did have unholy luck. After months of naval warfare, Howard and Brampton had managed to force Brittany to sue for peace. As part of the agreement, Tudor was to be returned to England, but Tudor, well served by either friends or fortune, had galloped across the border into France, his pursuers hard on his heels, and had reached France barely minutes ahead of them.

Richard had signed the truce with Brittany anyway, and tried to make a treaty of amity with France, as he was doing with Scotland. But France, though weak and divided by the problems of a minority reign, was united against him. They thought him an enemy of the realm, a notion bequeathed them by the Spider King. Louis had never met a man he couldn't buy, and he'd never forgiven Richard his defiance at Amiens. From beyond the grave he was making him pay. And so, France received Tudor with a hearty welcome and promises of aid. Richard's spies had sent word that he would invade England in the spring with a French army at his back.

London loomed against the horizon. Richard drew in his reins, stared mutely at the line of city wall, towers, steep roofs, and bridges that he had always hated. At the winding river crowded with boats, barges, and ships. At the dingy grey skies.

London, where the sun never shone.

He glanced back at Anne's litter and turned away with a heavy heart. He had the worries of a kingdom in which to bury his grief, but where would Anne find comfort?

Chapter Fourteen

*"Who is he that he should rule us?
Who hath proven him King Uther's son?"*

Illness was nothing new to Anne, but this time was different. This time she knew she was dying. She welcomed it. Death would be a release, not only from the pains of her body, but from something far worse: the affliction of her spirit. As she lay wasting in her bed, she thought of nothing else but the blessed release. It was Elizabeth who turned her mind to one whose suffering was greater than her own.

"My lady, may I speak?" Elizabeth asked hesitantly, wiping Anne's damp brow with rosewater. She handed the basin back to a tiring maid and knelt by the bed. "There is something you... something which..." she paused, rushed on, "I have no right to speak of it but... but..."

Anne turned puzzled eyes on the girl, who gazed at her earnestly. She blinked. For a moment Elizabeth had reminded her of someone familiar, but she couldn't place who it was. Then, with shock, she realised it was herself. Elizabeth reminded her of herself when she'd been young! The same colour hair, same honied complexion, same heart-shaped face. Strange that she had not noticed the resemblance before.

"Speak, child," Anne whispered with great effort, her voice laboured, breathy.

"My lady Queen, forgive me... 'tis about your lord husband, the King." Elizabeth lost her courage and dropped her lids. Anne gazed at her softly, seeing the lines of suffering that pulled at her mouth, the fingers that folded and unfolded a pucker of silk sheet. Summoning all her strength, she lifted her hand and placed it over Elizabeth's own. It had the desired effect.

"My lady, I fear for the King. He is in great pain but he mourns in silence. He needs you, Your Grace; he is so alone. The entire way from Nottingham, he rode ahead of your litter and cast back looks of such longing and sadness that I—I—" She broke off again, unable to meet the queen's gentle gaze. She couldn't tell Queen Anne how her heart had contracted to see the King's lonely figure riding ahead, how she had longed to gallop to his side, to take his strong sunburned hands into her own and comfort him. "You must get better or I fear the King… the King…" She swallowed, looked away in confusion.

The dainty hand squeezed her own with a touch as light as a bird's. "Speak," commanded the soft voice. Elizabeth lifted pained eyes to the wasted, once-lovely face. "Without you… I fear the King may not survive." She bit her lip to hold back the tears that threatened.

There was a long silence during which the queen merely stared at her. Then she nodded, tried to say something. Elizabeth bent her head closer to catch the words.

"Thank you, dear child," the queen murmured.

***

For a long moment after Elizabeth had made her revelation, Anne was stung with anger and jealousy. She had immediately seen through the girl's concern for Richard to the truth. Elizabeth loved him. And why not? Richard was handsome, kind, noble, chivalrous—everything a young girl would admire.

And Elizabeth was beautiful, young. Healthy.

Gazing at the full contours of the lovely face, Anne had been reminded of her own barrenness; that she was useless to Richard and to England. That she was dying, and the world would move on without her. Thankfully, that bitter moment of self-pity was short-lived. There was still enough generosity in her spirit to forgive Elizabeth her rosy cheeks, and Richard for one day forgetting her. She realised how selfish she'd been, and she was grateful to Elizabeth for opening her eyes.

That night when Richard came to her bedchamber at Westminster, she took a long look at him for the first time since Ned's death. He was dressed in plain black saye, unadorned by a girdle or mantle, and the tight-fitting cote and long hose that moulded his strong muscular body was unrelieved by any trimming. He wore no jewels except the sapphire she herself had given him, the gold griffin given him by her uncle, John, and his own signet ring. Lifting her eyes to his face, she nearly gave an audible gasp. He had aged terribly in the three months since Ned's death. His complexion was ghastly pale, his cheeks were sunken and sharply drawn, and pain was etched mercilessly in the lines around his eyes and mouth. Reaching out her hand, she drew him down beside her on the silver coverlet. The windows stood open to the warm August night; the gauzy bed curtains fluttered in the breeze, and the candles around the room flickered like tiny stars. She could smell roses and honeysuckle in the dark garden where moonlight cast dreamy shadows.

"'Tis a beautiful world, Richard, in spite of the sorrow."

Richard did not respond.

"We have overcome much in our lives, you and I. We shall overcome this." She spoke in a whisper, haltingly, for protracted speech was difficult. "With God's help, we'll learn how to live with our loss."

After a moment, in a low voice, Richard said, "We were young then. We had hope to light the way."

"My love… we have each other. God has not left us uncomforted."

"God," Richard murmured, turning to look at her with a curious expression. "I wonder sometimes, Anne, does God have a heart?"

"Richard, you've had much to bear these recent months," she whispered, in part from shock, in part to save breath for all she had to say. "'Tis why you doubt Him. But He has His reasons for taking our little Ned. One day we shall understand, as Job did when God revealed Himself to him." Richard looked at her in the dimness. She had lost much weight and was gaunt and pale, more frail than he'd ever known her. Her eyes loomed strangely large in her thin face and her fair hair hung limp in the coils at the nape of her neck. He couldn't let her go on torturing herself. He had to tell her the truth. The truth about Ned's death. He swallowed. "Anne… Tudor is not responsible. Ned's death was God's punishment on me. I had no right to the throne."

"You had no choice after Bishop Stillington revealed Edward's bigamy and—"

"Stillington has naught to do with it!" He ran his hands through his dark hair in abject misery. "I have no right to the throne! I took it anyway and God has made us pay with Ned!"

"No, Richard—" She stared at him blankly, "You have every right; you were next in line, descended from three of the five sons of Edward III. There was no question about your right."

He cradled his head in his hands. "My claim was false. I am no Plantagenet." He had never spoken the words in his life and he felt as though he had plunged a dagger into his own heart.

"No Plantagenet—! Richard, my love, what do you mean?"

His head twisted around and he looked at her strangely. "Who is he that he should rule us?... Who hath proven him King Uther's son?... This is the son of Gorlois, not the King. This is the son of Anton, not the King."

Stunned, bewildered, Anne finally comprehended. He was quoting King Arthur! Richard had always identified with Arthur, and now she understood why. Like that fabled king, he doubted his own birth. "You think the Duke of York was not your father?" *Love give me strength*, she thought. Struggling up to a sitting position, she took his shoulders and quoted the lines he had left out, "'For lo! we look at him, And find no face nor bearing, limbs nor voice, are like those of Uther whom we knew'—is that what you think?"

No response.

"Richard, you are not Arthur!" She caught her breath, rushed on. "Of all your father's sons, you are the most like him, so much so that Friar Shaa inserted it into his sermon at St. Paul's Cross to underscore your claim to the throne!" She felt depleted. The strain of speech was draining her, making her heart pound with an erratic rhythm. But she forced herself to go on, to finish what had to be said. "Did anyone laugh? Did anyone deny it? Holy Christ, how can you doubt your birth when no one else does?"

She took his hand in hers, looked into his resistant face. "You were the only dark one in a blond family; that is the reason you doubt. Aye, Richard, others noticed it, but they never doubted. My father once said that you were the only one to take after the Duke of York. You had his stature, and his temperament, and his heart.

He said that had you been born first instead of last, all would have been well for England."

"He said that?" Richard mumbled. The Duke of York had been an orphan and was raised by the Nevilles. Thrown together since early boyhood, the Duke and Warwick had become devoted to one another. Such a secret could never have been concealed, not from Warwick—there would have been whisperings. Rumours. There were always rumours.

"He said that, my love," Anne persisted. "And he would have known, wouldn't he?"

Richard passed a hand over his face, moistened his lips. "He would have known... Your father would have known." The fog in his mind began to clear.

"Now," she whispered, straining to touch his cheek with her hand, "think on our blessings... Katherine, and dear Johnnie, and little Edward. Soon Katherine shall be married to fine young Huntingdon, and grandchildren will follow to bring you—us—joy—" She panted heavily, strained by the exertion. "See, Richard... there is much to be grateful for."

He stretched out beside her and laid his cheek against her soft hair. She snuggled against him and he slid his arm around her bosom to hold her close. A great weariness engulfed him; he shut his eyes, and they fell asleep in each other's arms, in the position in which they had always lain together.

***

It is as if Satan has heard us, Anne thought. Within five days, Westminster had filled with tears and the smell of incense. Fourteen-year-old Katherine was dead. She had caught the sweating sickness that claimed its victims within twenty-four hours. In that time, a person either recovered or died. In London, the sickness was prevalent, and two London mayors had perished within months of one another, the last only a day after Katherine's death.

Richard had attended both funerals. Katherine was buried in her bridal gown, her corpse strewn with flowers, her auburn curls streaming around her. While young Huntingdon wept, she was laid to her rest in a stone coffin at Westminster Abbey. That night

Richard sat by Anne's bedside and gazed at her with hollow eyes. "I have fought all my life for what I believed right, and what has it brought me, Anne? I'm too weary to try anymore."

"No!" she cried out.

"'Tis hopeless, Anne..."

Anne reached up with a feeble arm to grasp his black cote, her mouth working in agitation. He bent his ear to her lips. "Never give up... to give up is to admit you've failed... we are God's soldiers and in the end what counts is how we fought His fight—" She fell back, gasping, spent.

His own words thrown back at him. The underpinnings of his life. He swallowed his choking misery, rose and brushed her cheek with his lips. He dragged himself over to the window seat. Taking his lute into his hands, he looked up at the dark heavens and strummed her favourite melody, one he had composed for her when they'd been newly wed: *Aye, aye, O aye... A star was my desire...*

***

Anne directed all her energies into getting better and forced herself to take nourishment. Though it made her nauseous, she swallowed hot broth, ate honey, and chewed boiled nuts and raisins. Exertion was taxing to the point of pain, yet she rose from bed and struggled to stand on shaky legs. She even managed to drag herself around. Richard was elated.

"My dearest," he said joyfully, taking her both her hands into his own, "now that you're better, we'll leave for Nottingham! I had no wish to leave earlier—" He broke off, averted his eyes. The truth was, doubting Anne would get well and facing a bleak future without her, it hadn't mattered much to him whether or not he met the threat of Tudor's invasion. "I know Nottingham is a gloomy place, but it's an invincible fortress in the middle of the country, and from there I can be anywhere on the coast quickly. At least there's Sherwood Forest, Anne."

Anne attempted a smile, but inwardly she felt the nauseating sinking of despair. His joy in finding her better was so poignant, it broke her heart. Whatever she had, it was fatal. What would become of Richard then? A suffocating sensation tightened her throat. She looked away.

Thinking he understood the reason for her sudden wretchedness—Nottingham was where they had received the news of Ned's death—Richard said gently, "We don't have to go directly—Windsor is on the way—we'll stop for a few days. We can celebrate the Feast of St. Bartholomew at Windsor. You've always enjoyed Windsor, my love."

The plaintive edge to his voice made Anne ache. Not trusting herself to speak, she threw him a quick smile and blinked to banish the memories. Only last year, in July of '83, soon after the coronation, they had spent three delightful days there on their way north for their progress. *North to Ned.*

"The gardens are splendid this time of year, and the fresh air will do you good," Richard added brightly.

***

While Richard was kept busy with state affairs, Anne, drawn by the beauty of Windsor's scenery with its rolling hills, emerald woods, and serene river, sat outside thumbing Richard's book, *The Vision of Piers Plowman*, about the weary plowman who dreams of a better world, one where injustice is remedied. Like all Richard's books, the flyleaf bore his signature, as was his custom, and the cover was plain, unadorned by precious gems, for he chose his books to read, not to impress. Its well worn pages declared to the world how dear the book was to Richard's heart. Here lay a smudge, there a notation... *Aye, he heeds its lessons, tries to remedy injustice wherever he finds it,* Anne thought, *but it has done him little good.* Last night, in his sleep he had clearly spoken a line from the poem—the saddest line of all. Anne forced the memory away. It pained her too much that he should feel this way, after all he had been through, all the good he had tried to do...

On the second day of their visit, with Elizabeth's help, she managed a short stroll along the river's edge and around the manicured hedgerows. Leaning heavily on the girl's arm, Anne reached the pleasure garden near the Round Tower. "What is the date today, do you know? I seem to have lost count," she said.

"The twenty-second of August," replied Elizabeth.

How fast the summer was drawing to a close! Her last summer. She glanced up at the vivid turquoise sky. No trace of a cloud. "Such a beautiful day," she whispered, almost to herself.

"You shouldn't be out, my lady, you should be in bed," urged Elizabeth. "The wind is chill. The King will not be pleased."

"The wind is chill, but the sun is hot." Anne smiled at her young niece, swept with affection. Lately Elizabeth had taken upon herself many of the duties of a lady-in-waiting, though Anne had summoned the girl to her side not to toil, but for companionship. "Don't fret, child. I can't stay in bed on such a day." She halted on the high grassy slope, suddenly winded. "We shall await my lord here."

Trailing servants set a high-backed chair next to a stone bench and withdrew a respectable distance. As she settled into her chair, Anne's glance swept the garden where she herself had directed the planting of flower beds and hedges the previous summer. It was alight with roses, lilies, and violets. Wood pigeons, wagtails, and larks chirped around her, and from the pastures outside the castle came the bleating of sheep. A yellow butterfly flitted past and she followed it with her eyes until it disappeared around the hedges. Down on the river's edge, two white swans glided in the jade waters. Swans mated for life; what did they do when their mate died?

She looked back at Elizabeth. The girl was standing stiffly, clearly ill at ease about the whole business. Anne forced a smile. "I can manage the King, dear child, and in any case I shall be all right. 'Tis warm even for August. The air will do me good. Now sit down."

Reluctantly Elizabeth bundled Anne's furred velvet cloak around her frail body, smoothed her own skirts, and took a seat on the sunny stone bench. She gave Anne another anxious look. "'Tis not what the doctors say, my lady. They say the air is bad for your fever—"

"Fie on the doctors; they would deny me everything. They think me already dead—" Anne broke off, shocked at her own bitterness. "Nay, anger serves no purpose. They mean well, but they can't help me. Only God can help any of us." She looked up at the sky where a flock of blackbirds soared with shrill cries. "And in this lovely place, I feel His presence." She moved in her chair and a white rose from a nearby bush caught in her cloak. She took it into her hands, bent her head to inhale its fragrance. It was in full bloom, the heart exposed. *A pity*, she thought; *it won't last the day*. She released it with a gentle touch, and the petals spilt to the ground.

She sank back in her chair wearily. At some level deep within herself, she realised she had always sensed how her life would play out. Maybe that had been the source of her childhood fears; the reason why Fortune had tried to keep her from marrying Richard; the reason why she had always feared for Ned. Because she knew it would come to this.

To this.

She became aware that Elizabeth was watching her, and with an expression that spoke far more than words. *The child has a good heart*, she thought. Raising a hand, she touched the girl's soft fair hair. With a sigh, she closed her eyes, lifted her face to the sun. For a long while she sat, quietly drinking in its drowsy warmth until, at length, men's voices and the trample of horses' feet shattered her peace. Opening her eyes, she squinted into the sun, in the direction of the noise.

From where she sat with Elizabeth, high in the pleasure garden near the Round Tower, she had an excellent view of the main entrance. A small troop of men-at-arms had appeared through a distant archway in the castle wall and begun a descent to the Norman Gate. In their midst a lone woman rode pillion. Thin, rigidly erect, wearing a wimple and dressed in black, there was no mistaking Margaret Beaufort. As if sensing Anne's attention, Stanley's wife turned her head and stared directly at her. Anne shivered.

Elizabeth also watched uneasily as Margaret Beaufort and her escorts descended to the main gate.

"You don't like her, do you?" said Anne, reading her expression.

Elizabeth averted her eyes hastily. "N-No, my lady, 'tis not so—"

Anne studied Elizabeth's sweet face. Though she was a Woodville, there was nothing Woodville about her. From the beginning, Anne had sensed a rare integrity in the girl. "You needn't pretend with me, Elizabeth. We are friends." She patted her hand. "The reason I ask is because she troubles me also."

Elizabeth's eyes flew open with surprise. "Your Grace—" said Elizabeth.

"*Anne*. Call me Anne."

Elizabeth inhaled deeply, "'Tis presumptuous of me to judge others—my lady—*Anne*—" her gaze returned to the Norman Gate and the joy vanished from her face, "but Lady Margaret has always seemed cold to me and—and—"

"Aye?" Anne prompted.

"And—" Elizabeth searched for the right word— "dangerous."

Anne's eyes widened. The same thought had come to her on her coronation day. "Lady Stanley had the honour of carrying my train at my coronation, yet she's been at the centre of two treasonous plots against my lord, the King, for which he has forgiven her both times." Elizabeth coloured fiercely and Anne remembered that Elizabeth's own mother had been at the centre of those plots alongside Margaret Beaufort. She reached out, took the girl's hand into her own. "Child, it was not your fault; you were not involved. One thing I've learned in life is that we can only be responsible for ourselves."

A grateful smile lifted the corners of Elizabeth's lips. "On my part, I've learned that, for all his sternness, the King is in truth a gentle and forgiving man."

"Too forgiving, and too gentle, and too easily fooled by showy piety." Anne tensed again. She returned her gaze to the gate. Though Margaret Beaufort was gone from sight, the chill she had felt when the woman had looked at her still lingered.

Elizabeth followed the direction of Anne's gaze. "Something about her troubles me… Could Lady Stanley be false of heart and using her devotion as a ploy to get her way with others?"

What wisdom the child has! Anne thought. "Aye, dear Elizabeth, her actions speak of her falseness. I know it goes contrary to what we are told, but I have long believed it is by our deeds, not only our words, that we will be judged."

"I don't even trust that she had a—" Elizabeth blushed a furious red and looked down at her hands in confusion. "Nay, I speak foolishly."

"I, too, have doubted that Margaret Beaufort had a vision."

The heavy lashes that shadowed the girl's cheeks flew up.

"It merely seemed... too convenient," Anne replied in response to Elizabeth's questioning gaze. "She had to choose whether to marry dull Suffolk or dashing Edmund Tudor. What better way to get her wish than to claim St. Nicholas appeared to her in a vision to demand it be Tudor? She's clever enough to concoct the story."

"I believe those who have truly been vouchsafed a vision would keep it close to their hearts, like a cherished treasure. Not boast openly of it to gain the praise of others."

"Yet I yearn to be wrong," Anne sighed. "It would be better for my lord husband if I were. If she does not deceive us, she must be without sin. Otherwise, God would not have chosen her for such honour."

"Nay, my lady, that need not be! God grants visions even to sinners, for St. Paul had his while persecuting Christians." She hesitated. "And I've had one."

Anne held her breath as she waited, but Elizabeth said no more. "Blessed Mary," Anne prompted with a small smile. "Must I always pry the words out of you, Elizabeth?" There was something endearing about the girl's shyness, and again Anne found herself wondering how the daughter could be so different from the mother.

"It was at Westminster, soon after my sister Mary died," Elizabeth began softly. "We were very close, Mary and I... One night I couldn't sleep, so I slipped out. It had rained heavily and it was dark, almost black, no moon at all, no light, not even any torches. I was sitting by the river, weeping, and suddenly there was a flash of blue light and I heard her voice call *'Elizabeth!'* She said my name only once, yet I knew it was Mary. I'd know her voice anywhere. And that flash of light, I didn't imagine it—" She dropped her gaze, her cheeks crimson. "I've never spoken of it before."

Anne looked up at the sky. If only she could hear Ned's voice again—one single word, that would be enough! Only half aware that she spoke aloud, she said, "Sometimes, late at night, when I pray, the candles flutter and I think I see out of the corner of my eye..." *Ned?* Her voice broke slightly, "I don't know what I see.

When I look, it's gone." She closed her eyes against the anguish that seared her heart.

Anne felt Elizabeth's gentle touch on her sleeve and lifted her gaze to the girl's sweet face. There was a depth of compassion in her eyes. "In no other way has God shown me special favour," Elizabeth said. "I'm certain there are many whom He loves better, who have never been granted such comfort."

Anne had the vague sensation that she was looking at herself, for again came that resemblance she had first caught at Westminster. Without forming a prayer or importuning the Blessed Virgin, in some far corner of her mind, a new knowledge took form, casting light into the shadows, filling her with hope and a calm strength. *In front of me all along lay the answer to my prayers, and I, poor blind sinner, have not seen!*

Anne took the girl's hand into her own. "'Blessed are they who mourn, for they shall be comforted.'" She closed her eyes, rested her head against the back of the chair, and let a smile curve her lips.

Chapter Fifteen

"The good Queen… saddening in her childless castle."

At Nottingham Castle, Richard descended the outer staircase from the great hall and crossed the inner court to the royal tower and his private apartments. The night was cool for mid-September, and few stars were visible in the cloudy sky. Torches flamed on the walls and guards walked the battlements, their footsteps resounding in the silence. He had rebuilt much of Nottingham in these months, yet in spite of the new tower's grace of proportion, the airiness of the coloured windows in the great hall, and the elegance of the stone corbels around the windows, it remained a gloomy place. As usual Anne was right: it had an air.

He trudged wearily up the stone steps to his bedchamber. It was late, and he had concluded much business that day. The Scottish envoys had arrived to sue for peace, and it was an impressive embassy that James III had sent. This time they would reach an agreement, maybe even seal the treaty with a marriage. He would offer King James' son and heir the hand of his niece, Anne de la Pole, Jack's sister. Richard faltered on the darkened stairway. A month ago, he had finally declared Jack his heir to the throne. He'd wanted George's son, who was both Plantagenet and Neville.

Like Ned.

He leaned a hand against the stone wall, shutting his eyes against the onslaught of pain. But Edward was a minor, and the realm needed a man. Besides, as his councillors had pointed out, Edward was simple-minded, as poor Henry had been. And so he had made the only choice he could. His twenty-four-year-old nephew, John de la Pole, the Earl of Lincoln, whom he fondly called "Jack." A fine young man, Jack. Pious. A good soldier. He held great promise. And he had youth and energy with which to tackle the demanding affairs of the realm.

He would need that.

He resumed his steps up the staircase, taking care to tread lightly.

He didn't wish to disturb Anne, if she slept. God be thanked, she did seem better. She was still too thin, too pale, too frail, but her spirits had mended somewhat. That was much to be grateful for. He reached the landing, surprised to find light flowing under the threshold. Anne was still up! He quickened his steps, pushed the door open, and stepped into the opulent solar, hung with bright coloured tapestries and furnished with carved chairs and tables covered in damask cloth.

Anne was sitting on a pile of red and purple silk cushions by the hearth where a warm fire crackled while their hound Roland slept nearby. *Like old times*, he thought with both joy and an ache. Her eyes loomed too large in her drawn face and she was so thin that she seemed overwhelmed by the topaz chamber robe that only last year had fit her well enough. He took a seat beside her on the pillows. "You should be asleep, my love. Are you not tired?"

Anne was exhausted from the strain of entertaining the Scottish ambassadors and Richard's great retinue that included the peers of the realm, Howard, Percy, Stanley, Chancellor Russell, many bishops, and all the knights and esquires of the body. But she had a pressing matter on her mind and time was passing; she couldn't afford to wait. She feigned a light heart as she offered him a goblet of wine.

"I haven't seen you in days—not *really* seen you—and I wished us to spend a little time together."

He eyed her suspiciously. Beneath the gaiety, strain was evident. "Anne, if there's something you want, you've no need to soften me up first. 'Tis yours, whatever it is."

"No, my lord," Anne lied, blushing and dropping her gaze. She had forgotten how he could read her. "I merely wish to talk… Is it so strange for a wife to expect a little of her husband's attention?"

Richard wasn't convinced, but it wasn't worth an argument. He stretched out and laid his head in her lap. He almost winced. It felt light as goose down. "You managed very well today at the banquet, my little bird," he said as brightly as he could. "All went very well indeed. Everyone seemed to have a splendid time."

"I thought so, too, Richard. The minstrels were especially fine, and I enjoyed watching everyone dance."

A silence fell. Richard turned his head away towards the fire. The last time they had danced together had been here, at Nottingham, on the Feast of St. George.

Anne saw Richard's mouth pull down with pain. Summoning the force of her will, she suppressed her own anguish and said gaily, "I thought the ladies had gone to much trouble to dress for the banquet. They all looked particularly lovely tonight."

Richard propped himself up on an elbow and sipped his wine. "I didn't notice."

Anne stroked his dark hair. "Surely, you must have noticed someone?"

"Like whom?"

"How about Ratcliffe's lady—she was all in gold to match her hair."

Richard shook his head.

"I do so enjoy watching those two. They're so in love—" She caught the wistfulness in her voice and immediately changed her tone. "Welladay, you must have noticed my Uncle John's daughter, Elizabeth—she was in violet, and I thought that was very becoming with her chestnut curls—" Elizabeth took after her mother and an image of sweet dead Isobel flashed into Anne's mind. She bit her lip, rushed on. "But of all my uncle's five daughters, Meggie is quite the most beautiful. You surely noticed her?"

"The one in royal blue?"

Anne made a show of clapping her hands. "Aye, to match her eyes! So you're not dead to our womanly charms? I do believe, Richard, that with her great beauty, she can hope for a splendid marriage." Meggie had inherited her father's deep blue eyes and dimples, and her mother's chestnut hair and milk-and-roses complexion. Before Anne could stop herself, she added, "She's much like them both, don't you think?"

Richard's eyes clouded. She had ruptured the mood once again. She blurted out, "I believe Joan Scrope is in love with Jack."

"If she is, 'tis too bad for her. As my heir, Jack must marry for dynastic reasons, not for love," he said tersely.

"'Tis sad that a king can't marry for love, Richard."

"Edward did, and his queen made England bleed."

"England bled not because he married for love," Anne replied gently, "but because he married the wrong woman."

"A Woodville."

"No, Richard. Not all Woodvilles are alike. Bess was simply unworthy." She stole a sidelong glance at him. "Take her daughter, Elizabeth, for example. She's nothing like her mother."

"Perhaps," Richard said curtly. "But she doesn't have to worry about being queen. She's a bastard."

"She's your niece."

"'Tis the only reason I tolerate her."

Anne assumed a smiling, musing manner, "Don't you think she's pretty?"

"I've never given it thought."

"Finding a woman attractive is not something to which a man gives thought." Anne wasn't about to give up, not now that she'd broached the subject close to her heart. "Either he does, or he doesn't."

He sat up abruptly. "Anne, what's this about? Why these foolish questions about that girl?"

"I just want to know, is all. Can't you humour me, Richard?"

"Very well then. She has fair hair like her mother."

"What does that mean?"

"Means she's a Woodville."

"Is that all you see when you look at her—a Woodville?"

"Aye. What else is there?" He picked up his goblet and downed a gulp.

"A truer beauty even than that of the face. Goodness of the heart... And she is of robust health. She'll bear her husband many fine sons—"

Richard slammed down his goblet, splashing ruby wine on the pillows. "Cease, Anne! Stop this torture!" He averted his face, pressed a hand to his brow. After a long silence he looked back at her and took her cold hands into his own. "Ned is gone, and the pain will never fade, for either of us. Every man prays for a son, but you were all I ever wanted, all I begged God for during those accursed years when our families broke with one another. I never asked for a son. Only you. Ned was a boon, a beautiful gift loaned us by heaven for too short a time. Aye, and now that he's gone, the days are black for it. But, dear heart, without you at my side I could not go on—could not—" His voice cracked. He pressed his head to her breast.

Tears blurred Anne's vision as she stroked the dark hair. She wanted to say, *But you must go on, my beloved. Help me to find you love, so I don't leave you uncomforted.*

"I could not—" Richard said again in a choked voice. Then it seemed to Anne that the fire dimmed and the candles flickered in the room and the shadows darkened, for she heard dread words uttered so faintly, she might have imagined them: *I will not.* She quivered. Bending down over him, she lifted his face in her hands as she used to do with Ned when he had been frightened. Looking deep into the heart-breaking dark eyes, she said, "Promise me—swear to me, on Ned's blessed soul—that you will never, *never* give up. Never, Richard. Not even if you must go on—" she hesitated, "alone. *Swear it!*"

Richard gazed up at the enormous violet eyes dark in the candlelight, pleading with such urgency, such desperation. He could not cause her more pain. He moistened his cracked lips.

"I shall not give up. I swear it," he said. "I must live to make Tudor pay."

Chapter Sixteen

"The vermin voices here
May buzz so loud—we scorn them, but they sting."

Richard spent two anxious months in Nottingham waiting for an invasion that never came. Finally in November, concluding that Tudor no longer posed a problem until the advent of good weather in the spring, he returned to London.

Royal bugles blared and bells rang for Tierce, but the crowds were respectfully quiet when Richard and Anne, clad in their dark mourning garb, approached Bishopsgate, followed by the royal procession of peers, knights, bishops, servants, and rumbling baggage carts. As always the air near London was thick with the smell of sweat, horse droppings, and butchered animals, and the skies that hung over the city were grey.

As if signalling the ill tidings that undoubtedly await, thought Richard dully.

On this chilly morning a bitter wind blew, bearing a dank, fishy smell from the river and the shops along Fish Street. He glanced at Anne with concern. Near the city she had transferred from her litter to her chestnut palfrey to make a more dignified entrance. She smiled at him between her furs, and he was reassured. At least her palfrey bore her sedately, not like White Surrey who, aware of the eyes on him, held up his elegant head and pranced majestically before the throng as befitted his royal status. Richard looked back to find the mayor and the aldermen riding to meet him in their ceremonial scarlet. He listened politely to the mayor's welcome and made the appropriate responses. The ceremony over, Richard invited him to ride at his side. "How goes it in my absence?" he inquired.

The tall, gaunt mercer shrank in his saddle. "My lord King, there's been a… a… spot of trouble."

Richard stared at him.

Disconcerted, the man lost his nerve and began to babble incoherently, "The—here—these—some—"

His nerves strained by the worries and work of the last months, Richard snapped, "A pox on this fiddle-faddle! Out with it, man! What trouble?"

"Placards," blurted the mayor, and swallowed.

"What do these placards say?" demanded Richard.

They turned into Watling Street. The mayor cleared his throat, launched into an explanation. "The p-placards have appeared all over the city—well, not exactly all over, but everywhere—well, not exactly everywhere—but everywhere that matters—on church doors. Mostly. T-these placards—" he cleared his throat again—"they bear a certain rhyme—"

Richard's prayed for patience.

"There—t-there it is again!" The mayor gasped with relief. "Speak of the devil, there it is!" He pointed to St. Paul's Cathedral where a crowd had gathered around a black-cowled monk reading a parchment nailed to one of the doors in the porch recess.

Richard turned to the body of knights behind him. "Fetch that placard!" he barked. One of them broke into a gallop, cantered up the steps of St. Paul's, and before the murmuring crowd, ripped the placard from the door and galloped back. "What does it say?" demanded Richard.

The knight paled. "Sire—I—"

Richard tore it from his hands angrily, and read:

The Cat, the Rat, and Lovell our dog,

Rule all England under a hog.

His hand shook, his face burned. He crushed the parchment in his fist. Somewhere in the crowd, someone tittered. Bile rose to his mouth and his pulse pounded furiously in his ears.

"Who dares?" Richard hissed through white lips.

The mayor swallowed. "We believe it is a Wiltshire m-man. A certain W-William Colyngbourne, an agent of Henry Tudor's. He was once an officer of your royal lady mother, the Duchess of York, Sire."

"I know him," Richard said tersely. Colyngbourne had been dismissed from his post and replaced by one of his own followers when Richard took the Crown. "Has he been apprehended?"

"Not yet, Sire."

"I want him apprehended," said Richard in a deadly voice.

"Aye, Sire! And he shall be, he shall. He's eluded us s-since July when he posted the f-first of these doggerels, but we're close now. Close, indeed."

"July?" Richard demanded. "Why was I not informed?"

The mayor coloured. "Sire, you—it did not seem—you were—it was—"

Anne leaned over and touched Richard's sleeve. She understood what the man was trying to say. Richard had not been informed because of Ned; they had not the heart. She met his eyes. Richard's rancour drained. "Lord Mayor, I thank you for your consideration of our grief." With a heart that weighed like stone in his breast, Richard nudged White Surrey forward.

The cavalcade neared Westminster. The holy song of the monks floated to him from the Abbey doors to the east. To the west, the rhythmic clatter of metal resounded from the composing room of William Caxton's printing shop, and the sharp smell of wet ink wafted on the air. His eyes fixed on the sign of the Red Pale. Sixteen months had passed since his coronation. The sign was swinging in the wind, as it had on that day when he'd walked to the Abbey with his heart filled with joy. Ahead had lain the future; dreams that could be worked into action; King Arthur's court that could be brought back to England for the glory of God.

Live pure, speak true, right wrong, follow the King—

Nothing had turned out as he had dreamed.

***

With slow, gentle strokes, Anne caressed Ned's little hound, Sir Tristan, who had curled up and fallen asleep in her lap. "We should be enemies, yet you're my dearest friend," she said, watching Elizabeth's fair head as she bent intently over her embroidery.

Elizabeth of York slid the needle through her tapestry and knotted the wine silk thread. She broke it with her teeth and smiled. "It seems another lifetime when I thought of you as an enemy. How strange life is."

"If we loved as easily as we hated, we could change the world," said Anne.

"You and His Grace have loved one another since childhood, they say." There was a wistful note in Elizabeth's voice.

"Aye, since I was seven years old... I remember the first time Richard came to Middleham. It was soon after his brother Edward was crowned. He was so young... so unsure of himself... and frightened." *And God help us*, she thought, *I see that same look now*. He's worked his heart out doing good, but his enemies lie about him, twist everything to blacken him, and give him no credit for the loyalty that is his strongest trait. And all those wounding slanders have shaken his belief in himself and destroyed what little pleasure might have been his.

Elizabeth's voice interrupted her thoughts. "Sometimes, though I could be mistaken—" she broke off in embarrassment. "No, 'tis foolishness."

"Tell me what you were going to say, Elizabeth."

Scarlet stained Elizabeth's cheeks. "Truly, it was nothing, my lady."

"I must know."

Elizabeth's fingers slackened around her embroidery. She turned her gaze on the river and a faraway look came into her eyes. "It's just that... sometimes... I see an odd expression on his face, when he thinks no one is looking."

"Aye?"

"Fear, and doubt, Madame. Forgive me, but I've seen that in his eyes, and it wounds me to the heart."

Anne caught her breath. After a moment she reached out and gently touched Elizabeth's gold hair, gathered beneath a silver circlet and gauzy veil. Once her own hair had been that bright. "Aye, child, I know."

"And I fear for him," Elizabeth whispered.

"Because you love him," Anne said.

The girl drew away in horror. "No, my lady, no!"

"You must not be ashamed of loving."

"I'd never do anything to hurt you— I'd give my life before I'd hurt you—" Elizabeth fell to her knees, seized Anne's hands. "Madame, pray believe me! You've been so good to me, I'd never repay you with such ingratitude!" Anne was about to reply when she felt suddenly faint. On the wind she had caught the sharp smell of the river, a foul pungent odour that summoned into her mind the memory of the sea voyage to Calais when she'd fled England for her life, and the filthy sailor who had coughed blood into her face. She pushed herself up from her chair on trembling legs. Sir Tristan jumped off with a start. The doctors had been baffled by her illness. Now she knew what she had.

The White Plague.

She clutched her stomach, assailed by a wave of nausea. Elizabeth leapt to her feet, seized her by the shoulders. "My lady, what is it?" she cried.

With a nod of her head, Anne indicated a far window that stood open to the rose garden. "There," she managed. Leaning heavily on Elizabeth's arm, she made her way slowly to the silver cushioned seat. There was no dark river odour here, only the sweet scent of roses and gillyflowers. She patted the empty space beside her.

"Why must you think you've harmed with your love, child?" Anne murmured when she felt strong enough to speak again. "All we take with us when we die is the love we leave behind."

Elizabeth regarded her with a puzzled expression.

"Love is all there is, dear child. All that matters… all that remains to warm the hearts we leave behind when we ourselves depart this world. We, in turn, take with us their love when we go." She looked out at the garden and her eyes fell on a distant tree. A majestic chestnut with wide, sprawling branches. Beneath such stately boughs she'd picnicked with Ned, and once, long ago, held court with Richard in their mythical childhood kingdom of Avalon. Her voice sank to a bare whisper. "Ned has my love, and I keep his— here—" She laid a hand to her bosom. "As long as I live, I'll remember his love—" A terrible pain seared her lungs, cutting off her breath. She gasped; the garden wavered in her sight.

"Madame, madame!" Elizabeth cried. "Are you all right?"

Through the darkness that engulfed her, Anne felt the girl's strong arms encircle her, hold her steady. Aye, Elizabeth was her gift to Richard. With Elizabeth's love and strength, she would rescue him from his hopelessness and despair, as surely as he had rescued her from that kitchen in Cheapside years ago.

The nausea, which had been coming on with increasing frequency of late, faded, but her breathing was still shallow and her chest hurt with each intake of air.

"'Tis nothing… merely a… passing pain." She spoke haltingly to conserve her energy. "Now… I've something to say… Then you must make me a promise." Again that resemblance to herself. Though the child had her father's eyes, with emotion they tended to darken, so that they sometimes seemed violet, like her own.

"Anything, Madame."

"Stop… calling… me 'Madame'," she breathed, "I am Anne."

"Aye, my dear lady Anne."

"We… must plan… for the future."

"The future?"

"Yours… and Richard's."

Elizabeth stared at her with uncomprehending shock.

"Daily I lose strength… It'll not be long now, I know," Anne whispered, her voice a bare tremor. "Some days are… difficult. If I could be at ease about Richard, I could let go… You're right, dear Elizabeth. He is so alone…" Her eyes returned to the tree and misted. "Alone with so much hate around him—" She broke off. She knew now what she had always suspected. She had an ill-divining spirit. The shadows she'd seen pressing around them on their coronation were real enough, not imagined. And the heaviness she felt surrounding Richard now would not be dispelled, except with love.

Elizabeth took her hand, giving comfort. She lifted her eyes to Elizabeth's face. "He'll… not survive, Elizabeth… without love… You must comfort him… help him. He'll need you…"

"For the King there is only you," Elizabeth cried. "He's not even aware I exist."

"Then… we must change that. Make… him aware. He's had much on his mind… but he wishes the Christmas festivities to be especially bright this year—" *Especially bright, to bury sorrow past bearing.* "We shall *make* him notice you… Aye, Elizabeth, you're what… Richard needs… What England needs."

"But I'm his niece—we cannot marry!"

"The Pope will grant a dispensation… if the price is high

enough..." For a while after Ned's death, she'd thought God was punishing her for having wed without a dispensation. She had long since rejected that notion. Though she knew she was edging perilously close to heresy, she simply couldn't accept the idea of a vengeful God. God was not Anger. He was Love. But Popes were men, and men were tainted with greed. "In truth, your blood bond... matters not. I have come to believe... that God sees no sin in love... except where that love brings pain to others." She paused to catch her breath. "Together... you shall bear him children and... turn his crown of sorrows... into a wreath of roses."

Her chest heaved with the effort of speech, but she managed to touch the girl's cheek in a loving gesture. "You shall... make a fine queen... Elizabeth." Then she smiled. For even the bleakest winter's day held the promise of spring.

Chapter Seventeen

"Things fall apart; the centre cannot hold."

A month after Richard arrived in London, William Colyngbourne, the maker of the impudent lampoon, was caught and indicted for his seditious, mocking rhyme, and charged with paying a man to deliver a message to the French court that Richard intended to make war on France and throw their envoys into prison.

"We must make an example of that traitor!" Richard raged. *That traitor* who had not only ridiculed him and his government before all England but had cost him the chance to make peace with France! *That traitor,* laughing at him like Trollope who had sworn fealty to his father, absconded with his battle plans, then led the Christmas ambush at Wakefield in which his father and brother were slain. *That traitor,* laughing at him, as Buckingham had laughed—

"Traitors embody all that's vile in man!" Richard kicked over a chair and swept an arm across the table, sending goblets crashing to the floor. "He must suffer before he dies!" He turned on his councillors. "He must suffer!"

Catesby, Francis, Rob Percy, Scrope, and Ratcliffe stood pale-faced, staring at him as though he had lost his mind. He pressed a hand to his aching head, sank heavily into a chair. "He must suffer," he said quietly. "He is a traitor."

Catesby cleared his throat. "Aye, Sire. That he is, and well we know it, and he must die the foul death of a traitor. But first he must be tried, so that the people will know justice was done."

"Catesby gives sound advice, Richard," said Francis. "Colyngbourne must be proven guilty by a commission of law. A fair-minded commission."

"I've always upheld the law!" snapped Richard, offended by the implication. Then, reflected in their eyes, he saw the scene in the Tower where Edward's friend, Hastings, once his own ally, had been rushed out of the council chamber and beheaded for his treason. Since the execution had been hasty, a log had served as the executioner's block. He looked away with shame.

"Colyngbourne shall have his day in court and it shall be as unimpeachable and impressive a commission as I can appoint. Men shall not say I indulged my malice."

Urgent hoof beats sounded in the outer court.

"My lord, it's the yeoman of the Chamber, William Bolton, whom you sent to Hammes to bring back Oxford," said Catesby, glancing out the window. "But Oxford is not with him!"

Richard pushed him aside and examined the group dismounting in the snowy courtyard. John de Vere, Earl of Oxford, was the greatest Lancastrian leader alive. If he had escaped to Tudor's side—

He crushed the thought. Footsteps sounded on the stair. William Bolton appeared at the threshold of the chamber. One look at his face and Richard knew.

Sweeping his hat beneath his arm, Bolton strode up to do his obeisance.

"Oxford has escaped," said Richard, before Bolton could speak.

"Aye, Sire. You were right to suspect the Lieutenant, James Blount. He not only helped Oxford escape, but fled with him to Paris. When a detachment from Calais was sent to investigate the situation at Hammes, they were refused admittance. The castle is now under siege."

Richard gazed out the window. Another dismal day. Grey, cold, miserable. And the snow, covering what yesterday had been green, or so it seemed. People hurried here and there below in the courtyard, carrying sacks, leading horses, hammering repairs, and out beyond the walls of Westminster Palace, in the crowded streets, beggars begged, vendors hawked their wares, ladies shopped for silks, and butchers slaughtered animals. Life went on as it had for centuries. With one difference. Chivalry was dying. He leaned his full weight on the stone embrasure of the windowsill. *Live pure, speak true, right wrong, follow the King*—The code of honour that had held good men together since King Arthur's days was fragmenting, dissolving. Oaths, loyalty, meant nothing. Soon man would sink back into the beast. The round table had been splintered by betrayals and feuds. Then, as now. What had changed?

Without a word, he strode out of the council room, leaving his men staring after him in stunned surprise. He crossed the snowy court and took the tower steps up into the massive Keep, unaware of the people who jabbed one another with their elbows as he passed. A chill wind blew through the stairwell from the battlements above. Voices came to him; men laughing at a jest, women chattering with gossip. He wondered if Anne would be in the privy suite. She was not. There were only the servants, polishing mirrors, beating the mattress, sweeping the rushes. One of his squires sat cleaning the jewelled sword that had been a gift to him from Edward before Barnet. The acid odour of vinegar pervaded the room and transported him to the past, and all at once it was his young squire, red-haired Johnnie Milewater, sitting there again, head bent, polishing his sword on the eve of battle.

The chambermaids straightened in surprise and the squire leapt to his feet. With a limp motion of the hand, Richard dismissed them. The door thudded shut. He went to the altar in the alcove. On the prayer desk stood his copy of Wycliff's translation of the New Testament. He laid his palm on its gilded brown leather cover.

He had ordered the laws enacted by his Parliament to be proclaimed in English instead of Latin so that his people would understand their rights. For the same reason, he owned a Lollard Testament, not because he was a Lollard and disavowed the miracle of transubstantiation or thought the church too rich and corrupt, but merely to read the Bible in English. To understand God's words more clearly. Yet never in his life had he felt so distanced from God as he did at this moment. Despite all his good works, he had failed to win His favour. For all his piety, his prayers fell on deaf ears.

He lifted his eyes to the gold enamelled triptych that stood below the altar, a gift from his mother on his ninth birthday, the year he'd left for Middleham. The left panel depicted the Kiss of Judas... Aye, he understood too well what it meant to be kissed by Judas... The right displayed the Last Judgement and the tortures of the damned. He winced, averted his face from their agony and the ruby drops of blood. He looked to the centre where the Virgin grieved over the dead Christ. In her stricken face he saw Anne, who grieved over Ned... Why had the Blessed Mother not protected Anne? Why did God not hear his prayers?

God.

He had taken Ned from him. Now He might take Anne. She was wasting away, with scarce enough strength most days to rise from bed. He raised his eyes to Christ's face on the silver cross, contorted with suffering, and sank to his knees. He tried to pray, but he could find no words.

***

"The messenger is here to report on the execution of the traitor Colyngbourne, Sire," announced the herald. The December morning was bitterly cold, yet Richard leaned out of the open window in the Painted Chamber, watching the snow fall and listening to the wind howl, oblivious to the icy wind lashing his face and whipping his furs.

"Tudor's agent died the foul death of a traitor, Sire," said the messenger. "He was hanged on a new pair of gallows, cut down while alive, and his bowels were ripped from his belly and burned before his eyes. He lived until the butcher put his hand into the bulk of his body, for he said at the same instant, 'O Lord Jesus, yet more trouble,' and then he expired."

Someone muttered, "So may all traitors end." To which many of his lords and a number of his officers and knights, murmured, "Aye, aye."

Richard gave a nod of dismissal and the messenger withdrew. He felt no satisfaction, only a terrible tenseness in his body. He moved back to the council table, picked up a document from a sheaf of papers and held it out to the messenger from Calais who had come with the ill tidings two days before. "I am granting the garrison at Hammes a full pardon. You will leave today and inform them of it."

"My lord, the wife of the traitor Blount was unable to escape with him. Do you wish her returned to England for punishment?"

"She is included in the pardon and may go wherever she wishes."

"Even to France?"

"Aye," said Richard.

"My lord, you are too merciful!" Sir Ralph Ashton exclaimed in a shocked tone, a hand to his dagger hilt.

"Except for Marguerite d'Anjou and Bess Woodville, women have no part in the troubles caused by men," said Richard dully.

"Traitors must be crushed, my lord. Make an example of them—or they'll breed like maggots and eat you alive!"

"No doubt you're right, Ashton, but that is not my way." He turned listless eyes on his secretary. "Kendall, issue commissions of array to the men appointed commissioners last May. They are to order my subjects to be ready to resist the rebels."

Howard shook his silvery head. "'Tis too early, my lord. Tudor can't launch another invasion 'till spring. There's time yet. The realm's weary of summonses to arms and talk of war. The Christmas season's a'coming—best not to remind them that peace is not at hand. Besides, there's no money." A loud murmur of assent greeted this response.

"What am I to do until then?" Richard exploded suddenly. *Sit and watch Anne die?* Unable to choke back the anguish that threatened his composure, he swivelled on his heel and left the room.

His councillors stared after him, stunned at his outburst which had had no prompting.

Chapter Eighteen

"And I, the last, go forth companionless
And the days darken round me."

The royal apartments teemed with as many people and as much business as Richard's council chamber. Anne was directing the preparations for the Christmas celebrations from bed. While Roland slept beside her, Elizabeth and the Master of the Wardrobe stood on either side, surrounded by servants who undraped fabric for her inspection. There were cloths of gold and tissue of silver, and silks and damasks of every hue—purples, crimsons, greens, blues, and apricot. She was nodding assent to a bolt of violet tissue when Richard walked in. The Master of the Wardrobe gathered up his fabrics and meinie and withdrew with a bow. Elizabeth blushed, curtsied and, avoiding his eyes, rushed past him.

"Stay, Elizabeth—" Anne called out, but Elizabeth was already gone. "She's so shy… Not at all like her mother." A coughing fit racked her chest and she gasped for air. Servants rushed to attend her. They held a silver basin to her mouth. Anne threw up bile and laid her head back on the silk pillows. A lady-in-waiting gently wiped blood-tinged mucus from her lips. Richard winced. He sat down on the velvet coverlet and took her hand. "You're not to tax yourself, my little bird. I can appoint others to the task and—"

"No, Richard," Anne interrupted, struggling up in bed. "I enjoy it. Elizabeth is helping me, and so is my mother. It shall be every bit as bright and splendid as you wish, Richard." He gave her a smile, though his heart felt as heavy as stone. Anne looked even more wan and pale than yesterday, if that were possible, and her hand felt as light as a flake of snow. Afraid she might read his thoughts, he averted his eyes and plunged into conversation.

"I've ordered an elaborate costume for myself of cloth of gold and crimson velvet, slashed with purple satin, and trimmed with ermine."

"You shall look very handsome, Richard."

"'Tis not why I chose it, my little bird. Sadly, the people judge the King as much by how he looks as what he does. Therefore, I must look most kingly and—and happy—"

Anne touched his cheek. "And I shall dress most queenly, dear Richard. We shall revel together most majestically." She managed a smile. As casually as she could, she said, "Elizabeth has been a great help to me. I don't know what I would do without her."

Richard said nothing, but the hand that held hers loosened its hold.

"You don't like her. Yet she favours you."

"'Tis your womanly wild imagining."

"Why do you say that?"

"She has no reason to favour me."

Softly, Anne murmured, "Love has little to do with reason."

Richard discarded her hand roughly. He went to the window and stared out. A tiring maid came to sponge Anne's brow. She waved her away; waved everyone away. The chamber emptied. "Why do you dismiss it so?" Anne panted. "As though it's an impossible thing... Is it because you think you're not handsome enough to be loved by a beautiful young woman, not tall enough, not blond enough—"

Richard swung around. "Cease, Anne! I've no wish to discuss it further."

"You're weary, Richard," she whispered, her voice cracking for lack of breath. "Come, sit with me. Drink. It'll do you good."

Richard took a seat by her bed and heaved a heavy sigh. "'Tis not you, my love, but the court. The incessant intrigue. The malicious gossip. The evil eyes always watching, waiting for their chance to wound. I can feel them like daggers in my back. How I hate London, Anne! How I wish to be in the North, with you and—" He broke off, bit his lip. He put out his hand to her and she took it into her own.

"Dear love, I know. But even here, in this gutter where rats congregate, there are good people. Elizabeth is one of them."

"Why must we talk of Elizabeth, Anne? Have you nothing to say to me?"

Anne felt the silence between them as heavily as the load of sorrow that weighed her down. When it's too painful to look back, and worse lay ahead, she thought, where do you go, what do you do?

She laid her head against Richard's shoulder and closed her eyes.

Chapter Nineteen

"Sir Mordred; he that like a subtle beast lay couchant with his eyes upon the throne, ready to spring, awaiting a chance."

On Epiphany, wearing their crowns, Anne and Richard sat on their thrones, presiding over the Christmas revelry in the great hall of Rufus which had been decorated with candles and evergreens. The air was fragrant with the scent of pine and bayberry, and the hall glittered with colour from the tapestries, silk carpets, and dazzling gowns and jewels of the nobles. Laughter, conversation, and singing resounded through the chamber. Richard had donned his sumptuous robes of crimson, purple and ermine studded with diamonds, and Anne a gown of violet and silver. On the dais where they sat, a fire crackled in the hearth. Even so Anne was cold.

"My dearest, your fingers are like ice. I shall warm them for you." Richard lifted them to his lips, kissed them tenderly and held them between both his hands. His heart twisted as he gazed at her. The special prayer that his confessor, Father Roby, had inserted into his Book of Hours from which he read his devotionals had made no difference… none at all. Thin and pale, Anne was so weak she had to be propped up in her throne with pillows. She had always been delicate as a flower, but now she was but a shadow of what she had once been. Richard could no longer fool himself. Anne was doomed. Crushed in spirit, always fragile in health, she would not survive much longer.

"Sire!" said a messenger.

Richard blinked. The man knelt before him. "I bring an urgent message from France, Sire."

Richard waited.

"Our agents beyond the seas report that, notwithstanding the potency and splendour of your royal state, Henry Tudor will, without question, invade the kingdom this summer."

After a pause, Richard said. "Nothing more desirable can befall me than to meet Tudor in the field at last." The man withdrew.

"Is that true?" asked Anne quietly.

"Waiting has never been my strength, my sweet. The sooner he comes, the better for me."

Anne felt a chill and drew her fur mantle closer. Richard was in no condition to defend his kingdom. He was pale, haggard, more careworn than she had ever known him. He barely slept anymore. She knew, because she feigned sleep for his sake, and he feigned it for hers, but as soon as he thought her asleep, he rose to kneel in prayer, or sit at the window and stare up at the heavens. She bit her lip. If he met Tudor in his condition, there might well be disaster. And Tudor, shrewd, ruthless, and cunning as he was said to be, no doubt knew that. Margaret Beaufort's son would be one who could smell his quarry's blood even from across the seas. She closed her eyes and raised a hand to her head. She felt suddenly dizzy.

"Anne!" cried Richard.

"'Tis nothing, my love, merely a passing faint," she managed. Looking at him, she remembered that blessed time when news arrived that Edward, only weeks before his death, had granted Richard the county palatine of Cumberland, making him virtually a sovereign prince independent of England. They had come so close to taking a far different path in life. So very close. But that dream had been spun of gossamer, shimmery and beautiful, and too frail to bear the burden of reality.

Anne's face had acquired a poignant, sorrowful look, and in an effort to distract her, Richard said, "Your gown is magnificent, dear Anne." In conversation there was a mindless solidity that kept dread thoughts at bay. "But why is it that Elizabeth wears the same?" He frowned in his niece's direction.

"Because I care for her," replied Anne. "And because she is eighteen and reminds me of myself when I was that age, and in love." Softly, she said, "Richard, will you not dance with her?"

Richard's eyes met hers. For a long time they held each other. Slowly, Richard transferred his gaze to his brother's daughter. She was conversing with Humphrey Stafford as she strolled gracefully along on his arm, turning heads as she went. She wore no headdress except a circlet of crystals and pearls, and her long golden hair shone like sunlight in the glow of the torches. She looked startlingly beautiful. Anne was right; there was a resemblance between them.

He heard Elizabeth laugh, a clear sound that evoked the ringing of bells. The past stirred in his heart and Anne's image flashed into his mind's eye, as she had been at his brother George's house, beneath the starry sky, by the river's dark edge. He gripped the side-arms of his throne and willed the memories away.

"Richard, what is it?" Anne whispered. He had blanched and his arm had jerked suddenly. When he turned his face to her, his grey eyes were filled with raw pain. "Nay, my lord," Anne cried softly, reading his thoughts. She clutched his sleeve. "'Tis God's will, Richard. Look not to the past, but to the future. 'Tis no use to dwell on what we cannot change... Dance with her, my dearest."

Like a man in a trance, Richard rose to his feet, gave Anne a small bow, turned and went down the steps. Music floated to him from the minstrel's gallery, but it seemed very far away. Someone asked him a question, which he neither absorbed nor would have answered if he had. As he walked past his guests, faces stared at him strangely; they blurred, faded away, were replaced by different faces. Directly ahead stood a familiar figure in a brilliant silver and violet robe that might have been Anne years ago. He went up to her and inclined his head. She blushed, sank into a deep curtsy. He offered his hand and she took it. He noted without emotion that her hand was soft as a flower petal. As Anne's had once been.

The minstrels broke into a lilting pavane. He led her to the dance floor. Trusty Lord Howard and his son, Thomas, fell in behind him with their ladies. Others followed: Rob, Jack, Ratcliffe, Brackenbury, Conyers, Catesby, the Lords Scrope of Bolton and of Masham, Francis, Greystoke, and the two Harrington brothers who were Knights of the Body. All his loyal, faithful friends, closing ranks behind him. The line moved up and down in rhythm to the melody; they turned, they twirled, they changed partners, and returned again. Ahead of him, Anne smiled at him; to the side, Elizabeth smiled at him. Violet and silver dress; gold hair and violet eyes; pointed chins and rosebud lips. Anne, as she had once been.

Silver-haired John Howard slapped his thigh and gave a roar of merriment, and such a joyous roar it was that it penetrated to Richard through the fog around him. He became aware of people. They were murmuring; stealing hostile glances at him and Elizabeth. He didn't care. What did it matter? Nothing mattered anymore.

***

Margaret Beaufort stood with her husband, Lord Stanley, Lord Stanley's son, George, and their henchman Reginald Bray. They watched carefully from the side of the room, as they had the previous Christmas. "What do you make of this spectacle?" inquired Margaret Beaufort with a raised eyebrow.

"We're about to have a new queen," Lord Stanley grunted. "He has dressed them the same to bring them to our attention. What else could be meant by it?"

"Indeed, Father, I believe you're right. Elizabeth of York will take Anne's place as his queen—and soon, I wager," said his son.

Margaret Beaufort glanced around the room at the faces of the prelates and the nobles watching the King dance with Elizabeth of York. "So think they all."

George Stanley bent his head, dropped his voice to a whisper. "I wonder, does he mean to do away with his queen in order to marry Elizabeth the sooner, and so thwart our Henry's plans?"

"I wouldn't be surprised," Margaret Beaufort hissed. "He may be poisoning her already. See how she looks. Like a skeleton in a coffin." She locked eyes with Bray who edged close, lowered his ear to her lips. "If she dies before my Henry can marry Elizabeth, it would foil our plans. We must crush this idea of his."

"By what means, m'lady?" whispered Bray.

"The trusted, tried, and true methods which we devised two years ago and which are exacting such a toll on our dear Richard." She smiled suddenly and her eyes glittered. "Placards," she hissed softly.

***

From the opposite side of the hall, the Countess' gaze moved between Anne, Richard, and Elizabeth, and back again. She left the Scropes and Richard's sister, Liza, with whom she had been conversing, and took the steps of the dais to her daughter's side. "I fear it was not a good idea. There are murmurings about you and

Elizabeth wearing similar dress. People are thinking the worst, dear child," she said heavily.

"People always do, Mother."

The Countess turned her gaze on the old sea-dog Howard shaking a merry leg and twirling his lady under his plump arm like a ribald youth, then at Richard, moving mechanically with Elizabeth. "Why can't they see the truth?... That some dance to remember... and some to forget."

Anne coughed, laboured for breath. Tears stung the Countess' grey-green eyes. "My dear one, what will I—will he—do without you?"

"He will carry on, Mother... with Elizabeth. Where there is love, life can begin again."

The Countess took her daughter's hand tightly in both of her own.

"Now smile, Mother. The eyes are watching."

The Countess forced her trembling lips to curve, tears blinding her vision.

Chapter Twenty

"O my soul, be comforted!"

In the dull greyness of the February dawn, Richard left his chambers and strode down the back staircase that connected to Anne's rooms. They slept separately now. The doctors had forbidden him to share her bed since January when she began coughing up blood. She was contagious, they said, and it was vital he keep his distance. He bowed his head, stepped through the arched entry into the side passageway that led to Anne's chambers, and encountered the Countess, leaving. "How is she?" Richard's heart did not beat as he waited for her answer. The Countess was silent for a moment, gazing at him with red-rimmed eyes. Sounds of coughing filtered from Anne's room. "She has not long, my lord."

Richard smashed his fist into the stone wall.

The Countess placed a gentle hand on his sleeve. "'Tis the will of God."

"No—!" he moaned, sagging into the wall. He turned bloodshot eyes on her. "Why is He doing this? Was Ned not enough for Him? What is enough for Him?"

"Hush, my lord! Don't let them hear you speak thus. You must not rail against God, my lord. Even a king must bow to His will." She glanced along the hall to the antechamber milling with servants, physicians, monks, and ladies-in-waiting. With an arm around his shoulders, she guided him in the opposite direction into a small room off the passageway. Two maidens sat in the window seat, chatting. Startled to their feet, they bobbed a curtsy and fled, their shock at Richard's condition evident on their faces.

Leaning on the Countess, Richard made his way to the window seat. "My lord," the Countess said, "'tis best you not see Anne until you are better yourself. She worries about you; all her thoughts are for you. It would break her heart to see you thus." Richard looked up at her pitifully. The Countess sank down beside him and took his hand into her own, tears rolling down her cheeks.

***

It was not until later in the day, after dealing with a host of problems with his council, that Richard felt composed enough to visit Anne. He paused at the door, forced a smile on his face, and entered. The bed hangings of silver brocade were pulled back and tied with ropes, and the sun, which had broken through the clouds, slanted into the room from the windows that stood cracked open for air. Dressed in a dark chemise and covered by a grey velvet coverlet embroidered with tiny silver roses, Anne lay propped up on white silk pillows, her arms stretched out woodenly at her sides. Elizabeth was with her, playing chess on the bed, and her pale gold hair and dress of emerald silk brightened the room as vividly as any of the jewel-coloured tapestries that hung on the stone walls.

"The knight," Anne whispered.

Elizabeth moved the knight. "Very clever, my lady. Now let me see how I can salvage myself—" Thoughtfully, she cupped her chin in her hand and examined the board.

Richard's heart filled with gratitude to Elizabeth.

Anne glanced up, caught sight of him at the door. "My dearest lord!" she cried with delight. She tried to rise, fell back, choked by a fit of coughing. Then she gagged. Elizabeth leapt to her feet, grabbed a silver basin, and held it to her mouth. The room filled with the stench of vomit. She smoothed Anne's damp hair, helped her lay back against the pillows.

Richard strode to Anne's side, snatched a damp towel from an approaching maidservant. "I'll do it," he barked. The woman bowed her head, stepped aside. He dabbed the gilt-edged cloth to Anne's mouth, and winced as he wiped away blood. He accepted a clay cup from a monk. The foul-smelling liquid, thick as oil, offended his nostrils. "What is it?"

"A tincture of bitter aloe, black poppy juice, and bethony, Sire. Good for bleeding and cough, and to ease pain and procure sleep." Richard slid his arm behind Anne's shoulders and supported her while he tilted the cup to her lips. She was so weak, she could barely swallow. Much of the foul liquid slid out from between her teeth and dribbled down the side of her mouth. She pushed the cup away, seized by another coughing spell. He handed it to the monk and gently wiped her mouth. Anne laid her head against his shoulder. "Is it bad today, my love?" he asked. From the corner of his eye, he saw Elizabeth leave. The servants followed and the Countess, the last to go, shut the oak door behind her, leaving them alone.

"Not now... when you're here, Richard," breathed Anne. "I always feel better when you're here, my love." He sat down on the bed, stretched out beside her. He tightened his hold of her. *The doctors be damned*, he thought. He took Anne's small white hand into his own and rested his cheek against her brow.

Anne said haltingly, "How goes it, Richard... with Tudor, I mean?"

Richard tensed. "No news."

"But there is trouble... isn't there?" Anne insisted.

His gaze went to the window. The rippling blue Thames flowed past, dotted with colourful barges and masted ships. It was by sea that Tudor would come. All he needed was a fair wind. "There's always trouble in the realm, but nothing that need worry your sweet head." He kissed the top of her brow and stroked her hair.

"Richard, it worries me... far more... when you... keep things from me."

"Truly, 'tis nothing, little bird..." His eye rested on John's old hound, Roland, asleep in the corner, "merely the memories, which seem weightier today. Maybe because it'll soon be spring." *Spring*. He bit at his lip. Once there had been joy in the spring. No use looking back. *In last year's nest there are no eggs*. John smiled down at him against the backdrop of a vast sky, the wind whipping his hair. He blinked. "I find myself thinking of your uncle John a great deal lately," he managed over the tightness in his throat. Looking back was dangerous, he reminded himself. He mustn't look back. He couldn't go forward if he looked back.

"Aye, Richard," Anne said, hardly able to lift her voice above a whisper. "His was a tender heart, for all that he was a soldier... He fixed my wood doll once... though he lay in bed, wounded in the shoulder by an arrow..." Her voice trailed away.

The laughter of children playing in the court below filled the silence. Aye, Richard thought with aching grief, they'd managed to lose the past in that sun-drenched place they'd shared with Ned.

Then they'd moved—barely, slightly, imperceptibly—and the past had found them again.

Church bells tolled in the Abbey and were echoed down river and across town. He winced. They had been tolling with increasing frequency since Christmas, for Anne. His hand dug into her shoulder.

"I know, Richard…" Anne breathed. "If only we could erase the past… start over, rewrite it ourselves, as we would have it be… Then all would be joy, not sorrow."

"But it wasn't all sorrow, Anne," Richard replied with surprise. "Not after I met you. You changed everything." Scattering caution to the winds, he did what he had vowed never to do and spoke the words he had always turned away. "I remember when— I remember when I rode into Middleham for the first time and saw you and heard your voice… You have a beautiful voice, you know—Flower-eyes." He had purposely used his pet name of happier times to comfort her, unaware that his own mouth had curved at its mention.

"Just so you looked at me that day I showed you the injured little owl," she smiled.

"I remember as if it were yesterday. I think that's when I fell in love with you, but I didn't know it, of course. I was too young. Only nine."

"Two years older than me when I fell in love with you."

"All this time, you never told me when that was."

She placed her cheek against his and gazed out the window. "When I first saw you practising with your battle axe alone in the rain." She paused for breath. "You were so determined—not like the other student knights, playing marbles and sharing jokes by the hearth… I often stole out after that, just to watch you—and caught many a cold and was scolded for it."

Richard smiled. "I remember when…" he said again, and suddenly the stone walls of the chamber melted, the years rolled away, and they were laughing together, sheltering in the hollow of their chestnut tree, holding court in their childhood realm of Avalon while rain fell in torrents around them. He tightened his hold of her hand and she joined her memories to his, and in her voice and her laugh echoed the melodies of old songs they had sung together.

He could smell the sweetness of fresh-cut grass, hear the wind tear through the towering forests of the North, see birds wheel with dizzy freedom across the autumn sky. The music rose in volume and all at once they were dancing in the castle halls, and hounds were yelping as they ran across the moors and back to a castle filled with the smell of almond-cakes and sweet cinnamon wine at Yuletide. Those they had loved returned to greet them, smiling as though they'd not been dead all these years: John with his dimples and deep blue eyes calm as the sea at twilight, praising him in the tiltyard; Warwick, smiling down from a fine height; Desmond, Edward, George...

Ned.

Richard swallowed on the constriction in his throat and the light went out of his eyes.

"What is it, my love?"

He bit his lip and disengaged his arm. He moved to the window, stood with his back to her. "If only Ned—"

A long silence fell, broken only by the song of the birds.

Anne stared at his back. "Aye..." she whispered, "these are the things we would change... if we could." A vast weariness came over her. She leaned back, closed her eyes.

Richard left Anne asleep and tiptoed from the room. Heads turned in the antechamber. The Countess half-rose from her seat. He raised a finger to his lips and she nodded, sank back down. He slipped out into the passageway and was about to take the stairs down to the inner court when he halted. Elizabeth sat in a window seat in a small alcove off the private chapel, engrossed in a book. He went to her.

"Elizabeth—"

She jumped up with a gasp and her book fell to the floor. She made no effort to retrieve it.

"I didn't mean to startle you. I meant only to thank you for what you've done for my lady queen," he said awkwardly, feeling strangely at a loss.

Elizabeth blushed. "I wish I could do more, Sire." Her blue eyes filled with tears. She dropped her gaze. "I have prayed but—"

Dimly he noted that she didn't call him uncle. But then, why should she? He had never treated her as a niece, or thought of her as blood. A Woodville, that's all she'd ever been to him. He stood stiffly, unable, or unwilling, to leave. He realised now that he'd never really looked at her before, never really spoken to her or listened to her, or even seen her. Not as a person. A woman. Anne was right. She was beautiful. And she reminded him so much of Anne. He couldn't take his eyes off her. The happy, lost past suddenly seemed very near.

Elizabeth lifted her eyes. They were Edward's eyes, blue as the summer sky.

She said, "You were dear to my father's heart."

"And he to mine." His pulse quickened. What was happening? This made no sense.

Elizabeth cried out, "If we both loved him, how can we hate one another?"

"I—" Richard tried to speak but the words wouldn't come. It pained him to think she hated him, but he couldn't deny that his loathing of her mother had coloured his perception of her. He pulled his gaze away with effort.

Outside, river birds mewed, bargemen shouted, and a young couple laughed in the court below. Richard was assailed by a terrible sense of loneliness. He brought his eyes back to Elizabeth. She was flushed, her trembling lashes were lowered. "By your leave, Your Grace," she said. "I will see if the Queen needs me."

"She is asleep," Richard said. He felt inadequate, and utterly miserable, and sick with yearning for he knew not what.

Elizabeth stood twisting her slender hands together. "Then I shall see if the Countess needs me."

He hesitated. He didn't want her to leave. He didn't want to be alone; feared it suddenly more than anything else in the world. But he knew she should go. He gave a terse nod. Elizabeth almost broke into a run. She brushed past him with a rustle and he caught the whisper of a fragrance. Lavender. Anne's fragrance. He looked down at the book that Elizabeth had dropped. He bent down, picked it up. *Tristan and Iseult.* His book; it bore his signature and motto on the flyleaf, *Loyaulte me Lie... Richard of Gloucester.* The marker was still in place. He opened the worn leather volume, moved to the window, and read.

Gone was Iseult's hatred, no longer might there be strife between them, for Love, the great reconciler, had purified their hearts from all ill will, and so united them that each was as clear as a mirror to the other. But one heart had they—her grief was his sadness, his sadness her grief. Both were one in love and sorrow, and yet both would hide it in shame and doubt.... Heart and eyes strove with each other; Love drew her heart towards him, and shame drove her eyes away.

He lifted his gaze and stared in the direction in which she had disappeared. Sinking into the seat she had left, he gripped the book in his hand and read on.

Chapter Twenty-One

"But hither I shall never come again
Never lie by thy side, see thee no more—
Farewell!"

That night, alone in his bedchamber, Richard sat in a window seat, making no effort to sleep. By the light of the flickering candles, he read *Tristan and Iseult*. When he was done, he closed the leather-bound covers and wrenched the window open. The pale blue glow of moonlight reflected off the snow in the cold night. A few frosty stars twinkled in the sky. He could smell the dampness of the river and hear the water lapping below. He took a deep breath. He didn't know why Elizabeth had intruded into his thoughts. She meant nothing to him. He loved Anne. Elizabeth was his niece—and a Woodville. He had always hated Woodvilles.

He glanced down at the book in his hand.

No, he cared nothing for Elizabeth, but around her swirled memories. In her eyes he saw a river's edge and a girl with fair hair clinging to him beneath a starry sky. In her hair and the lift of her mouth, he saw a golden laughing god clattering into a cobbled court to embrace a small, fearful brother. He had noticed Elizabeth because Anne had forced him to notice her; and now, each time he looked at her, he saw Anne and remembered the sweetness of love; saw Edward, and remembered the warmth of brotherly affection.

He laid the book aside and stirred from the window. Soon another day would dawn, and there was much business to attend on the morrow. In his mind, he heard Anne urge him to bed, as she used to do.

***

In scarlet and gold, partly to disguise his low spirits, partly to raise them, Richard strolled with Elizabeth in the wintry gardens. Together they crossed the palace cloisters and passed the snowy central garth where a group of fur-clad nobles and ladies amused themselves tossing a gilded leather ball. Their laughter was subdued and their sober dress reflected respect for Anne's condition, but still Richard was irked. The old cry of his childhood would not be crushed: *It isn't fair!* Time was a friend to these strangers, bringing them pleasure, and it was an enemy to him, conquering Anne and taking away a piece of her each day. Already it was February. Without a miracle, how much longer could she survive?

He stole a glance at Elizabeth. They had been walking along in silence for some time now and he knew he should say something, but he didn't know what. He was assailed by a tumble of confused thoughts and yearnings, swept with loneliness and despair, and there were no words to convey to her what it meant to have her company for this short while.

"'Tis a fine morning, my lord," Elizabeth said, a blush creeping into her cheeks as she hastily dropped her gaze. "The sky has never been more blue."

"It will soon be spring," Richard replied, the terrible ache in his heart growing with each step they took. She was dressed sedately enough in green and wore no jewellery besides the silver clasp of her cloak and gilt circlet over her hair, which was pulled back at the nape. Yet the contrast of her robes with the shining gold of her hair only heightened the beauty that reminded him of Anne. He cast a look behind him, to the high window in the white-stone palace where Anne lay ill.

"I saw the first jonquil this morning; it broke through the snow," Elizabeth said softly, catching his glance. "I picked it for the Queen. The joy on her face was—" her voice cracked and she fell silent.

Richard nodded, his throat too constricted to speak.

They took the path down to the river, continued to walk along in awkward silence, past strolling clerics and knights with their ladies, and others seated on benches amongst the hedges. Ahead, the great fountain splashed noisily. Swathed in furs, several young damsels sat on a carpet spread around its smooth stone rim, their admirers grouped at their feet, one strumming a lyre, another playing a flute. A love song floated on the wind. Richard was aware of the eyes that followed them, and he read their thoughts. As always, they didn't understand, assumed the worst. The curse of God be on the fools! What did they know?

"It seems a long winter this year," Elizabeth offered. "I shall be glad enough of spring."

Richard cast about for an answer, but all he could find was, "Aye." Her closeness was comfort, so why this confusion? He knew he should leave, yet he was unable to tear himself away from her side. With Elizabeth time didn't seem such an enemy, but with Anne each moment was wracked with suffering as she groaned with leg cramps, fought for breath, and struggled to spit up the bloody flux from her lungs—while he watched helplessly. He was King, and he was helpless. The shadow of Anne's loss drew nearer around him, darkening the world like an eclipse.

A group of courtiers bowed. He acknowledged them with a taut nod.

"I hear Lady Scrope had another girl," Elizabeth said. "That makes three daughters."

He felt a rush of guilt. She'd been making effort at conversation, he none. He longed to sweep away the prattle, to tell Elizabeth of his love for Anne—of his regrets for her own losses; losses for which he bore responsibility—

"Aye, three," he said. "I shall have to consider what gift to send." He bit at his lip and clasped his hands behind him as they strolled in silence once more. Gratefully, he thought of a question, "You know her well; do you have a suggestion?"

She threw him a shy glance and blushed again. "Perhaps some cloth of gold—" Shrieks of delight interrupted her and she looked towards the Thames where a group of children played with a dog on the riverbank. "Or a hound," she said with a wan smile. "My father, God assoil his soul, gave me a shaggy hound on my sixth birthday, and she brought me much joy."

Richard winced. For some reason, Edward's memory pained him this day.

"I shall send her cloth of gold," he said more curtly than he intended.

Elizabeth looked at him sharply. Their gaze met and locked. His heart jolted in his breast and his whole being filled with waiting. A line from *Tristan and Iseult* came to him: *Each knew the mind of the other, yet was their speech of other things.* He tore his eyes from hers. *God's Blood, this is Edward's daughter—my own niece!* He said, "My lady, I must leave you now. The Queen has need of me."

Elizabeth fell into a deep curtsy.

He was half way down the snowy path when she arose. Swept with a wretchedness of mind she'd not known before, she watched him, his bleak, solitary figure. For some inexplicable reason, all she could think was that her father had loved him, too. Without warning, tears started in her eyes and rolled slowly down her cheeks. Today was her nineteenth birthday, and she couldn't help remembering.

***

February gave way to bitter March. Wednesday, the sixteenth, dawned cold, but sunny. After Compline, Richard stole a few moments from his council chamber to go to the chapel. He had barely begun his prayers at the altar when he heard a commotion in the nave, the sound of footsteps on the stone floor, the clink of metal, the rustle of garments. He tensed, jerked around.

"Sire, the Queen—" Ratcliffe broke off. The Archbishop of York was with him.

Richard's breath caught in his throat at the sight of Archbishop Rotherham. He gripped the wooden transept fiercely with both hands.

"No, my lord," the Archbishop said. "She is still with us, but failing fast."

Richard shut his eyes on a breath, nodded thickly. They withdrew. He turned back to the altar. Pressing his palms together, he lifted his moist eyes to the crimson and gold image of the suffering Christ.

O God, help me! Show me the mercy we don't find on earth, he prayed in his despair. The candles flickered unsteadily. His vision blurred and he could barely make out the cross. He blinked, but he still couldn't see. Had God hidden His face from him? With a choked gasp, he flung himself from the altar.

Sounds of chanting came to him as he neared Anne's room. At the threshold of her chamber, his legs failed him. He grabbed the pillar for support. The stone felt cold and dank to his touch. He pushed himself forward, stepped through the open door. At the far end of the room, their dark cowled figures barely visible in the shadows, four Benedictine monks were singing the prayers he had found so soothing when he had heard them in the abbey churches. Now they sharpened his panic. He turned his gaze on Anne.

The silver curtains were tied back. She lay stretched out on the great bed, eyes closed, a pale, diminished, almost lifeless figure in white. Candles burned around her and a large silver crucifix hung on the dark silk-draped wall over the bed, glittering with menace in the flickering light. Once another crucifix had glittered so. *In the Tower, the night Henry had died.* Richard blinked to banish the memory. Was that the sin for which he was being punished now? He had tried to atone by transferring Henry's body from shabby Chertsey Abbey, where Edward had buried him, to the splendid Chapel of St. George at Windsor. But like everything else he had done in his life, it hadn't been enough.

He passed a hand over his face and looked back at the bed. The Countess sat at her daughter's side in a tapestried chair, her back to the windows. Sunlight illuminated her figure from behind and her face would have been in darkness but for the light of the candles. She lifted her eyes to him and he saw his own torment reflected there.

He moved to the bed, only vaguely conscious that the Countess rose as he did so, that the doctors retreated, the servants slipped away. He absorbed all this in slow motion, for time had lost its measure. At Anne's bedside, he took a seat and reaching over the velvet coverlet, clutched one cold hand in both of his. Her breath came in short, laboured pants. He tightened his hold and deepened his own breathing, in order to breathe for her, to keep her alive with the vital force of his own body.

Sensing his presence, she opened her eyes. She tried to speak. He bent his ear to her lips. A whisper of ice touched his cheek.

"Sing to me—" she gasped, fighting for breath, "of the North—"

Emotion threatened to overwhelm him. His lips were parched. With difficulty he forced them to move, to form the words. The song, slow at first, gathered force and flowed freely from his soul. He sang of the deer, the twilight, the wind and the water; the song he'd always carried in his heart and never had time to pen:

Aye, aye, O, aye the winds that bend the brier!
The winds that blow the grass!
For the time was may-time, and blossoms draped the earth...
Wine, wine—and I will love thee to the death
And out beyond into the dream to come...

She calmed. Her lips curved into a smile. Time hung suspended. He watched her, grateful for each peaceful breath, for the absence of pain. Gladly would he sit here forever, if that were the only way to keep her with him. She gave a moan. Ice spread through him. "My little bird, what is it?"

"I will wait—" she said, each word dragging forth with pain, "for you... in heaven."

Words from the letter beneath the chestnut tree. Richard bent his face to hers, brushed her hair and cheeks and brow with his lips. "My love," he whispered, "my dearest love..."

A voice at his shoulder said, "Sire, 'tis time." He looked up. Archbishop Rotherham stood in his gold and white robes, the Holy Book in one hand, a jewelled crucifix in the other. Richard's heart pulsed in his ears and a rising pain choked off his breath. His agonized cry pierced the chamber. "*No—!*"

"Sire," said the Archbishop, "the last rites must be performed."

Richard stared up at him, but his face wavered in and out of focus, hurting his eyes. He shifted his frantic gaze back to Anne. "It can't be time. Not yet, not yet!" *Never*. If she received extreme unction, she would leave him.

"I pray you, my lord. The Queen must not die unshriven."

Die. The dread word he had denied all these months echoed through him, a loud, distorted, evil drumbeat: *Die, die, die...* He tightened his grip around Anne's frail body and laid his head against her breast. Through his own heavy breathing, he heard her whisper, "I pray you, Richard..."

He lifted his head and looked at her. Her eyes were scarcely open, her small nose pinched, but her expression told him what she had no strength to ask. He reached out to the curtain for support, struggled to his feet, but his unsteady legs buckled beneath him and only the gentle arms of Anne's mother held him so that he did not fall. "Come, dear lord," said the Countess, her face wet with tears.

Barely able to breathe, Richard looked up at Rotherham's dry countenance. "Hurry, I must be with her when—"

The Archbishop inclined his head. Leaning on the Countess' arm, Richard dragged himself from Anne's chamber.

***

Though it seemed an eternity, it was only a short while later when the Archbishop opened the door of the chamber. Richard rose stiffly, heavily, made his way to Anne. Her eyes were closed; she was barely breathing. He knelt at her side. The monks resumed their low chanting.

"Richard…" she murmured feebly.

"I am here, Flower-eyes," he said, brushing her damp brow with his lips. "I won't leave you, Anne… I'll never leave you."

"Elizabeth… she loves you," she said, straining for breath. "Where… there is… love… life… can be born… anew."

"Hush, Anne, hush." He took her cold hand into his own. Through ashen, quivering lips, he whispered, "I want only you. Anne stay with me—stay, I beg you!" Anne opened her eyes wide and looked at him. Pure violet, those eyes. Lit from within with a golden light. "No need for tears, my beloved Richard," she said in a strong, clear, steady voice. He gaped at her with astonishment. Hope flooded his breast; a smile broke across his face. She would be well! God had heard his prayers! He would work a miracle after all! "Flower-eyes, my Anne—" he cried joyfully.

She lifted a hand, touched his cheek.

"I shall see Ned," she smiled, the light dimming from her eyes. Her hand fell limp.

"Anne!" Richard cried in panic. *"Anne—!"*

Silence.

His head on her breast, he clung to her with a choked moan. Only he heard her last words, her final breath; faint, falling away, like an echo along a distant passageway fading into deepest night, "Oh, Richard," she sighed. "'Tis beautiful, Richard…"

But for Richard there was only anguish and pain so excruciating that his entire body vibrated with it. He didn't see the Archbishop lift his great jewelled crucifix and make the sign of the cross over Anne's body; didn't hear him intone "*In Manus Tuas, Domine—*" then break off to look up at the window and gape at the sky. He didn't see the monks lift their heads and follow the Archbishop's gaze or hear the gasp of horror that ended their song. He didn't see the servants who knelt in prayer cross themselves for fear. All he saw was Anne, lying on the bed, pale as a marble effigy and as still, in a room gone suddenly dark and silent and cold. All he felt was that a shadow had fallen across his shoulder, that ever more for him it would be night. He knew it was noon, that the day had been bright when he had entered, but there was no light anymore, only a dismal gloom lit by the flickering light of candles, and a strange, eerie silence. No birds sang; no church bells pealed; there was no sound from man or beast.

He lifted his head, turned behind him. Everyone, including the Countess and the Archbishop, stood immobile, their faces uplifted to the heavens. He pushed himself from his knees, moved to the window. Outside, snow covered the trees and garden wall with glaring whiteness. He felt the cold as if he were part of the landscape, a thread of water hanging frozen from the bare tip of a branch, immobile, going nowhere. He looked up, stared at the sky.

The world was as black as night, and where the sun had shone, only a shadow remained. The mighty sun had been darkened by the Hand of God.

His breath caught in his throat. *This was God's answer to him!* He buried his face in his hands.

A low, sweet voice broke through the horror. "So many angels came down to guide her to heaven," the voice said, "that their wings darkened the sun." He heard them through his shattering grief and they sounded to him like a melody plucked on a harp. Who was there who could give such comfort? He dropped his hands from his face. Elizabeth smiled at him through her tears, though her heart broke to look at him. Pain was carved in merciless lines across his brow, at his mouth, around his eyes. *Jesu*, but he had aged ten years in an hour. She went to him, touched his sleeve, "She has been rescued from this dark world, my lord. God has one more angel at His side this day."

They looked for a long moment into each other's eyes and between them lay their love for Anne and all that they had shared. Richard took a step forward mutely, collapsed against her and smothered his face in her shoulder. Her arms went around his head and she held him like a suffering child.

With tears streaming down her cheeks, the Countess turned away and the servants bowed their heads, sniffling. Only Archbishop Rotherham remained aloof, dry-eyed, gazing sourly on them, his face contorted with disgust. First the King had dressed his niece like a second queen at Yuletide. Then had come the shocking stroll in the garden. Now they embraced for all the world to see. They were like lovers, King Richard and his *niece*. Never, in all his years, had he thought to witness such a scandalous sight. He drew himself to his full height, swept with an icy resolve. Tudor had to be informed.

Chapter Twenty-Two

"But how to take last leave of all I loved?"

Beneath drizzling grey skies, the funeral procession wound its way from Westminster Palace to the Abbey. Anne's bier, covered with black and white velvet and drawn by four black horses, rumbled slowly across the cobbled court, escorted by four knights bearing torches. For once the eternal church bells hung silent and there was no sound but the hoof beats of the horses, and the weeping. Anne had much endeared herself to the poor by her acts of charity and goodness, and the common people had come in great numbers to pay their last respects. Pressed against the walls and gates, they watched the solemn cortege.

With dragging steps, clothed in plain dark saye without girdle or trimming, bareheaded and unadorned by any jewels save Anne's small sapphire ring, Richard walked behind her coffin, remembering their coronation when she had walked behind him. Just twenty months had passed between. There had been hundreds of candles and tapers, then as now. Monks had chanted, then as now. The Archbishop had led the procession; the lords and ladies had followed from the Palace to the Abbey.

Then as now.

Searing pain shot through him. To safeguard the two he loved best in the world, he had taken the Crown, and paid for it with their lives. A line from King Arthur came to him: *And I am blown along a wandering wind, and hollow, hollow, hollow all delight!*

He shuffled forward.

Inside the Abbey it was dark and cool. The smell of burning incense filled the nave and curls of smoke wafted to the gold bosses on the soaring vaulted ceiling, misting the air and lending a sense of unreality. The monks' chant rose in volume and their song resonated against the stone floor and soaring arches. Slowly the funeral procession wound along, torches flaring, past the shadowy Sanctuary and the High Altar, past the tombs of other Plantagenet kings of England: the Henrys, the Edwards, the Richards... He didn't glance at Henry V's tomb and painted wood effigy of silver and gilt, erected to his memory by his widow, Katherine of Valois, Henry Tudor's grandmother, but at the tomb of Richard II he looked up at the carved marble figure.

It was a mild, child-like face with winsome curls that had sown the seeds of the Wars of the Roses between Lancaster and York. For nearly a hundred years England had paid in blood for his murder. The realm had thought the dynastic struggle ended with Henry's death; it had not. Edward had thrown away the gains by marrying a Woodville—

No, Richard corrected himself. By marrying Bess Woodville. Anne had pointed out the difference, and Anne had been right. He had hated all Woodvilles because of Bess; had blamed them for the ills that had befallen him, the Nevilles, and England. But no longer. Elizabeth was part Woodville. If only Edward had married someone like Elizabeth.

An ache for the past, for all that was, was not, and might have been, descended on him with crushing force. He shut his eyes and forced a long breath. When he opened them again, he found himself gazing at the effigy of Richard II's queen. *Anne*. Richard II had buried his Anne in a frenzy of grief, they said. He tore his gaze from the soft face and bit down against the wrenching of his heart. History had a brutal way of repeating itself. He dragged himself forward.

Near the south door leading into the shrine of Edward the Confessor the procession came to a halt. There, in that place with its carved stone screen and gold feretory, he and Anne had knelt together to be crowned. Now her tomb yawned open before him, a cavernous marble pit set on a stone bier. The monks raised their voices to chant the solemn masses and dirges of the Requiem. When it was ended, Archbishop Rotherham stepped forward, opened his psalter, and droned the Pater Noster.

Richard stared at the unyielding stone and felt he would strangle on the pain in his throat. In his mind's eye he saw the child Anne, who had taken him to her little injured owl and run up the grassy slopes of Middleham with him, laughing... Anne, untroubled and teasing, on the cusp of maidenhood, waiting for him beneath the boughs of the old chestnut tree. Anne, the young bride, riding pillion as they tore over the thundering River Tees and made love in the tender grass…

Anne was gone, vanished like the beautiful sparkles of hoar frost he had taken for diamonds in the sun as a child. Into that blackness, she would be sealed forever. Anne, who had shared his dreams and his youth and his beginnings. And so many of his endings. *Oh God, God—*

Raw, primitive grief overwhelmed him and the last shreds of his iron will, which had held him together through the batterings of his childhood, through his exiles and the wars, through the loss of all his kin and the death of his only child, ruptured like old silk sliced by a sword. His shoulders trembled and the tremors became heaves; choked sobs assaulted him and scalding tears blinded his eyes. Standing at the foot of Anne's tomb, surrounded by his nobles and the prelates of his realm, Richard broke at last and, covering his face with his hands, he wept.

Chapter Twenty-Three

"Accursed, who strikes nor lets the hand be seen!"

In his chamber at Westminster Richard turned away from the window, ready to meet his councillors waiting for him in a council room off the south court. He had shut himself away for a full week since Anne's death, but the moment he had dreaded could no longer be put off. The time had come to resume his duties, and rule alone. Alone… A line from Malory came to him: *The goodly apples, all these things at once Fell into dust, and I was left alone And thirsting in a land of sand and thorns.*

Silence pervaded the halls as he made his way down the stairs, through arches, past pillars, across the court. An icy wind blew from the river, tearing at his mantle and beating him back. He hunched his shoulders and fought his way forward with determined strides. It was quiet in the Palace cloisters. Sombre dress and solemn faces met him everywhere. Even the dogs seemed to have sensed the mood in the castle and lay quietly watching. He turned a corner, pushed open the door, and entered. A tapestry protected the chamber from the draft. He thrust it back. Candles burned in silver sconces on the long gleaming table but failed to pierce the gloom. Silence here, too, and grave faces. He threw his gauntlets on the table.

Ratcliffe came forward, handed him a placard.

Richard's councillors watched him anxiously as he read. Jewels flashed on his fingers, around his crimson collar, and on the turned-up brim of his hat, but for all the magnificence of his elaborate royal robes, he looked terrible. His face was sickly pale, his mouth tight and pinched, and beneath his bloodshot eyes ran deep black circles. It was clear that he had slept little since his queen's passing. And there would be no respite. Within days of her death, placards had appeared on St. Paul's and the rumour had reached the far corners of England that King Richard intended to marry his niece. Against their will, the royal council had no choice but to confront him with it.

Richard looked up. His hand trembled as he laid the placard down.

"Sire, you must deny this, deny that you ever considered such a step," Ratcliffe said. "Not only is such a marriage impossible—the Pope would never grant a dispensation—but to marry Elizabeth of York would give the lie to your title as King. If she is legitimate, then so are her brothers—" Ratcliffe hesitated. "My lord, there is talk that you poisoned the Queen in order to wed Elizabeth of York. Unless you deny this marriage rumour, even the people of the North will turn against you. Queen Anne was much loved in York."

Richard stood immobile and it seemed to the men around the council table that he didn't comprehend. Then without warning, he crashed his fist on the table, nearly toppling the heavy silver scones. "That vile bastard! That lying, scheming Tudor! Is there nothing he'll not say, nothing he'll not do, to steal the Crown of England for his bastard head?" His eyes glittered. He seized Ratcliffe by his doublet. "Do you believe Tudor's lies, Ratcliffe? That I schemed for the throne? That I murdered my brother's sons? That I poisoned Anne?" He thrust him back. "And you, Catesby? Rob? Conyers?—Aye, and you, Francis?"

Everyone shrank back; once before a man had died in the face of such rage.

"Sire," said Francis through parched lips, "you cannot doubt us?"

"Why?" Richard swung on him. "Wasn't Caesar murdered by the one he loved best? Didn't Buckingham aim to destroy me? Why should you be different? Why should any of you? Treason is in the air. It hangs like ripe fruit, ready for the picking and tempting all! Tell me that lies and betrayal are not the swords and shields of Tudor's war! Tell me chivalry isn't dead! Tell me there's still loyalty in this world—in this stinking, rotten charnel house of a world... Tell me that!"

Silence. The March wind howled outside and rattled the windows.

Richard rammed his fist on the table again. "Lying bastard... Foul, lying bastard!" He kicked chairs over and pounded the table until his knuckles bled. Depleted, he slumped into a chair and let his head drop to his chest.

Everyone watched helplessly, wanting to comfort but finding neither the courage nor the words. It was Francis who finally went to him. "My lord, we are not traitors," he said softly, dropping to a knee, "none of us—not Rob, Catesby, Ratcliffe and I, nor Brackenbury either, not Conyers nor Scrope of Bolton and many others you know well. They're all good men and go back a long way with you... *Live pure, speak true, right wrong, follow the King—*"

Richard lifted his head. It was the code of their boyhood dreams. The shape of their lives.

"Not only are you my King, but my friend since earliest boyhood. Together we listened to tales of King Arthur and together we learned to wield the sword... You are my true sovereign and gladly would I give my life for you. I swear this oath before Christ and His Saints, that I have ever been loyal and will remain so unto death. *Loyaulte Me Lie.*"

Richard gave a choked moan. He flung himself from his chair and embraced Francis. An audible sigh of relief swept the room.

"My lord," said the royal councillor Catesby, "if you marry off your niece, it would blunt Tudor's hand. Then he could no longer boast of a marriage that would unite the red rose with the white."

A sudden weariness engulfed Richard. His back ached between his shoulder blades and the old wound from Barnet throbbed. He moved to the window, looked out at the mournful river. "You forget, Catesby, the red rose and the white were united long ago when my mother, the granddaughter of the Duke of Lancaster, married my father, the Duke of York. As for marrying off my niece to spite Tudor—" he swallowed, willed himself to go on. "As for marrying off my niece, I won't give Tudor the satisfaction of thinking that I care a whit for his plans."

"But it would be good statecraft."

"Statecraft has never meant anything to me. You should know that by now. I've given my best. If that's not good enough for England, then she's welcome to the bastard." He strode to the sidetable, swept up his gauntlets, and made his way to the door.

Ratcliffe called after him. "My lord, what about Elizabeth of York?"

Richard froze in his steps. His eye went to the tapestry directly in front of him that concealed the door to the chamber. Deer and fern. A knight in golden armour at the feet of a fair-haired maiden. Blazing with the jewel-toned colours of rubies, emeralds and bright blue sapphires, it lit up the grey room like a torch. *Tristan and Iseult.*

He shut his eyes.

"Make a proclamation… There never was, and never will be… plans for a marriage between us." He flung the tapestry aside and stepped out into the bitter March wind.

Chapter Twenty-Four

"Sir, there be many rumours on this head;
For there be those who hate him in their hearts."

Within days it became clear that a written proclamation was not enough. Richard would have to denounce the marriage rumour in person. Summoning the mayor, aldermen, and chief citizens of London, his lords temporal and spiritual, and leading the officers of his household, Richard rode to the hospital of the Knights of St. John in Clerkenwell. He had chosen it deliberately. Students were schooled in the law here, and it was a place familiar to him, one he understood. He respected the law, and law was the foundation of his rule. The people needed reminding of that. In a loud, distinct voice, he stood before them and denied the rumour spread by Tudor.

Along the way back from Smithfield, through the Strand and the Fleet to Westminster, Richard rode wearily, his heart heavy as lead, and the crowds who stared at the colourful royal procession seemed to him a swarm of flies come to settle on a wound. Later that night he sat at a table in his candlelit solar, sharing a cup of wine with Francis. Sleep seldom came to him these days and he'd dismissed the servants for the night, seeing no need to deprive them of their rest as well. Behind him a fire crackled in the hearth. He had purposely set his chair so that he sat with his back to it and had no view of the silk cushions strewn about the floor where he used to sit with Anne.

"More wine?" he asked Francis, picking up the ruby-studded flagon.

"Maybe just one." Somewhere in the garden an owl hooted. Francis smiled apologetically. "'Tis late even for owls, Richard."

It was past the midnight hour and Richard knew he should let his friend go. Francis had to leave for Southampton at first light, to secure the southern coast against Tudor's invasion. But memories weighed heavy on him this night and he dreaded the morrow. Come morning, there was something he had to do that he couldn't bear to think about. He poured wine and set the flask down beside the hourglass. From the corner of the room John Neville's old hound, Roland, caught Richard's gaze. Roland gave him a soulful look and wagged his tail.

"I find myself thinking a great deal about my cousin John lately," Richard said, drawing the hourglass near. Grains of sand drifted down in a fine stream, inexorably marking the passage of time. Nowadays when he looked back, it seemed to him that his path had been paved with graves. Of them all, after Anne and Ned, it was John he mourned most. *Aye, 'tis on a winter's night, when it is freezing, that we think most of the sun…* "I owe him my life. If it hadn't been for John, I'd have died at eighteen."

"Aye," Francis said softly, "he gave his life for yours."

"He taught me how to fight with my left hand… showed me how to overcome my handicap."

"He was a valiant soldier. A true knight."

"I miss him, Francis. Always have… All these years. It doesn't get better. It gets worse. Edward shouldn't have taken away his earldom."

"A miscalculation. Edward was angry with Warwick. John was his brother. Edward paid for it."

A single hoot from the owl sounded again in the night, and another more distant owl answered. Richard looked down at his right hand, at the gold griffin ring John had given him that day long ago at Barnard's Castle when they had sealed their kinship by mingling their blood. *"Brother to Brother, yours in life and death,"* they had vowed as the wind blew and the birds shrieked.

"We've all paid for Edward's miscalculations," said Richard, with a swallow of wine, "and I fear we are not done yet. John should be here with us now, Francis. Not Percy or Stanley." He upended his cup and poured himself another. Turning his head, he stared out the window. It was a clear night; a full moon silvered the sky and torches flared along the battlements. Had it looked that way at Pontfract the night John made his decision to trade his life for Richard's?

Richard glanced at Roland. The hound returned his mournful look. "John didn't like Stanley, though Stanley was married to his own sister at the time," Richard murmured. "'He's not a man I'd want standing at my back,' is what he said. His exact words." Richard licked his lips. "Exact," he repeated with a slur.

"John was right. You must keep your eye on Stanley."

"John also said, ''Tis not what you are but what you will become that counts.'... What have I become, Francis?"

"King Arthur, my friend."

Richard mulled his wine. "King Arthur failed." He downed a gulp. "Once I believed winning or losing made no difference, it was how you fought the fight that mattered. Now I know better, Francis."

In the morose silence that followed, Richard's thought churned. Thanks to Tudor's lies, he was losing the battle for men's hearts on which he had rested the justification for the crown he wore. He remembered the morning at Clerkenwell, the faces of the crowd watching him as he rode back to Westminster. The crimes of which they accused him! It was in their eyes as he rode past in the streets, and their whispers, which ceased abruptly when he appeared. Every unspeakable crime that could be conjured in the dark corners of their minds—treason, incest. The murder of his brothers, his wife, his nephews. All lies concocted by Tudor. And they believed them. It lifted them up to see another brought low. He was coming to believe that man was a blight on the face of the earth. He slammed down his cup.

"I know what they say about me, Francis. They call me foolish because I pardon my enemies instead of slicing their heads from their shoulders. They say the world I wish to create is impossible because I believe in justice and fight against corruption. They think me mad for it. No doubt I am."

"Your lunacy is to see life as it ought to be, Richard, instead of as it is." Francis picked up the flask and poured Richard a full measure of wine. He pushed the cup to him.

Richard drank deeply. "Indeed, until—" *until Ned's death*— "recently, I believed that virtue always prevailed—" He waved his cup around, sang drunkenly, "*Onward to glory I go*—'Tis a damned bleak world in which we live, Francis. The worst crime of all is to be born. For that, you get punished all your life."

Francis touched his sleeve. "Nay, Richard. We will suffer. We will despair. But we will go on, and we will be resurrected."

Richard shot him a twisted smile. "You have more faith than an archbishop, Francis."

They fell thoughtfully silent.

"It was Buckingham's revolt that changed everything and gave Tudor hope," Francis said after a time. "Whatever possessed you to hand him such power, Richard?"

"I thought that obvious. He was like George." Richard toyed with the hourglass again. The hour was almost spent, and except for a few grains, the sand lay on the bottom.

"Aye. That he was," said Francis. "Like George."

Richard threw him a look. Francis was not thinking of smiles and golden curls. "I should have known, should have seen it, Francis. But I wanted George back as he used to be. I thought I'd found him in Buckingham. I couldn't let myself see… I couldn't let myself see a lot of things."

Francis dropped his gaze. Richard gave the hourglass an angry shove; it slid along the table and came to a halt perilously close to the edge.

"The trouble with learning from experience, Francis, is that we always learn too late."

***

After a wretched night of little sleep and bad dreams, Richard felt a desperate need for confession. Maybe that would gird him with the strength to do what had to be done this day. He summoned his confessor, Brother John Roby, to his private chapel.

"They say the grey whale travels thousands of miles in winter, seeking warmth and sunlight. Where do I go, Brother?"

The friar regarded him gently. "The cold will not last forever. 'Tis the wild beast's utter faith in the return of spring that enables him to survive the winter. The sun will come again. Frozen rivers will melt. Flowers will bloom….Faith will sustain you."

Then he listened to Richard's anguished confession about Elizabeth and murmured soothing responses about sinful thoughts, assuring him they were deplorable but human, and that God would forgive in the face of true repentance.

"I have another confession... My hatred for Henry Tudor." The man who had poisoned his peace; who had filled his days with vile rumours and his nights with demons. "I've fought a hundred enemies in the field. But this malice, this slander—it has no face, no name— it maims without killing—" He looked at the friar with pained eyes, "How do I fight this?"

"You fight lies with truth," replied Brother John, "and with goodness. If these are not enough to win, then perhaps the test lies in the battle itself."

"Battle," echoed Richard, seizing on the word, giving it an interpretation the friar had not meant. *"Battle—"* In the outcome of battle lay the judgement of God. *Redemption or Death.* Soon there would be battle between him and Tudor. Aye, there was the answer! Battle that would end his torment. One way or the other.

"Remember," Brother John warned, "evil can be more powerful than good, yet you must not fight evil with evil. Hold on to virtue at all cost. That is the true test, and the hardest one of all."

But Richard did not hear. Like a man in a trance, he repeated, "Battle... True test is battle... Redemption or death... Battle."

Brother John regarded him with a depth of pity. After a moment, realising he could offer no further comfort and all else was useless, he made the sign of the Cross.

"Dutiful child of God, I grant you absolution—*Nomine Patri, Filii, Spiritus Sancti.*"

Chapter Twenty-Five

"There will I hide thee 'till my life shall end,
There hold thee with my life against the world."

Richard stared at the small group he had summoned to the royal suite. He stared at them in order to imprint their image on his mind, as indelibly as it was imprinted on his heart.

The Countess wore her dark robes of mourning. Beneath her wimple her face was aged, deeply etched by sorrow, but she held herself gracefully erect with the same dignity she had always shown. Little Edward stood at her side, dressed in black velvet. He was nine now, and nothing in his face or manner resembled George or Bella or his proud grandfather Warwick, for there was nothing gay, or proud, or bright about him, and he did not dream great dreams. But his heart was gentle and would always remain so, since it would forever retain the blessed innocence of childhood.

His son, his love-child, John of Gloucester, would be fifteen in May. How time sped past! It seemed only yesterday that he stood in Kate's house, gazing on his new-born infant. Johnnie was a mixture of Kate and himself, with his own dark hair and her green eyes and rosy cheeks. A handsome boy, he realised suddenly, taking in the strong, square jaw, the broad shoulders, the long muscular legs in blue hose. He would be tall. The thought gave him pride. Aye, Johnnie held great promise. He had a fine mind and he could laugh as easily as Edward had. His cheerful disposition would stand him in good stead. God be thanked, there was no need to worry. No one would hurt him. There was no purpose in it. He had no claim, no rights, no lands, nothing. He was a bastard.

God be thanked for that.

He let his gaze pass to Elizabeth, but only for a moment, for the sight of her brought heavy woe. She wore his favourite robe of deep green, and her pale hair shone in the dimness. That was all he would allow himself to see.

"You must go to Sherriff Hutton, you'll be safe there," he said thickly, avoiding Elizabeth's eyes, "all of you."

Elizabeth nudged little Edward forward. He fumbled with his hands shyly. "Uncle, I would s-seek… a favour of you."

Richard's heart ached for the boy. Gently he said, "Dear nephew, whatever it is, you know I will try to grant it."

"I w-w-wish I c-could fight for you…" Edward drew a deep breath, made fists with his hands in an effort to suppress his stammer. He succeeded, and the words poured forth like a waterfall, "I wish I could fight the bastard Tudor, dear lord Uncle, but as I am too young to help you slay him, will you take my banner into battle instead of me—?" He hung his head, embarrassed by his emotion and the effort it had taken him to get the sentence out.

Elizabeth placed her arms around his little shoulders, nodded to a servant in the corner of the room. The man brought the folded banner to Richard, knelt and unfurled it. A blaze of gold tassels and golden embroidery on white silk shot across the carpet. In the centre stood a nut-coloured cow.

Richard stared at the Dun Cow of Warwick. When he had last seen that emblem, it had been in the fog of Barnet and he had fought on the opposing side. He winced.

"We've been working on it all winter," Elizabeth said. "Cousin Edward helped in the design. He is talented in things artistic."

Richard knelt, took the child's hands in his own. "I shall bear your banner at my side and my thoughts shall be of you, Edward, and of your noble grandfather, Warwick the Kingmaker, and all those of the House of Neville whom I loved so well." A loud sob escaped from the boy. Richard pulled him close in a last embrace and felt the wet of his tears against his neck, then realised that they were not Edward's, but his own. He swallowed, clenched his jaw, imposed iron control on himself. He would have need of his strength a while longer. There was still Elizabeth.

He rose stiffly. "Go now, Edward. Worship God devoutly, remember to apply yourself to your studies, and never forget knightly conduct. For there is wisdom in prayer and learning, and a great lord has need of both." He gave the boy's hand to the manservant and watched him leave. His heart contracted violently in his breast and he felt a sudden need to call to him, "May God be with you, fair nephew!"

One sad backward glance, and Edward was gone.

Richard looked at John. "Father!" his boy cried on a sob. Richard clasped him to his breast, long and silently. Then he forced himself to loosen his grip. "Fare thee well, my dear son," he said, his voice cracking. John fled his arms, stifling a moan as he ran.

The Countess stepped forward. They gazed into each other's eyes a long quiet moment. "Dear lady, whom I have loved as a mother," Richard whispered, taking her gently into his embrace. "I thank you for the comfort and the love you have ever shown me."

Tears sparkled in her eyes, rolled slowly down her cheeks. "You were the son I never had, Richard." Her voice trembled. "I shall pray for your victory."

He bent his head and stood motionless as she left him, and in the rustling of her garments he heard the rustling of the wind through the trees of Middleham, the call of the wild, the rush of the rivers. He bit his lip until it throbbed like his pulse. When he had regained control of himself, he lifted his head and looked at Elizabeth. Her eyes were red-rimmed, swollen. With a motion of the hand, he dismissed the servants and waited until the door thudded shut behind them.

He said thickly, "I regret the death of your uncle Anthony. I know now he bore me no ill will. He was but an unwilling pawn."

"Aren't we all?" she whispered.

"Can you—can you forgive me, Elizabeth?"

"I forgive you, Richard," she said, gazing at him through her tears. "Because I love you."

"No!" he said roughly, sharply. "No, don't—I'm old, finished. God has taken everything from me, left me alone, barren. But you are young. You have your life before you. You'll change. You'll forget me."

"You can't believe that! This is no childish infatuation. I'm a grown woman and I love you, Richard. Anne wanted us together—she made me promise—"

Richard held up a hand. "You must not say these things. I must not hear them." Despite his resolve, his eyes stole back to her. "It's impossible, Elizabeth," he whispered hoarsely.

They stared at one another, and without warning they were in each other's arms. He held her close, her cheek against his and he could taste the salt of her tears and knew that his own were on her lips. Despair swept him and he felt his grief like a burning in his blood. He thrust her from him.

She stood, face flushed, breasts heaving. "I crave a favour, my lord!"

He waited.

"I wish a portrait of you. A miniature… It would be a comfort to me."

His throat ached. Anne had used those same words when she had begged a portrait of him, but he'd never found time to pose. There was always so much work to attend. *Oh, my Anne!*

Elizabeth spoke again, her voice a tremulous whisper, "—and your book, *Tristan and Iseult.*"

He held his back rigid and cast around for some bulwark against the rising tide of pain. His lids came down over his eyes. He managed a nod. There was silence for a long moment, then he felt a touch on his cheeks, a touch like butterfly wings where Elizabeth's lips rested for a fleeting second.

"I'll never change," she whispered. "I'll go to my death loving you, Richard."

And then she was gone, nothing left but a trace of her fragrance. Lavender. Anne's fragrance.

Richard heaved his shoulders back, lifted his face to the cold air that blew in through the window, and again he was back on the windy moors. But this time it was winter and there was nothing all around but desolation and despair and the wind that howled a single thought: *If Tudor won, he would marry Elizabeth.*

"Damn you, Tudor! Bastard! Vicious lying Lucifer—" He kicked the stone pillar, pulled the brocaded cloth from the table. A dozen small glass ornaments smashed to the floor. He strode to the mirror, flung it from its stand and it shattered into a thousand fragments. "You have no right to the throne. Bastard!… Whoreson!… No right to Elizabeth—the curse of God be on you!"

His crown lay on a carved table against the wall, resting on a satin pillow. He picked it up into his hands and held it high. It glittered in the low light, seemed to wink at him. He threw his head back, gave a shrill howl like a wounded animal, and laughed. *The curse of God is on myself!*

***

On the night of the tenth of May, while the palace slept, Richard entered the south door of Westminster Abbey and went quickly up the transept towards the shrine of St. Edward. He had come to say goodbye to Anne. Tomorrow he would set out for Nottingham, maybe never to return. He was not afraid. Once his heart had been filled with fear. Now there was nothing left to fear because there was nothing left to lose. Except a battered crown.

With his face half hidden in his hood, he stood before the guards around Anne's tomb and, not trusting himself to speak, dismissed them with a wave of the hand. They filed past silently with their torches, leaving gloom behind. The door shut with a resounding *clang* that echoed for some seconds through the empty halls of the Abbey. He threw back his hood and sank to his knees before Anne's tomb.

Tapers flicked unevenly, throwing shadows against the walls and the marble effigy of Anne that he had designed himself. She lay on a pillow, draped gracefully in a sheet, a crown on her flowing hair, a soft smile curving the corners of her lips. She held a lily in her hand and doves encircled her. She had always loved their gentle cooing at her bower. He reached out a trembling hand and touched the stone face. "Anne," he whispered, "Anne, Anne… I've come to bid you a last farewell, Anne." Though he knew it was only the trickery of the candlelight, in the agony of his soul he wanted to believe the statue moved. "Dearest love, my sweet wife… we had so few days together on this earth, but always your tender love watched over me and gave me strength… Now there is no comfort. Your image lives within my heart, yet I cannot feel your warmth—" He swallowed the choking tightness in his throat. "May merciful God reward thee for the faithfulness and kindness thou hast ever shown me, my gentle, beloved Anne. My little bird—"

Chapter Twenty-Six

"Now must I hence.
Thro' the thick night I hear the trumpet blow."

When the cock crowed in the darkness over London, Richard was already up and dressed, ready to leave Westminster. He'd spent most of the night by Anne's tomb and had bid all whom he had loved farewell, except one. His mother, "Proud Cis," the "Rose of Raby." It was to see her that he was journeying to Berkhampsted.

In the crisp sunshine of the May morning, the royal cavalcade rolled out of Westminster soon after breakfast, clarions blowing, horses clip-clopping, baggage carts rumbling. Beside him rode Kendall, Catesby, Ratcliffe, and Rob Percy in a tight group, bobbing in their saddles. John Howard and his son Thomas were in Essex, guarding the region against invasion, and Francis was in Southampton, on watch in the southern counties, attending to the refitting of the fleet. They would join him later. He had committed the defence of London to Brackenbury's capable hands, the white-haired Merlin who'd been Constable of the Tower when young Edward had disappeared.

His gaze moved past his friends to a stout figure in a furred scarlet mantle and feathered black velvet cap riding ahead in a smaller group. Stanley had been at his side since he'd taken the Crown, had not requested leave from court, and had given him no reason to doubt his loyalty. Yet the Wily Fox remained a dangerous uncertainty in spite of all the favour Richard had shown him; all the lands, wealth, and offices he had granted him in an effort to win his heart. There were measures that would neutralize Stanley's threat to him, but he had refused to take them. In testing his success with Stanley, he was testing himself and the success of his reign.

Dogs barked, children laughed, and the townsfolk cheered. The royal procession wound past Charing Cross and the little church of St. Martins in the Field. They were taking the west road out of London, going to Berkhampsted by way of Windsor. Though Barnet would have been a more direct route, he had no heart for Barnet.

There were memories whichever way he turned, but Anne had been fond of Windsor.

They approached the Mews where his falcons were kept, and proceeded into St. Martin's lane. They passed the fair homes of his knights. Ladies stood at the windows to wave their husbands farewell, and many were weeping. It was a scene sickeningly familiar. He had tried to spare his people war, and he had failed. Once more Englishmen would gather to kill Englishmen; friend to slay friend.

The minstrels broke into a stirring march with drums and flute as they neared St. Giles. White Surrey snorted, lifted his crimson-plumed head higher. Richard glanced down at his noble destrier, prancing to show off his burnished hoofs. Proud and beautiful, his silken white coat shimmering in the sun, he attracted as much attention as Richard himself. Richard was reminded of the day twelve years ago in the courtyard of Barnard's Castle when Anne had gifted him with the stallion, not knowing that white was an unlucky colour for a war horse. To his gilded saddle she had pinned a piece of parchment that carried a verse from Apocalypse: *I saw heaven opened; and behold a white horse; and He that sat upon him was called Faithful and True, and in justice He doth judge.* Richard closed his eyes on a breath: *I tried, Anne...*

He leaned forward and patted White Surrey's fine neck. He was an exceptional beast, a rare blend of strength and intelligence. At Middleham on that last day there had been sorrow in those velvety eyes.

The lilting march ended and the minstrels switched to a different melody. Plaintive and sweet, it was one he had heard many times in the halls of Middleham. His thoughts turned to Anne. She had believed that love cured all the world's ills, but she had forgotten that love was a double-edged sword. It cut as well as healed.

He forced his mind to the conversation around him, so he wouldn't dwell on memories.

"...Never did I think to see the day come when a no-good French-Welsh bastard would dare lay claim to the Crown of England," one of his knights was saying. A chorus of angry shouts met this remark and someone cursed Tudor. "The only true claim he has is to being a bastard," offered another knight. "Aye, true bastard lineage on *both* sides—not many can boast of *that!*" Everyone laughed.

Richard's hands clenched around his reins at the name he'd learned to hate. Tudor had destroyed all he'd loved and left him nothing. He had tempted Buckingham away and forced him to send Elizabeth north. He was behind every traitorous plot, behind every foul rumour. Maybe even behind Ned's death. He winced. *If Ned's death, then Anne's death.* Hot pain flooded him.

Tudor was a phantom without a face, the winged dragon of his nightmares with fiery eyes the colour of blood. He gritted his teeth. One day he would look into those dragon eyes, lift his sword, and plunge it down that devil's throat, straight into that black heart. He would do it, by God, if it were the last thing he did on earth.

***

At Berkhampsted bells pealed for evensong when the royal cavalcade approached the gates and crossed the drawbridge into the castle yard. The odour of cooked meat stung Richard's nostrils and his stomach contracted; he'd had little appetite in months and the smell of food now elicited a touch of nausea.

He was met by his mother's chamberlain leading an entourage of her officers. Richard had arrived during evening prayers, the man explained apologetically, and the Duchess could not be disturbed, for distraction was an enemy to the peace and inner stillness she sought. The household routine rested strictly on religious observance, and as was her custom, at the first stroke of the bell, she had taken a drink of wine until her chaplain was ready to accompany her in reciting the evensongs, and as the bells died away, she had entered the chapel to hear vespers chanted by the choir. She would join him afterwards in the solar before supper, if that was acceptable to the King. Richard inclined his head in assent.

He was led through the great hall being set for dinner, and up to the royal apartments. The room was elegantly, if sparsely, furnished. A bed with a dark silk coverlet and bronze damask curtains stood against one wall; a table with a silver ewer and basin on the other by the window; and a writing desk and chair before the hearth. No bright tapestries of courtly love adorned these stone walls, but a dark series set forth the Passion and the tale of St. Mary Magdalene.

He undressed with his squire's help, splashed rosewater over his face and neck, and washed his hands before donning a fresh grey velvet doublet, dark suede hose, and a jewelled collar. He shrugged into a black velvet mantle and put on his black velvet cap, pinned with his emblem of the boar. The sun was setting as he finished his toilette. He left his squire and took the steep winding steps to the western battlements. A fierce wind blew, refreshingly cool, carrying the sweet smell of grasses and wildflowers. It was May, the season of rebirth. He dismissed the guard and stood for a long moment, gripping the stone turret.

This time last year, Ned was buried in Sherriff Hutton.

He rested his weight on his hands and gazed over the lovely rolling meadows and the broad river, glistening like molten silver in the sunset. A flock of magpies flew overhead, black against the violet sky, mewing noisily, and from the distance floated the faint bleating of sheep and tinkling of bells. The earth was bathed in a divine tranquillity. Once he had understood such beauty, had felt it strike a resounding chord deep within him. Now there was only an aching despair, a yawning loneliness.

The soft murmur of voices came to him. He looked down at the courtyard. A large gathering of ladies was leaving the chapel, led by his mother's tall slender figure in plain black silk. Her white hair was barely visible beneath a veil of stiffened black gauze and at her waist hung the chaplet of gold beads his father had given her. With the aid of a silver walking stick and steps slower than he remembered, she crossed the courtyard and mounted the outer staircase to the great hall.

He left the battlements and took the worn stone steps down to her solar.

***

Cicely, Duchess of York, bent to kiss her sovereign's hand but Richard restrained her. He lifted her slender hand to his own lips.

"But you are King," she said a trifle sharply.

"I come not as your king but as your son."

Her wrinkled mouth, still well-shaped, softened. He followed her across the woven silk rugs, past the long wall of flaming torches and tapestries depicting the legends of St. George and St. John the Baptist, and they took seats by the west window, on gilt chairs set near a pre-dieu. She adjusted her skirts with a smooth, elegant gesture. As he waited, his eye strayed to the tapestry displayed on the south wall: the Wheel of Fortune.

His gaze lingered on the familiar scene woven in golds, topazes, and darkly mysterious greens. It was the solitary profane subject among all the religious series, and it spoke for his mother's life as vividly as the religious scenes betokened the lives of the saints, for she had been raised to many a dizzy height and dashed down to many a dismal depth. In a way, the Wheel of Fortune carried almost sacred significance for them both.

"Wine?" his mother inquired.

Richard shook his head. The servant went over to a table beneath the tapestry where a little malmsey pot resided next to a blue velvet primer and a white leather psalter. He removed the cover of silver and gilt, carefully poured wine into a silver goblet, and brought it to her. She took it and dismissed him from their presence. After a delicate sip, she set the goblet down on the table beside her. "'Tis good to see you, my son. It has been a long time."

"Since before my coronation," Richard replied.

She made no response and her face was unreadable. She sat erect, her hand gripping the carved armrest, her head held high, gazing at him steadily with her bright, blue Neville eyes. An image of Warwick flashed through his mind, and for an instant and with a stab of despair, he saw John clearly.

"I'm here to tell you three things," said Richard. "First, that you were right."

"If that is what you thought I wished to hear, you are mistaken."

"You were right, my gracious lady mother," he repeated, "and I wish you to know that I have sent Bishop Langton to Rome for a Papal dispensation. I intend to have Edward's children declared legitimate. As soon as it is granted, I'll proclaim Richard of York my heir to the throne."

"Ah."

"You're not surprised?"

"I am never surprised when you do what you believe is right. You have always striven to do right, even at your cost. Like your father before you."

Richard was speechless in his astonishment.

The Duchess spoke again. "Have you thought how young Lincoln will react? You shall have to set him aside."

"Jack knows. He's sworn to act as Protector and to safeguard the throne for little Richard, and if anything happens to him, for George's son."

"He is an honourable young man." She regarded him steadily. "What is the third thing you came to tell me?"

"Farewell."

Her lips parted in surprise. "Farewell?"

"I go to battle. Whether I return is up to God."

"You have been to battle before and seen no need to take special leave of me."

"Those were different times."

"And now?" she pressed. "What is different now? No King of England has died in battle since Harold at Hastings."

Richard pushed out of his chair and went to the window. He couldn't tell her that this was his last battle; that this would be to the death—his or Tudor's. For him there was no other way. He would not plunge England into a civil war to keep his throne.

Blue twilight had fallen over the countryside and little lights were appearing down in the village. He heaved a deep breath, turned back, scrutinized his mother. She sat rigidly erect, with the aura of a queen, but more remarkable after all the years and all the losses, was her serenity. She was old; she had greyed; her health had not been good of late; yet she exuded peace. Gazing at her, it was easy to remember why she had once been called "The Rose of Raby." But there was more than faded beauty in her face. There was strength, and the grace that comes from a tranquil heart.

"How do you do it, Mother?"

"Do what, Dickon?"

How long since anyone had called him Dickon! They were all

dead now; all who had called him Dickon. "Bear all the death... You lost my father, your brother, and Edmund in a day. Of four sons, I am the only one left." He didn't add, *and the least loved.*

Her eyes widened and for a moment she seemed unable to reply. He had surprised her. Never had he asked her anything of so intimate a nature. There had always been a barrier between them, stemming from her clear but unspoken belief that to be royal was to be different; royalty never displayed or discussed feelings.

But despite her outward calm, Cicely Neville was deluged with emotion. By devoting herself to prayer and contemplation of the Divine, she had severed herself from the trials and tribulations of normal daily life and found spiritual repose, yet from the moment she had set eyes on the ravaged face of her last-born child, she was deeply affected. Memories flooded her of her little changeling child, the dark one hanging back from his golden siblings as though he felt himself an intruder; of the trembling seven-year-old who had clutched her hand fiercely at Ludlow but held his head high, determined at all costs not to let his terror show.

She had always had a special regard for Dickon who, almost from birth, had seemed a lost soul. He had struggled to live, struggled to belong, to measure up, to earn what had come to the others without effort. And clearly, that struggle had failed and the failure was carved in terrible lines on his comely face. Gaunt and pale, his eyes encircled by dark shadows, he was a man sore wearied by care and watch, and it hurt her deeply to see his pain.

She rose, came to him, placed a hand on his sleeve. "I do it with the help of God."

"And what if God is set against you?" he cried suddenly.

"Why do you believe God is against you, Dickon?"

Emotion overwhelmed him. He averted his face. "You know why."

"No, I do not."

Richard heaved a deep breath and it seemed to him that the air seared his throat. "God turned a deaf ear to my prayers. He took from me everyone I ever loved. Anne—Ned—Katherine—" His voice broke.

"'Tis through suffering that we find Christ, my son."

"You're not hearing me, Mother. God has condemned me! He darkened the sun at the hour of Anne's death—to show me—to show the world—" he swallowed, fought for breath, continued, "His disfavour."

"I see."

He watched her return to her seat, the silver walking stick thumping the cream and umber tiles softly, his father's gold beads jingling at her waist. She arranged herself gracefully into her chair and looked at him.

"There was an eclipse of the sun when our Lord died on the Cross," she said.

Richard gazed at her without comprehending.

"Perhaps it was not His *disfavour* but His *favour* he wished to show. Perhaps He wished to show the world that He Himself lamented this one death... where there had been much suffering... and much love."

Cool fingers seemed to ease away the hurt in Richard's breast. Elizabeth had comforted him with similar words, and comfort had come to him that night at Anne's tomb. Though he knew solace failed to last long beneath the weight of sorrow, he accepted the balm his mother offered with a grateful heart.

"Elizabeth said God sent so many angels to take Anne to heaven that their wings darkened the sun."

"Aye, there was about Anne a deep sense of love, a truly gracious regard for all living things. God took note of her."

Richard turned his head to the window. Night had fallen, and a faint sliver of pale light still streaked the horizon, but in the near total darkness there appeared a sight he'd never seen before: In the gardens and the deep woods a few trees glowed silver-white with a strange iridescence. He had never known vegetation to shine with light amidst total darkness, had not even thought such a thing possible. The moment seemed unreal, dreamlike, portentous and almost divine. He went to his mother and knelt at her feet.

"Give me your blessing, Mother," he said, remembering that she had once refused it.

She reached out, touched his face tenderly. "You must understand that what has happened is not your fault, anymore than Christ's tribulations were His. Our lives are part of a mighty plan, and though God cannot always alter it and grant us relief from loss, He can send us strength, if we but accept His will... Dear son, I grant you my blessing." She made the sign of the Cross over him. "Now, let us pray together."

She removed the chaplet from her waist and offered it to him. He stared down at the rosary given her by his father. Six sets of ten gold beads separated by six square enamel stones, all engraved with the figures of the saints and completed by a gold cross and a scalloped shell of jet—the scalloped jet Anthony Woodville had brought her from his pilgrimage to Compostella. He winced. Aye, there was much to be forgiven, but the burden of guilt no longer seemed as heavy. He took the rosary and together they moved to the pre-dieu to recite their devotions.

***

"I'm concerned about Richard, Francis," said Rob.

"He's exhausted, is all," replied Francis. "It's nothing a rest won't cure."

"It's more than that." Rob leaned forward, lowered his voice to a hushed whisper. "Nothing matters to him anymore."

"What foolery. Tudor matters. Richard's determined to make Tudor pay for what he's done."

"No, Francis. Since Anne's death, he doesn't eat, doesn't sleep. He barely functions. He can't go on like this." Rob fell silent, pondered the table thoughtfully, and looked up with anxious eyes. "He cared for Elizabeth, Francis. He's worse since she left. Much worse. The fits of temper—" He shook his head. "He smashed his crown after her departure."

Francis stared at him in disbelief. "His *crown?*"

"He must have. One of its points was dented... You've been away, you don't know. He's moody, distracted, irrational. His judgement's poor and he won't listen to reason. If he doesn't come to his senses soon... I fear, Francis."

"Richard will protect the kingdom. He's always answered the call of duty."

"You don't understand! Tudor has only one chance to win

England—he's having a devil of a time getting gold from the French to finance this invasion and they'll not support another. But Richard's a reigning monarch. He has the power of the realm behind him—men, arms, money—yet a single battle is all he says he'll allow himself. It's insane." Rob swallowed hard, ran a hand through his thatch of red hair. "What if we lose, Francis?"

Francis stirred uneasily in his chair and turned his face to the dark sea.

***

Heavy clouds blanketed the night. Francis hobbled up the worn tower steps to his chamber. He had been in Southampton for months now, refitting the fleet and preparing the southern coast for Tudor's invasion. There was always so much to do, so much to worry about. But this news about Richard... He halted in his steps. This was not good.

He resumed his uneven gait up to his room. If it were true—if Richard were cracking—then they were doomed. At the threshold of his chamber, he pulled up sharply. Where was everyone? Torches flared, a fire burned in the hearth, but the chamber was empty of servants, though the coverlet had been turned down for him. Strange... there was something on the pillow. He knitted his brows together, approached cautiously. A letter... And a rose.

A red rose.

Tudor had sent him a missive.

Chapter Twenty-Seven

"For I, being simple, thought to work His will."

Light morning mist hovered over the countryside as Nottingham Castle loomed into view on its rocky prominence. Richard reined in White Surrey and stared at the brooding towers and long line of battlements, words from a favourite poem echoing in his mind:

'Tis the Castle of Care
whoso cometh therein
May mourn that born he was
In body or soul.

The quote came from a ballad about the sorrows of the poor, but what about the sorrows of kings? He gave a sigh and nudged White Surrey forward.

In two days it would be the eleventh of June, Anne's birthday. He remembered the dread that Anne had felt the last time they had come to Nottingham. Somehow she had sensed what was to befall. He himself had no wish to return to this place that was laden with memories, but he had no choice. There was little love for him in the manor houses where the names of Stafford and Hastings were mourned, and though there were some good men who were staunchly loyal, like Lords Ferrers of Chartley, Grey of Codnor, and Lord Zouche, a strong royal presence was necessary. The North was for him; the South, against him. These strategic midlands would determine whether his kingdom would be won or lost.

The two weeks since Berkhampsted had confirmed his decision. He would not deviate from the test he had set for himself. In Stony Stratford he had calculated what was right for him and the realm, and it had brought disaster. From now on he would leave everything in God's hands. If God wished foul Tudor to rule England in his place, then so be it. He would submit to His will, whatever His plan.

He clattered over the drawbridge and through the arched gates into the courtyard. The castle chamberlain delivered a lengthy welcome. He listened politely and made a gracious reply. After giving White Surrey over to the Master of the Grooms, he embraced Francis, who had come up from Southampton to visit. Followed by his retinue of knights and squires of the body, he climbed the staircase to the great hall.

The high ceilings and tall stately windows of the wood-panelled chamber darkened and weighed down on him with fierce oppression. Here in this gloomy room as they drank and made merry on the feast of St. George, was brought the news of Ned's death. *Always with the hand that gives, is the claw that takes back.* He laid his gauntlets down.

"'Tis the Castle of my Care," said Richard, almost to himself.

His men averted their gaze. Francis said, as lightly as he could manage, "Aye, and a frightful dismal place. The day is fine, Richard. Let's leave here and go hunting."

Richard didn't respond. He moved to a window and pushed it open. A warm breeze caressed his face. Leaning on the latch, he looked out over the emerald forest stretching away on the northern horizon where Robin Hood had made his stand for loyalty and justice. And away to the east, over the hills and dales, crouched Tudor, awaiting his chance. Soon he would pounce.

He slammed the window shut. "Send to Wales for hawks and falcons. By God, we're going to hunt in style and let that Welsh bastard know we lose not a moment's sleep over him!"

***

For Richard, every day without Anne seemed to last forever, and the day of her birth was torment. He spent much of it on his knees, at a prayer vigil in the chapel hearing masses, and privately at the small altar in his bedchamber. That night, alone by the fireside where he used to sit with Anne, he read from the Book of Ghostly Grace which his mother had given him as a parting gift. It bore an account of the visions of Cistercian nun St. Mathilde of Hackeborn, one of the earliest mystics of the Sacred Heart, in which she described the state of former friends as she beheld their souls after death.

Richard lowered the book in his hand, remembering Anne's account of Isobel's death. Everyone had thought Isobel was imagining John's presence, but according to St. Mathilde, she might indeed have seen him. Staring into the shadows of the night, he whispered, "Come to me, Anne, come to me—" But there was no flicker of movement from the darkness; no answering response from the silence. Wearily he rose from the fireside and fell into bed. And for the first time since her death, he dreamed of her.

In his dream she laughed and took his hand and they ran into the moonlit woods together and made tender love beneath their chestnut tree. As dawn broke, she gathered her filmy white robes about her. "Don't go—" he cried in panic. "Don't leave me in this empty place!" She stood in the morning mist, gazing at him, the breeze stirring her gown. "I will wait for you in heaven, my love," she said, and faded with the mist. "Anne—" he cried. "Anne!—"

He awoke to find himself clutching a pillow to his breast. He hurled it away and sat up in bed. He bowed his head into his hands.

***

In the sun of springtime, Richard hunted and hawked with friends, seeming not to have a care in the world as he rode out into Nottingham Forest each morning, his yapping hounds at his heels, a falcon on his wrist. He seemed not to be aware that Henry Tudor was rigging his fleet at Harfleur, or that France was giving Tudor men and money as well as ships. But Tudor was never far from his thoughts during the idle sunny outings with his lords and the long dark summer nights alone. That Tudor would come soon was as certain as death itself, but when he would strike his blow, and where he would land, Richard's agents had been unable to discover. In the council chambers at Nottingham and riding to and fro from Nottingham Forest, the question was the subject of endless debate among Richard's advisors. The day after Anne's birthday, returning to the castle at sunset with their tired horses and dogs, the argument raged fiercely.

"Wales," said Ratcliffe quietly with a wary eye on Lord Stanley riding ahead. Though Richard gave the Wily Fox the benefit of the doubt, he himself didn't trust Tudor's stepfather. "He'll land in Wales."

"Not Wales," said Francis. "Rhys Ap Thomas' the main chieftain there and he's sworn fealty to Richard. And Huntingdon's there. He'd never let Tudor past him."

Richard winced at mention of that name, flooded by memories. Sweet Kate, lying in her coffin, clad in her bridal gown, and young Huntingdon weeping beside her, as he himself would soon weep for Anne.

Ratcliffe said, "If Ap Thomas goes back on his word, there's not much Huntingdon can do. Wales has always been trouble for the Crown. That's why Jasper Tudor was able to hold Harlech Castle for Lancaster long after the rest of the land was Edward's." He paused. "I fear the Welsh favour Tudor. His emblem is King Arthur's Dragon, for he's half Welsh, and claims descent from a line of Welsh kings."

"He claims a lot of things," laughed merry Sir Richard Clarendon, his golden head shining in the bright rose sunset. "Including that he's not a bastard."

A loud round of laughter applauded this remark and Richard smiled. Will Conyers said, "One thing's for certain: a chicken or a weasel would better fit his blazon than the dragon he sports." He rode tall in his saddle, a hand on his hip, an expression of contempt on his handsome square-jawed face. Richard gazed at him, at his compelling blue eyes and the confident set of his powerful shoulders, which had always reminded him of John. There was a certain nobility about the Neville clan, he thought. A pity so few survived.

"'Tis said he's more at ease scheming in a pansy French court than fighting on a battlefield," Conyers added, "and that he avoids feats of arms like the plague."

"Then it should be short work to slit the Dragon's throat," offered the Black Knight, Ralph Ashton.

Dragon. Richard flinched. Strange that the dragon of his childhood nightmares should have acquired a real-life aspect in Tudor. He remembered the warnings of wise-eyed Thomas Hutton after his return from the court of Brittany. Hutton had been right;

the Devil protects his own. The Dragon had escaped them and slipped into France, just as their grasp had touched his slimy hide. It would be no easy matter to slit his throat. But where would he land? That was the question. The Welsh chieftain, Ap Thomas, had sworn fealty, yet who could be sure? Once an oath had bound a man to the death and honour had meant more than life itself. But the old world was vanishing, and in the new one that was being born, oaths were broken daily and there was little place for honour. He hated this new world, and understood it even less.

Chapter Twenty-Eight

"I hear the steps of Mordred in the west,
And with him many of thy people and knights
Once thine, whom thou hast loved, but grosser grown
Than heathen… spitting at their vows and thee."

In his royal apartments in the Keep that he had enlarged and brightened with oriel windows, stone carvings, silk carpets, and colourful tapestries, Richard paused only long enough to remove his hunting clothes and wash, intending to go down to the chapel for Compline. He had just shrugged into the grey mantle his squire held for him and picked up his psalter when there was a knock at the open door.

"Ah, Stanley," Richard said pleasantly, trying to suppress the sense of unease that suddenly gripped him at the sight of the red-bearded, stocky figure.

"My lord," replied Stanley, with a smile on his shrewd face that didn't reach his small green eyes, "may I have a moment?"

Richard dismissed his squire with a wave of the hand. "By all means," Richard said. "You are welcome." He waved him to a chair.

"I prefer to stand, my lord. I've been sitting all day and my legs require stretching. Much as I enjoyed our hunt today, you can't know what a day's ride can do to a body full of years." He gave a chuckle.

"You may have more years than I, Stanley, but few men would wish to engage you in battle. In my campaign against the Scots, I never had a more worthy captain."

"I thank you for your confidence in me, my lord, and would have you know it's returned. I hold you in high regard, not only as King, but as the most admirable general and valiant knight I've e'er known in battle. 'Tis to my great honour that you call me friend."

"Aye… friend," murmured Richard, studying his face. Half in anticipation, half in dread, he said, "'Tis why I made you steward of my royal household… so that you would always be in close attendance on me."

"My honour, and also my pleasure," said Stanley with a slight bow.

"So what brings you here at this late hour?"

"Sire, as you know, I have been at your side since before you became King." He paused, then continued. "'Tis a long while. Much business attends me on my estates. Your Grace, I beg leave to retire to Cheshire for a brief respite. I have long been absent from family."

"I see," murmured Richard. Stanley's eyes told him nothing, and the smile behind the red beard was in place. He settled his gaze on the window. The garden was dark; no stars were out. He gripped his psalter tightly in his hand. Had he not always known this request would be made? He had hoped to win Stanley to him with favours and justice and mercy; had hoped Stanley would serve him with the same assiduous loyalty he had shown Edward for over ten years. And for over two years Stanley had done so. For two years he had refrained from requesting leave to depart court and Richard had not had to face the possibility of his disloyalty.

Now it is clear, he thought with a sick plunging of his heart. No matter how virtuous his court, no matter how hard he tried, no matter what manner of man Tudor was, Stanley was Tudor's stepfather and he would side with Tudor. At best, he might take no side at all; at least until he knew who the winner would be. In either case, Richard had failed. He felt paralysed, numb. "Your family?" he said. "Lady Margaret?"

Stanley shook his head. "My lady wife maintains a separate household in Lincolnshire. As you know, our marriage was made for the usual reasons, unlike yours with Queen Anne—"

Richard winced.

"There is little affection between us, my lord," Stanley added gently. "'Tis my sons and my brother, William, I wish to see."

Richard fought to control his swirling emotions. Oh, how he needed to believe Stanley! To believe that he was loyal! That there was still goodness to be found in man! And yet... and yet—

"Invasion is imminent," Richard said without inflection. He met Stanley's small shrewd eyes.

"Well I know that. The moment there is news, I shall rush to your side to crush the disreputable bastard."

"Your stepson," said Richard.

"I've never met the man. He's dear to my wife's heart; not to mine."

Richard averted his eyes. "I shall present your request to the council." Stanley's footsteps receded down the stairwell. He sank into a chair, a hand to his head. He was drained, weary to exhaustion. He couldn't think, couldn't plan, couldn't feel. Nothing mattered, or would matter ever again. The cold would last forever.

Chapter Twenty-Nine

"Ill doom is mine to war against my people and my knights.
The king who fights his people fights himself... and the stroke
That strikes them dead is as my death to me."

"You can't grant Stanley permission to depart, my lord!" said Catesby as he stood at the council table, his long face pinched and white in the dimness of the gloomy stone chamber. "He intends to betray you! 'Tis the only reason he makes the request at this time!"

Ratcliffe said, "My lord, it would be madness to let him leave now." He spoke quietly, but beads of perspiration glistened on his face and his eyes were anxious. "He is a cunning man, unworthy of your trust. He could muster a great army and bring it to the field against us. You must not grant permission."

Richard sat listlessly at the head of the table. He made no response. Rob hunched over the table and focused his hazel eyes on Richard, "Stanley's a man with a finger to the wind, ready to change sides if Fortune blows the other way. It would be folly to let him go. You know full well what he intends!"

"No," said Richard, "I only suspect. Suspicion is not enough on which to judge a man." Twice before he had condemned on the basis of suspicion alone. It would not happen again.

Kendall looked up from his papers. Richard's secretary was now a full member of the royal council, had been tested through many trials, had proven true, and Richard valued his judgement. "Sire, the Stanleys have always juggled their allegiance to their benefit," he said. "Trust is a word they barter for their own gain."

"Aye!" urged Conyers. "'Tis how they've survived four kings and grown ever more powerful in an age that's claimed the lives of men far better than they. He must not be allowed to depart at this critical juncture."

Still Richard said nothing.

"Richard," Rob persisted, "if Tudor triumphs, Stanley will be stepfather to a king. He made cause against you with Hastings, and if Buckingham's revolt had succeeded, he would have betrayed you, and well you know it. When Warwick won, he was at his side, and when Warwick faltered, he betrayed him." Rob waited. Still no response. Richard sat staring absently at the window, a faraway look in his eyes. "Would you," Rob added urgently, "having kept this most cunning lord under your care this long, let him depart on the very eve of Tudor's invasion? The solution is simple. Hold him in custody until the invasion is over."

"Aye, aye!" cried Richard's councillors with one voice.

Richard stirred, heaved a sigh. He went to the window, unlatched it, pushed it open. The rain had ceased and the morning air felt fresh and cool against his cheek. Sparrows flew below the window, building nests in some far corners of the castle wall. He watched as they disappeared around the bend. In a small garden below a woman hung up her washing and an old man played chess with a young boy beneath a tree. He let his gaze wander over the thatched roofs of cottages beyond the castle walls to the swans gliding along the River Trent and the long fields of barley and rye that stretched on either side of the river. The hillside was pastoral with sheep, and windmills turned, white cloths billowing in the wind like sails. He looked north, to the rich green of Nottingham Forest, and back to the machicolated town walls. All along the high road to the castle people went up and down, carrying their wares on their backs, dragging their mules and their carts. Chickens clucked; sheep bleated; dogs barked. And men betrayed. So it was in King Arthur's time. So it would always be.

He turned back to his councillors.

"Last Christmas I dispatched commands to Cheshire and Lancashire that they were to obey Stanley in the event of invasion. If I trusted him then, why should I not trust him now? He was Tudor's stepfather then, as he is now. I have always known his history. What has changed? He's done nothing against me." Softly, he added, "I intend to grant the permission he seeks."

A shattering din of voices arose. Francis slammed a fist down on the table. "'Tis a damnable folly! Your blind clemency will be the ruin of you, Richard!"

Silence fell. Richard gazed at him with shock and he was dimly aware that everyone in the room was staring at Francis with mouths agape. Never had his friend spoken to him in this way, never forgotten that he was his overlord and King. Never, in fact, had Richard witnessed his gentle, mild-mannered friend lose his temper with anyone, yet now Francis' face was blotched red with fury. "Are you so blind you don't realise what's been going on? Tudor made me an offer to betray you—lands, titles, whatever I desired! What do you think he's offered his own stepfather?"

Richard stared at him mutely, mouth slack with disbelief. He tried to speak, but no words came. He swallowed, licked his parched lips. "Tudor dared approach *you?*"

"In Southampton! I found a missive on my pillow with instructions where to leave my answer."

Richard held his breath. His chest felt as if it would burst. "And your answer?"

"I'm here, aren't I? I told him to slither back to hell, where he came from! You can be sure he fared better with Stanley."

Richard threw his head back, and laughed, but his laughter was sharp, without mirth, edged with bitterness, and it broke off abruptly. *Foul Tudor dared approach Francis!* Such daring intimacy meant that spies and informants were all around them, had infiltrated his household and government at every level. It meant that Tudor feared no one and nothing. That Tudor was so bold—and Richard so vulnerable—he'd even come after Francis, his boyhood friend. A sardonic voice spoke in his head. *And why not?* it said. *Didn't he score before, with Buckingham?*

"Damned, vile, whoreson—God rot his lying soul! He sought to strike at my bosom, like the loathsome viper he is!" He made his way to the head of the table, took a seat, motioned his councillors to do the same. He took a moment to compose himself, said as steadily as he could, "As you all know, I never sought the Crown. It was our dream—Anne and I—to put distance between ourselves and court. Contrary to Tudor's lies, I set aside my brother's sons unwillingly... For the good of the realm... For the safety of those I loved... And because I set them aside, the Crown has weighed heavy on my head—"

His hands, resting on the table, trembled. He removed them from view and forced himself to continue. "I have pursued justice for my people. I have tried to earn my right to the throne. 'Tis all I can do. The rest is God's will." He looked down at his ringed fingers. His ruby signet caught the morning sun and glinted. He thought of blood. Ever since Barnet, rubies made him think of blood. "Stanley must be allowed to ride away, so that his allegiance be freely given. Freely, or not at all. God's will must be done."

"But—" a chorus of voices objected at once. Francis' rose above them all. "But," he said, "you are a commander, my lord. The outcome of battle is God's will, yet no commander goes into battle without a plan, without strategy, and expects to win. Or disables himself to give the enemy a foolish advantage."

"I will not circumvent God's will. I will not force myself on England."

"By releasing Stanley, you're challenging God." exclaimed Rob. "You're stripping yourself of armour and handing Tudor a sword to slay you with. Is that what you want? After all Tudor has done to you, do you want him to win?"

"Aye, 'tis so!" agreed everyone in the room.

"All I have left is my humanity." Richard crushed the quaver in his voice and met their gaze. "I won't let kingship strip me of that, too."

"Let us compromise, my lord," said Catesby. "Let Stanley give us his eldest son as surety for his good behaviour."

"Aye," agreed Kendall. "At least then we'd have something. He may not give us his support, but at least he won't give it to Tudor, either."

"His son? A man would never endanger his son. I might as well keep Stanley himself." Richard looked from face to face. He saw the fear, the desperation, and the hope. He was talking about their lives, too, he suddenly realised. By demanding Stanley's son, he was blunting the test he had set for himself, but these men had put themselves and all that they cherished into his hands. He owed them something. "Catesby, my clever lawyer, you have your wish. We shall inform Stanley that since decisive events are approaching, I need men of experience about me. He cannot leave until his son is here to act as his deputy during his absence."

Sighs of relief resounded around the table.

***

Lord Stanley sent for his son, George, and Richard welcomed the young man warmly. There was thunder in the hot summer air as Stanley mounted his destrier in the courtyard and Richard stood by to wish him Godspeed. Their eyes met and held. *He knows his son is a hostage,* Richard thought, *and he knows I know it.* Lord Stanley doffed his velvet hat and crinkled his ginger beard in a smile. “Farewell, my lord King.”

Richard watched him ride westward with his retinue and disappear into the hazy heat of summer.

Chapter Thirty

"I know not what I am,
Nor whence I am, nor whether I be King;
Behold, I seem but King among the dead."

High on his rock, alone with his thoughts, Richard posed for his portrait in the Castle of his Care. He found himself increasingly at the mercy of his moods of late, and often he cut the sessions short, much to the painter's dismay. When he couldn't keep the memories at bay by force of will, the only remedy was change: a plunging into activity where there had been solitude; solitude where there had been activity. He knew his erratic behaviour was unsettling to his men, but he was unable to control himself. Idleness was alien to his nature, and for most of his life, there had not been enough time to do all that needed to be done. Now time, empty and meaningless, moved the days slowly and allowed his mind to fill with thoughts of the past.

To aggravate matters, August was hot and sweltering, rendering Nottingham Castle more oppressive than ever. On the tenth day, he decided on impulse to move five miles north, to the lodge in the park of Beskwood in Sherwood Forest. Not only was it cooler there, but relieved of the painful reminders that Nottingham was wedded to in his mind, posing for his portrait at Beskwood Lodge became a soothing pastime, despite his restlessness.

Maybe it was the earliness of the hour, he thought, gazing over the treetops to the hills ringing Sherwood Forest. The lodge had not stirred yet, and birdsong and splashing fountains made music on the fresh morning air. Sometimes he imagined he heard Anne's laughter in the water, and sometimes he saw Elizabeth's gentle smile in the pattering of the rain on the foliage. Here, in this chamber, at this hour, the past came alive in a comforting way. He inhaled deeply. Ah, the past; when he was young. Grief was fiercely felt then; but so was joy. There had been hope then.

He brought his gaze back to the painter dabbing at his portrait. He liked the old artist and enjoyed his company, though he missed

Francis, who had returned to Southampton a few days after the council meeting. But Rob was with him, and Humphrey Stafford, Scrope of Bolton, and Jack, and others dear to his heart. Though he was unable to find pleasure in their pursuits, he went hunting with them in the afternoons, and he shared their evenings in the great hall where they drank and made merry to relieve the tension of waiting for Tudor.

It seemed to him that his entire life had been spent waiting for Tudor. What would happen once he landed? The realm had seen enough of war and, as long ago as Barnet, men had failed to answer the call to arms. Would they heed his summons now? And what of Stanley? He had wilfully armed Stanley. Would those arms be turned against him? He twisted his signet ring.

The painter was laying down his brush. He moved to the canvas. An uncanny likeness. He studied it a long time. It was a strange feeling to see himself reflected so clearly through someone else's view. When he looked into a mirror, he didn't catch the sadness in his eyes, or notice himself toying with his ring. The artist had captured a depth unknown even to him.

"You do an excellent likeness, Memling," he said.

"'Tis all in how you hold the brush, Sire."

In Richard's mind, John said, "'Tis all in how you hold the sword, Dickon. See—"

Richard forced the memory away. "Until tomorrow, then, my good—" Frantic footsteps interrupted him. Amid shouts, the door was thrust open. Jack, Scrope, Ratcliff, and Rob burst into the chamber. Jack's doublet was unbuttoned at the neck, as if donned in haste, his curls unruly, his eyes wide with alarm. Francis was with them, looking dusty and weary. Richard blinked in bafflement.

"Francis? What are you—" In a heart-stopping moment, he knew what had happened—knew with every instinct of his being; knew before Francis fell to his knees and spoke the words.

"The waiting is over!" cried Francis. "Tudor has landed! Sire, Richard—Tudor has finally landed!"

***

The next hours were frenzied. While his followers attended to the business of preparing the army to march, Richard sent urgent dispatches to John Howard, Percy, Brackenbury, Stanley, and his other captains, summoning them to his side. At the same time, he took his leave of Jack, sending him north, to Sherriff Hutton. His nephew was his heir to the throne. They could not both take part in the battle, and Elizabeth and the children would be glad of his company. Meanwhile, details poured in about the invasion.

Waving the red and green dragon banner of Cadwallader, Tudor had landed at Milford Haven with fifteen ships and a force of some two thousand men released from the prisons of Normandy. One could not find anywhere, came the reports, a more evil lot. Such was the contribution of the court of France to Tudor's effort. In return, in the event of his victory, Tudor had promised to cede to France the territories of Calais and Guisnes. His commanders were his uncle, Jasper Tudor, and the Earl of Oxford, and among his English band of followers were many who had fled to Brittany after Buckingham's rebellion, such as the four-hundred-pound seven-foot giant, John Cheyney. But, noted Richard inwardly, Bess Woodville's son, chicken-livered Dorset—of no use even to vile Tudor—had been left behind as a pledge for the money that the French King had loaned the Dragon.

On the fifteenth day of August 1485, at Beskwood lodge, while Richard carefully observed the sacred Feast of the Assumption of the Virgin Mary, he received Lord Stanley's reply to his summons.

He was closeted with his advisors in a small upstairs room that functioned as an informal council chamber. Though it was lit by many tall tapers and opened onto a wide passageway with mullioned windows along the length of one side, the room was dark and filled with shadows. The wood walls were hung with blue silk fabric, the plank floor covered with dull reed matting, and there was only a single window. A summer storm was brewing and the dismal morning heightened the gloom of the chamber. The guard at the door admitted Stanley's messenger. Not trusting himself to read his dispatch, Richard passed it to Francis, who cut the white ribbon with his dagger and broke open the seal. He scanned the contents and the colour drained from his face.

"Stanley says he's suffering from the sweating sickness and is unable to join you at this time."

Richard's mind spun. It wasn't possible! What manner of man places his son in danger? Epithets and cries of *Traitor!* raged around him. He shook himself to clear his head, realised that someone had seized the messenger. With enormous effort he lifted his hand, waved the man gone. "He's had no part… in this." Even speech was difficult. He dropped into a chair. "Catesby, bring me… George Stanley." Catesby had no chance to comply, for at that moment, amid a rumble of thunder, footsteps sounded in the passageway. Black-garbed Sir Ralph Ashton appeared at the door.

"Sire! Urgent tidings!" He strode across to Richard, gave a quick obeisance. "George Stanley tried to escape. I apprehended him in the attempt. He has already confessed—I lost no time getting it out of him." Over Richard's head, Ashton exchanged a meaningful glance with Francis. Though Richard had welcome Stanley's son warmly and made him an intimate, Francis had made sure he was carefully watched by able men before he'd left for Southampton.

Richard roused himself from his lethargy. He lifted his head and looked at Ashton. Like Buckingham, Stanley would be quick to confess before such a man. Dressed in black, with his hard rheumy eyes, bloodless complexion, and purple scar slashing his cheek, Ashton's demeanour was fearsome. In any case, Stanley's son was not one to throw himself away for a cause. Richard waited for his Vice-Constable to continue.

"He and his uncle Sir William have plotted with Henry Tudor to betray you, but he swears his father intends to stay true. He's thrown himself on your mercy and implores permission to send Stanley a message."

"It'll do him… little good." A man who would gamble his son's life was a man without humanity. "But let… him try." He knew he was mumbling. His mouth was dry and his tongue, like his head, his hands, and the rest of his body, seemed suddenly an ungainly weight. He motioned for wine. Gripping the cup with both hands, he drained it, not caring that he spilt more than he swallowed.

"My lord," said Catesby, "we must notify the sheriffs of the realm to proclaim William Stanley a traitor!"

"My lord," said a voice at the door. One of his Esquires of the Body held a black velvet package in his hands. "This comes from the Red Pale at Westminster, Sire." At a nod from Richard, the man drew out his dagger and cut the cloth. He handed Richard a small leather volume.

"'Tis Malory's tales of King Arthur's court, a first printing," said Richard with a glance at the gold lettering. "Caxton has retitled it *Morte d'Arthur*." He opened the book at random and read aloud: "And slowly answered Arthur from the barge, 'The old order changeth, yielding place to new, and God fulfils himself in many ways. If thou shouldst never see my face again—'" He stared at the words, read softly, "'Pray for my soul.'" He shut the book, lifted his eyes. His friends were gazing at him silently.

A voice rang out. "Sire!" A messenger entered, bearing the badge of the Silver Lion, Howard's livery. He bent a knee. "Sire, the Duke of Norfolk sends hearty greetings and would have you know that he will be at Leicester poste-haste, with a thousand men at his own cost!" Richard's mouth softened. Faithful Howard; Friendly Lion. Loyal friend who honoured oaths and promises. "Tell Norfolk he shall know our thanks."

Another voice came at the door. "My Liege!" A dusty youth stood between two men-at-arms. His face was familiar. Richard frowned, trying to place him. "He comes from Brecon with urgent news, Sire," said one of the men. *Ah, Brecon.* He was the lad who'd come about Buckingham. Richard tensed in his chair. The youth entered, fell to his knees.

"Rhys Ap Thomas, he's betrayed you, Sire—gone over to Henry Tudor, he has! Tudor promised him Wales if he deserted you, m'lord!"

Richard turned disbelieving eyes on Francis. "But he swore to stand true. Swore Tudor would have to pass over his dead body to enter Wales—" he broke off.

Francis stared at him helplessly. Thirty years of civil war had broken the sanctity of oaths, and Richard knew it. Yet he kept hoping to be proven wrong, kept appealing to man's higher nature, and they repaid him by answering the call, not of loyalty, but of greed. Was he truly so naive? Could he really believe that man was better than he was? Had he forgotten that Judas sold Christ for thirty pieces of silver?

Thunder growled ominously in the distance. All at once rain pelted from the skies. A sudden wind slammed the window open. Francis latched it shut. "Which way is Tudor headed?" Richard demanded unsteadily.

"He entered Shrewsbury three days ago unchallenged," replied the lad.

Tudor had penetrated nearly to the centre of his kingdom! Was there no one who would stand up for him? He looked at his advisors. "Sir Gilbert Talbot of Shrewsbury… I showed him much favour—"

Francis couldn't bear it any longer. "No doubt it's for personal, not political, reasons that Talbot went over to Tudor's banner, my lord. Lady Eleanor Butler was his kinswoman, and the revelation of King Edward's marriage pre-contract caused his family much shame."

Richard sank in his chair, laid his head against the high back. Two other men appeared at the door. Richard gazed at the tall one with the weather-beaten face and his young companion, men from York whom he'd met on happier occasions. "Sponer, Nicholson, welcome. What brings you here? Good news, I pray. We're in dire need of it…"

Sponer looked at him strangely. "My Liege, the lack of news is why we come. 'Tis rumoured that Henry Tudor landed in the southwest on the seventh day of August, but there's been no official word. If that's true, the council wishes to know why Your Grace has not sent the city a summons to arms."

Richard met Francis' eyes and knew he'd had the same thought. Percy had been entrusted with the commissions of array for the East Riding—Percy, whose loyalty he had been wooing for nearly fifteen years; Percy, who had sent word a week ago that he was coming with all possible haste, and had not come. Not even plague in York had deterred Stonor and Nicholson, and not even plague would have prevented the men of York from answering his summons. There was only one reason why they hadn't come. Percy hadn't told them. He wanted to exclude the men of York because he intended to stand aloof from the conflict. As he had at Barnet. As he had during Buckingham's revolt.

Richard's shoulders sagged beneath his doublet. "Express my thanks to the Lord Mayor and the city of York for their loyalty. Tell them that I am in sore need of what men they can send me, for I will give battle to the enemy within days."

"Sire, if that is so, then I will stay. Nicholson can relay your message."

Richard nodded; they withdrew. His councillors drew close.

"The Stanleys are playing their usual game of waiting to see who'll win," Scrope of Bolton said. "You can neutralize them, my lord. Force them to unite openly with the enemy. Many of their men will desert and they won't be able to intervene against you in the battle."

Richard made no response.

"Aye—as for that damned Percy—" exclaimed Rob, forgetting for the moment that he was a Percy himself, "he, too, can be forced to declare himself before it's too late. Better still, place him in custody. Most of his men will readily follow the royal banner if his treason is made public."

Richard said nothing.

Francis gazed at the still, melancholy figure in the chair staring out into empty space. Richard's grey eyes had darkened and he looked exhausted, far older than his years.

"Richard," Francis said gently, "there's been no popular rising for Tudor, not in England or even in Wales. There's no need to rush into battle. Time is on our side. You've ordered a hasty mustering and we're not at full strength yet. The realm is answering your call to arms, but many of those who wish to fight for you are still assembling their retainers and supplies. Others—men like Stonor and Nicholson—haven't yet heard your call to arms. If we wait, Tudor will lose strength, and we'll gain it."

No response. The silence filled with the pounding of rain.

"Sire, Francis is right—time is on our side!" Catesby blurted. "Don't rush to give battle. Crush Tudor and live to enjoy a long reign!"

Thunder rattled the windowpanes and a flash of lightning lit the room. Richard didn't seem to notice. The men exchanged glances with one another. Conyers came, knelt before him. "My lord, my King... the people need you. What'll become of them under a man like Tudor should you lose this battle on which you have decided all must depend? If you don't allow us more time to undo the mischief Percy and the Stanleys have done, you'll be marching into an ambush you've allowed these lords to set for you."

Clutching the carved armrests of his high-backed chair, Richard shut his eyes. Aye, he might manage affairs well enough to win against Tudor, but that would not be true redemption, for he would be subverting God's will by helping himself. And what then? What lay ahead for him then?

A marriage with the Duke of Lancaster's great-granddaughter Johanna of Portugal, to unite the white rose with the red. Johanna, who wished to be a nun, who spoke no English; who was nothing like Anne. Was this the redemption he had begged God to grant him? To live in a world without love; to rule in a realm without loyalty?

He felt like a man shipwrecked, and the lightless years stretched before him like an endless sea. He lifted his head, gazed at his senior statesman. Tawny hair, now tinged with silver at the temples, eyes blue as sapphires, strong jaw, a mouth made for smiling. A noble countenance. Aye, there was much Neville in this Robin of Redesdale; much to remind him of John. Would this be John's counsel if he were alive? If he had not been sacrificed by Edward?

Edward.

Out of the distant past, Warwick's words echoed in his ears: *What man ever trusted Edward and was not deceived?* He had given Warwick's warning scant thought at the time, but now he saw Edward at Barnet, fog rolling in at his feet, and heard him laugh, *'Tis a fool thing Warwick's done, to come to me when all he had to do was wait—he's played into my hands!* In his mind's eye, he saw Warwick in a tent at St. Alban's, cradling his head. Why had Warwick chosen chance over certain victory by turning south to his enemy, Edward, instead of north to his ally, Marguerite? At the end of the long, hard road, had betrayals left him bereft of hope, yearning for death? *Don't let them destroy you, too, Dickon,* he had warned. Had he meant to include Edward with the Woodvilles? Edward, who had made Bess his queen, and by so doing doomed all who had trusted in him?

His eye fell on Caxton's book on the table beside him where he had dropped it. He fingered the leather cover. A line from Malory drummed in his head: *My house hath been my doom.* King Arthur's words. He roused himself from the numbness that weighed him down and forced himself to his feet.

"You give wise counsel and no doubt you're right. There's only one thing—" Flies buzzed in the hot, humid room, the walls wavered in his sight and the gloom grew so oppressive, he wanted to cry out. His breath quickened as the familiar, desperate realisation swept through him: his friends were at his side, but he was alone. He would always be alone. "I cannot wait."

***

As Richard stepped out into the open courtyard and the pouring rain, several Esquires of the Body ran to join him and startled grooms appeared from the stables. "My horse!" Richard shouted. He knew he was a frightful sight with his wet hair clinging to his face, but he didn't care. White Surrey was rushed out. He mounted. His men-at-arms scrambled into their saddles. "I ride alone!" he yelled over the crackling thunder.

"But Sire—Tudor—"

He swung on them, eyes flashing with fury. "Do you see an army here?"

The men exchanged nervous glances with one another. "Nay, Sire—nay."

"If I were afraid of that damned Welsh bastard, do you not think I'd have an army here?" he shouted.

"Aye, Sire, aye!" they replied in unison.

He spurred White Surrey into a wild gallop, past the raised beds of flowers and herbs, beneath the branches bowed low with rain and fruit. Down the hill he galloped, into the meadow, past houses and fields where sheep huddled for shelter beneath the trees. The distant hills disappeared into drenched green foliage.

On he flew through Sherwood Forest. He didn't realise how far he'd gone until White Surrey reared beneath him in protest, foaming at the mouth. He reined him in, stroked his soaking neck.

For the first time since he'd left the lodge, he became aware of his surroundings. He had emerged into a clearing. The rain had ceased and the sun was struggling through. In every direction there was nothing but forest and sky, and where the green swept up the steep hill perched Beskwood Lodge, wreathed in greenery and barely visible through the trees. Though dark clouds hung over it, to the west they were edged with pink and the sun broke through in shafts, sending rose-coloured light falling to earth.

He raised his face to the sky and watched a flock of blackbirds fly across the rolling clouds. Their cries pierced the silence and seemed suddenly more melodious than all the songs of minstrels at court. For an instant his heart soared with them. He closed his eyes to smell more deeply of the damp, cleansing freshness of the earth and lifted his face into the wind. The rustling of pines came to him loudly. Middleham.... His lips lifted at their corners.

Middleham.

His eyes flew open as pain exploded in his breast and the wind turned vile in his nostrils. *Vile with incense that failed to mask the stench of rotting human flesh.*

He spurred White Surrey into a gallop. The clearing disappeared into the thickness of woods. Cold wind blew at him; thorny branches caught at him. Bruised, bleeding, breathless, he sped White Surrey out again. He raised his stained face to heaven. "My house—" he cried, his voice breaking, "has been my doom!"

Chapter Thirty-One

"Howbeit I know, if ancient prophecies
Have err'd not, that I march to meet my doom."

Sunday, the twenty-first day of August, dawned bright and windy.

To the marching tunes of drummers and pipers, the royal cavalcade trooped out of Leicester where they had spent the night and headed to Market Bosworth, clarions blaring, baggage carts rumbling, pennants flying. In the narrow streets, the townspeople watched silently. Clad in full armour and riding his proud white war horse, Richard bore a golden crown upon his helmet so that all might know he was King. Above him floated his banner of the White Boar, displayed along with the Cross of St. George and the White Rose in a sunburst of the House of York. Ahead fluttered his little nephew's banner of the Dun Cow, carried by a herald in a tabard quartered with the royal lilies and leopards.

There had been no response to his summons to arms from Stanley, the mightiest of his lords. Percy had finally arrived late the previous evening with his excuses. Many other nobles had not answered his plea, but Howard and his son had been waiting in Leicester with their contingents, true to their word.

Good, trusty Howard has always been loyal to York, Richard thought, warmed by affection as he glanced at the barrel figure riding next to him. The man he had in childhood nicknamed "the Friendly Lion" rode bareheaded, his thick mane glistening with crystalline brilliance in the sun. Richard suddenly had a sense that he'd been here before, done this before. Aye, indeed he had, he thought; as a twelve-year-old he'd ridden to Bosworth with Howard at his side, just so, leading an army to his brother Edward. He remembered being captivated by the faery beauty of the tiny village, while Howard had sensed menace. They had shared much together since then, and with his caring ways and jovial manner, the old duke had done much to fill the hollow space in Richard's heart that his father and John Neville had left behind.

He turned in the saddle to look at his many friends. All the northern lords and most from the midlands had answered his call: Zouche; the Scropes of Bolton, of Upscale, of Masham; Ferrers of Chartley; and Dacre. As for Greystoke, that good man had brought a mighty contingent with him. Even Brackenbury was here, though the gentle Merlin had had to lash his horse from London to reach Leicester in time. His gaze ran along the length of spikes and spears stretching behind him as far as the eye could see. Men had streamed in to join the royal army until late into the night. Loyal men, Richard thought; and tomorrow, many of them would pay for their loyalty with their lives. He glanced at his boyhood friend, Francis, riding at his side. "Since Roman times armies have marched along this road, men to kill other men, Francis. When will it end?"

"When greed ends, Richard. And that, I fear, will be never."

Greed, Richard reflected, swaying in the saddle to the rhythm of his horse's hoofs. Greed for power and material gain had driven Marguerite d'Anjou and the Woodville queen, splintering the realm. Greed had fuelled his cousin Warwick's ambitions, and his brother George's follies. Now greed propelled the bastard Tudor to reach for a Crown to which he had no right.

"Aye, Francis. Greed is surely the root of all evil."

They were nearing the west bridge over the River Soar. All at once White Surrey balked. Rearing and plunging as if he'd seen a phantom, he neighed wildly and refused to cross. Richard slammed his knee and struck his golden spur against a stone column as he fought to restrain his spirited destrier in the narrow space. At length he subdued the proud beast and they clattered across. Barely had they cleared the bridge when a disturbance made him turn. Amid shouts, someone had raised a sword.

"Halt!" roared Richard over the din of marching men and music of minstrels. The sword froze in its hand and was lowered. A handsome knight galloped up through the ranks.

"What happened there, Clarendon?" demanded Richard.

"My lord," said Clarendon angrily, out of breath, his armour glinting in the sun, his fair hair shining. "There was a wise-woman sitting by the bridge, and I asked her of the success of our enterprise."

Richard looked at him steadily. "And what did she say?"

"My lord, she said—the accursed witch said that where your spur struck the stone," the knight swallowed visibly, "your head will be broken on the journey back."

Richard sat very still, remembering another wise-woman who had foretold his early death, just as ancient prophecies had warned King Arthur of his doom. What had been Arthur's reply?

But let what will be, be.

He squared his tense shoulders, ignoring the old wound from Barnet that ached again. He glanced towards the stone column of Leicester's bow bridge that White Surrey had refused to cross, then at Clarendon whose green eyes blazed with outrage. "For this, you wished to strike her dead?"

"Aye, my lord, for she lies!"

"Soon enough you'll have your fill of bloodshed."

Richard jerked his tasselled bridle and spurred his war horse westward, to Market Bosworth.

Chapter Thirty-Two

"Now must I hence.
Thro' the thick night I hear the trumpet blow."

A soft breeze blew. The moon was as fine as gold thread, scarcely a moon at all, and the sky glowed with stars.

Richard paced the far reaches of his camp, noting men's faces in the firelight, the condition of their gear. He came to a halt near a thicket on the slope of Ambion Hill. Ahead in the distant dark, enemy fires glittered like stars in the night firmament, and across to his right, almost equidistant between Tudor's army and his own, the fires of Lord Stanley's men flickered uncertainly. From the horses tethered at the rear of the camp came neighing and snorts. He heard a dog bark, and thought of Roland, who had died a month before. Somewhere someone played a flute. The haunting melody floated over the murmuring of men's voices and the chirping of crickets, evoking a deceptive tranquillity. The air smelled of smoke and cooked meats on the spit.

Tomorrow, Richard thought, it would smell of blood.

Men with torches climbed past him, moving horses and weapons, dragging supplies. He greeted them with a nod. They disappeared into the darkness. He thought of the last time battle lines had been drawn this way. *Barnet*. He shut his eyes.

"Such a night is made for love, not war," said a voice.

Richard looked up with a start. Francis limped out of the shadows. Like himself, he wore a dark doublet and hose, unadorned save for a jewelled dagger at the belt, so that he almost melted into the night. His dark hair stirred in the breeze, and there was a pensive shimmer in his eyes as he gazed at him.

"It's my fault we're here, Francis." Richard's voice faded to a whisper.

"No, Richard. Fortune is to blame."

"Fortune," Richard murmured. "Have you thought, Francis? We struggle, we fight, we make choices, and in the end, Fortune decides for us... But for a chance meeting beneath an oak, there would be no battle tomorrow."

Francis heaved an audible sigh. "Aye, Bess Woodville would never have wed Edward, but for that chance meeting. On such trifles do our lives turn... At least we outnumber them. That's a comfort." Richard turned his gaze on Stanley's campfires in the southwest. "Depends how you count," he said. "There are three armies here tonight. Who knows what Stanley will do?"

"You should have executed him for his first treason," Francis grunted.

"I've mangled everything I've touched," sighed Richard.

"Nay, Richard! You've done your best to set things right. Like Arthur."

"And like Arthur I war on my own people." He turned abruptly and strode up the hill. Francis fell in at his side. Their boots crunched on the hard earth. "They think we're going to lose, Francis. That's why they're not here."

"They're not here because they think we're going to win, with or without them. Those like Jack's father, the Duke of Suffolk, have too much at stake should we lose."

"If—the Saints forfend—Tudor is victorious," Francis resumed when Richard made no answer, "it'll stir the realm into action. Those who stayed home today will join your side tomorrow."

"Not my side, Francis. This is my last battle."

"So you say, yet you know that the loss of one battle need not be serious. Let strategy guide you instead of your heart."

Men tramped past with their torches. Richard took in their expressions. "There's been enough fighting, Francis."

"Richard, for God's sake, think of England!"

"I have done my best for England, Francis. Now 'tis time to look to my own heart... 'Tis time to end it, one way or the other. Englishmen have been killing Englishmen for thirty years. This will be my last battle. Tomorrow God will render final judgement."

"If Tudor wins, I'll fight on! For England! For York—"

"Men flock to the winner these days. If we lose, his army will swell like a belly-heavy dragon. Do what you must to survive, Francis."

"I took an oath to you. Never will I bow to that bastard."

"After tomorrow, you're absolved of your oath."

"Would Lancelot have followed Mordred? Answer me, Richard!"

They had reached a tree. Bare of leaves in golden August, blackened as if by fire, it stood alone on the ridge of the hill. Richard halted, placed his hands on his friend's shoulders. "You've not seen war, Francis. I have. I've seen blood running from the wounded. I've seen the dead in the mud, villages destroyed, children starving. I've seen the agony of mothers and wives..." He swallowed. "I hate war, Francis. Let it end."

"Some things are worth fighting for, Richard."

The hammering of steel and twanging of bowstrings rose in volume as archers and men-at-arms checked their equipment for the morrow. Metal flashed in the light of campfires; men were cleaning weapons of steel that could sever arms and rip out entrails. There was little conversation, some nervous laughter. Without exception, the men were subdued, their faces pensive. Only a madman felt no fear on the eve of battle, Richard thought. His shoulder throbbed. He dropped his arms.

"Is death our reward, or our punishment?" he asked softly. The question hung in the air for a long moment.

"No one knows what death is," replied Francis at length, "whether it's not perhaps man's greatest blessings, yet people fear it as if they know it to be the greatest of evils."

"I believe it is our reward," said Richard quietly.

Across the dark meadows drifted the silver chimes of nearby Sutton Cheney Church where they had prayed at Vespers earlier. The breeze had picked up. Richard looked at the lone, blackened tree, bereft of life, yet standing firm, its maimed branches held high. He stretched out a hand, leaned against it. Charred bark crumbled beneath his weight, disintegrated in his fingers, and fell to the ground. Richard withdrew his hand. "Have you ever wondered, Francis?" he whispered.

"Wondered?"

"How small a part of life is taken up by treasured moments... how large a part is suffering?"

"It'd take a dull mind never to question such a thing. Even the barbarian infidels have considered it. They believe every soul must pass through seven valleys before reaching God. Like seven dark nights… Only after its greatest suffering, in a place they call the abyss, does it reach the valley of hymns and celebration."

In the silence that fell, the chirping of crickets blanketed the night. The clear notes of a lyre floated on the summer air and so sweet was the melody that men hushed to listen. A flute joined in and a woman's rich voice began to sing a plaintive refrain, filled with yearning. Richard let his eyes seek the shadows as images floated before him. He saw Anne smile at him, eyes tender and loving, and heard Ned's laughter echo through the castle gardens. Again from his father's torch-lit halls came the deep tones of troubadours recounting tales of noble knights. He closed his eyes against the memory of those dazzling moments, lit by the reflection of so much joy. They had been, he thought now, like rose petals flung over one long, endless funeral cortege.

The song rose in volume. Richard knew the words. It was the lament he had sung as a boy at that long-ago banquet at Middleham. He added his rich voice to hers,

Love, thou art bitter; sweet is death to me,
I fain would follow love, if that could be;
I needs must follow death, who calls for me,
Call and I follow, I follow…

The notes faded into the darkness.

"Camelot was a dream," he whispered. "Were we fools to dream such dreams, Francis?"

"What would life be without dreams?" Francis said as softly. "But the truth is that man is flawed. Camelot was destroyed by greed and ambition. Evil often triumphs over good."

"Yet the dream does not die. Arthur still lives and there will always be those who believe, who will strive for ideals against all odds. Surely that counts for something in the end?"

"Maybe, in the end, the quest is all that matters."

"You've been a good friend, Francis."

Francis' eyes glistened.

Through the thin, sparse branches of the suffering tree, Richard looked up at the dark sky crowded with thousands of glittering silver stars. They poured out of the deep blackness towards him and seemed so close, so very close, that if he put out a hand, he felt he could touch one. He reached up, but all he caught was a stunted branch of the burned tree. It snapped in his hand with a loud, brittle crack.

"Tell them, if anything happens to me— tell them I tried, Francis—"

Francis had no chance to respond. A messenger was rushing down the slope.

"My lord, Sir John Nesfield has arrived! He awaits in your pavilion."

Richard tensed, looked at Francis. "'Tis that matter I told you about, Francis. Come."

He spun on his heel and climbed the distance to his pavilion, with Francis in pursuit. He pushed the flap open and entered. Inside, by a table, in the flickering light of the candles, stood the trusty knight and his charge, a beautiful golden-haired boy in black velvet. Nesfield bent a knee in obeisance and the boy gave a low bow.

"Nephew," said Richard, inclining his head in cordial greeting. "Welcome." He sank down on the cot and drew the boy to him by the shoulders. "There is much to be said and little time, so I shall be brief. This is my friend, Francis Viscount Lovell. 'Tis important that you know his face."

The boy stared dutifully at Francis, trying to commit him to memory. Richard sat very still, watching. He remembered the day at Greenwich Palace in the garden with Meg and the boy in gold and white satin who tripped out of the hedges after his ball. Meg had been taken with little Richard but he'd felt no kinship with his namesake. His own words echoed in his ears: "He is a Woodville." He blinked, forced the memory away.

"I wish you to know that I regret what has happened, nephew, and I intend to make amends. Once Tudor is dead, the danger to you is past. I have sent to Rome for a dispensation to declare you legitimate. If victory is mine tomorrow, I shall acknowledge you as my heir. But if I fall—" He faltered, found his voice again. "If I fall, you must flee over the seas. When the time is right, you'll be sent for. 'Till then, 'tis death to be a Plantagenet." Richard dropped his hands from the boy's shoulders and rose. He went to his desk, withdrew a key from inside his doublet. Unlocking a silver casket, he took out a small square of parchment attached to a circle of ribbon. The document bore a large red seal from the Great Seal and a smaller one from his signet; a rare double seal.

"Take this with you and keep it safe always. If I am vanquished, use it to convince the crowned heads of Europe and my royal sister the Duchess of Burgundy that you are indeed my rightful heir to the throne of England." He hung the document around the boy's neck, tucked it carefully inside his doublet. He searched his face. "One more thing. Did your mother give you a password?"

"Aye, my lord uncle. She gave me one when we parted in Sanctuary. It's—"

"Don't tell me! Don't tell anyone! Keep it secret until the time is right. Do you understand, nephew?"

The boy met his gaze steadily with his own clear intelligent eyes, which were so blue they might have been Neville eyes. A rush of sudden pain twisted Richard's heart. Another eleven-year-old prince had once taken his measure with just such a look, but those eyes had been filled with rejection and fear. How different might it have been!

"My lord King, I do understand—" The boy's voice came to Richard as if from across a vast distance. He roused himself from his thoughts.

"—and I thank you." The child's tone was strangely old for his years, and by the stress he laid on the last word, Richard knew he understood, and forgave, and might even bear in his heart a trace of affection for his uncle. Thanks to Elizabeth, he thought. Sweet, gentle Elizabeth.

"You must take a name to hide your identity," said Richard. Gazing at the boy he was flooded by memories: the death of his own father; the flight across the seas with Warwick to Burgundy; the long, endless days of exile when he hadn't known if Edward lived or died, or what would become of him. He'd felt like an orphan, yet he'd had George with him. This boy, little older, had no one.

"Your last name shall be Warbeck," he continued. *Warbeck*,

Flemish for "orphan." It was bitterly apt. "Your first, 'Perkin'." There had been a boy named Perkin in Bruges, a likable boy, son to Philip the Good's Master of the Wardrobe. "You will live with a Portuguese Jew named Sir Edward Brampton. Have no fear. Brampton has my full confidence and is loyal to York unto death." He nodded to Nesfield who arranged the boy's cloak around him and tucked his golden hair carefully beneath his hood. He took his hand.

"Guard him well, Nesfield," said Richard.

"With my life, Sire."

"And keep well away until you know the outcome of the battle. If you must flee, Tyrell will give you safe passage through Calais to Burgundy. Tell Brampton the future of England lies in his hands. He must not fail."

"Aye, Sire."

Richard watched them cross the tent. At the flap, little Richard turned. "Farewell, dear uncle. I shall pray for thee."

"And I for thee, Dickon," Richard replied in a husky voice. How strange to hear himself call another by that name! "—that God keep thee safe and grant thee a long and fruitful life."

The boy looked at him for a long moment, his mouth quivering, then went out into the night. Richard stood silently, head bowed, gripping the side of the table. Finally he brought his gaze to Francis. "Your friendship has meant a great deal to me, Francis... I thank thee from the bottom of my heart."

Francis did not respond immediately, shaken by a rising dismay as he stood regarding Richard: the dark hair bobbed at the ears, the cleft chin and firm set of the jaw, the sad turn of the wide mouth. And the intense grey eyes. Such unspoken pain glowed in those eyes that his own misted looking at them. Blessed Heaven, could it be true that past the morrow he might never again see this face he had loved as a brother? He took a step forward and in a lightning flash, they were in each other's arms, clasped in a fierce embrace.

"If there's any justice in the world, victory is yours tomorrow," Francis whispered in a choked voice.

"Pray for my soul," said Richard, thickly, unsteadily.

Then Francis was gone.

Alone in the tent, Richard sank down on the bed, his head in his hands, staring at the ground. He bent over, picked up a handful of the red earth at his feet, let it spill slowly through his fingers. *Is death our punishment or our reward?* Caxton's book lay on the desk beside the silver casket. He reached out, picked it up, flipped it open to Arthur's death:

Then spake the bold Sir Bedivere:'My King!
...he who hates thee, he that brought
The heathen back among us, yonder stands,
Mordred, unharm'd the traitor of thine house.'
Then spake the King: 'King am I, whatsoever be their cry;
And one last act of knighthood shalt thou see
Yet, ere I pass.' And uttering this, the King
Made at the man.
Then Mordred smote his liege
Hard on the helm... while Arthur at one blow,
Striking the last stroke with Excalibur,
Slew him, and, all but slain himself, he fell

Richard fingered the last line, remembering a plank table in a dim parlour of an inn long ago. In his mind's eye, Anthony Woodville smiled at him. *Your favourite part?* he'd asked. His own answer came to him unbidden. *When Arthur slays Mordred. For justice is done.*

Truer words he'd never spoken. Aye, death wouldn't be so hard if he could take foul Tudor with him! Foul Tudor who had attacked his honour with his damnable lies and destroyed his happiness with his evil plots; Tudor, the dragon of his nightmares who had shorn him of hope. By God's blood, tomorrow that dragon would be no more, for he would set his eyes upon its hideous hide and slash it into a thousand bits!

He rose, flung the book aside. It struck the casket, which fell to the ground, spilling its contents. He seized his sword from where it rested against a coffer and unsheathed it from the scabbard. He held it up to the flickering candlelight. It glinted wickedly. Did he want to die? No more than he wanted to live. John's words echoed in his ears: *You can't go forward if you keep looking back. In last year's nest, there are no eggs.*

True, but if he lived, what he tried to forget, he would always remember.

He threw his sword on the bed, sank down beside it, and dropped his head into his hands. His eye fell on a small object at his feet. He picked it up. The miniature likeness of himself that he had promised Elizabeth had fallen from the casket. There was something else. A book... *Tristan and Iseult.* He reached under the bed, pulled out the small leather-bound volume. He dusted the grains of red earth off the cover. The flyleaf bore his inscription, *Loyaulte me lie, Richard of Gloucester.* The book fell open in his hands:

Close visor, lest an arrow from the bush
Leave me all alone with Mark and hell.

He blinked with disbelief. Elizabeth might well speak those words to him, were she here. So many coincidences. Meaningless coincidences. How had Anne explained it? Like a map drawn in duplicate, blurring the lines and rendering the map useless. The map of our lives.

He rose wearily. *Just a little further*, he told himself. He summoned a messenger, gave him the book and the portrait, and directed him to Sherriff Hutton.

He lay down on the bed and closed his eyes. Soon it would be dawn.

Chapter Thirty-Three

"But let what will be, be."

Sleep would not come to Richard. The last candle had burned itself out when someone called his name. He answered, and received no reply. He rose from bed, looked around, but could discern nothing in the deep darkness of the tent. He went to the opening, pushed back the flap. It was a black night, utterly silent. He froze. Holy Ninian! The camp was empty! What had happened to everyone? Had they all deserted him, every last man? He shut his eyes on an anguished breath. *Treason!* He took an unsteady step forward and halted. From his distant right came the thunder of hoofs. He peered into the night. Something glittered in the darkness like stardust. Strange... it was armour! So they were knights. But whose? His, or Tudor's?

He emerged to gain a better look. The glitter brightened, burst into a glow that lit up the night as horsemen closed the distance between them. They were indeed knights, but neither his, nor Tudor's, for their armour was not steel, but crystal. *Crystal?* How could that be?

They sat their mounts proudly, sword arms down, eyes fixed firmly ahead. Somehow he knew they had come to do him homage. Falling one behind the other, they encased him in a circle. He watched, fascinated. They were a beautiful sight, these crystal knights on their white horses. The circle completed, the knights lifted their sword arms in one swift motion. He had been wrong, he thought suddenly. They had not come to honour him, but to slay him! He braced himself for their blows. But there were no swords in those hands—only roses. Red roses.

Richard watched in amazement as a rainbow emerged. Tinged with the purest hues of rose, lavender, and violet, the rainbow grew wider, more vivid, reflected off the crystal knights and shattered into an array of glittering, glowing colours that filled the night with the most exquisite beauty. He had never seen so much beauty. So much beauty, he could scarcely bear it!—

He opened his eyes.

He was in bed. There was darkness in the tent. He threw back the covers and sat for a moment on the edge of his cot. It was Monday, the twenty-second of August, the eve of the feast of St. Bartholomew. He had been awakened many times in the night by fierce and terrible nightmares, but never by a dream of such rare beauty. A dream that left such sweetness and peace in its wake. And hope… But this was the day of battle, and of judgement, not of hope. Once there had been hope… A year ago on this very day, he had been with Anne at Windsor and she had sat in the garden for the first time since Ned's death, and he had been hopeful of her recovery.

He became aware of the sounds of the stirring camp: the stamping and neighing of horses, the clanking of armour, the murmur of voices as officers awakened sleeping men to eat breakfast and check their gear. His squire, Gower, appeared at the entrance with a candle. "My lord, 'tis time. Almost dawn." Richard clenched his jaw to still the racing of his heart. The knight held his candle to the oil-lamp, flooding the area with light. Richard regarded the man who had once been John Neville's squire. "Have you ever had a dream so beautiful it woke you up, Gower?" he asked softly.

"Why no, my lord. Never. I never even knew such a thing was possible."

"Neither did I."

The older man waited, as if expecting Richard to say more. When he didn't, he set the candle down on the table and picked up the ewer. He splashed water into the silver basin. The cold water felt good against Richard's face and neck. He took a seat on the campstool while Gower shaved him, brooding on the dream and its meaning. If he didn't know better, he would say it signified his victory in battle, but there had been too many omens to the contrary. Besides, the roses had been red, the colour of Lancaster… Maybe it was a triumph of another kind… Yet, if he lost the battle, what other triumph could there be?

Gower held up the mirror for his inspection. Richard's jaw slackened in dismay. It was a ghastly stranger who stared back at him, with skin the colour of mould and a face that was startlingly livid and frightful in the greyness of dawn. The sooner he hid himself beneath his helmet, the better. Pushing himself to his feet, he stood to don his armour, the same white armour he had worn at Barnet. He noticed the older man's hesitation, the sorrow in his eyes. So must Gower have looked at John that morning of Barnet, he thought. John's words echoed back to him across the years: *Aye, we're alike as brothers in many ways and our lives seem to take the same turns.* Richard had a sense of time barrelling backwards, then flashing forward. They had come full circle and now he stood where John had stood at Barnet, the end of the road.

He looked down at the golden griffin he wore on his finger. *John, old friend, more than ever I need you now. If only you were at my side to give me courage. If only you could see me wield my axe once more.*

"Your gauntlets, my lord."

"What?—" He had let his mind wander again. "Ah."

Gower hooked the latchets and buckled the straps that fastened Richard's mailed gauntlets. Richard rested a grateful hand on his shoulder for a long moment. Then, stifling his emotion, he said, "Summon my captains."

From the camp came the hammering of steel and twanging of bowstrings. They were drowned out by shouts. Gower rushed back in. "'Tis my Duke of Norfolk, Sire! Something's happened!"

The Silver Lion flashing on the azure tabard over his armour, Howard stormed into the royal tent, waving a placard in his hand. He was red-faced, fuming. Richard had never seen him in such a state.

"This was pinned to my tent in the night!" Howard roared, holding the placard out.

Richard took it and read:

Jockey of Norfolk, be not so bold.
For Dickon thy master
Has been bought and sold.

Richard felt the blood drain from his head. Trembling with fury, he crumpled the doggerel in his fist, his breath burning his throat.

Was there no end? No end to the foul treason? Even in his own camp! Even on the eve of battle! For the love of God—

"Accursed Tudor!" he raged. He kicked the table, and the oil lamp would have toppled but for Gower. "Accursed Tudor! By Christ's holy wounds, where were my sentries? Your guard? How in the Blessed Virgin's name weren't the traitors caught? Had you done your duty, Howard, this could not have happened!"

Howard turned crimson and a vein throbbed in his forehead. "Duty, Sire, is what's kept me here!" he retorted angrily.

Richard jerked his head around and glared. Abashed, Howard said, "Forgive me, my lord—'tis that I'm not accustomed to having my loyalty questioned."

Richard dropped into a campstool. "Why, Howard? Why are you still with me?"

"I'm no traitor!" Howard bristled again, his pride bruised.

"Why stay? When by doing so, you risk so much?" Richard asked wearily.

Now Howard understood. In a soft tone, he said, "You mean, what makes me different from the others? Aye—" He gave a sigh and sank his ample bulk down on the cot, "I could've carved a fine settlement out o' Tudor for my support. He approached me, as you know—" He paused at Richard's expression. "So you didn't know? No matter. I turned him down flat cold."

"Tell me why you stay, my friend," Richard repeated.

"'Tis a black day when a man is asked why he chooses honour over dishonour… I stay because you're my king, because you've been good to me, because it's the right thing to do." He slapped his palms on his knees and rose. "Now, my lord, I must away. My men await."

Richard nodded.

Howard strode to the opening, pushed aside the flap, turned back thoughtfully. "There is one other reason, my lord."

Richard waited.

"Because you have my heart."

***

Brother John Roby's expression was wretched as he gazed at his King. "Sire, we can't perform Mass. We have no bread."

"A minute ago you said we had no wine!" Richard fumed.

"That, too, my Liege. We left Sutton Cheney in such haste we forgot to—" His voice died away. "There are no chaplains, either."

"Get out of my sight! Out, out!" blustered Richard, boiling with impotent rage.

Before the man could move, Ratcliffe rushed into the tent. "My lord, there's no time to be lost! Tudor's advancing! It seems he would seize the initiative!" A sombre-faced Scrope appeared beside Ratcliffe. "The men're upset about Mass, m'lord. 'Tis bad enough they'll miss their breakfast, but Mass—" He swallowed, continued in a lower tone, "'Tis a bad omen and causing much murmuring and fear in the ranks. There were many defections in the night. More may slip away before we give battle."

Richard put on his helmet so the men wouldn't see his face. He pushed up his visor and thrust the tent flap open. The August morning was cool, fresh; the day gave promise of fair weather. He strode out to the troops assembling on the crest of Ambion Hill. Their lances and bills bristled in the grey light of dawn and the brightly coloured standards glowed. The murmurings died away. He went across to White Surrey, whom Gower held by his gold-tasselled bridle. His war horse gave him a snort of greeting. He mounted and positioned his prancing destrier to face his troops as red dawn streaked the sky.

"There will be no divine service by my order!" he shouted so all could hear. "If God is with us, we have no need of Mass! And if He is not, Mass will not help!" He noted the looks on men's faces as they gazed at him. Shock. Horror. Fear. Steeling himself so that they should not see their own emotions answered in his own face, he turned to Gower.

"My crown!" he called.

"Sire—" protested Conyers in a shocked whisper. Francis cantered forward. "Sire, you already stand out thanks to White Surrey, you must not wear the crown. It'll mark you as a target for every archer in Tudor's ranks." A chorus echoed his concern.

Richard looked at Francis and Conyers, at the sombre faces of his other loyal friends, Rob and the lords Scrope of Bolton and Masham; his advisors, Ratcliffe and Catesby; his secretary, John Kendall; gentle Brackenbury, loyal Humphrey Stafford, and the many others who had kept the faith and stood by him. He wished he could make them understand, but there were no words to express what was in his heart: this day was his Day of Judgement.

"Fetch my crown, Gower," he said.

A hushed silence fell. Gower went into the royal pavilion, emerged with the crown on a velvet cushion. His footsteps crunched on the hard red earth. Richard looked down at the circlet of gold. The rubies glinted darkly. He had always hated rubies. He reached out, took the crown into his trembling hands, set it squarely atop his helmet. "This day I live or die as King of England!" he cried.

His friends glanced away wretchedly.

"Brackenbury!" said Richard. "Dispatch a message to Lord Stanley. Tell him to come if he values the life of his son!" Brackenbury galloped off. Percy's retainer rode up. "What is it, Tempest?" demanded Richard.

"My lord, the Earl of Northumberland proposes that his mounted force take up a position in the rear. That way he can fall on Stanley's flank if he moves against Ambion Hill, and he will be close enough to you to provide reinforcements if you need them."

Richard stared quietly at the man. So this was Percy's game, to stay neutral. He could deny his request. Reveal his treachery. But what good would that do now?

"Very well," he agreed tersely. Better for Percy to be neutral in the rear than in front of the line where his stance would demoralize the royal army. He would have to manage without Percy's three thousand. He looked back at his men. They were silent, waiting for his final address. It struck him more forcefully than ever before that it wasn't only his life he was wagering in this battle, but theirs, too. It wouldn't happen again. There would never be another battle for his accursed Crown.

"If Henry Tudor wins this battle, England, as you have known it, will change!" he said, straining to speak loudly despite the depth of weariness that weighed him down. "Justice, the common man, matter not to Tudor. He is reared in France and has learned from

King Louis. He will rule England with fear and an iron fist. He will be a ruthless despot, as Louis was to his people, and he will wreak vengeance upon you—" They were all looking at him with grave, desperate eyes. He wished he could give them encouragement, but he owed them the truth. "I have tried to be a just prince to you. But if I triumph, England will also change. No longer will I seek to rest my rule on good will. Opposition will be crushed. Traitors will be shown no mercy. I will be ruthless in demanding obedience—for the security of the realm."

He fell silent, sick at heart. There was no more to say and he would not give them false hope. Without Percy and the Stanleys they were outnumbered by Tudor eight thousand to six. Only if the Stanley brothers remained neutral, did they stand chance of victory. How likely was that?

Horses' hoofs thudded on the hard ground. One of Howard's azure-jacketed men was riding up on his left.

"The Duke of Norfolk is ready to deploy, Sire!"

Richard inclined his head and watched the man return to Howard's vanguard. The banner of the Silver Lion sparkled in the rising sun, pointing the way. Trusty Norfolk. Bless him, loyal knight.

Turning White Surrey, he followed Howard. He himself would lead the centre of his army. Let Percy rot in the rear.

Chapter Thirty-Four

"'And one last act of kinghood shalt thou see Yet ere I pass.'
And saying this the king Made at the man.
Then Mordred smote his liege Hard on the helm..."

Richard stood with his army at the summit of Ambion hill. Above him fluttered the banners of England and St. George, his own White Boar, and young Edward's Dun Cow of Warwick. Birds wheeled in the sky, squawking loudly, and golden wheat fields glistened in the sun. From distant Sutton Cheney Church where he and his men had prayed at Vespers the night before came the chiming of church bells, ringing for Prime. There was the bleating of sheep and the whinny of horses. A few dogs barked.

Richard could see all three armies of his enemies. Tudor was below in Redmore Plain, directly south, less than six hundred yards away and closing the distance, his standard of the Red Dragon of Wales waving in the wind as he marched with his army of two thousand men. The Stanley brothers, together numbering about six thousand, were to Richard's right, across a valley and a stream to the southwest, their red-jacketed men motionless. Lord Stanley was further north than his brother and remained on foot, as was customary, while William Stanley, positioned closer to Tudor, was mounted and on the ready.

Traitors, he thought with disgust, turning away as the wind shifted and the heavy smell of dung assailed his nostrils. He focused on Howard's azure ranks to his left. The vanguard was flowing downwards and taking on the shape of a bent bow pointing south to the enemy, and Howard was pushing his cannon to higher ground and arranging his men-at-arms between his archers. An impenetrable swamp protected Howard's flank on the northeast but the hillside was too small for the huge royal host of six thousand men to stretch out across. Howard had to assemble his division further down the slope than it should be.

Too late to worry about that now, Richard thought. He set about disposing his own men along the ridge. The hillside was a splendid sight, ablaze with Lilies and Leopards, the White Boar and the Sun of York, and Richard's colours of berry and grey. But that was because men stood crowded on the tight ledge. Maybe this high ground had not been a good idea. If only John had been here to advise him!

Enemy trumpets shrilled the battle-cry, drums rolled, heralds sounded fanfares. Howard's trumpets answered and his captains shouted orders. On Tudor's side commands rang out in French, Welsh, and English. Frantic hoof beats sounded on Richard's right. It was Brackenbury, returning with Stanley's reply. He drew his stallion to a halt. "Sire, Lord Stanley says he cannot join you at present."

Shock rendered Richard momentarily mute. "Did you warn him that his son will die if he refuses?"

"I did, my lord," said Brackenbury. "He said to tell you he has other sons."

Richard stared. It was impossible! Inconceivable! Could a father care so little for his own son? "Catesby!" roared Richard, eyes blazing.

"Aye, Sire?"

"Execute George Stanley!"

Catesby paled. "My lord, if we do, we'll force the Stanleys to throw in their lot with Tudor—"

"They plan to do that anyway. Carry out the execution!"

"Aye, Sire," said Catesby miserably, turning his horse.

"Catesby, wait!" He couldn't do it. How would he go on, if he couldn't do what had to be done? "Let the battle decide his fate." He trotted his horse forward to where the knights of his household waited in their shining armour. Behind them stretched the ranks of his reserves, a thousand strong.

A chorus of blood-curdling yells erupted. Battle was joined. The Earl of Oxford appeared beneath his banner of the Star and Streams, guns thundering. Stone cannon balls bounced against Howard's position on the hill. Howard answered with a rain of arrows and a burst of cannon fire from his one gun, taking a toll on the Lancastrian front line. Richard cursed himself. He had not thought of bringing more guns, since guns had never proved much help to Warwick. Oxford's foot soldiers gained ground rapidly and poured half-way up the hill. The two armies clashed on Ambion Hill with an earth-shattering din of metal. Though Oxford was protected on his right by the swamp, his left flank was open—unless William Stanley supported it. Richard glanced over to his right. The Stanleys hadn't moved.

He scanned the reserves behind Tudor's lines. Henry Tudor was there somewhere. Watching. Hiding. He was no soldier. He wouldn't risk his neck. That kind never did. Richard turned to his men. "Find out where Tudor has stationed himself!" He focused his attention back on Howard's side. The armies were locked in fierce combat. Tudor had committed the bulk of his troops to Oxford's vanguard, and Howard's line was weaker than the enemy. In the centre of the fighting, the Silver Lion bobbed against Oxford's Stars and Streams, now and again pushing forward, but more often giving ground. Despite the fire maintained by Howard's archers, Oxford continued to advance. Howard's bow shape turned into a crescent, thinned dangerously.

"Send reserves to Norfolk!" commanded Richard. He watched, his heart pounding.

The centre held. Slowly Howard recovered, began to beat Oxford back. Oxford's trumpets blared retreat. Commands sounded above the noise of battle. The enemy fell back. There was no more clash of steel. No arrows flew. A lull descended on the field. Could Oxford be withdrawing after only a half-hour battle? Why wasn't Howard in pursuit?

Richard's men were murmuring the same thought. He rose in his stirrups to gain a better look. Howard was evidently confused, thought it might be some kind of a ruse. Richard could see him looking along his line with his son, the Earl of Surrey, and his captains, the lords Zouche and Ferrers.

Oxford's men gathered around their standards. He was getting reinforcements and reshaping his army's ranks into an arrow-head pointed at the hill. Howard had missed a chance for a rout! He must have realised his mistake, for Zouche raised a steel-gauntleted arm and the royal trumpets sounded the battle call again. Howard led his men in a charge down the hill. They threw themselves on the enemy. Richard could see the barrel figure in shining silver armour exchanging sword thrusts with a knight in the thick of the fighting. Howard was discharging himself like a true lion, thought Richard, his mouth softening. His eye went to two other men nearby, fighting side by side; yeomen, from the look of them, with their leather jerkins and rusty steel sallets. They fought like war gods, bringing men down quickly with a few well-aimed lance-like thrusts of their pole-axes. A knight rode up, raised his sword to cut one of them down, and was somehow unhorsed. Those two had felled a knight in full armour! Richard almost cheered. There would be a knighthood for them!

"Anyone know those men? Richard asked.

"I know them, Sire!" a young knight called from behind him. "They are the Brechers, father and son, from the West Country."

Somewhere a distant memory stirred. Richard's heart constricted. These were the people who had given them shelter when he and Anne had run away from Barnard's Castle and were lost in the rain.

"I know them, too," he said, softly.

"Sire!—"

Richard twisted in his saddle, looked down at the man.

"Sire! We've found him for you—Henry Tudor!" cried the scout. "There, to the west, on the rising ground opposite—" He ran forward, pointing.

Richard trotted White Surrey a few paces and peered into the dusty air of combat. "The one standing by the red-dragon standard?"

"Aye, Sire!"

As he watched, a messenger ran up to the figure, did obeisance. *Tudor!* Richard clenched his teeth, tightened his grip of his reins. Hate swept him with such force, he could almost taste its vile bitterness in his mouth.

"Richard, what is it?" Francis' voice.

"That's Tudor," he said, without turning.

Francis followed his gaze.

"He won't get away this time," Richard said. "I'm going to slay the dragon."

Francis grinned. "Allow me to give you a hand." Richard looked at him gravely. With a calmness he himself knew to be strange under the circumstances, he said, "You won't be at my side, old friend. You can't take part in the fighting. If anything happens to me, you have to be there for Jack… and Warbeck."

"But—" Francis fell silent. Their eyes met and held. He gave a nod, swallowed visibly and transferred his gaze to the fighting on Howard's side. All at once he gave a bounce in the saddle. "A mute point, Richard! Looks like Howard will slay the beast for you!"

Howard's lines were still washing back and forth like a tide, but he was fighting fiercely, gaining steady ground. *Forward, my brave Lion,* urged Richard silently. *Forward!* Then, before his eyes, Howard disappeared and there was a swirl of fighting around his banner. Shouts arose. Howard's son, the Earl of Surrey, was swinging his sword furiously but the royal ranks were giving way. Richard rose in his stirrups. He still couldn't tell what was happening! A messenger galloped up, reared to a halt.

"The Duke of Norfolk has been slain, my lord!" cried the man. "The sun was in his eyes—he didn't see the arrow coming!"

Richard reeled. He collapsed into his saddle, tightened his hold of the reins. *The sun was in his eyes.* He hadn't considered the sun when he'd faced his army south! He hadn't considered a lot of things. It was his fault Howard was dead. *His fault.* He'd never fought a pitched battle of this magnitude, and now good Howard, the Friendly Lion, was gone. Just like that. His eyes stung. If John had been at his side this would never have happened. John had never lost a battle, except Barnet, the one he'd had no heart to win.

He swallowed on the constriction in his throat, found his voice, "Send reserves to Surrey's aid!" As one of his esquires galloped off to give the order, another messenger rode up. Richard held his breath.

"Lord Ferrers has fallen, my lord!"

Black rage swept Richard. He cursed, turned his head, sought Tudor. A horseman was galloping furiously across Redmore Plain. That would be Tudor's messenger, bearing the news of Howard's death to Stanley. The foxes smelled blood. "Send to

Northumberland!" ordered Richard. "Command him to advance at once in support of the royal army!"

***

Flies whined in Richard's face. The day had grown hot.... so hot. He felt dizzy, could barely breathe beneath his armour, and his throat ached. He needed water.

A small crowd stood around the well behind his standard. He slid from the saddle. They rushed to assist him. He shoved them aside. He could stand. He just needed water, that's all. Someone offered him a cup. He drank, but it was not enough, did nothing to assuage his thirst. He removed his helmet, passed it to Gower. He stumbled to the well, leaned his weight on the rough stone edge until he managed to catch his breath. He grabbed the bucket and drank greedily, spilling more than he swallowed. That was better. He looked up at the sky. Dust. No birds. His standard of the White Boar and Edward's Sun-and-Roses beat loudly in the wind.

Howard was dead. Ferrers was dead. And maybe Zouche— How many more? He rubbed his bleary eyes. That damn Tudor. *Lucifer.* He had to do something before they were all dead. All his knights.

Rob rode up, flung himself from his saddle. "Richard! Are you all right?" Richard gripped his shoulder, as much to support himself as in friendship. "I'm going to get him, Rob. I need to get him."

"Tudor?"

"Help me into the saddle," he whispered.

"Richard, you're in no condition—"

"I'm tired, that's all. Help me, Rob—"

Rob assisted him onto White Surrey. No sooner had he taken his reins than his men shouted that a rider was approaching from the north bearing the Silver Crescent badge of Henry Percy on his helmet. Richard held himself very still; the muscles of his forearm tensed beneath his armour. Percy's herald dismounted, bent a knee. Impatiently, Richard motioned him to rise.

"Your Grace..." said the man uneasily, "my Lord of Northumberland bids me tell you that he feels it his duty to remain in the rear in order to guard against Lord Stanley, in case he moves against your flank." He looked down at the trampled grass at his feet.

Men cursed; others spat. Two men seized the herald; a dagger flashed. Richard raised a hand. Silence. Richard stared at the man's bent head, at the Silver Crescent he bore. Richard had displaced Percy in the North and Percy had never forgiven him. Despite all the favour he had shown him, all the generosity and the courtesy, there had been no gratitude. Only resentment; a bitter, grim resentment. He turned and looked at Percy, far in the distance, sitting still as a statue on his horse, glum and sullen. It should be John there, he thought. If John were Earl of Northumberland, everything would be different. This was Edward's doing. His revenge from the grave. By sacrificing John all those years ago, he had reached out into the future and sacrificed him as well. Richard was surprised that he should feel no emotion; nothing at all. No fear, and no hope.

Let what will be, be.

He looked at his men. Others had joined him: noble Ratcliffe, fair Clarendon, gallant Conyers, gentle Brackenbury, faithful Kendall, and many trusted retainers and esquires. And there was dear Rob. And Francis.

Francis; ever at his side.

Catesby ran up, pushed his way through to Richard. "Sire, Lord Zouche is dead! The battle's all but lost! The Stanleys will advance against us at any moment. You must seek safety in flight!"

Richard smiled. They all looked at him strangely. They didn't understand. "I'm going to charge Tudor's position," he said.

There was disbelief for a moment, then gasps and shocked murmurs.

"Sire, it's too dangerous!" protested Conyers. "To get to him, you must pass directly in front of the Stanleys' position!"

"For that reason I'll not order any man to come with me. I ride to seek Tudor. Alone, if need be. You can each choose whether to follow."

After a moment's silence, Rob trotted his horse beside Richard. Clarendon raised a mailed arm in salute. "*Loyaulte me lie!*" A chorus echoed his refrain. *Loyalty binds me.* A smile lifted the corners of Richard's mouth. Men burst into action. Horses were led forward;

knights and squires calmed their excited mounts, tightened armour plate and saddles. Gower put Richard's battle-axe into his grip. Their eyes locked, grey to brown. *Farewell, friend; and thank you.* Richard slammed his visor shut. He drew himself up in his saddle, saw Francis standing by the boar standard, watching him. Richard sat very still, his eyes soft. He nodded his crowned helmet in Francis' direction, in farewell.

"Loyaulte me lie!" he cried, turning his horse.

***

South-westward down the hill he led them, gathering speed, a bright figure in shining white armour on a white horse, his golden crown flashing on his helmet. In a wide arc he swept them past the southern end of the battle line. Ahead lay the flatland of Redmore Plain. The noise of the battle on Ambion Hill faded, grew ever more distant. He felt at one with White Surrey; at one with his men. They were all with him, all the men of his household, almost a hundred brave, loyal knights, ready to battle the mass of the enemy reserves. To kill the dragon leader.

Live pure, speak true, right wrong, follow the King—

This was what it was all about. Loyalty. Justice. To fight for right.

Through the eye-slits of his visor, he glimpsed the banner of the White Hart, William Stanley's blazon. Straight across Sir William's front, he galloped, hoofs thundering behind him. Stanley's men were a stream of blood-red jackets on his right, hundreds and hundreds of them, all staring, mouth agape, scarcely a bow-shot away and unable to believe the evidence of their own eyes. He felt exhilarated. He wanted to laugh. To roar with laughter. He wanted to clasp every one of his men to his heart and tell them he loved them.

The ground was rising. They were nearing Tudor's position. Men had been caught by surprise. They scattered, ran for their horses, tried to get into formation. Richard heard their cries; the shouted orders. Ranks closed around Henry Tudor. A mighty figure charged forward. It was the giant, Sir John Cheyney, nearly seven feet tall and three hundred pounds. Richard swung his battle-axe in an arc, made contact with a crash of steel. Cheyney's horse reared; he lost his balance, fell to the ground. Another knight advanced to take his place. Richard raised his battle-axe again and brought it down on his helmet. Ratcliffe and Rob hewed their way to his side. All around him was the crash of metal. His ears throbbed with the screams of horses in pain, the cries of men, the thumping of his own heart. Ahead waved the standard of the Red Dragon borne by William Brandon. Ahead was Tudor.

He could see Tudor!

Tudor was on foot. He wore a breastplate but no helmet, and there was fear on his face. He recoiled, looked as if he were about to run. Oh, God, it felt so good to see the fear! Richard plunged forward. Brandon blocked his path with his sword. Richard whirled his axe. Steel crashed against steel. Brandon fell dead. Richard's men were all around him now in a tight group, slashing their way forward. *Just a little further!*

Shouts erupted; someone sounded an alarm: *All is lost! Save yourselves!* Richard paid no heed. Someone else seized Richard's bridle. It was Ratcliffe. He was gesturing behind him. Richard turned. Through the narrow slits of his visor and the swirling yellow dust of combat, he saw the blood-red jackets of Sir William's men. They were thundering down on them. Richard shook his head. He wouldn't flee! He had to get to the Dragon before Stanley reached them. He spurred White Surrey forward. His men swung round to meet the onslaught. There was yelling, an ear-deafening crash of steel on steel. But even as Richard chopped through the masses of weapons, he realised that all around him his men were falling. All at once White Surrey gave a shrill, piercing scream and sank to his knees in the dust. *Oh, God, no, not White Surrey—!*

He slipped from his saddle, swung his battle-axe wildly, desperately, cutting his way to Tudor. Someone grabbed his arm. He looked up. It was the young knight Clarendon. Conyers was with him, leading a fresh horse. He shook his head again. *Not while the Dragon lived!* He smashed onward with his battle-axe. Conyers and Clarendon turned to protect his back from Stanley.

Suddenly Richard found himself face to face with the Dragon.

For an instant he couldn't move, he was so surprised. There

was nothing fierce-looking about this beast. Tudor was thin-lipped, with a long uneven nose and lank, straggly brown hair. The most astonishing feature in his nondescript narrow face was his small grey eyes, which were strikingly pale and stretched wide in naked terror. He was more hare than dragon, this miserable worm, this lily-livered coward! Richard raised his axe. A terrible pain exploded in his arm, knocking the breath from his body. He whirled round, swinging his battle-axe with his left. Clarendon and Conyers had fallen. Red jackets were all around him.

"Treason!" he cried, thrusting for his life. *He'd almost had him!* But for Stanley's treason, he would have had him! Rob, Ratcliffe, Kendall, Brackenbury; they were dead. Howard, Zouche, Ferrers were dead. And Tudor lived.

Tudor lived—

It wasn't fair! He struck out blindly in all directions. *Virtue always prevails.* His own words, spoken with such bland assurance to Anne a lifetime ago, pounded in his head, mocking him. *Stand on your throne and tell your people that,* a voice yelled in his head. *Tell Stanley and Percy! Tell Rob and Howard and Conyers!*

"Treason!" he cried. "Treason!" He saw the gloomy chamber at Ludlow, the candles that threw menacing shadows across the stone walls and illuminated the faces of his father's kin. There was Salisbury, Warwick, young Thomas Neville, and his own brother Edmund. Andrew Trollope loomed over them, laughing; an earring in one ear. He heard his father's voice, loudly, clearly, "Treason!" cried his father.

"Treason!" cried Richard, flailing about him against the masses of swords and spears pounding his armour. There was such pain, he couldn't hold his battle-axe any longer; couldn't stand. He was so tired; so very tired. He sank to his knees. "Treason!" he whispered. There was a roaring in his ears. Sweat poured into his eyes. He blinked, surprised it was red. Red was everywhere. Then there was no more red, only black, and he was cold, so cold. He laid his head down in the dust.

Through the shaking earth and the din of battle he heard music, distant at first; a familiar refrain, but too faint to recognise. His eyes shot open. What was this? How could this be? He tried to lift his head but some great weight kept him down. The music rose in volume and his heart lifted. It was the Song of the North, sung by a thousand voices, pure and magnificent, harmonizing more melodiously than he had thought possible. An exquisite warmth radiated through him; he listened enraptured.

Richard!

Joy exploded in his breast. *Where are you, Anne? I can't see you—*

I'm waiting for you in heaven, Richard. Ned is with me. Come, my love; it's beautiful here.

I'm… coming… Flower-eyes.

Epilogue

"Thy shadow still would glide from room to room."

Westminster Palace
February 11, 1503

Elizabeth shifted her weight on her prie-dieu and her eyes strayed to the coffer where she had hidden Richard's portrait. It was hopeless. Her thoughts were not with God; they were with Richard. For some inexplicable reason, he felt so near at this moment, as if he would walk into the room in the next instant. Today the years had fallen away and the ache of the past had returned more acutely than ever before, maybe because today was her birthday, and birthdays always carried her back to her happy youth, to the beautiful days when the palace halls rang with her father's laughter and life sparkled with golden warmth and the promise of endless sunny tomorrows. To when sweet Anne had welcomed her to court with a loving smile, and Richard had strolled with her in the snowy garden.

A sharp pain sent her doubling in agony. She clutched her abdomen and gasped. Her lady-in-waiting appeared at her side. Elizabeth shook her head, waved the woman back to the settle. She hesitated, retreated with reluctance. Elizabeth clasped her palms together and leaned her weight on the velvet-covered rail. There had been much difficulty with this birth, her seventh; a girl, born two weeks ago and dead only days later. She brushed a tear away. Fixing her eyes on the image of the suffering Christ hanging on the wall before her, she murmured fervent prayers for them all: her three dead babes and Arthur, her beloved boy who had died last year at seventeen, and taken with him what was left of her heart.

Then she whispered a prayer for Richard.

She had said Masses for his soul every day of these eighteen years since the black tidings of Bosworth Field were brought to Sherriff Hutton. Sometimes there was solace to be found. At other times, like now, prayer availed her nothing. She made the sign of the Cross and rose from the prie-dieu. She turned to her lady-in-waiting. "Leave me, Lucy."

"But, my lady, you know I am ordered not to leave your side. What if you collapsed again? No one would know, and the King—"

"I am well enough," interrupted Elizabeth. "Well enough, Lucy. Go, now. I'll pull the bell cord if I need you."

The lady in waiting hesitated. "What if you can't reach it in—"

"I'll pull the bell cord if I need you," repeated Elizabeth firmly. The woman sank into a curtsy and withdrew. Elizabeth waited until the door thudded shut. She went to the coffer. Slowly, heavily, she let herself down, withdrew a key from inside her bodice, and removed the silver chain from around her neck. She opened the chest. Her treasured, worn copy of Richard's *Tristan and Iseult* was where she had hidden it, safe in a false drawer at the bottom. Another spasm of pain rippled in her side. Leaning on the coffer, she gripped the book tightly in her hand until it passed.

She made her way past the tall traceried windows to the brocade-covered writing table in the corner and sat down in the carved chair. The sun poured into the chamber in long panels, fell across the table, bathing her in warmth. A sudden wind stirred the ivy on her bower. She closed her eyes and softly hummed an old tune from the past.

Aye, aye, O, aye the winds that bend the brier!
The winds that bow the grass!
For the time was may-time,
and blossoms draped the earth—

The song had haunted her all day, though she had heard it only once. It was Richard's Song of the North, which he had sung to Anne on her deathbed.

Wine, wine—and I will love thee to the death
And out beyond into the dream to come...

Emotion threatened to overwhelm her. She blinked back the tears that stood in her eyes. Shouts drifted up from the garden, and she looked down, grateful for the distraction. Eleven-year-old Harry was playing football in the snowy court. She gazed at him, thinking of her beloved Arthur. Ginger-haired and heavy-set, Harry was nothing like Arthur, or like her, or like any on her side, not even in temperament. From babyhood he had been a difficult child, wilful and calculating, with quicksilver moods that turned him from cherub to fanged adder in an instant. Sometimes she thought Harry hated her. At nine, he'd stolen on her like a fox on prey and surprised her studying Richard's portrait. Startled, she'd cried out and dropped the miniature. Harry had picked it up and handed it back to her. A look had come into his eyes; a look which was often there now, when he turned his gaze on her. She shivered despite the sun. She didn't know what to make of Harry. Yet Harry, to his credit, hadn't told his father—maybe because they liked one another even less.

She opened the book, careful not to spill the few grains of red earth that came from the field of battle. Even that was dear to her. Gently she traced Richard's inscription with the tip of her finger: *Richard of Gloucester, Loyaulte me lie.*

"Richard..." she murmured, touching all that was left of him. He had such beautiful handwriting: strong, clear, each letter elegantly formed. Good that he didn't know that day at Bosworth Field how it would all end: his body despoiled; his memory vilified; his friends and those of his blood hunted down and murdered. Lovable young Edward, George's poor son, had died for his Plantagenet blood, and so had Richard's own sweet boy, Johnnie, who was a bastard and no threat to anyone, save another bastard. By the time Henry was done, there would be nothing left of the pure strain. Even those who had loved Richard were dead, with the possible exception of Francis. He had disappeared after the first rebellion and no one knew what became of him.

The early years had been hard on Henry, filled with unrest, but he had survived. He was a born survivor. Jack's rebellion of 1487 had failed, along with the succession of others launched from Ireland and led by a certain Perkin Warbeck who claimed to be her brother, Richard of York.

She drew a sharp breath. Dear God, she didn't want Warbeck to be Dickon! Not even though he was said to have the same drooping eyelid as little Dickon, the same face and lineaments of body as her father! Meg had received him as her nephew and backed his invasions for six long years, but then Meg would support a bowl of porridge if it made trouble for Henry. She'd never learned why her own mother, Bess, had thrown her support to that first rebellion when she'd had so much to lose. Henry had banished her to a nunnery where she was carefully watched, and there she had died seven years later, in poverty. During these years, other princes of Europe had stepped forward to uphold Warbeck's claim. James of Scotland had even permitted Warbeck to marry into his royal family.

No, she refused to believe it was Dickon! She couldn't bear the thought of Dickon dying a traitor's death at Tyburn: of being hung on the gallows, drawn apart, and cut into sections while still alive. It was too horrible. A dizzy spell sent her swaying in her chair. She held a hand to her head until it passed.

Aye, Henry had made his throne secure, had kept it longer with his iron fist than Richard ever could with his tender heart. What Henry lacked as a warrior, he made up for with a slyness of mind that did honour to his mentor, King Louis of France. A line from Malory echoed in her mind: *Catlike thro' his own castle steals my Mark.* He had learned much from Louis; he was much like Louis. He even wore the same hat: a flat affair with a peak in the front... Henry hadn't wished to wed her, if the truth be known. He'd delayed their marriage as long as he could, in part to be sure she didn't bear Richard's child. Henry was like that. Full of fears and secret suspicions, cold as a Northumberland winter. Even after all these years, she still recalled her revulsion at the first touch of his body on hers; the feel of his sweaty skin; the smell of his offending breath. In time, her repugnance faded, reduced to near indifference by familiarity. She was grateful for that small mercy.

She flipped to the back of the book where she had hidden Richard's miniature portrait... Dark hair, wide sensitive mouth, strong square jaw. Eyes looking into the distance: earnest eyes, filled with terrible sadness. His last words to her echoed in the dark stillness of her mind: *You'll change! You'll forget me!* He had been wrong. She had neither changed nor forgotten. Nothing could remove him from her heart. Not time; not life. She would never forget a detail of his face.

She set down the miniature and drew the book to her. She remembered herself at eighteen, after Richard's death at Bosworth, removing a pen from a sand cup, dipping it carefully into the ink and opening the flyleaf. *San Removyr,* she had written beneath his inscription. It was her motto, used only once in her life, when she was neither princess nor queen. *Without changing.* Only he would understand. She brought his portrait to her lips, implanted a kiss. It was said that he'd dreamed of triumph that last night before battle, but his triumph had not been of this world. She lifted her face to the bleak winter sky. "Richard, if you have been greatly hated, you have also been deeply loved—"

The sudden constriction in her chest stopped her breath. Oh, God, she couldn't faint! She had to hide his portrait! She rose heavily and struggled to her coffer, each step dragging forth with pain. She located the secret compartment and slipped the book into it. There, the portrait was safe! She locked the chest, hung the key around her neck, pushed it deep into her bodice, her heart racing. Sagging against the coffer, she drew ragged breaths. Something was terribly wrong with her sight. She rubbed her eyes, looked down at her skirts.

A thick pool of bright red blood swam at her feet.

***

Elizabeth's body felt as heavy as marble. She couldn't move any part of it: not her hands, feet, or even her eyelids. There was no pain, but breathing was slow and difficult. Though she could hear voices and recognise them, everything seemed far away, as if from another world with which she no longer had a connection. A flurry of sounds dimly penetrated her consciousness: footsteps, a medley of hushed voices, the rustle of fabric permeated by a stale odour. She held her breath. Someone leaned over and she heard them murmur, "My lady, 'tis the King."

A wild joy erupted in her breast, filling her cold body with the heat of sunshine and an ineffable, inexplicable lightness. Her eyes opened, her head lifted, and a wide smile came to her lips; it seemed to her that she could even raise her arms.

"Richard!" she cried.

In the motion of bending down to kiss her cheek, Henry Tudor stiffened and his face twisted in disgust.

"I am too late, I see."

A sobbing lady-in-waiting stepped forward and closed Elizabeth's eyes.

Afterword

Richard's bloody body, naked and with a felon's halter around the neck, was slung contemptuously across the back of a horse. As it was borne across the west bridge of the Soar, the head was carelessly battered against the stone parapet, as the wise-woman had prophesied. For two days the body lay exposed to view in the house of the Grey Friars close to the river, then it was rolled into a grave without stone or epitaph. At the dissolution of the monasteries, his grave was despoiled and his bones thrown into the River Soar.

Henry Tudor came to London in a litter, peering at his subjects from behind the curtains. By dating his reign from the day before the battle, he was able to attaint and hang for treason the men who had fought for Richard, including a Brecher father and son whose bravery had been noted by the enemy.

Francis, Viscount Lovell, was offered, and rejected, all of Henry Tudor's overtures of pardon, including a role in Tudor's coronation. With an army of Irish foot soldiers and German mercenaries, he and Lincoln invaded England in 1487 and almost snatched victory at the Battle of Stoke. He disappeared after the battle and was last seen riding his horse across the River Trent. It was thought that he had drowned. In 1708 a secret underground chamber was discovered at Minster Lovell and the skeleton of a man was found seated at a table on which there were set a candle, paper, and a pen. All dissolved into dust as the door opened. It is now generally accepted that he was given refuge by a trusted servant and died of starvation as a result of the old man's own death. However, the position of Francis' body does not support this theory. It would be difficult, if not impossible, to remain upright in the final stages of death by starvation. For this reason it is possible Francis died more mercifully, of wounds sustained in the battle.

John de la Pole, Earl of Lincoln (Jack), was noted by his enemies to have fought with great valour and skill at the Battle of Stoke, as did the German mercenaries who died with him to the last man. His Irish supporters, who composed half his army, likewise fought fiercely, but poorly clad and equipped only with clubs and scythes, they "fell like beasts before the enemy's armour and swords." In 1501, when Henry Tudor began to exterminate those with Plantagenet blood, Lincoln's younger brother, Edmund, Earl of Suffolk, fled to the Continent. Tudor managed to get him back, and Henry VIII executed him. A third brother, William de la Pole, died in the Tower. The youngest brother, Richard, sought refuge in France, where he came to be known as the last "White Rose."

Margaret Plantagenet. George's daughter married into the Pole family. When her son fled to France to escape Henry VIII and refused to return, Henry had her executed in her son's place. By all accounts she died barbarically. It is said that she fled from the executioner and had to be chased down at Tower Green. It took five blows of the axe to behead her. She was sixty-eight. She was later regarded by Catholics as a martyr and was beatified in 1886 by Pope Leo XIII.

Edward, Earl of Warwick. George's tragic son was picked up from Sheriff Hutton immediately after Bosworth and taken to the Tower. He was executed by Henry VII on a pretext of treason in 1499, along with Perkin Warbeck. He was twenty-four.

John of Gloucester. Henry Tudor granted him a small pension, but just before Stoke, he was picked up for receiving a letter from Ireland. He disappeared into the Tower and was never heard from again.

Henry Percy, Earl of Northumberland. The North never forgot Percy's gross betrayal of Richard. Four years after Bosworth, while travelling near York to collect ever-higher taxes for Henry Tudor, he was pulled from his horse and murdered. His retainers watched.

Sir William Stanley. After the Battle of Bosworth, William Stanley retrieved Richard's battered crown from a thorn bush and crowned Henry Tudor with it. Despite his critical intervention in the battle and this grand gesture, he was never trusted by Tudor, who blamed him for taking too long to come to his aid. In 1495 Tudor executed William Stanley for supporting Perkin Warbeck.

Lord Thomas Stanley. Henry Tudor gave Stanley the earldom of Derby, but never entrusted him with the power he had enjoyed under Richard and he faded from the scene. Stanley's wife, Margaret Beaufort, soon abandoned his bed by taking a vow of chastity, and on one occasion Henry Tudor found an excuse to extract from his stepfather the lofty sum of six-thousand pounds in fines.

John Morton, Bishop of Ely, became one of Tudor's most trusted and influential royal advisors and enjoyed enormous power. Tudor appointed him Archbishop of Canterbury in 1486 and secured him a cardinal's hat in 1493. Despite all his achievements, his only claim to fame is for "Morton's Fork," a sophisticated argument that justified the extortion of taxes from both rich and poor for Henry Tudor.

Lady Margaret Beaufort died in 1509 wracked by pain and "praying and weeping many tears" in concern for her immortal soul. Her confessor, Cardinal John Fisher, was executed by her grandson Henry VIII in 1535, taking her secrets and her sins to the grave with him.

Bess Woodville. Though thrifty Henry Tudor did not restore Bess' property after Bosworth, he did grant her the pomp and privileges of a Queen Dowager. With the birth of her grandson Arthur in September 1486, she enjoyed a proud position at Tudor's court as the ancestress of kings. Just before Lincoln's rebellion in 1487, her situation changed abruptly. Stripped of her few possessions, she was thrown into confinement at the nunnery of Bermondsey Abbey. For the rest of her life, it was considered dangerous to even attempt to see or talk with her. The general belief is that she was detected aiding the cause of the rebellion.

She died five years later, impoverished and bemoaning the fact that she had nothing to leave her daughters but her blessing, and "small stuff and goods." Her wood coffin was conveyed to Windsor by boat at night and she was buried with only three distant relatives present, "no ringing of bells," and so few candles that a disappointed sightseer who witnessed the event commented upon it in his journal. Though her son Dorset and three of her five daughters did visit her privately at the chapel two days later, the funeral service that followed their departure was done cheaply and shabbily. No royalty attended.

The Marquess of Dorset was sent to the Tower at the same time that his mother was taken to Bermondsey Abbey. Released after the Battle of Stoke in 1487, he made sure he never incurred Henry Tudor's displeasure again. He died in 1501. The ill-fated Lady Jane Grey, the nine-day queen, was his great-granddaughter.

Robert Stillington, Bishop of Bath and Wells (Book Two,* The Rose of York: Crown of Destiny*) was incarcerated immediately after Bosworth. He was pardoned by Tudor's parliament and arrested again after he threw his support to Lincoln's rebellion. He died in prison in 1491.

Sir James Tyrell didn't participate at Bosworth because Richard left him in charge of Calais. He retained this position under Tudor until he gave hospitality to the Earl of Lincoln's two brothers, the Duke of Suffolk and Richard de la Pole, on their way to Burgundy. Hesitant to return to England, Tyrell was given a safe conduct by Henry Tudor but was arrested as soon as he came aboard ship. He disappeared into the Tower and was beheaded on Tower Green in 1502. In 1504, Henry Tudor gave out the story that Tyrell had murdered the princes, but he produced no evidence.

Sir Edward Brampton remained true to the House of York, settled in Bruges after he fled England, and became a merchant. Margaret, Duchess of Burgundy knew him well. In Perkin Warbeck's confession, extracted under torture, Warbeck states that he went to Portugal with Lady Brampton, possibly in an effort to shield Sir Edward Brampton. Elsewhere Warbeck states that he was the son of a Jean Warbeck, a "converted Jew" and merchant.

Anne, Countess of Warwick. In December 1487, Henry Tudor restored her lands so that she could legally sign them over to him. She fought in the courts for Middleham Castle, and won, but Tudor never returned the property. She died in 1492 at the age of sixty-six.

Cecily, Duchess of York, lived to be eighty years old and died in 1495 at Berkhamptsted, a virtual nun. She was buried in Fotheringhay Castle beside her husband and son, Edmund.

Margaret, Duchess of Burgundy, dedicated the rest of her life to supporting and fomenting rebellions against Henry Tudor.

John Sponer. The day after Bosworth, John Sponer brought the city of York news of Richard's overthrow. To the mayor and aldermen hastily assembled in the council chamber, "It was showed by John Sponer that good King Richard, late mercifully reigning upon us, was piteously slain and murdered, to the great heaviness of this City."

This is Richard's epitaph, written at great personal risk by the men who knew him best.

Author's Note

This book is historical fiction based on real people of the period and real events. Though details that cannot be historically verified are the product of my imagination, no fictional characters have been invented and, with the exceptions noted below, I have adhered to historical facts when these are known[1]. Time, place, and character have not been manipulated for convenience, and the actual words used by the historical figures represented here have been integrated into the story whenever possible. However, as there is much that remains unknown about this period of history, I have connected the dots and filled in the blanks, and the interpretation of events is mine. By the use of handwriting analysis, noted graphoanalysist Florence Graving provided invaluable insights for me into the characters of these major historical figures whenever their handwriting samples were extant.

I first became interested in Richard III when I saw his portrait at the National Portrait Gallery, London. (That portrait is reproduced as the cover of book two of this series: *The Rose of York: Crown of Destiny*.) His noble features and gentle expression gave the lie to Shakespeare's description of him as an ugly hunchback, and the more I read about Richard III, the more difficult it became to reconcile the actions of his life with his reputation in history as an evil villain. To the contrary, his life brimmed with honourable actions that spoke of idealism and faith in God.

My research on this period took ten years. I visited university libraries across the nation from Stanford University and Berkeley on the west coast to Harvard and Boston College on the east, and I went north of the border to my alma mater, the University of Toronto. In England, I was honoured to be granted privileges at the British Museum where I perused various documents, as well as books from Richard's library, notably *Tristan*, which Elizabeth of York clearly read as a young woman at a time of crisis in her life when she was neither princess nor queen, since it bears an intriguing motto and her signature. A copy of *Consolatione philosopiae* by Boethius also carries notations by her in the margins, and is inscribed on the flyleaf with a fascinating combination of Richard's motto, *Loyalte Me Lye*, and Elizabeth of York's first name, both in her handwriting. To further my research, I visited Ricardian sites in both England and Bruges numerous times, and interviewed several notable Ricardian authorities, including Peter Hammond and Bertram Fields.

For the ease of the modern reader, the quotations used come from Tennyson's *Idylls of the King,* not from Sir Thomas Malory's *Morte d'Arthur,* written in Richard's lifetime. I have followed Richard's itinerary as king.[2] Dates given are correct, even as to the day of the week. There was indeed an eclipse of the sun on the day Anne died, and insofar as possible, I have checked the details I describe, such as the moon on the eve of Bosworth, which was a five-percent moon, barely two days old and therefore scarcely visible.[3] According to tradition, Richard did ride a white horse, despite the fact that the color white was commonly regarded as bringing bad luck. For me, this provided an important insight into his character.

One question I have been asked with some frequency regards Anne's vegetarianism. It may come as a surprise to many that there were, indeed, vegetarians in the fifteenth century. This fact is documented by John Stowe in *Stowe's Survey of London,* which has been regarded as the prime authority on the history of London from its initial publication in 1598.[4] Stowe reports that at a Christmas feast in the ninth year of Henry VII's reign, sixty dishes were served to the queen, Elizabeth of York, none of which were "fish or flesh."

Other facts may prove of interest. The garden Richard installed for his ailing wife survives at Warwick Castle, as does the window at Barnard's Castle (described in *The Rose of York: Love & War)* and Richard's book, *Tristan*. Richard's breakdown at Anne's funeral is well documented, and Anne Neville and Elizabeth of York did appear in the same gown on that last Christmas of Richard's life, giving rise to rumours of an illicit love affair. An emotional involvement is suggested by Elizabeth's mysterious motto, *sans removyr*, "Without changing"—never used by her again—inserted into Richard's book, *Tristan*, below his ex libris.[5]

The death of Richard's son and heir, Prince Edward, came a year to the day of King Edward IV's own death. This uncanny coincidence, coupled with the fact that it was sudden, of a belly ache accompanied by great pain, lends credence to the contemporary rumours of poison, and might explain Richard's desperate attempt at Bosworth to engage Tudor personally.

As to whether Richard had a deformity: no one who knew him during his lifetime ever mentioned one. The Countess of Desmond, who danced with Richard at a banquet, is reported to have said that he was the handsomest young man in the room besides his brother the King, and a German ambassador who visited England in 1484 left a detailed description of his visit and of Richard III himself, describing him as "two fingers taller" than himself. Shakespeare's immortal image of the limping hunchback with the withered arm shouting, "A horse, a horse, my kingdom for a horse!" is also disputed by Richard's surviving portrait[6] and the tributes awarded him for his valour at Bosworth. Even Henry Tudor's hired historian admits that Richard was killed fighting bravely in the thickest press of his enemies.

After every conflict the victor rewrites history, and Henry Tudor was no exception. Having won the throne by right of battle, he set a dangerous precedent for his own future. The legend of the hideous, villainous monster was deliberately initiated during his reign in order to justify his usurpation. He hired an Italian historian, Polydore Vergil, to paint his predecessor as evil and forge his propaganda into history, and Sir Thomas More absorbed the Tudor version from Richard's old enemy, Bishop Morton, in whose household he was reared as a child. More's account of Richard's reign, unfinished and broken off in mid-sentence, was published posthumously and taken up by the Tudor historians Hall and Holinshed. Shakespeare's play sealed the legend. As soon as the last Tudor was dead, the people of the North rallied to right the injustice done to Richard's memory. George Buck was the first, then came Horace Walpole. With *Historic Doubts*, Walpole created a debate that rages to this day and includes both historians and novelists.

While much is known about the historical figures of this era, some major gaps exist. Of Anne, little has survived beyond the tragic outlines of her brief life, but if a wife influences the man her husband becomes, then it is possible to glimpse Anne's essence in the great works Richard effected. Perhaps her influence extended even to her dear friend Elizabeth of York, who may have emulated her both in her humanitarian acts, and by touching "neither flesh nor fish." This is how I derived her character. No information exists, however, on the identity of the woman, or women, who might have borne Richard's two illegitimate children. I have taken Rosemary Horrox's suggestion that it was Katherine Haute.[7] It is known that the children came to live with Richard at an early age, and when I came across a reference to his vast, and puzzling, generosity to the Benedictine nunnery of St. Mary in Barking, Essex, I became convinced of the reason.[8]

Francis Lovell is not known to have had a club foot, but in view of his noble birth, his training, and his relationship with Richard, Francis' knighthood was conferred strangely late in life, and by Richard, not King Edward, so an impediment of some kind may have been present. Francis is not known for deeds of arms, and this makes his survival of both Bosworth and Stoke even more curious, unless he had reason not to participate in the fighting (see below).

A final question remains: were the princes murdered, or did they survive?

Henry Tudor was as plagued by rumours that the boys were alive as Richard was by rumours that they were dead. Did Richard murder them? Volumes have been written on the subject and for those who wish to delve deeper, I provide a list of reading suggestions below. In the absence of surviving evidence, however, it is important to keep in mind that it is impossible to resolve some of the contradictions, and all accounts of Richard's reign ultimately dissolve into interpretation. As such, they are subject to dispute. Documents that could exonerate Richard, such as Perkin Warbeck's letter of identity, or Edward IV's royal order to Bishop Stillington to perform a ceremony of marriage with Lady Eleanor Butler, may have existed, but apparently failed to survive. This is not surprising. Both Stillington and Perkin Warbeck were imprisoned and at

Tudor's mercy, and it is known that Perkin Warbeck was subjected to torture. Henry VII pursued the destruction of any documents unfavourable to his own version of events, including the Titulus Regius. It is indeed fortunate for posterity that one obscure copy was overlooked.

Though the Tudors were anxious for history to believe the princes were murdered and that Richard III committed the deed, there are some compelling pieces of evidence in favour of Richard's innocence. A fact often overlooked is that Richard had three little nephews who were legally barred from the throne. The Tudors would have us believe he murdered two of them, but not the third—Clarence's orphaned son, Edward Earl of Warwick. Richard brought this child to live with him in his household, and as soon as Richard was slain, Henry Tudor imprisoned the boy, then eleven, in the Tower of London. Thirteen years later, he beheaded young Warwick on a pretext of treason, so that his son, Prince Arthur, could inherit a throne unchallenged by a rightful heir and marry Catherine of Aragon.

The treatment of young Warwick alone speaks volumes about the difference in character between these two kings. And in the actions of Elizabeth Woodville and her daughter, Elizabeth of York, it is possible to find further evidence of Richard's innocence.

Elizabeth Woodville must have believed Richard didn't murder her boys since she came out of Sanctuary and wrote her son Dorset that all was well and to return to England. A year into Henry Tudor's reign, she suddenly incurred Tudor's disfavour and was locked away in an abbey where she was held virtually incommunicado until her death. She must have lent her support to the rebellion, but was it because she'd learned her son, Richard of York, was alive, or was it because she'd learned that Henry Tudor, or his mother, Margaret Beaufort, was responsible for the death of her boys? And why did Henry Tudor, who defiled Richard's body and his reputation so brutally, never formally accuse Richard of the murder of the boys? Was it because he knew Richard was innocent?

As Henry VII's queen, Elizabeth of York won the hearts of her people with her charity and generosity, much as Anne Neville had done. It is unlikely that such a woman could have loved a man she knew to be the murderer of her brothers, yet a case can be made that love him, she did.

Another consideration may lend weight to the theory that at least one of the princes escaped with his life. Francis survived both the Battles of Bosworth and of Stoke. As Richard's devoted friend, we would expect to find him at Richard's side at Bosworth—unless there were good reasons why he could not participate in Richard's suicidal charge. At Stoke, the fighting was fierce and everyone fell to the last man. Either Francis stayed on the sidelines in both battles, for a higher purpose as I have outlined in this novel, or he was greatly skilled in arms, which is unlikely, for the reasons explained above.

For some, the most convincing evidence that the princes died in Richard's reign is the fact that no one ever saw them after July 1483. However, in *Richard of England* (Kensal Press, 1992) Diana Kleyn makes a compelling case that Perkin Warbeck was indeed who he said he was. For those interested in pursuing the topic further, Audrey Williamson's *The Mystery of the Princes* also provides an intriguing, and authoritative, analysis.

Finally, I would like to make certain acknowledgements. Richard's "I hate war" comment to Francis on the eve of battle is taken from the National World War II Memorial in Washington, DC, as spoken by President Franklin D. Roosevelt.

The reference to the lark on page 47 is purposely drawn from Shakespeare's Romeo and Juliet. My intent in so doing was to suggest a certain similarity between Richard and Anne's love affair depicted in *The Rose of York: Love & War*, and Shakespeare's most romantic play, written a hundred years later. It is not known for certain where Shakespeare found his inspiration for his *Romeo and Juliet* (just as it is not known for a fact whether Shakespeare wrote his own plays) but perhaps it was in these two young lovers, torn apart by war and brought together by love. During the course of my research I was struck by a remarkable coincidence: Shakespeare used Richard and Anne's time period for his *Romeo and Juliet* tragedy and a title belonging to Anne's family, viz. *Montagu*. As his drama is set in Verona, Italy, it is curious that he would choose to call his protagonist by a name that is clearly not Italian.

Richard III bequeathed us a precious legacy of rights in the two short years he was King, yet his memory has been defiled and many believe him to be Shakespeare's embodiment of evil. History has taken from Richard his good name, for which he sacrificed so much while he lived, and denied him the presumption of innocence that was one of his gifts to us. In this context, the words of Richard's father, the Duke of York, spoken before his death in 1460, acquire a poignant significance. Let us hope the Duke was right when he prophesied that the truth shall not perish.

S.W.

Endnotes

1. It is thought that Richard's sister Anne may have died before 1483, but this is not known for certain.
2. Edwards, Rhoda, *The Itinerary of King Richard III 1483–1485*, Alan Sutton Publishing for the Richard III Society, 1983.
3. This information was kindly calculated for me by Bruce Green, 1997 doctoral candidate at the Los Alamos National Laboratory. His computer program established that the moon on the night of August 21, 1485, was as described.
4. *Stowe's Survey of London*, (Introduction by H.E. Wheatley); Everyman's Library, Dutton, New York, p.415
5. At least on the part of Elizabeth. For *Tristan*, signed by Richard III, and by Elizabeth of York, see the British Library Manuscript Harleian 49, f. 155. An intriguing discussion of this subject has been undertaken by Livia Fisser-Fuchs in The Ricardian, No. 122, Sept. 1993, pp. 469–473. Also see Anne E. Sutton and Livia Visser-Fuchs, *Richard III's Books*, Sutton Publishing, Great Britain, 1997.
6. There is evidence that his only surviving portrait was doctored to give Richard uneven shoulders.
7. Rosemary Horrox, *Richard III: A Study of Service*; Cambridge University Press, 1989, p.81
8. Charles Ross, *Richard III*, University of California Press, 1981, p.130

Bibliography

NON-FICTION

Armstrong, C. A. J; *England, France, and Burgundy in the Fifteenth Century*; Hambledon Press

Barber, Richard; *The Paston Letters*; The Folio Society, London 1981

Bennet, H. S.; *The Pastons and their England*

Bennet, Michael; *The Battle of Bosworth*;

Blake, N. F.; *Caxton and His World*

Brooks, F.W.; *The Council of the North;* Published for the Historical Society by George Phili[& Son, Ltd, 1953

Campbell, Lord John; *The Lives of the Lord Chancellors and Keepers of the Great Seal of England;* vol. 1, John Murray, London, 1848

Cheetham, Anthony; *The Life and Times of Richard III*; Shooting Star Press, 1992

Chrimes, S.B.; *Henry VII*, London 1975

Chrimes, S. B.; *Fifteenth Century England*

Chrimes, S. B.; *Lancastrians, Yorkists, and Henry VII;* St. Martin;s Press, 1964

Clive, Mary; *This Sun of York: A Biography of Edward IV*; Sphere Books, London, 1975

Cornwallis, William; *Encomium of Richard The Third*; ed. A.N. Kinkaid, 1977

Dockray, Keith.; *Richard III: A Reader in History*; Alan Sutton, London, 1988

Druitt, Richard; *The Trial of Richard III*

Edwards, Rhoda; *Itinerary of Richard III, 1483-1485;* Alan Sutton Publishing for the Richard III Society, 1983

Fields, Bertram; *Royal Blood: Richard III and the Mystery of the Princes*; Regan Books, New York, 1998

Flenley, R. ed.; *Six Town Chronicles of London;* Oxford, 1911

Foss, Peter; The Field of Redemore: The Battle of Bosworth, 1485; Rosalba Press, Leeds.

Gairdner, J.; *Richard III*; Cambridge University Press, 1898

Gillingham, John, ed.; *Richard III: A Medieval Kingship*; A History Today Book, Collins & Brown Ltd., London, 1993

Green, Mary Ann; *Lives of the Princesses of England;* New Haven, Connecticut Research Publication 1975

Gairdner, J.; *The Historical Collections of a Citizen of London in the Fifteenth Century. (Containing William Gregory's Chronicle of London)*. Camden Society Publications, new series 17; London; 1876

Griffiths, R. A.; *The Making of the Tudor Dynasty;* St. Martin's Press, New York, 1993

Griffiths, R. A.; *The Reign of King Henry VI;* Sutton Publishing Limited, Great Britain; 1998

Griffiths, R. A.; "Local Rivalries and National Politics: The Percies and the Nevilles and the Dukes of Exeter 1452-1455" *Speculum,* vol. 43 (1968) pp.589-632

Hammond, P. W.; *Edward of Middleham, Prince of Wales*; Gloucester Group Publications, 2nd Edition, 1973

Hammond, P. W. and Anne Sutton, ed.; *The Road to Bosworth Field;* Constable and Company Ltd., London, 1985

Hammond, P. W., ed.; *Richard III: Loyalty, Lordship And Law;* Alan Sutton Publishing and Yorkist History Trust; London, 1984

Hammond, P. W. and Anne Sutton, ed.; *The Coronation of Richard III: The Extant Documents;* Alan Sutton Publishing, London, 1983

Hanham, Alison; *Richard III And His Early Historians 1483-1535*; Clarendon Press, Oxford, 1975

Hicks, Michael. A.; *False Fleeting Perjur'd Clarence: George, Duke of Clarence*; Alan Sutton Publishing, London, 1980

Hicks, Michael.A.; *Richard III And His Rivals: Magnates and Their Motives;* Hambledon Press, London

Hicks, M.ichael A.; *Richard III: The Man Behind the Myth;* Collins and Brown, London, 1991

Hicks, Michael A.; *Who's Who in Late Medieval England (1272-1485)*; Shepheard-Walwyn

Horrox, Rosemary; *Richard III: A Study in Service*; Cambridge University Press, 1989

Jesse, John Heneage; *Memoirs of King Richard the Third and Some of His Contemporaries*;

F. A. Jesse, John Heneage; *The Last War of the Roses*; Nicholls, Boston (Rice University Microfilm)

Jenkins, Elizabeth; *The Princes in the Tower*; Coward, McCann & Geoghegan, Inc. New York, 1978

Jones, Michael K., and Malcolm Underwood; *The King's Mother: Lady Margaret Beaufort, Countess of Richmond and Derby;* Cambridge University Press, 1992

Johnson, P.A.; Richard *Duke of York 1411-1460*; Oxford University Press, 1988

Kendall, Paul Murray; *The Yorkist Age: Daily Life During the Wars of the Roses;* W.W. Norton & Company, New York, 1970

Kendall, Paul Murray; *Richard The Third*; W. W. Norton & Co., New York, 1956

Kendall, Paul Murray, ed.; *Richard III: The Great Debate*; W.W. Norton & Co., New York, 1992

Kendall, Paul Murray; *Warwick The Kingmaker*; W.W. Norton & Co., New York, 1957

Kendall, Paul Murray; *The Universal Spider: The Life of Louis XI by Philippe de Commynes,* trans. and ed. by Paul Murray Kendall; London Folio Society, 1973

Kleyn, Diana; Richard of England; the Kensal Press, Oxford, England; 1990

Lamb, V.B.; The Betrayal of Richard III; Alan Sutton Publishing Inc., U.S,A.; 1991

Lancelott, Francis; *The Queens of England And Their Times; From Mathilda, Queen of William The Conqueror to Adelaide, Queen of William The Fourth*; D. Appleton & Company, New York, 1848

Lamb, V. B.; *The Betrayal of Richard III: An Introduction to the Controversy*; Alan Sutton, New York, 1991

MacGibbon, David; *Elizabeth Woodville*; Arthur Barker Ltd., London 1938

Mancini, Domici: *The Usurpation of Richard III*; translated by C.A. J. Armstrong, ed.; Alan Sutton, London, 1989

Maurer, Helen; *Margaret of Anjou;* Boydell Press, Great Britain; 2003

Meyers, Alec; *England in the Late Middle Ages*

Meyers, Alec. R.; *English Historical Documents*; Eyre & Spottiswoode, London, 1969

Mitchell, R.J.; *John Tiptoft, Earl of Worcester;* Longmans, Green and Co., London 1938

Murph, Roxane; *Richard III: The Making of a Legend;* Scarecrow Press, Metuchen, N.J., 1977

Nicholls, John; *Richard The Third*

Pollard, A. J.; *Richard III and the Princes in the Tower*; Alan Sutton Publishing, London, 1995

Petre, J.; *Richard III: Crown And People;*

The Ricardian: Journal of the Richard III Society, Nos. 83-145

Rawliffe, Carole; *The Staffords, Earls of Stafford and Dukes of Buckingham 1394-1521;* Cambridge University Press, 1978

Ramsey, Sir James H.; *Lancaster and York: A century of English History*; Clarendon Press, Oxford, 1892

Richardson, Geoffrey; *The Hollow Crowns*; Baildon Books, England, 1996

Richardson, Geoffrey; *The Lordly Ones; A History of the Neville Family;* Baildon Books, England, 1998

Richardson, Geoffrey; *The Deceivers*; Baildon Books, England; 1997

Richardson, Geoffrey; *The Popinjays; A History of the Woodville Family;* Baildon Books, England, 2000

Richardson, Geoffrey: *A Pride of Bastards: A History of the Beaufort Family;* Baildon Books, England; 2002.

Ross, Charles; *Richard III*; University of California Press, 1981

Ross, Charles; *The Wars of the Roses*; Thames and Hudson, London, 1986

Scofield, Cora; *The Life and Reign of Edward IV*; 2 vols. Longmans, Green and Co., London, 1923

Scott, Kathleen L.; *The Caxton Master and His Patrons;* Cambridge University Library, 1976

Strickland, Agnes; *Lives of the Queens of England*

Storey R.L., *End of the House of Lancaster;* Stein and Day, New York; 1967

Storey R.L.; *The Reign of Henry VII;* Walker and Company, New York, 1968

Stowe's Survey of London; Intro. By H.B. Wheatley; Everyman's Library, Dutton, New York, 1970

Tudor-Craig, Pamela; *Richard III*; Ipswich, 1973

Waters, Gwen; *King Richard's Gloucester: Life in a Medieval Town*; Alan Sutton Publishing, London, 1983

Weightman, Christine; *Margaret of York*; St. Martin's Press, N.Y., 1989

Weir, Alison; *The Wars of the Roses*; Ballantine Books, New York, 1995

Williamson, Audrey; *The Mystery of the Princes*; Alan Sutton Pub;lishing, London, 981

Wheatley, H. B. ed.Woodhouse, *Life of John Morton*

NON-FICTION: MEDIEVAL LIFE

Aldred, David; *Castles and Cathedrals: The Architecture of Power*; Cambridge University Press, 1993

Bayard, Tania; *Sweet Herbs and Sundry Flowers for the Medieval Gardens and the Gardens of the Cloisters;* The Metropolitan Museum of Art, New York, 1997

Bishop, Morris; *The Middle Ages*; American Heritage Library/ Houghton Mifflin, Boston; 1987

Black, Maggie; *The Medieval Cookbook*; British Museum Press, 1992

Carey, John ed.; *Eyewitness to History*; Avon Books, 1987

Coghlan, Ronan; *The Illustrated Encyclopedia of Arthurian Legends*; Barnes and Noble Books, 1993

Dyer, Christopher; *Standards of Living in the later Middle Ages*; Cambridge University Press, 1989

Englebert, Omer; *The Lives of the Saints*; Barnes and Noble Books, 1994

Gascoigne, Christina and Bamber; *Castles of Britain*; Thames and Hudson, New York, 1980

Gies, Frances & Joseph; *Life in a Medieval Castle*; Harper & Row, New York, 1974

Gies, Frances and Joseph; *Life in a Medieval City*; Harper Collins, 1981

Gies, Frances and Joseph; *Life in a Medieval Village*; Harper & Row, New York, 1990

Gies, Frances and Joseph; *Women in the Middle Ages;* Harper Collins, 1980

Gill, D. M.; *The Exquisite Art of the Medieval Manuscript*: Illuminated Manuscripts; Barnes & Noble Books, 1996

Hanawalt, Barbara A.; *Growing Up in Medieval London: The Experience of Childhood in History*; Oxford University Press, 1993

Harpur, James and Elizabth Hallam; *REVELATIONS: The Medieval World*; Henry Holt, New York, 1995

Heller, Julek and Deirdre Headon; *Knights;* Schocken Books, 1982

Herbs for the Medieval Household; Metropolitan Museum of Art, 1971

Heriot, James; *James Heriot's Yorkshire*; St. Martin's Press, New York, 1979

Hopkins, Andrea; *Knights: The Complete Story of the Age of Chivalry from Historical Fact to Tales of Romance and Poetry*; Quarto Publishing, London, 1990

Howarth, Sarah; *The Middle Ages*; Viking, 1993

Images of Britain; Longmeadow Press

Maynard, Christopher; *Days of the Knights: A Tale of Castle and Battles*; DK Publishing Inc., London, 1998

Price, Mary: *Medieval Amusements*; Longman Group U.K. Ltd; 1988

Reader's Digest *Everyday Life in the Middle Ages*; 1992

Reeves, A. Comptom; Delights of Life in Fifteenth Century England; Richard III Society, Inc., 1989

Ross, James Bruce and Mary Martin McLaughlin; *The Portable Medieval Reader;* Penguin, 1977

Rowling, Marjorie; *Life in Medieval Times*; Berkley, New York, 1979

Ruby, Jennifer; *Costume in Context: Medieval Times;* B.T. Batsford Ltd., London, 1993

Turnbull, Stephen; *The Book of the Medieval Knight*; Arms and Armour Press, London, 1995

Ward, Jennifer C.; *English Noblewomen in the Later Middle Ages*; Longman Publishing Group, London, 1992

Willett, C. and Phillis Cunnington; *The History of Underclothes*; Dover Publications, New York, 1992

FICTION

Chaucer, Geoffrey; *The Canterbury tales*; Bantam, 1981

Christine de Pizan: *The Book of the Duke of True Lovers*, trans. by Thelmas Fenster; Persea Books, New York, 1991

Langland, William, ed. A.V.C. Schmidt, *The Visions of Piers Plowman,* Everyman-London; Charles E. Tuttle-Vermont, 1997.

Lytton, Sir Edward Bulwer; Last of the Barons; R. Worthington; New York, 1884

Malory, Sir Thomas; *Le Morte D'Arthur,* vols.1 and 2

Shakespeare, Wm; *The Tragedy of King Richard The Third*

Tennyson, Lord Alfred; *Idylls of the King*;

Author Biography

Sandra Worth graduated from the University of Toronto with a double major in Political Science and Economics, and has won numerous writing awards and prizes for her work. Her debut novel, *The Rose of York: Love & War*, about Richard III's childhood and his love affair with Lady Anne Neville, was published in 2003 and has garnered eight of the ten awards thus far bestowed on *The Rose of York* trilogy.

Sandra spent ten years researching the period, making nearly a dozen trips to England and Bruges to examine Ricardian sites. In addition to her alma mater in Canada and the British Library in London, she visited numerous university libraries across the U.S. and obtained privileges at the British Museum. She also interviewed several notable Ricardian scholars, including Peter W. Hammond and Bertram Fields.

Sandra divides her time between Austin and Houston, Texas, and is currently working on her fourth book on the Wars of the Roses, a prequel to *The Rose of York: Love & War* set in the 1450s.

Printed in Great Britain
by Amazon

35964673R00155